Trouble

ALSO BY LEX CROUCHER

Gwen & Art Are Not in Love

Infamous

Reputation

Trouble

A NOVEL

Lex Croucher

ST. MARTIN'S GRIFFIN
NEW YORK

First published in the United States by St. Martin's Griffin, an imprint of St. Martin's Publishing Group

TROUBLE. Copyright © 2024 by Lex Croucher. All rights reserved. Printed in the United States of America. For information, address St. Martin's Publishing Group, 120 Broadway, New York, NY 10271.

www.stmartins.com

Design by Meryl Sussman Levavi

Library of Congress Cataloging-in-Publication Data

Names: Croucher, Lex, author.
Title: Trouble : a novel / Lex Croucher.
Description: First U.S. edition. | New York : St. Martin's Griffin, 2024.
Identifiers: LCCN 2023038226 | ISBN 9781250323965 (trade paperback) |
    ISBN 9781250323972 (ebook)
Subjects: LCGFT: Romance fiction. | Novels.
Classification: LCC PR6103.R673 T76 2024 | DDC 823/.92—dc23/eng/20230825
LC record available at https://lccn.loc.gov/2023038226

Our books may be purchased in bulk for promotional, educational, or business use. Please contact your local bookseller or the Macmillan Corporate and Premium Sales Department at 1-800-221-7945, extension 5442, or by email at MacmillanSpecialMarkets@macmillan.com.

Originally published in the United Kingdom by Zaffre, an imprint of Bonnier Books UK

First U.S. Edition: 2024

1 3 5 7 9 10 8 6 4 2

For Hannah

Trouble

Chapter One

THERE WAS SHIT ON THE HEEL OF EMILY'S BOOT. HORSE, PRE-sumably. She had tried to scrape the edge surreptitiously on the step as she ascended into the coach, but had only half succeeded. The presence of the (probable) horse shit wouldn't have mattered if it weren't for the large family crammed into the coach with her; they clearly considered themselves rather genteel, but they weren't dressed well enough to excuse the expressions of pure disdain on their faces—the puckered mouths and wrinkled noses as they glanced at her sidelong, having decided she must be the source of the smell.

The fact that they were right was not softening Emily toward them. If the opportunity presented itself, she had already de-cided that she would rid herself of the shit by wiping it on the gentleman's soft fawn breeches, or the lady's muslin, which was far too pale for traveling in anyway. They could hardly imagine themselves so far above her in station when they were sharing the same carriage, the cheapest Emily had been able to find to the coast that didn't require strapping herself to the roof and making her body into a very straight line to lessen wind resistance. Even that might have been a more pleasant sensory experience than this: trapped in close quarters with these strangers and all their scratching, their breathing, their *fidgeting*, all the while judg-ing *her* as she sat perfectly still and, yes, smelled very slightly of manure.

Emily despised people who put on airs. If this family thought her low and common, then low and common she would be. She crossed her arms. She glowered. She noticed the small, snub-nosed boy in front of her glance over and flinch at the expression on her face, and felt only grim satisfaction. Good. Let him be afraid. Let all children cower before her, and keep their grubby hands to themselves, and know that they were not to cross Miss Emily Laurence.

"Where are you traveling to?" asked the lady opposite. "Fairmont House?"

"Yes," said Emily.

"To take up a position?"

Emily gritted her teeth and nodded.

"Which?"

"Governess."

"Oh," said the lady, glancing between her child and Emily and frowning slightly. "Won't that be . . . pleasant."

It would not. Emily had never taken to children, nor dreamed of having a clutch of her own, and had circumstances been different she would have laughed at the very thought of taking up a position minding anybody else's.

Her sister, Amy, was the natural caregiver. The empath. She brewed tea whenever there was an emergency of an emotional nature; mopped brows and brought pots for vomit when the ailment concerned the body. She was kind to the elderly without wincing. She voluntarily asked questions in dull company, prompting further conversation, when Emily was perfectly happy to let the interaction wheeze, rattle, and die.

Amy also genuinely adored children. She found them *winsome*. Even when they were awake. Even when they were talking to her!

It was not to be borne.

"I had a governess," said the little boy. "I did not like her."

"Where is she now?" Emily asked conversationally. "Dead?"

"Mmm," said the boy, thinking. "The baby . . . ate her."

"The baby did not eat her," said the boy's mother, tutting at him and reaching over to straighten his collar.

"Ah," said Emily. "She ate the baby."

"Good God," said the family's patriarch.

The various members of his family fell silent. Apparently, this signaled the end of their conversation.

Emily was all too relieved for the excuse to adjust her position—she was pressed very tightly against the door of the carriage, so she had to revolve jerkily on the spot to make any progress—and gaze out of the small window at the countryside whipping past. Greenish-gray fields hemmed in by dark gray stone walls, the sky graying grayly above. It had been much the same for the past three hours, but it was somewhat soothing to be reminded that the world outside this four-wheeled hell still existed.

She had allowed herself to be vaguely excited by the prospect of seeing the sea for the very first time, but when it did come into view, it took her a long time to realize that she wasn't just looking at another vast gray field. With her only diversion a severe disappointment, Emily misplaced the will to carry on, and the carriage started to feel very hot. The bony girl-child sitting next to her smelled strongly of lavender, but it did not quite mask the base notes of mackerel and milky vomit. The road was getting rougher, so that they were all bouncing out of their seats.

Emily clenched and unclenched her hands, and started counting the things around her in an attempt to slow her breathing. Six pleats in each ragged curtain. Four large gouges in the roof above them, possibly made by a werewolf or an escaped Pomeranian. Three horrible children. One moth squashed into the upholstery just above the gentleman's head, so that every time he bounced near it, he risked making a hat of it.

"Have you met Captain Edwards?" said the lady, trying to

catch Emily's eye encouragingly. Apparently she was very diffi-cult to put off.

"Have *you*?" Emily countered.

"Oh," said the lady. "No. We are not . . . acquainted."

This Emily translated to mean that she *desperately* wanted to be, but had never received an invitation to become so.

Emily had an invitation, of sorts. It was actually addressed to her sister, but this was merely an issue of semantics. The house-keeper had written to *a* Miss Laurence to confirm her position as governess at Fairmont House, and *a* Miss Laurence would be keeping the appointment.

Amy had been too ill this morning to get out of bed, even to see Emily off. She had tried to pretend she was simply terribly sleepy, but Emily had always been the liar of the family. She had told Amy quite a few lies as she'd left, to try to ease their parting.

That it was all temporary. That she had written to Fairmont House to explain, and that they had inexplicably accepted Emily's help until Amy was well enough to travel. That Emily would be pleasant and amiable, and would not hold it against these people that they were gilded and landed and able to put out advertise-ments for *staff*, while the Laurences could only afford to send for the (mediocre) doctor when things were looking especially dire. That she would try not to be so angry.

Even in the fog of fever, Amy should have been able to see through that one. Emily was always angry.

"Do be kind," Amy had said, as Emily clasped her too-hot hand, her own chest painfully tight. "And let them be kind to you, idiot."

"I will," Emily had lied. "God, I'll miss you."

That one had been the truth.

She had taken their mother aside and given her the sort of de-tailed instructions one might provide when leaving an acquaintance in charge of a beloved pet. Their mother had frowned at her all the while.

"You are aware that I live here?" she said wearily, once Emily had finished. "And that I am your mother, and that Amy is my daughter, and that I know where we keep the soup ladle?"

Emily was not entirely convinced. Their mother was prone to long stretches abed, evenings spent staring unseeing into the fire with her needlework abandoned in her lap, swollen joints frozen halfway between a stitch. Emily was the one who surreptitiously checked if Amy was feverish each morning, and heaped more vegetables into her portion of stew, and opened the window when the bedroom was getting too stuffy. Emily was the one who kept the accounts, went to the market, set money aside as often as she could in case they had to call for the doctor. Had she told her mother about the windows? Perhaps she could write, just to make sure.

"And have you been a governess long?" said the lady in the carriage, her knee accidentally knocking against Emily's as they weathered a small hillock. "You cannot be more than . . . five-and-twenty?"

She was attempting to be kind. Emily was nine-and-twenty, and looked every minute of it.

"Yes," she said. These people might not be acquainted with Captain Edwards, but if she was going to play the part of veteran governess, she ought to start at once. "I recently cared for the children of a local family."

"What age were they? The children?"

". . . Six?" Emily would have done a better job, but the coach had just experienced such violent turbulence that her stomach was attempting to leap out of her mouth.

"What—all of them?"

"Most of them," said Emily.

"*Most* of—?"

It was a blessed relief when the carriage crashed.

Chapter Two

Emily was no expert in carriage-driving, but she was relatively sure that the back wheels weren't supposed to leave the ground.

Everything lurched forward, reticules and hats and children flying through the air like flower petals at a parade; when they finally came to a stop, Emily found herself wedged between seat and indeterminate limbs. She scrambled to disentangle herself as her fellow passengers did the same with grunts and squeaks of discomfort, and after a stunned pause, all three children burst into tears in discordant harmony.

"Stop it," Emily said breathlessly to the nearest child, who blinked at her and then made a concerted effort to cry harder.

Once it was ascertained that nobody had been seriously perforated or snapped in half, they all clambered out into the mud so that the coachman could attempt to dislodge his vehicle by encouraging the horses with intermittent cajoling and threats of horrible violence. He even had the gentleman from within the carriage—whom Emily now learned, against her will, was called Mr. Sandler—attempt to lead the horses while he pushed the carriage from behind. Unsurprisingly, this did not make any discernible difference to their circumstances.

When it began to rain, Mrs. Sandler, who had up until that point been bravely taking charge of her dirtied, weeping children, let slip a small wail of despair.

"It's no good," said the coachman, with the grim practicality of a man who had weathered worse than this and was silently imploring them to not be dreadful little babies about it all. "I'll run ahead to the house for help."

"Oh," said Mr. Sandler, his voice entirely devoid of feeling. "No, no, I shall do it."

The coachman did not bother engaging with this pretense, and immediately departed.

"Well, that was rather rude," said Mr. Sandler, roused to true emotion. "Offer the man my help, and he won't even entertain the idea!"

"Oh, Malcolm," said Mrs. Sandler, in a tone so perfect for the chiding of children that Emily made a note to replicate it when the time came to eke out discipline.

It seemed silly to sit out in the rain with a perfectly good carriage available to hide in, so Emily went back inside to collapse into the lower altitude seat, and was horrified when a few moments later Mrs. Sandler reopened the door and put the youngest of her children on Emily's lap.

"If you could just sing something to him," she said desperately. Behind her, the scrawny girl and the snub-nosed boy were caked in dark gray mud and screaming with impressive resonance, considering their respective sizes. "I'd have Malcolm take him, but he's afraid of sheep."

Whether this phobia belonged to her small child or her adult husband was not made clear.

By the time help arrived, Emily and the silent toddler were staring each other down in a fraught stalemate, sitting with their arms crossed on opposite sides of the carriage.

"Miss Laurence?" said the coachman, peering in and looking discomfited by the general atmosphere of malevolence. "Er . . . reinforcements have arrived."

Emily picked up the small child as one would heft a dirty pot or a box full of spiders, and returned him to his rightful owner the moment she exited the carriage. It was growing dark around them, the wind picking up, the colorless landscape losing all of its light to a flock of gathering clouds.

There were three additional people standing around the carriage. One was a short, well-curved Indian woman of middle age, with an umbrella in one hand and the other on her hip, like she was about to start issuing instructions. She glanced up at Emily and frowned very slightly, as if she'd seen something she hadn't expected. This, of course, made no sense—Amy had never met any member of the household staff, so it was impossible that they'd know just by looking at her that Emily was an imposter. Perhaps this woman simply sensed the hostile energy that was coming off her in waves and did not think it befitting of a governess.

The second new addition was a thickset, ruddy-faced frown of a man who must have been at least fifty, with what looked suspiciously like bloodstains on his shirt, his expression pinched as he assessed the wheels. He was far more believable as a man of action than Mr. Sandler had been; in fact, Emily would have believed him capable of lifting the carriage with one hand if the mood had taken him.

The last of the newcomers was a man in perhaps his mid to late thirties, with gently weathered skin that had tanned halfway to tawny, and silver hair at his temples. He had a sharp, striking face, full of stern angles and overenthusiastic cheekbones. He was wearing leather riding breeches that might have once been white but had been abused all the way to a murky beige, and a shirt that hadn't fared much better—hand-me-downs, perhaps, past their best before he had ever donned them.

He didn't bother with a preamble—he simply gestured to the coachman and the frowner, and then braced himself against the back of the coach to push. They joined him, and the woman went to help direct the horses, and within a couple of minutes of coordinated shoving the coach was free.

"Can't thank you enough," said the coachman, enthusiastically shaking both men's hands.

"You must be Miss Laurence," said the Indian woman, coming over to do the same to Emily. "I'm Miss Meera Bhandari. We've been corresponding. I should have thought to send word about the mud—it's always tricky in this spot when it rains—but anyway, the good news is that we're only a quarter of a mile away from the house. You'd be able to see it, if it weren't for the slope of the land."

Emily tried to channel her best Amy impression. She smiled. She ducked her head. She said "Oh, how pleasant!" for the first time in her life.

Miss Bhandari gave her another odd look, but didn't question the pleasantness of the situation.

"You're shivering," she said instead.

"Not on purpose," said Emily.

"We must get you back to the house. Where are your things? Joseph will take them. Don't mind his face, it always looks like that. Joe, could you please see to Miss Laurence's . . . Oh, he's already doing it." Joe was apparently the brawny, red-faced older gentleman. "Is that your trunk, Miss Laurence? Excellent. I suppose we'll just—"

"I shall take her," said the man who wasn't Joe. He had rolled his shirtsleeves up to his elbows and was standing with impeccable posture. "I need to return to the horses, anyway." He was the groom, then—and if Amy had been corresponding with her, Miss Bhandari must have been the housekeeper.

One of Mrs. Sandler's small children suddenly fell face-first to the ground, and everybody else rallied around to make noises of consternation and offer advice.

"Right," said Miss Bhandari, lingering for a moment before going to join the fray. "Very good."

At this point Emily realized that she had managed to overlook the presence of an additional horse. Said horse had been standing out of sight behind the carriage; now the sharp-faced groom who was apparently to "take" her went to fetch it. He didn't do anything so polite as *ask* if she minded clambering onto a horse with him. He just bent and cupped his hands so that she might use him as a human ladder.

"I'm very muddy," she warned him. He just glanced down at himself, wet through and similarly dirtied, and then raised his eyebrows at her. "Well. I did warn you."

Emily hadn't ridden a horse since childhood, and she wasn't entirely sure how to arrange herself: both legs astride seemed sensible, although difficult to achieve with a dress. She wriggled into position and then discovered that doing so had hitched her skirts up so high that quite a large portion of stockinged calf was visible.

The groom glanced at her legs and then looked pointedly away and cleared his throat.

"Sidesaddle is traditional," he said, his voice slightly strained; Emily thought he might be holding back laughter, and immediately resolved to hate him.

"I was . . . injured, in the crash," she lied, her head held high. "Sidesaddle would not be comfortable."

The groom caught her eye, and she saw a flash of something softly puzzled in his expression before he nodded curtly.

"As you wish."

Luckily, he did not press further on the issue of an invented injury that necessitated one's legs being open; he simply got up behind her and took the reins.

It really was a very short ride to the house, but Emily spent every second of it preoccupied with the disconcerting feeling of a strange man at her back. She couldn't remember the last time someone who wasn't her sister had been this close to her. Her mother had probably hugged her at some point in the past year, and Emily might have suffered it momentarily before leaping from her grip like a sliver of soap, but that was all.

There had been the men at the textile mill, but even they hadn't dared to put more than a single hand on her, usually in the realm from elbow to shoulder blade—a decision they had quickly regretted.

This man did, at least, seem to be trying to touch her as little as possible.

They cantered along the lane and down the gentle slope that had indeed hidden the house from view; once she saw it, it was impossible for Emily to look at anything else, mostly because there was nothing else to look at. The landscape was nigh on featureless in all directions: just a few trees and then fields, fields, and more fields, ending abruptly in cliffs to her left.

The house was very rectangular and symmetrical, made of red brick that was noticeably faded on the side that faced the sea, the windows and doors framed in pale neoclassical trim. It looked quite silly in the middle of all this waterlogged land, as if it had been picked up from somewhere more sensible and dropped here by accident. The late summer sun was still an hour or two from setting, but the thick cloud cast such a blanket of gloom over everything that candles had already been lit in the downstairs rooms; the little squares of light seemed rather pathetic, unable to keep all that dreary, sea-swept isolation at bay. The grounds looked surprisingly ill-kept, the hedges running wild, a large tree at the end of the drive glumly cradling a broken limb.

Although it was somewhat diminished by the landscape, the house was actually very large. Large enough to house hundreds of people, probably. Far too vast for just one family and their servants. Emily thought of the bed she shared with her sister and felt momentarily overcome with murderous intent.

There were a few outbuildings clustered to the right of the house as they approached, and the groom pulled the horse to a dramatic stop and then dismounted, offering her his hand in a perfunctory manner and removing it immediately once she was on solid ground.

He looked slightly alarmed when he realized she was staring at him, awaiting further instruction.

"One of the horses is unwell," he said.

"Oh," said Emily.

"So I'll . . ." He nodded toward the stables, taking the horse by the reins to lead it away.

"What's it like here?" she blurted out, putting off the moment she had to enter the house for just a little longer. "Are they dreadful? I suppose they must be, with a house like this."

He stopped and looked back at her, impassive, and she realized with a sinking feeling that he was one of *those* sorts of employees: ones who refused to hear a word against their masters, as if they owed them real loyalty because they provided meager pay and a lightly chewed attic room to sleep in.

"You don't have to pretend for my sake," Emily tried again. "I've encountered naval officers before. I know them to be deeply self-important. Is Captain Edwards a classic of the genre?"

Another of those minute, inscrutable expressions passed over his face. Emily couldn't place it. Surprise? Amusement? Barely repressed horror?

"Yes," he said neutrally, after a beat. "I suppose he is."

"Damn," said Emily. "I mean . . . Ah, well. That's a shame."

He stared at her for a moment longer, but didn't say anything further, and then he abruptly turned and walked away with the horse, leaving her standing there, wet and apprehensive.

"Ugh," she said to nobody, wrapping her clammy arms around her to keep the cold at bay. She briefly entertained the idea of trying to find a servants' entrance, but if the entire point of involving the horse had been to get her inside and dry as quickly as possible, it made far more sense to trail mud through the front door instead.

She rang the bell as she entered, but found nobody rushing to greet her in the very white entrance hall. There wasn't much in the way of furniture, but what there was looked expensive enough: a mahogany and satinwood inlaid table, a single cream and cobalt vase, a dramatic family portrait framed in intricate loops of gold on the far wall. She took a few steps forward, then glanced behind and discovered that she was leaving brazenly dark smears all over the black and white diamond-patterned tiles. She supposed she couldn't keep walking through the house, ruining everything she touched. It would not make a particularly good first impression.

She found herself stuck.

Five minutes passed, during which her only entertainment was listening to drops of muddy water fall from various corners of her person as they hit the floor.

Somebody burst through a door on her left, startling her, and then strode across the hallway and disappeared through the door opposite without seeming to see her. Emily waited, frozen, and a few seconds later a man with floppy hair roughly the color of a lackluster walnut retraced his steps and stared at her.

"Ah. You're . . . Miss Laurel?"

"Miss Laurence."

He nodded thoughtfully. He was wearing a very nice coat in myrtle green, and boots that had been recently buffed and polished. He was also very handsome, in the way that an optimistic illustration of a fairy-tale prince might be handsome.

"Damn, everything's a bit . . . and I'm in the most frightful rush. I'm not sure where Meera is, she's the one who—"

"My carriage broke down," said Emily. "Some of the staff went to help."

"Of course they did," said the man. "Gluttons for punishment. Well, I'm sorry not to be of more assistance, Miss Laurence, but I have a prior engagement and I'm already running forty-five minutes behind schedule . . ." He was already on his way out again.

Emily tried to remember herself. What would Amy do?

"It was a pleasure to meet you, Captain Edwards," she said, smiling and going for a very belated curtsy.

The man reappeared.

"Hang about," he said. "A pleasure to do what to whom?"

"Er . . ." said Emily, unsure how she'd made a mess of this. "To . . . meet you?"

"Captain Edwards?"

". . . Yes?" Emily said. "Sir."

"Oh," said the man. "Well . . . no."

"No?"

"Not the man in question."

Emily just blinked at him. This conversation was like navigating a hedge maze designed by a fanciful baby.

"Oliver. Fletcher. Valet."

"But you're . . ." Emily gestured vaguely at him. "You're dressed . . . and you said you were . . . going out?"

"It's my night off," Oliver said, flashing her a grin. He adjusted the sleeves of his very nice jacket, then froze. "*Fuck!*"

The shouting and the profanity caught Emily so off guard that she twitched, splattering more watery mud from her sleeve onto the already tragic tiles.

"Good God, Oliver, *language*," said Miss Bhandari, bustling through the door behind Emily. "And in front of our new governess! Another sixpence for my jar, please."

"Meera, there's a hole the size of a gentleman's fist in my coat, and I am half an hour late to my engagement—"

"Forty-five minutes," said Emily.

"Well, exactly. You can forgive me a little coarse language when the situation does *so* call for it."

"I cannot. Put a sixpence in my jar and stop letting gentlemen put their fists through your coat," said Miss Bhandari cheerfully. "All right, Miss Laurence—I sent Akia to fetch towels, I'm sure she'll only be—ah, yes, here we are."

A tall, slender Black woman with her tight curls coiffed into a bun entered, holding spotlessly clean towels ripe for ruination.

"Miss Laurence, this is Akia—Miss Akia Smith. You must excuse us, but we have fallen into bad habits. It's all first names here, we are too familiar for our own good."

Meera looked anxious, as if Emily might be horrified by this transgression; she supposed a *real* governess would be, but Emily could not quite rouse herself to feign disdain.

"Good evening," said Akia, handing Emily a towel with a smile. "I was in a carriage crash once. I bounced off the roof and accidentally swallowed a lady's earring. It was actually very harrowing, but I find that in the retelling of such stories, it often helps soothe the mind to make them comedies rather than tragedies."

Emily had absolutely no idea what to do with this information; luckily, Miss Bhandari—Meera—clapped her hands together to reclaim their attention.

"Baths, I think," she said, "or the cold will get into our bones, and we'll be no good all evening. You take the first turn, Miss Laurence, and I will take a quick dip after."

"But . . . don't you have jobs to do?" said Emily, keen on this talk of baths but baffled by the very casual attitude they were all displaying to working hours.

"Not on our night off," said Oliver, aghast at the very idea. "Damn the bloody coat, Meera, I'm just going to have to leave it as it is, I'm twenty minutes late—"

"Fifty minutes, now," said Meera. "And that'll be another sixpence for the jar, thank you."

"Fuck the jar!" Oliver said as he disappeared through the doorway.

"Oh, Oliver," Meera said, shaking her head. "I hope it was worth a shilling."

They all seemed quite agreeable, really, but no matter: Emily wasn't there to make friends.

She planned to steal what she could from this house, then head home to Amy and never look back.

Chapter Three

THE HOUSE CONTINUED TO BE LARGE AND OBJECTIVELY impressive. Emily continued to be unimpressed.

The kitchen she was hustled into was less ostentatious, being as it was very concerned with the practicalities of cooking. It was big, and the fireplace was cavernous, but there was nothing particularly glamorous about smoke stains and old pans, even if you had amassed quite a lot of them. Large and grumpy Joe had changed his clothes and immediately taken up residence cutting vegetables, and Emily deduced that he was likely the cook, although she hadn't met any men in the profession before. She avoided him and his very big knife as she skirted the room and went to lift one of the buckets of water Meera and Akia were preparing for heating.

"Oh, no, please—you don't have to do that," Meera said quickly.

Emily stopped short. She had made yet another blunder; apparently *governesses* would not lower themselves to hauling water. Now that her fingers were already on the handle it was too late to take it back, so she improvised.

"I'm not afraid of hard work. I think it . . . builds character. I want to be useful, in any way I can. Truly."

Meera exchanged a glance with Akia, and Akia raised her eyebrows back.

"Well," Meera said slowly, "we *are* actually rather short-staffed, so if you're sure . . ."

Her reluctance, as it turned out, was extremely short-lived.

Emily helped with the buckets, and then dutifully heaved them into the small servants' parlor next door, where the bathtub was pulled very close to the fire.

"Go on," said Meera. "You were wettest the longest."

Emily didn't need telling twice. She soaked for what was probably an impolite length of time and left the water looking positively brackish for the next bather. Her trunk had been delivered to her, so she rummaged inside for a dress and found one that was a rather pretty, muted copper color, painstakingly mended under the arms so that you could hardly tell it had ever been torn.

One of Amy's, obviously. None of Emily's dresses could have been described, even charitably, as *rather pretty*. Amy was the one who kept her dresses in immaculate condition, and chose with care whenever the opportunity arose to procure one secondhand. She had already been halfway through packing for Fairmont when it became clear that she would not be going, and had insisted that Emily take the trunk and its contents with her instead. Emily felt a brief pang as she put the dress on, and then straightened up and went to face the household.

"Ah, Amy," Meera said as soon as she emerged. Emily faltered, taking a moment to catch up with her lies. *Right.* Amy must have included her Christian name in her correspondence. Unfortunate. "Do you mind if I call you Amy? I'll show you to your room, and then once you're situated you can meet the children."

"Am I not . . ." said Emily. "I thought I'd be introduced to Captain Edwards."

She had *no* desire to meet the man, really, but the longer she put it off, the more she'd be on edge, looking for uppity gentlemen around every corner. The incident with Oliver the valet had been humiliating enough; she intended to be prepared when she really did meet the master of the house.

"Captain . . . ? But you have already met him," said Meera.

This was demonstrably false. The only men Emily had met were Joe the cook, Oliver the valet, and . . .

"Not the *groom*?" said Emily.

Meera looked gently disapproving. "He's certainly *not* the groom. We do not *have* a groom anymore. Oliver and Captain Edwards share responsibility for the horses."

"Oh," said Emily. "Oh, God. I stepped on him."

She had, in fact, done worse than that, but she did not want to admit to the housekeeper that she had also enthusiastically insulted him into the bargain.

"You . . . ?"

"Ah . . . I stepped on him. Captain Edwards. I put my foot on him."

What was it that she had called him? Self-important? And hadn't he *agreed*?

It was only what he deserved, really. But the entire point of coming all this way to live in this too-big estate and look after horrid children was to *keep* this position and appropriate what she could from the house until her luck ran out, not to lose it all immediately. They needed this money. *Amy* needed this money.

"Did you do it spontaneously, or did he request it? The foot?"

"He . . . requested it, I suppose."

"Well then. No harm done. Now, your room . . ."

Emily's room was at the very end of the first floor, tucked into a corner of the house. It was twice as big as her room at home, with a full-sized dresser and a little desk by the window, upon which somebody had put a vase containing a generous bunch of pink sea thrift. The wallpaper was cheerfully floral, and there was a fire lit under the unadorned white stone mantel.

She was left alone to unpack her things and "get her bearings." The unpacking took all of five minutes, her handful of dresses taking up less than a quarter of the space allotted, and then Emily lay down on the bed to test the mattress and accidentally had half a nap, only occasionally dipping into true unconsciousness, telling herself whenever she surfaced that she was simply resting her eyes.

When Meera returned, washed and changed, Emily was groggy and out of sorts and absolutely *not* ready to meet the children. All she knew of them from Amy was that there were two, and they were motherless.

"I did tell Aster to stay put, but it's like asking a frog to answer the front door—she seems to derive absolutely no meaning from anything I say . . . Right, here we are. This is the schoolroom. It's where you'll be teaching your lessons."

Ah, yes. Her lessons. Emily was expected to impart wisdom. She hadn't gone so far as to plan what that wisdom might be yet. Her primary fields of study of late had been subjects like Intermediate Lock-Picking, and Soup Studies: How to Make One Batch of Broth Last a Week, neither of which would be suitable. She would probably just have to improvise, which was sort of like regular lying but with an additional element of the theatrical. She had listened around half of the time when Amy told her about the lessons she'd taught the children at her last position, and could probably cobble something passable together from what she had retained. Perhaps she could fill the first few weeks by simply asking her charges to demonstrate what they had already learned. Either that, or she'd just make them read from *The History of England*, as her own teacher had made them do back when the Laurences had been in healthy enough fortune to afford such luxuries as education.

It was only a matter of time before she was discovered as a fraud, but she thought her wits could at least get her through a month or two as long as nobody challenged her to provide a historical fact on the spot, or asked her to explain the correct order of spoons to use at a dinner engagement.

The schoolroom was extravagantly large for its purpose and papered in Aegean blue. It had been scattered with scholarly props—a globe here, an easel there—but otherwise looked like a pretty drawing room, with a table and chairs at one end and soft furnishings arranged around the fireplace.

There were two young ladies sitting by said fireplace, in very different states of readiness.

Emily's first thought was that they were hardly *children*. The younger was maybe fourteen, the elder perhaps two years her senior. She could guess which was Aster on sight; the older sister was slumped dejectedly in her chair, entertaining herself by making the large tear in her stocking even bigger, and seemed to be covered in a fine spray of white paint. The younger was beautifully turned out, her hair the same drab brown as her sister's, but set in perfect curls. She was smiling hopefully at Emily in a way that made her feel deeply uncomfortable.

"Miss Laurence, this is Miss Grace Edwards and Miss Aster Edwards. Girls, this is Miss Amy Laurence. She has had a hard journey to get here, and I trust you'll make her feel welcome."

"What sort of a hard journey?" said Aster, sitting up slightly, as if energized by the prospect of Emily's misfortune.

"My carriage got stuck in the mud a little way down the lane," said Emily.

"Dull," said Aster. "Why'd you have to say it like it was interesting, Meera? It should have been highwaymen."

"Aster," said Meera. "Let Miss Laurence settle in for a week or two before you start setting violent brigands on her in your mind."

"Shan't," said Aster. "May I be excused? I was painting in my room."

"Aster," said her younger sister, sounding pained. "Don't be rude. I am so very sorry to hear of your troubles, Miss Laurence, and I am grateful to you for making the journey. It is so difficult to travel in this inclement weather! We rarely have true summer days here—it is something to do with the coastal climate. Meera, might we have some tea?"

She sounded positively middle-aged—as if she'd been hosting people for tea and exchanging small talk about the weather for decades. It was unnerving. Emily glanced at Meera to see if this was out-of-character behavior, but she was nodding approvingly.

"Sit down, please, Miss Laurence," said Grace. "I want to hear all about you! We have been looking forward to your arrival ever since Meera told us you had accepted the position. Do you mind if I call you Amy?"

"Is it not a little . . . informal?" said Emily, hoping to cling to *Miss Laurence* for as long as possible.

"Oh, we hardly mind things like that here! Even Father says *Meera*, not Miss Bhandari."

"And what do you call him?" Emily asked Meera.

"I call him Captain Edwards," said Meera primly. "As should you. I'll send Akia with the tea."

Emily sat down in an empty chair. She wished she could lounge uninterestedly, as Aster was doing, but she forced herself to sit upright and fold her hands neatly on her lap.

"I love your hair," Grace said, and Emily couldn't stop herself from snorting. "Oh, don't laugh! I mean it—such a lovely yellow."

Emily knew her hair to be the sort of blond that put one in mind of soiled straw and puddles of questionable origin. Grace Edwards was obviously very practiced at conjuring compliments for the irredeemable.

"Thank you," she said, with great effort. "Your hair is also very . . . pretty."

"Akia did it," Grace said, beaming at her. "She's marvelous."

Marvelous Akia came up with the tea and wouldn't stay, no matter how much Grace begged her to.

"But it's your night off!"

"No, it isn't, Grace. Oliver and Meera take tonight off, and me and Joe will take tomorrow."

"Joseph and Meera never really take nights off," Grace said ruefully.

"That's because Joe thinks his knives are his children, and would marinate anyone who touched them in boiling wine," said Aster, confirming the impression Emily had already formed of the cook. "And Meera hasn't relaxed since 1807."

"*You* must take time off, Amy," said Grace.

Emily wasn't getting any better at looking suspiciously startled any time somebody used her sister's name. Nobody in this house seemed aware that *taking time off* was not usually part of a lowly employee's repertoire; at Emily's last place of employment, you *took time off* only if you had been dismissed or recently lost a limb or phalange, and even then you were expected back as soon as you'd stanched the bleeding.

"It's true," said Aster. "If the last governess had taken more days off, perhaps she wouldn't have lost focus and died in that horrific boating accident."

Emily looked helplessly at Grace.

"There was no boating accident," Grace said reassuringly. "Father said she just needed a . . . rest." This was somehow *more* alarming than the story with the boats. "Have you seen the house? Has somebody given you the tour? Oh, I would love to do it myself, but I'm not at my best today."

"Grace is sometimes unwell," Akia said.

Grace screwed up her nose, as if she outright rejected this assessment of her health.

"Akia, you needn't say it like that," she said, sounding more ill-tempered than Emily had imagined her capable of. "I am hardly *unwell*. I just get a little tired sometimes. Let she who has never been a bit sleepy at midday cast the first stone!" Her tone brightened. "Aster will give you the tour, Amy."

"Aster will not," said Aster. "I'm painting."

"How wonderful, to have a pastime you enjoy," said Emily, once again attempting to channel Amy's steely sunshine in this spikier sibling's direction.

"How wonderful indeed," said Aster, with a penetrating look Emily couldn't parse. She should have guessed that simpering geniality was not the way to Aster's heart; it certainly wouldn't have worked on Emily herself.

Aster was handsome in a very hard way, thick brows and sharp angles only slightly softened by puppy fat, unlike her sister, who looked as if she should perpetually smell of roses and milky chocolate.

"Not much else to do around here in the way of hobbies," Aster continued, "unless you want to go mad or die of exposure."

"Aster!" said Grace, sounding genuinely upset. "Why would you say such a terrible thing? Stop it at once—you're ruining Amy's first day, when I have already decided to like her very much."

"You decide to like *everyone* very much." Aster gave Grace a friendly pat on the shoulder when she got up to leave. Her brief glance at Emily was . . . less friendly. "It's nothing personal, *Amy*, but I don't need a governess, and the sooner we come to an understanding about that, the better."

Emily blinked at her. It was exactly the sort of thing she might have imagined a difficult child would say to a governess, so much so that it felt comically trite.

Aster gave Akia a brief nod of farewell and then sauntered away. If she'd had pockets, Emily fancied she would have stuck her hands in them and whistled.

Despite herself, Emily had found her amusing. She didn't *like* her, exactly, but she could respect her particular brand of hostility. There was a naive, anarchistic spirit about her that would no doubt be stamped out by the time she reached true womanhood.

"Please do ignore Aster," said Grace. "She's at a difficult age."

"Yes," Emily said awkwardly.

There was a silence, and then Akia cleared her throat.

"I shall take you on the tour."

Extremely grateful for an excuse to leave the earnest focus of this tiny hostess, Emily jumped up to say her goodbyes.

The house was a house. It had various large rooms, decorated ornately but without any sense of personal taste, and with quite a few large gaps where it looked as if more furniture might have once stood. It seemed as if Captain Edwards or his late wife had perhaps ordered their remaining decor at random out of a newspaper. *This* would only be to Emily's advantage. If they had no idea exactly which antiques adorned which surfaces, they could hardly be expected to notice if one or two small trinkets went astray.

She didn't plan to clear them out, after all. She couldn't hope to, without getting caught. The way to do it, she had decided, was to be slow and quiet. To watch and wait until the moment was right to spring. She would say *like a cat*, but she'd seen how stupid cats could be. Like a spider, perhaps. Or a snapping turtle. Something that went unnoticed, even *after* the moment of ambush. She would pocket things here and there, never too much at once, and then perhaps take the coach a few towns over on one of these convenient *nights off* to find somebody in a pub who didn't mind purchasing objects of questionable origin.

There was no shortage of nooks and crannies to pillage in a place this enormous; Emily's house could have easily fitted into the disused ballroom, with room to spare for a small garden around the edges. At home they had one room downstairs and two up, and they spent almost all of their time gathered close to the hearth, the world shrunk down to a small circle of firelight. Fairmont House had a fireplace in every room, and at least ten rooms on the ground floor alone.

Those at the front of the house had a view of the cliffs and the distant watery horizon out of every window, and the littoral spirit seemed to have infiltrated them; they were mostly decorated in blues and greens, the wooden furniture leached of color until it looked more like driftwood than mahogany. There seemed to be a breeze frisking through the rooms, even though the windows were firmly closed, as if the sea air could not be kept at bay by mere brick and glass.

The more sparsely furnished rooms had little in the way of easily pocketable fripperies at first glance, but when she ran her eyes surreptitiously over the glass-fronted cabinets and the lower shelves, she saw the glint of crystal and china—the promise of long-forgotten heirlooms and impulse purchases that hadn't seen the light of day for years.

Much more interesting than the house was Akia, who kept up a gentle commentary as they walked from room to room, and was surprisingly entertaining.

"This is the smaller drawing room, if you can believe it. They only use the larger one, so if you need a moment to collapse quietly, this is the place to do it. Just don't let Meera catch you with your feet on the pouffe . . . I'm mostly lady's maid to the girls, but we do split the cleaning as we're short-staffed, and now that you've been foolish enough to be helpful, you will almost certainly be asked to muck in with the schoolroom and the bedrooms. We end up doing lots of this and that . . . The other week Oliver tried to get me to hold one of the horses still, and when I got distracted the horse sat on me, so if he asks, best to pretend you have a deathly fear of horses . . . I certainly do now. Would you describe yourself as more even-tempered or nervous and uptight, do you think?"

"Pardon?" said Emily.

She had been distracted by the *smaller* drawing room, which was at the back of the house and was the color of anemic strawberries. It made her feel very plain and dirty, despite the fact that she'd just washed. She hated that feeling. These people weren't *better* than her just because they had a very large house. She didn't want to sit on their hideous brocade sofas anyway.

"I'm just wondering. The house is a delicate balance, you see. I take things as they come. Meera is Meera, Oliver can relax with the best of them on a good day, but he's a secret neurotic, and Joe is a fiend in the kitchen, but I think it helps as an outlet for his rage, because the rest of the time he is actually quite serene . . . Which are you?"

An unpleasant, unsociable aspiring thief, thought Emily. *I'm not sure what that'll do to the balance, but I can't imagine it'll be anything good.*

"I am . . . generally good-spirited," said Emily. It wasn't quite what Amy would say about herself, but it was an accurate description of her sister nonetheless. "Although I am quite . . . solitary. I find ways to amuse myself."

She didn't want these people poking around in her life, trying to befriend her. They wouldn't find anything to their liking anyway.

"I see," said Akia. "Ah, well. Perhaps you'll accidentally amuse me if I happen to be standing near you when you're doing something droll."

"What happened to the last governess?" asked Emily, as they walked into the large dining room, which was already laid for dinner. So much silver. So much crystal. It was obscene.

"Oh," said Akia. "She was not . . . to Captain Edwards's liking."

Emily had hoped that Captain Edwards perhaps paid so little attention to his staff and children that she might escape scrutiny; the idea that she could be dismissed for the crime of *unlikability* was grave news indeed, especially as she'd already put her foot on the man.

She knew she was deeply unlikable. She just didn't care.

"Do you mean that he did not like her personally?" said Emily, as they walked the length of the table.

"Hmmm," said Akia. "No, I don't think it was that. There have been quite a few governesses over the years, and none have been up to scratch." She paused, and seemed to realize that nothing she was saying was particularly reassuring. "Just don't do anything foolish, and I'm sure you'll be fine."

A low bar, and yet one Emily did not plan to clear.

"When Miss Grace Edwards is unwell," she said, to change the subject, "does she require additional assistance?"

"Not that she'll allow you to administer," said Akia. "She suffered from the same consumption that put Mrs. Edwards to rest. We expected to lose her, too—you know how that terrible business goes; once you have it, there's no getting it out of you—but somehow she pulled through. Only surviving case the doctor had ever seen in the whole county."

"She doesn't *look* ill."

"Appearances can be deceiving," said Akia. "Joe has dedicated his life to the task of feeding her well, and she has every comfort and treatment available, when she'll accept them."

It wasn't this child's fault that she got to be luxuriously ill—ill in an enormous feather bed, with a doctor at her beck and call, a cook downstairs determined to keep meat on her bones and color in her cheeks—but Emily hated her a little for it anyway.

Amy's limbs were starting to look like birds' legs, startlingly thin and not at all plausible as a means for staying upright. She shivered on summer days and wore her veins like blue lace at the surface of her skin.

Emily would not waste any of her sympathy on this child, reclining in her sick chair that might as well have been inlaid with gold.

"You look like you want to bite me," Akia said mildly. "Come on. Let's go and fetch you something more suitable for dinner."

Chapter Four

WHEN EMILY AWOKE THE NEXT DAY, SHE HAD ABSOLUTELY NO idea where she was. She experienced a moment of bleary panic, reaching across the bedclothes to try to locate Amy's sleeping form, before she opened her eyes and realized that she wasn't in her bed at home at all.

She wondered if her mother would go up to check on Amy in her stead: watch from the doorway to check for the regular rise and fall of her chest, as Emily did every morning from the next pillow, or check if her cheeks were flushed with the threat of fever.

Amy found these habits of Emily's *extremely* vexing. If she noticed Emily watching her, she would tell her in no uncertain terms to go away, or make a rude and unseemly gesture with her hand if she was feeling particularly spirited. It was Emily's fault for teaching her that gesture in the first place; she'd had somewhat of a reeducation at the mill, primarily in all the ways you could tell somebody to go to hell.

The previous night at dinner, while Emily tried valiantly to stay awake, Meera had told her that she'd be expected at nine o'clock in the schoolroom to begin lessons.

"The captain often takes his meals with the children," she had explained, doling out soup, "and I was not given the impression that he wanted to alter this arrangement, so I hope you don't mind breakfasting and eating your dinner down here with us on occasion."

Emily had no idea that she was *supposed* to mind. It seemed strange to her that governesses considered themselves so much above the other staff of the house; having never been a *lady*, it made perfect sense to her that she would take her meals with everybody else employed in the running of Fairmont. Amy had spoken of the housemaids and valets at her last position in such friendly terms that Emily assumed she had spent plenty of time rubbing elbows with them—but then again, Amy could befriend a bear that was attempting to eat her. Anyway, surely only a pretentious sort of ninny would split hairs about exactly what sort of servant they were, when it all boiled down to the same thing.

When Emily arrived in the schoolroom a little early to get the lay of the land, she was relatively unsurprised to find Grace already waiting for her, dressed as if expecting an important visitor.

"Good morning, Amy! I have been up since five, I was so looking forward to our day."

"Er ... good morning," said Emily, wondering what could have gone so wrong in this girl's life that she was *excited* about her lessons, and then remembering—ah yes, deceased mother, lingering illness. She supposed that if you were overly fond of your parents, the loss might be quite significant.

Emily's father had been a dedicated drinker, perpetually out of the house attending to "business" and only aware of his daughters in an absent-minded, passing way; sometimes he came home feeling particularly sentimental and would tell stories from when the girls were small, mixing up the key details, casting himself as the heroic pinnacle of fatherhood in every one. In truth he was a *father*, not a papa. Their mother had been the steadier fixture; she was very fond of Amy and slightly alarmed by Emily, and had never bothered to hide either of these facts. Emily remembered her as practical and unfussy, but weak-willed when it came to her husband, and inclined to prioritize keeping the peace over all else.

Mrs. Laurence had given up entirely after her husband died and had faded into the background of Emily's life, unable to come up with any sort of plan to improve their fortunes. Emily had never forgiven her for it. Her own grief at her father's passing, complicated as it was by the confusing impression he had made on her life, had quickly turned to resentment and anger at the state he had left them in.

She wondered what form Grace's grief had taken at the loss of her mother. *She* certainly didn't look angry and resentful right now. In fact, she looked disconcertingly thrilled, although her expression twisted briefly into regret as she spoke.

"Aster is . . . Well, I seem to have misplaced her. She *was* here, looking for a book, and I tried to sort of block the door with my body so she couldn't leave, but she just waited and took her chance as soon as I sat down again."

"I see," said Emily. "We will do without her, for now. What were you studying with your last governess?"

"Music lessons," Grace said, with a hint of distaste. "And social etiquette. I wouldn't have minded—I love music and I dearly look forward to parties—but I'm afraid she was not . . . musically inclined, or particularly convincing as a potential party guest."

"Why don't you just find something you've been reading," Emily said, sure that she would be exposed at once if she tried to start with music and etiquette, "and tell me about it?"

"Really?" said Grace, her face brightening. "I've been reading *Udolpho*! Have you read it? It's about a young lady called Emily St. Aubert, and she's having a miserable time of it."

Emily didn't even blink at the sound of her own name. She was improving already.

The number of miserable Emilys in the room doubled as Grace explained the plot of *The Mysteries of Udolpho* in great detail; Emily had not read it, but Amy had, and had recounted the entire thing to her in great detail even as Emily pressed her face into the mattress and begged her not to. At least simply listening to Grace and prompting with a few well-placed exclamations of "And why do you think *that* is?" was infinitely preferable to attempting any real teaching.

Grace *loved* reading. Emily knew because Grace had told her so three times. She wondered what it might be like, to have so much time dedicated to leisure that you could have favorite hobbies; Emily had always been so focused on the practicalities of life that she would have had no idea what to say if anybody had asked her what sort of things *she* liked to do.

She seemed to be endearing Grace to her without any effort on her part at all. Apparently nobody had ever asked her to talk at length about a book she was enjoying: this alone secured her, as Grace told her repeatedly, the top spot of all the governesses ever employed at Fairmont House.

Aster only strolled in when the time came for luncheon. She looked as if she was attending an entirely different occasion from Grace, in a simple day dress with something misshapen and hand-knit thrown over the top. Emily wondered if Grace had knit it, and if anybody had told her that she should never attempt the feat again.

"And what have we been lecturing on today?" Aster asked Grace, apparently pretending Emily didn't exist.

"Emily and Valancourt!" said Grace.

"Ah, yes," Aster said gravely. "The foolish Monsieur Valancourt. What a mawkish little harlot."

"*Aster*," Grace breathed, horrified.

Emily pressed her lips together and said nothing, and Aster leveled a very cutting look at her, waiting for her to react.

"Luncheon," she said, her eyes flitting back to Grace again when Emily stayed silent.

"But we should have luncheon with Amy," said Grace.

"Father has summoned us."

Grace almost pouted. "But I want to enjoy lively conversation and witty anecdotes over my luncheon!"

"I am extremely lively," Aster said, as lively as a flattened badger.

"You know as well as I do that we will answer Father's questions about our morning, and then it'll be nothing but silence until dessert. Incidentally, what *have* you been doing with your morning?"

"Pushing the boundaries of artistic expression," said Aster. "Making obscene shapes out of clay."

Grace tried one more time. "I really do think that Amy—"

"If *Amy* desires company, I am sure she will feel very at home among the *servants*," said Aster.

This immediately obliterated any goodwill Emily had been feeling toward her for being occasionally witty. Whatever quirk of personality had resulted in Grace treating the staff as real people clearly hadn't been genetic, because Aster was looking at her as if she was a household pest trying to make off with her sandwiches.

"Aster! It's cold cuts today, anyway, remember, because Joe is taking the day off."

Joe was certainly not taking the day off. During breakfast, Emily had seen him walk into the kitchen and line up all of his knives for sharpening, humming tunelessly under his breath. She still had yet to speak to him and didn't plan to do so while he was gazing lovingly at his extensive collection of blades.

"The temperature of the cuts makes no difference," said Aster. "Good day, Miss Laurence."

Emily looked from Grace's consternation to Aster's disdain and then returned a curt "good day" and left.

It rankled her to be dismissed when *she* was the one who

wanted to leave—*she* certainly had no desire to eat luncheon while listening to Grace's constant prattling and fielding Aster's misdirected ire. To hell with them. Perhaps she wouldn't eat luncheon at all.

She did, because it was there and she was hungry, but she refused the offer of company with the staff and took the thickly sliced bread and pink ham and cheese up to her room, looking out the window at the dreary view.

This only took approximately ten minutes to accomplish; with hours still until she'd be expected back in the schoolroom, she started drifting around the house like an ill-intentioned ghoul. The rooms felt cold, even in late summer with the fires lit. It was something about the sea air; it made everything feel perpetually harsh and bracing, even when it was just whistling through small, undetectable gaps in the windows. It was also noticeably salted, the taste white and hot on her tongue. If she wasn't careful, she'd end up brined, like a grim and solitary herring.

Emily passed through the smaller drawing room—the *spare* drawing room—and on this sweep paid particular attention to a cabinet full of what looked like expensive curiosities. It was in a dark corner, tucked behind one of the doors. A long-forgotten trinket in a hidden cabinet in a disused room seemed exactly the sort of thing that might go for years—perhaps even decades—without being missed. It was perfect.

On her way back down the hall, she heard voices from inside the dining room and slowed to listen.

". . . and we were talking about *Udolpho*, Father, which I have nearly finished. I think she's going to end up marrying him even if he has lost everything and ended up in a French prison. I think she'll do marvelously."

"Who?" said a man's voice. It was deep and brusque. It must

have been Captain Edwards, of damp horseback riding infamy—
not that he sounded particularly familiar to Emily. He'd barely
spoken to her at all.

"Miss Amy Laurence!"

"Miss Laurence was in a French prison?" said Captain
Edwards.

"No, Father, you're not listening to me—Amy wasn't in
prison."

"That we know of," said Aster.

"Aster," said Captain Edwards warningly.

"She looks like she fell off the back of a wagon, Father. Didn't
Meera say that her father was a gentleman? I don't believe *that* for
a second. Her hands are pitiful. She looks like she dressed herself
in the dark at the burlap sack factory."

Emily looked down at her hands. It hadn't occurred to her
to hide them, but she realized now what Aster would have seen:
cracked skin, calluses, little pink pockmarks that had once been
shallow injuries. *Not* the hands of a lady, reserved for gentle
things. They were the hands of somebody who'd had to work hard
to survive.

"Aster, just *stop it*. How can you be so unforgivably mean-
spirited! It's not her fault if her hands are sore and she doesn't
have any nice clothes. And it is hardly as if you *care* what anybody wears. I saw you last week, wearing those—"

"Quiet, Grace," Aster said sharply.

"Aster," Captain Edwards said again, stern with a hint of weariness. "Enough."

"It's all right for you," said Aster. "You don't even have to
talk to her! And count yourself lucky you don't—there's nary a
thought behind those eyes."

Emily had heard enough. She walked away, fists clenched
tightly at her sides, no longer caring if her footsteps were audible
from inside the dining room.

She could not remember if there was a special hell reserved for children, or if they were simply assimilated into the general population, but regardless—Aster Edwards would get on there very nicely.

If Grace noticed that Emily was a little colder toward her as they sat down that afternoon, she didn't say anything; she did glance at Emily's hands, however, and Emily forced herself not to flinch and to keep them steady on the book in front of her. It was a beautiful edition of childhood fairy tales, decorated with a whole meadow of gilt flowers, and Emily had taken it down from the shelf, thinking of trying to ascertain its worth, before finding herself distracted by the meticulously inked illustrations.

"Finish *Udolpho*," she said, "and we shall have silence, please, until you are done."

Grace picked up the book and turned the pages with utmost concentration until she found her place. She carried herself very carefully; Emily had thought that it was simply an obsession with bearing and good manners, but looking again she realized that every movement was calculated to conserve energy. Not for her the explosive dramatics and skipping of most girls her age, if skipping was indeed still the done thing (Emily had not kept up with the fads). If only Grace's desire for moderation had carried over into her style of conversation, her company might not have been so tiresome.

As it was, she found it impossible to go more than five minutes without voicing some inane thought aloud.

"I should never think to describe myself as a *nymph*, even if I were the heroine of a novel. It seems presumptuous," and what felt like only a few moments later, "When somebody is described as *springing* across a room, I can only imagine them being flung as if from a trebuchet and colliding with the opposite wall," and then, "I have never met a real nun. They feel as mythical to me as witches, or dragons, and I do so covet their floppy hats."

Emily said, through gritted teeth, "I recall that I asked for silence."

"Yes," Grace agreed. She managed an entire ten minutes of silence, during which Emily intended to replace the book she was holding to look for other valuable tomes, and instead accidentally read an entire story about an unscrupulous princess, before Grace said, "Everybody in France seems to have a lot of feelings."

"That affliction is not contained to France," said Emily, closing her book irritably.

"I must confess I do indulge in many myself," said Grace, "but I try to stay quiet about them, rather than running around the countryside in paroxysms of emotion. It makes Father uncomfortable when I cry, and Aster always seems to want to *do* something about the problem, even when nothing can be done."

"Well . . ." said Emily, but nothing else followed, and eventually Grace picked up the book again and engrossed herself in French feelings until Meera knocked on the schoolroom door.

"What are we learning?" she said cheerfully.

"That feelings are an affliction," Grace offered.

"Ah," said Meera, her smile faltering as she looked quizzically at Emily. "I am sure that I have missed some further context."

"No," said Grace happily. "Meera, have you ever met a nun? Do they really and truly exist? They aren't like . . . leprechauns, or minotaurs?"

"There is only one minotaur," said Emily, taking the rare opportunity to display some of her meager academic knowledge.

"Surely not," said Grace. "How did they make the first one? Surely the process could have been repeated."

"Grace, I think it might be prudent if you rest for a while before dinner," Meera said quickly.

Grace grumbled a little, but eventually acquiesced; she left, but Meera didn't. Emily pointedly picked up her book again.

"I am sorry about the eating arrangements," Meera said. "I know it must not be what you are accustomed to, and I hope you know it is not meant as a slight."

"Mmm," said Emily.

At the mill, she'd sometimes eaten outside leaning against the wall, watching rats gather the courage to come and wrestle for her crumbs.

"You can join us for dinner," Meera said, "and you are very welcome to sit up with us afterward if you like. We play cards. Oliver cheats. I'm sure we'd all like to get to know you better."

"Thank you," said Emily. "I won't."

Meera didn't push the matter, but Emily saw the steely resolve in her expression and knew that it would not be the last time she was asked. She would *not* be press-ganged into socializing, no matter if Meera employed guilt or cajolery or even light weaponry. It was a waste of her time.

There wasn't any point dressing for dinner, as she was already wearing one of her best dresses, and she was only sitting down with the servants anyway. She did re-pin her hair so that it wasn't quite so lopsided, avoiding looking directly at her face as she always did, not particularly interested in what she might see squinting back at her. She was sure she looked tired, although she had hardly earned it, having spent most of the day sitting down and not even attempting any sort of real teaching. It seemed to Emily that the higher in position and wage you became, the less actual work you were required to do, which was such a fundamentally backward way of doing things that it could only have been designed and enforced by the idle rich.

On her way downstairs she paused for a moment on the first floor landing, peering through an open door into a guest bedroom that looked to have a glut of expensive trimmings. She was just wondering if there was a market for stolen cushions when she heard footsteps coming from the other direction and moved quickly on.

It was Captain Edwards, who *had* dressed for dinner, and looked strikingly different from the last time Emily had seen him: his jacket was dark and snug at the shoulders, the waistcoat a spotless cream, his stock crisp and white. If she had seen him in *this* outfit, there never would have been a moment of doubt about who was the master of this house.

He was walking directly toward her. She prepared herself for a proper introduction—to greet him, to try to say something that might placate him after the debacle of their first meeting. When he reached her she curtsied, her gaze dipping to the floor, but by the time she raised her head again she realized that he had simply . . . walked straight past her.

As if she did not exist. If *she* were part of the furniture that they seemed to be halfway through selling off.

Emily watched his retreating back, slightly agape, and then, for a brief and very serene moment, imagined taking a taper from the fireplace and setting the house alight, starting just outside his bedroom.

It was probably a sign of enormous and disappointing naivete that she was at all surprised.

She was resolutely silent when she sat down opposite Oliver the card-cheating valet in the servants' dining room, and tried not to listen as he talked about the previous evening's adventures, oscillating wildly between good humor and mild fits of pique.

"And then they told me that it *wasn't that sort of pub*. I was wearing my finest jacket! If you don't want people to drink whiskey, don't *provide* whiskey."

"And I s'pose if they don't want people to stand on the tables," said Joe in a gravelly, monotonous voice, "they shouldn't have tables."

"Yes," said Akia. "And if they don't want people to change all the words to 'God Save the King' to be about the removal of stockings with one's teeth, why write the song at all?"

"Oh," said Oliver. "How did you hear about all that?"

"Delivery from Mr. Khan," said Akia, grinning at Meera, who held her gaze defiantly but went a little red. "He *lingered* somewhat."

"He was helping me with the cucumbers," said Meera.

"I'm *sure* he was," said Oliver.

Apparently the saga of Meera and this Mr. Khan had backstory, mythology, even recurring side characters; Meera sat looking extremely disgruntled and sporadically trying to urge them to stop, but they kept teasing her in the good-natured way that only came from years of coexisting in close quarters.

These people clearly knew one another well; had weathered hard things together, celebrated small victories, gathered up their wages and walked to the pub so that they could knock their drinks together and tell the same stories over and over again against the backdrop of an oft-frequented bar rather than the servants' dining table. They could probably tell one another's moods from the sets of mouths and shoulders, knew exactly where to prod to get the strongest reaction in a squabble, and how to smooth over hurts with a well-timed word or a cup of tea made to exactly the right specifications.

Emily could not imagine anything worse.

She let it all wash over her—the bickering, the well-worn camaraderie—as she stewed, feeling as if there was a chasm between her and the others.

It wasn't exactly as if she'd come expecting this household to be a delight—she had expected to hate it here, had hated it before she had even seen it—but to have all her theories about the sort of people who lived in houses like this one confirmed within a day was even worse than she'd expected. Captain Edwards was the vilest sort of snob. Aster was a nightmare, a parody of a wayward ward. Even Grace openly pitied the state of Emily's hands and passed judgment on her clothes.

When dinner was finished, everybody helped clear the plates; Emily tried to pick up her own, but Meera stopped her at once, leaving Emily the odd one out, sitting uselessly at the table and wondering how long she had to wait before she could escape. Eventually Joe opened a bottle of cheap wine, Akia fetched glasses, and Oliver started dealing out cards. Emily slipped away before anybody else could beseech her to join in their merry-making, listening to the sound of their soft chattering and laughter grow quieter until it gave way to silence.

It suited her far better; she was not feeling the *least* bit merry.

Chapter Five

ON HER FOURTH DAY AT FAIRMONT HOUSE, EMILY SAT TAPPING her dry pen idly against parchment, watching the sky brighten over the sea.

It was impossible to know what to write to Amy about her new life, but just as impossible not to send anything at all. The Laurence sisters had been inseparable throughout childhood, right up until the day, seven years earlier, when Amy had traveled the vast distance to the wealthiest household on the outskirts of the next village—six miles, practically an ocean away—to take up a position as governess to their children. She had sent daily notes, drawings, anecdotes about the children that she clearly thought were charming and that Emily found patently horrifying, and Emily had replied cheerfully, threatening violence if she did not come to visit soon.

Six miles did not seem such a long distance now. If Fairmont House had been six miles from the Laurences' home, Emily would likely have been able to see her house from her position here at the desk by the window. She imagined the slant of a roof, the curling smoke from a chimney, the knowledge that even if she could not find horse or carriage, she could be home in an hour and a half on foot if needed. Hell, she could do it in an hour if she hiked up her skirts and didn't stop to right any of the people she flattened on her way.

In reality, there were no familiar landmarks to be seen from her new bedroom. Everything here was alien. Emily's mind was adaptable to change—she could adjust to almost anything if she needed to—but her body seemed to be lagging behind, leaving her feeling discombobulated and frustratingly thin-skinned.

She could not even bring herself to tell Amy that she missed her. Instead, she described her bedroom in great detail, dashed out a couple of vague lines about the children, and ended with an ill-advised joke about falling over the cliffs that she regretted as soon as the letter was sealed.

Her second and third days as a governess had been just as strange as her first. She had instructed Grace—still her sole student—to read for most of the day, and to recount some of the things her previous governess had been teaching her in more detail, in the hope that she might be able to replicate some of those lessons well enough to not be declared a fraud in her very first week.

So far, it seemed to be holding. She was speaking to Grace as little as possible, which was partially to prevent revealing her deficiencies and partially because Grace was damnably annoying. Grace seemed to have noticed this cold front; she had not flagged in her dedication to prattling but was at least self-aware enough to cut these musings short when she saw the lack of amusement on Emily's face.

There was a sort of rhythm to Fairmont House as it awoke each morning, even if it was uneven and prone to minor disasters due to the lack of staff. Emily woke up far too early, a habit ingrained in her from six-o'clock starts at the mill, and stayed in bed until she heard the distant creaking of floorboards and gentle opening of shutters that meant the servants were preparing the rooms for habitation. She could not actually hear the kitchen fire being lit, but she fancied that she could feel when Joe started coaxing the heart of the house into being; it was the spring from which ran everything that sustained them—tea and hot water and breakfast—and Emily did not emerge from under her bedclothes until it was in full flow.

She knew perfectly well that they could have done with her help, just as she now knew that offering that help was considered firmly beneath her; she was willing to make herself useful, but not *that* useful. If proper governesses only came downstairs in the morning when the honey cake was ready to be cut and the bread toasted golden, then a proper governess she would be.

Apparently proper governessing also involved walking the children as if they were dogs. On their third day together, Grace had inquired as to why they had not yet gone for a turn about the grounds or a stroll along the coastal path, and instead of answering, Emily had said that they would go on the morrow.

The morrow had arrived too soon, as such things tend to do, in direct proportion to how much you dread them. Unlike walking a dog, there was a whole process required before one could even step out the door—the right bonnets, coats, and cloaks to be found, the lacing of the correct boots—and Emily stood downstairs in the hallway waiting for at least half an hour after their proposed start time for Akia to assist in the unearthing of all of these particular articles.

Somebody enterprising had clearly managed to grab Aster by the scruff and force her into her own cloak, because *both* Edwards siblings appeared at the top of the stairs looking far too bundled up for a temperate August day.

"Oh, Amy, I am ever so sorry about the wait," Grace said as she descended the stairs. "We couldn't find my gloves, and then Aster was telling me this story . . . Do tell Amy the story, Aster."

"No," said Aster, glancing behind her to see if she was being watched and then immediately removing her bonnet and throwing it over the banister, so that the cream ribbons fluttered sadly through the air before it came to land behind a credenza.

"Remember what we talked about," Grace said sternly; she was looking at Aster instead of where she was going, and almost tripped over the hem of her cloak on the bottom step. Aster threw out an arm to catch her, and then propped her back upright.

"It was a linear narrative," she said, not looking at Emily, "with a beginning, middle, and end. The genre: a comedy of errors. Lessons learned by the protagonist: none."

"But *you* were the protagonist!" said Grace. "And the boat sank!"

"Exactly," said Aster. "And I would do it again. Look where you're going, Gracie, or you'll lose a nose."

"That's all right, I have a spare. Now, here we all are. Shall we set off?"

Setting off! Such a novel idea! Emily turned and fiddled with her own bonnet, so that neither of her charges would see her rolling her eyes. She probably should have insisted that Aster fetch her hat back, but the idea of going three rounds against her over a *bonnet* seemed foolish when she was sure she would need to conserve her energy for further fisticuffs.

It was a perfectly pleasant day outside, which was to say that it wasn't raining, windy, or entirely gray. The watery sun bled through the clouds, and in the distance the sea looked almost blue, a vast improvement on Emily's first glimpse of it.

Grace kept up a stream of chatter in her ear.

"Where should we go? There is the coastal path, but it does all sort of look the same. Sometimes there are seals, but they are private creatures, and do not respond well to catcalling. Have you seen the garden yet? Oh, then we shall start there!"

They walked around the outside of the house—ridiculous, Emily thought, that it should ever take more than a minute to travel half the circumference of the place you lived in—and entered the garden.

It was somewhat sheltered from the coastal wind, although it was clear that the bordering trees bore the brunt from their stooped posture and general broken-backed weariness. The ground sloped gently away from the house, so it was a downhill walk along the length of the flower beds, which had likely once been neat and regimented and were now absolutely overflowing.

Emily had never been particularly well versed in types of flowers, but she could see many varieties of roses, overgrown and grappling for space; shocks of marigolds and soft lavender; a vast quantity of plump, furry white and purple daisies. They were the constant in every bed, and in some places had succeeded in defeating the other flowers entirely in a very thorough coup.

"Aster," said Grace, reaching out to touch one with gentle fingers.

Aster didn't say anything, and Emily was momentarily confused.

"They're aster flowers, I mean. Our mother planted them when Aster was born. She loved the garden. Much more than she liked the house."

Aster the person was grimacing, as if it was deeply embarrassing to be surrounded by the flower you had been named for, but Emily felt momentarily knocked askew as she looked back at the garden around her. She hadn't thought much about the late Mrs. Edwards, but it struck her now how strange it was to care for someone—to plant hundreds of flowers for them—and for those flowers to keep growing so determinedly after you were gone that it was impossible for anybody to gaze upon your garden and not see how much you had loved them.

Amy was the only person Emily could ever imagine loving that much, but demonstrating it with flowers was so saccharine that Amy would probably try to summon a doctor for *her* if Emily ever so much as seeded a daisy in her name.

"There are no *Grace* flowers, of course," said Grace sadly. "She did plant rue, though, the herb of grace."

"Yes, and it turned out that it smells absolutely foul and

blisters the skin," said Aster. "We should have swapped names—it would have been far more apt."

"You do not smell foul," Grace said, and then followed it up with a considered, "very *often*, anyway."

"But I do blister the skin," Aster said, flashing her sister a smile that seemed calculated to look as devil-may-care as possible. Unfortunately, it wasn't entirely convincing: the Devil did care just a *tiny* bit; he just didn't want anybody to know.

"Come along," Emily said stiffly, wanting to put some distance between herself and the wild clouds of asters. She set a brisk pace, not checking to see if the children were following. It was all too *sentimental*—the flowers, and the memory of their mother, and the easy back-and-forth between the Edwards siblings. There was a pitted wall at the back of the garden, with a gate that led out to a track; it was only once she reached it that she realized that neither of the girls was with her.

Aster was the first to catch up.

"You are walking too fast," she said, her voice laden with vitriol. "Slow *down*."

Emily took a breath. She counted to three.

"Aster, if you wish to say something to me, there is no need to—"

"The things I wish to say to *you* could be listed at length on a speck of dust. Just pay *attention*, would you?"

Emily glanced back at Grace. She was walking at a brisk pace to try to catch up. She looked mostly at ease, if a little short of breath.

Amy had once told Emily that cats were so good at hiding injuries that it was almost impossible to tell that they were hurting; she had been talking about the tomcat who lurked behind their house, mousing and romancing, who had a gash in his leg but was maintaining a stiff upper lip about the whole thing. It was a defense mechanism, born from an instinct not to show weakness at any cost, lest the wolves descend.

Amy had also once told Emily that assuming someone with an illness was constantly on the verge of swooning was the sort of base foolishness that made her want to unravel people's knitting, which was about as close to true violence as Amy came.

Perhaps Grace was perfectly fine. Perhaps she was not.

Aster seemed to think not.

"If you are remiss in your care of my sister in any way," Aster said quietly, "I will most probably kill you."

Emily flushed hot with the force of her indignation, but before she could say anything, Grace caught up with them, and Aster's face smoothed over in an instant.

"What, pray tell, are you two discussing so seriously?" Grace said. Her cheeks were slightly pink, but it *was* a warm day.

"Shakespeare," Aster said, without pause. "Particularly the part in *Lear* where Cornwall scoops Gloucester's eye out."

"Ugh," said Grace.

"He steps on it, too. Must have felt like popping a big grape. Come on, Gracie, let's get back to the house. I tire of the wonders of the natural world. I wish to retire gracefully, to achieve repose and look only upon the mundane wallpapers of life."

That evening, when Emily had once again been invited to spend time with the servants, and once again declined without bothering to be polite, she made the mistake of going for a walk around the house. She was just *looking*, she told herself—just *checking*. The Edwards family were all abed, the servants preoccupied. There was no better time to start thinking seriously about her first foray into a life of crime.

It was quite late, the house silent on the upper floors, even more of a gaudy mausoleum without the bustle of distant industry. Em-

ily walked through the empty dining room, along the length of the
table three times the size of the one she had eaten her own dinner
at, and thought of Aster and Grace sitting in these very seats, making snide comments about her hands and her dress and the contents of her mind. She went on into the drawing room—the *spare*
drawing room—which looked more maroon than strawberry in
the light of the low-burning fire, and imagined how well her sister
would look, sitting by the hearth on one of these pink armchairs,
warm and happy and wanting for nothing.

All thoughts of being patient and sensible, of waiting for the
right time to strike, were driven from her head by her urgent
desire to *take* something from these people.

She paused, listening. There were no footsteps from the floor
above or telltale creaks of floorboards from the hallway. The only
sound came from the fire, the soft noise of something shifting in
the grate as it put itself to bed.

The glass-fronted cabinet she had spied earlier in the week
wasn't locked. The doors did squeak slightly as she opened them,
but Emily saw that as a good sign: if they were often used, somebody would have thought to drizzle a little oil on the hinges. She
glanced over her shoulder at the doorway, found it unoccupied,
and bent to peer inside.

She understood immediately why nobody had bothered sticking their head in recently. It was mostly shiny clutter: the sorts of
things that looked impressive at a distance, but revealed themselves to be tarnished upon closer inspection. But behind the rows
of ancient, cloudy crystal glasses and goblets, the dented engraved
teaspoons, and a single gold and amethyst earring cushioned in a
velvet case, she found a box no bigger than the palm of her hand.
It was a baroque monstrosity, made of chiseled bronze and inlaid
with glimmering purple jasper, dotted with gemstones of various
colors like you might stud a ham. It was honestly one of the most
hideous things Emily had ever had the misfortune to look upon,

and had clearly been hidden at the back to prevent others from suffering the same fate.

It was perfect. Too dreadful to be missed, but with plenty to be stripped and sold without having to try to convince them of the box itself, which would be far too easy to identify.

Her dresses might not have been to the Edwards children's standards, but they did contain something that made up for aesthetic deficiencies: *pockets*. Amy had sewn them in herself. Of course, if she had known what Emily would go on to use them for, she would have immediately taken up the seam ripper.

Emily pocketed the box and was closing the cabinet doors when somebody spoke.

Her blood ran cold. Her stomach did an athletic little flip. She lost feeling in her fingertips, and possibly also her nose.

"There's a hand mirror on the top shelf that matches, if you'd like to steal any more of my late wife's things."

Emily had to step farther out into the room to see him. Captain Edwards was sitting in the corner in a high-backed armchair, with a candle stub on the table next to him and a closed book in his hand. The door had blocked her view of him, and she had been foolish and vexed enough not to conduct proper reconnaissance before she started putting her hands where they did not belong.

"I was going to take it to Miss Edwards," Emily said immediately, trying to keep her voice steady. Captain Edwards was perfectly still in his chair, the side of his face that was lit calm and expressionless. "To Miss *Grace* Edwards, I mean. We were just discussing baroque design during our lessons this afternoon, and I thought I'd find something to demonstrate . . . to surprise her with tomorrow morning so that we could . . . discuss it. I am sorry not to have asked, but . . . I thought everybody had gone to bed."

"I see." Captain Edwards didn't sound as if he particularly

believed or disbelieved her. He had undressed a little after dinner—no stock, no jacket, just a partly open shirt and a waistcoat
that was surprisingly plain. Emily tried not to drop her gaze from
his eyes to the surprisingly vulnerable strip of skin from throat
to chest; avoiding eye contact was probably what a guilty person
would do.

It was quite hard to *maintain* eye contact, though. His gaze
was so piercing that she felt lightly gut-stabbed.

"If it pleases you," she said with conviction, "you can sit with
us in the morning, and lend your voice to our discussion."

This was the sort of risk that made Amy call her sister "an
audacious blockhead," but Emily was too deep in the lie now to
do anything other than barrel recklessly onward.

"That won't be necessary," said Captain Edwards, finally un-
pinning her from his gaze as he opened his book. "Give it to
Meera after your lesson, and tell her to put it in with the lot for
auction next week."

"I will," Emily said, not quite believing her luck. She paused.
"Good night, Captain Edwards."

He said nothing.

With a very heavy pocket, Emily fled.

Chapter Six

IT WAS DIFFICULT TO SLEEP, EVEN IN SUCH A COMFORTABLE bed, with something probably worth the combined incomes of a small village sitting on top of her dresser. Captain Edwards had inadvertently given her the perfect cover: Meera did not know about the proposed sale of the box; the captain himself did not seem concerned enough about its future to think of it again. It could slip from the house without notice, and everybody except Emily would assume that was exactly where it was supposed to be.

There had been a time when she and Amy had owned nice things. Nothing as gaudy as this box—it really was hideous, even worse when she held it up to the candlelight, sort of like a square, iridescent insect with lumps—but things that were *incidental*. Fripperies. Trinkets. Items that served no purpose or function other than to look pretty or to be given as a token of affection, and then kept on display to prove that somebody had once liked you enough to spend a handful of shillings on you. The Laurence family had never actually been *wealthy*—she thought of herself and Amy at Grace's and Aster's ages, fighting over their one good new dress of the season, often envious of the girls they saw in the street with all their fashionable, fine things—but for the most part, they had been happy. They always had enough to eat, even if it wasn't the best cut of meat; there were always a few gifts at Christmas.

That was before their father died, and their mother gave up, and every avenue they should have explored in an attempt to keep hold of a modest income shrank until it became impassable. Mr. Laurence had trained as a barrister, his lavish education funded by a particularly generous and forgiving uncle who had inherited well and believed his nephew to be capable of greater things; unfortunately, he had not proved himself worthy of such hopes. Rumors—which were true—that he liked to drink and gamble his earnings, that he had been known to turn up to work still as drunk as a wheelbarrow, *and* that he was not clever enough to hide these facts as well as some of his colleagues, did not make him a particularly popular choice among solicitors. Nor did the fact that he owed many of those solicitors debts. By the time Emily was grown, Mr. Laurence's fortunes were already picking up speed as they trundled downhill.

She did not understand the extent of it until he died, very suddenly, when she was eighteen. He expired in disgrace, owing a great many people a lot of money that he'd never had in the first place. It was embarrassing, but Amy and Emily were to discover that there was something far worse than being embarrassed—being genuinely afraid.

While her father had been alive, some part of Emily had always believed that she would be all right. Nothing truly bad had happened to her, and even when times were lean, they had always been able to make do. After Mr. Laurence died, however, and their mother spent most of her time weeping and decidedly did not attempt to find matches or situations for either of them—and after it turned out that the pleasant young man Amy had been gazing at across the packed halls of dances had a father, too, and that he was in fact one of the people Mr. Laurence had been in a lot of debt to—things became much . . . darker. The world narrowed. Possibilities were no longer endless, and it became clear they never really had been. Nobody wanted to marry one of Mr. Laurence's daughters. Life was a mine shaft with no bottom, and if you took a misstep, you could trip over the edge and keep falling forever.

Emily had determined not to care about her lack of marriage prospects, but she knew it hurt Amy—Amy, who was so kind and funny and beautiful, and would have made somebody a wonderful wife. It was horribly unfair.

They sold their house, which had not been particularly lavish in the first place, and moved somewhere even smaller. Mrs. Laurence was able to pay off a few debts, but the amount owed was so vast, it was like spitting into a well in the hope of eventually filling it. Their fortunes dwindled. Mrs. Laurence became a sort-of seamstress, when she remembered, picking up jobs here and there. Emily and Amy held out for two years, and then they faced the reality of their new situation and went to work.

Looking back on that time in her life, Emily *liked* to think that she had simply squared her shoulders and walked straight to the mill without hesitation, but if she was honest with herself, it hadn't been quite that simple. She had tried to find work elsewhere at first. She had avoided the mill, had turned her head when she walked past, as if just by looking at it she might be sucked in like a mouse down a drain.

Eventually, she had given in. Her mother had emerged from her stupor long enough to be horrified, which had actually helped harden Emily's resolve to see it through. It was taking far too long to find decent positions, and she knew that if she started earning a wage—meager as it was—it would buy Amy a little more time to find something more suitable.

The argument that had ensued with her sister was quite possibly the worst they'd ever had, but once Amy understood that Emily's mind was made up, that was that.

It had been worth it, in the end, when Amy had become a governess for the Turners, which was what she had wanted from the moment they started discussing the possibility of work, while lying under the blankets of their shared bed. Their parting had been painful, but Emily had put on a brave face and smiled and told her sister that she should fill her pockets with sweets, in case she needed to throw them as a distraction and run, and that she should draw little marks on the children at her new house if she had trouble telling them apart.

When Amy fell ill, Emily tried to call her home and forbid her from working at all, but Amy could not countenance the idea of sitting by the fire sewing with her mother while Emily worked long days among the looms. The work at the mill was bitterly hard. Her peers were other tired, hard-faced women and the young boys who had not yet been elevated to true mill hands. The girls who worked there were never offered such a station. They mostly moved on at some point, because their bodies were exhausted or because they were no longer suited to the factory floor.

Emily did not move on. Work was still scarce, and she had nowhere else to go.

She was sure, in the same dogged, unshakable way she clung to all of her truths, that Amy would have returned to full health if she hadn't refused to slow down or come home to rest. Amy argued that the money was too good, and that it was not as if she was working as hard as Emily; in the end, she had only come home when it was truly impossible for her to continue. Emily did not ask what exactly had precipitated this realization, but she saw the concern with which Mr. Turner delivered her personally from his carriage back into Emily's care.

It had seemed that Amy might be well enough to work again just as the position at Fairmont House became available. It paid even better than the Turners had, and she had written to inquire at once. They could not afford to lose Fairmont, even when Amy took a turn and clearly could not go.

This was why Emily had to be far more careful and not let her temper take the reins. She had to think like Amy, talk like Amy, *breathe* like Amy—at least until she was named an incompetent or a fraud and sent away. *Amy* hadn't let the world harden her. Amy was kind, even when life wasn't kind to her.

Emily couldn't be soft or sweet or kind, but she could try to remember who she had been at eighteen, and who she might have become if it hadn't all gone so wrong.

At breakfast, the morning after Emily's first successful theft, Akia turned to her and handed her a thick wedge of firm, yellowish fruit.

"It's pineapple," she said. "Have you tried it?"

"No," Emily said, her mind fuzzy from a night with too little sleep. "Where did it come from?"

"I know a man," Akia said, winking at her. "Not really. I mean, I *do* know a man, but there's nothing untoward about it. He has connections to a house with a pinery. And he owes me a favor, because of the time he almost ran me down in his wagon, and I was only saved because the horses were startled by a seagull and swerved at the last second."

"A seagull?" Emily said faintly.

"Yes. Anyway, that's not important. A favor was in order. That favor is now half a pineapple."

"But why are you giving it to me?" said Emily, perplexed.

"You looked dead," said Akia. "You know—on the inside. And it tricked you into talking to me. Eat it before it browns."

Ignoring this indictment of her looks, Emily did. The pineapple was delicious *and* hurt her tongue, which was interesting enough to entertain her until Akia started clearing the plates. She found herself actually listening to the idle chatter between the servants; watching Oliver pack his pipe while telling Meera about an argument with the horse veterinarian that had almost resulted in fisticuffs; noticing that Joe winced when he bent to poke at the fire, his hand going to his back.

The morning passed without incident, Grace being well-behaved enough that Emily sometimes forgot she was there at all.

When she returned to the schoolroom after luncheon, she discovered that Aster had deigned to join them, which dampened her mood instantly.

"Thank you for joining us, Aster," she said, which she thought was very big of her, considering.

Aster just glared at her.

"I think we will have a splendid afternoon," said Grace, apparently immune to the glare.

"I did consider driving a nail into my hand very, very slowly instead," said Aster, "but this was preferable only because I could not locate a hammer."

"There's one in the kitchen," Emily said, before she could stop herself.

Aster tried to behave as if she hadn't heard this, but the slight upward jolt of her eyebrows betrayed her.

Grace had finished *Udolpho*, which meant that Emily could simply ask her to recount her feelings about it and then let her go and go. Aster got up and perused the bookshelves as she did, finding what she was looking for—a dense-looking tome about sixteenth-century Italian art—and slumping back into her chair.

". . . and now I think I would probably not like to marry him," Grace finished eventually. "He is probably the sort of man you *like* to think you would marry, but who would actually be entirely useless in reality and spend all his time moping and exclaiming and not knowing where the accounting book is kept."

"I see," said Emily.

"Do you?" said Aster, looking up from her book with a very penetrating look in Emily's direction. "I notice you have not told us what *you* think of *Udolpho*. What are the themes? The moral lessons? What is the symbolic meaning of the black veil?"

Emily swallowed her discomfort and smiled thinly.

"I am interested in Grace's thoughts on the book, Aster, as I am already perfectly aware of my own."

"There is no need to get testy," Aster said, in the sort of infuriating tone that was a test of its own. "I just think it rather odd that you have been here for five days and all Grace has done is read her book while you . . . Well, what exactly have you been doing? Sleeping with your eyes open?"

She shouldn't have put the idea of driving nails into hands into Emily's mind. Now that she was angry, all the world was hammers.

"I have been enjoying our lessons," Grace said firmly.

Aster rolled her eyes; Emily knew that she had been granted a reprieve and should hold her tongue, but her tongue had other ideas.

"Why don't you tell us a little about what *you've* been reading, Aster? Have you read *Udolpho* recently? Enlighten us on the *themes*."

"I can't read," said Aster, closing the book she had been idly flicking through.

"Well, I know that's not true," said Emily, trying to keep the edge out of her voice. "You seemed as if you wanted desperately to tell us your thoughts on the black veil."

"Can *you* not read, Miss Laurence?" Aster said sharply. "Is that why you're getting so embarrassingly vexed?"

"I was lucky enough to receive an education, as are you. I know you think all this somehow beneath you, Aster, but there are many people who would love a chance to spend their mornings sitting and discussing literature. Alas, they're working in the mills and the mines. Perhaps you'd like to swap places? I can just *picture* you down a mine."

Aster sat up a little straighter.

"*That* was rather ill-mannered, Miss Laurence."

"I am simply trying to educate you, Miss Edwards."

"Don't call me that," said Aster, her facade of indifference crumbling for a moment.

"Call you what?" Emily said, genuinely confused. "Miss Edwards?"

"Oh, *go to hell*," Aster said, her tone laced with genuine malice. "If you can even navigate your way there. You are clearly an idiot of poor breeding incapable of following basic instructions."

Emily saw red. She saw a color *beyond* red, as yet undiscovered.

"I *beg* your pardon?"

"I think you heard me quite clearly."

"I'm giving you a chance to reconsider being such an insolent little *bitch*."

She regretted it immediately, all the air leaving her lungs at once. This was not a scrap with somebody trying to overcharge in a street market, or a disagreement on a factory floor. This was certain to lose her the position. There had been no point unpacking after all; she'd be gone before the clock struck twelve.

"You are the lowest sort of swine," Aster said, her face contorted into something hurt and ugly, "and you can go and *fuck* yourself."

In the silence that ensued, Emily listened to the ticking of the marble clock and swallowed the burning in her chest, locked in the fiercest eye contact she had ever endured in her entire life.

"I think I should like to read *The Italian* next," Grace said desperately, her voice thin and high, "now that I have finished *Udolpho*. Although perhaps . . . Should I take a break from—"

Aster stood up, scraping her chair back with force, so that it shrieked painfully against the floorboards.

"Tell Father I tried," she said to Grace, before she stormed out.

"I'm so sorry," Grace said faintly. "She . . . doesn't really like Gothic literature."

"Yes," said Emily, still catching her breath. "Well. I . . . I should not have lost my temper. I can only apologize."

"That's all right," said Grace, valiantly attempting normality. "I am sure that by tomorrow we will all have forgotten it and be great *friends* again."

Chapter Seven

𝓛ARGE AS IT WAS, THE HOUSE FELT TOO SMALL TO CONTAIN Emily's anger.

She did not attend dinner with the servants that evening, choosing instead to go to bed early and pull the blankets up over her head and seethe steadily until she fell asleep. She half expected that any moment Captain Edwards would kick down the door and demand that she left at once for the crime of insulting his precocious daughter, but the captain did not appear, and her door stayed intact. She could only surmise that she had somehow remained employed, at least for the time being.

Meera took one look at her at breakfast the next morning and gently suggested that she might take the afternoon off.

"The doctor is visiting Grace after luncheon, anyway," she said cheerfully.

"The doctor?" Joe said, pausing with his knife half sawn through a hunk of bread.

"Just to check on her progress," Meera said, giving him a reassuring smile. "No cause for concern."

Joe resumed sawing.

"What is there to do?" Emily said. "If I take the afternoon off, I mean."

"Oh, well, there are all sorts of places, although most of them are either cliff or beach . . . You have not been into the village yet, have you? It isn't very large, but at least it isn't made of rock, grass, or sand."

"I think it actually is made of rocks and sand," said Akia. "Is that not what houses are made of?"

"Unless they're made of mud and horse shit," said Oliver.

He paused, then sighed, reached into his pocket, and pulled out a coin, which he slid toward Meera without further comment.

"There's a pub," said Meera. "Although the food is—"

"Don't eat the food," Joe said gruffly.

"Unless," suggested Akia, "you are trying to urgently rid your stomach of poison. In that case, there's no better fare in the whole county."

With these glowing reviews in mind, and after a claustrophobic morning spent in the schoolroom watching Grace sketch intense, lopsided puppies, Emily set off to the village.

It was a brisk half-hour walk, and something lightened in Emily's chest as she put the house behind her. It was a relief to be anonymous and unobserved, accompanied only by jagged coastline and squabbling seabirds and the crash of the surf below. She could slouch, and put her hands in her pockets, and swear at the sky if the mood took her (which it did, and often). The landscape, which she had previously written off as one long stretch of gray, was actually broken up by bright, scrubby patches of gorse and heather, and it wasn't long before hedges and stone walls rose up with the promise of civilization ahead.

The road down to the village sloped so much that Emily dreaded having to walk back up it; when the village itself came into view, it was nestled down by the sea like a bird's nest built optimistically into the cracks of a cliff, the buildings a collection of squat gray sentinels guarding a small market square against the coastal wind. There were boats moored at one end of what could not even charitably be called a harbor, bobbing on the gentle waves.

It did not seem to be a market day, and yet there were still a few stalls set up selling freshly caught fish and local cheese, which was a pungent combination. Emily walked past the scrum of shouting fishermen and their customers, then the small line outside the haberdasher's, and entered the Rose and Crown.

It was a tiny warren of a pub. It had many oddly shaped corners, tables squeezed into nooks, and old men nursing their drinks in crannies; quite a few of them looked up at her as she entered, and then tracked her progress toward the bar. Emily wished hellfire and damnation on all of them.

She fingered the handful of sixpences in her pocket that she'd slipped out of Meera's swear jar, and then ordered a pint of strong beer.

She had never been a drinker—certainly not of *beer* in *public houses*, even after her station had experienced such a rapid decline that it would not have been strange for her to join the other mill workers for a drink at the end of a shift—but the week had already been too long, and it wasn't even over yet.

Besides, this beer was good, insofar as beer *could* be good. Halfway through the pint Emily stopped feeling on edge and shrinking from every glance thrown her way. Her gaze wandered to the walls, where somebody had attempted to improve the interiors by wonkily nailing up a few framed etchings; some of them looked as if they had been torn from a newspaper.

One of them was of Fairmont House.

It looked nicer, etched. Less lonely. You could almost imagine that the front drive gave way to lush, well-kept grounds instead of endless coastal moorland. You could pretend the people living inside it weren't obnoxious pudding-heads. You could pretend they had all died in a fire.

"That's Fairmont," said the pretty, plump barmaid, leaning toward Emily as she polished a glass with her rag.

Emily shifted minutely back. "Yes."

Satisfied that they shared this knowledge, the barmaid nodded. "They've a new governess," she said.

Emily did not react. She supposed that the bartering of information like this was a key part of the barmaid's trade. Perhaps she was expecting something in return. Perhaps she was just bored.

"Scrawny, odd-looking thing, apparently. The Sandlers saw her on the way in. Underfed. Big lampy eyes, like a runt kitten. I suppose it's as well to have a plain governess, though, so that nobody gets any ideas—'specially with the captain a widower nigh on four years now."

Emily ducked her head, focusing carefully on her drink. *Odd-looking?* Thanks ever so, Mr. and Mrs. Sandler. She should have opened that carriage door and let their baby slide out into the mud.

She didn't reply, and eventually the barmaid bustled off to bother somebody else. She was left alone for all of ten seconds before somebody sat down next to her at the bar. Emily did not look at him, so all she got was a vague impression: warmth, reddish hair, a dark coat.

"For what it's worth," the man said quietly, "I happen to like your eyes."

Emily stiffened. She still did not look. She picked up her pint and knocked back the last of it, then made to get up.

He put his hand on the bar next to her.

"Wait," he said. "I apologize. That was too bold of me. What I really meant to say was . . . good afternoon."

It was a valiant effort, but Emily was not so easily fooled.

"By way of apology," he continued, undeterred, "let me buy you a drink. You do not have to talk to me while you drink it."

"I know I don't," said Emily, before she could stop herself. Damn.

"Ah." She could hear a smile in his voice. It was annoying. "Good. Then we have a deal."

As he leaned forward to catch the barmaid's attention, Emily glanced at him. He had dark auburn hair that curled gently down to his neck, a neat mustache that matched, and was incongruously tanned in the same way that Captain Edwards was. Another seafaring man, then, or perhaps a soldier—something had kept him dallying out of doors. He looked to be around forty, give or take a few years either side.

When the pint appeared, he slid it toward Emily with a knowing smile, and she looked away.

"Did I win, then?" he said quietly.

"Win what?" said Emily, taking a sip and then using her sleeve to blot her mouth in a very unladylike manner. "I am drinking your pint. I was led to believe that I could do so without a running commentary."

"Not that," said the man. "You're the mysterious, underfed governess, yes? You were very good, but you twitched a little and it gave you away."

Emily took another long drink. "Yes," she said eventually. "The mystery is how I find my way around with such odd, 'lampy' eyes."

The man laughed at once, light and easy. "We have already established what I think of your eyes. How are you liking Fairmont?"

Emily did not quite roll her much-discussed eyes, but it was a close thing.

"I like Fairmont just fine."

"Goodness, I can tell. Is Captain Edwards treating you well?"

"Who?" said Emily.

The man laughed again. "Giving you the cold shoulder, is he? Sounds just like the old bastard."

Emily let out a surprised huff of laughter, disturbing the froth of her beer, and then stopped very abruptly.

"Outlawed laughing now, too, has he? Well, he'll never get that through the Lords."

"Do you know him?" Emily said, a little surprised by all of this familiarity and laid-back lambasting.

"Yes, yes. Not that well, but our paths crossed in the navy a few times. I was actually thinking of sending him a note—will you deliver it for me, if I go and scribble it now, or will you set fire to it in front of me and then drop it into my pint?"

Emily shrugged noncommittally.

"Of course, I could not ask you to do so without compensation. I have . . . hmmm. Three shillings and some lint. I am partial to the lint, but the three shillings are yours."

It felt important to Emily that she wait at least a few seconds before answering, and that she sound frankly bored when she did.

"Fine."

"Fine," said the man, pleased. "Excuse me for just one moment."

He was only gone for a few minutes; when he returned, Emily looked at him properly. He was handsome in a piratical sort of way. She did not exactly *trust* him, but she trusted him to be untrustworthy, which was a sort of assurance in its own way.

"Here," he said, placing the folded note down in front of her, sealed with a blob of candle wax. He had tucked the three shillings into it, so that it was heavier than she expected when she picked it up, and she nearly dropped one of the coins.

"Careful you don't lose a hand when you give it to him—he bites."

"I'm sure he doesn't," she said, emboldened by the beer and this new comrade in captain-hating. "*Biting* would be far too interesting. I could tolerate biting, as part of a broader repertoire of personality traits."

Emily liked making him laugh, because he didn't do it out of pity and it wasn't aimed *at* her; he laughed in a sort of quietly awed way, as if he had discovered something exciting and was pleased to be the first to witness it.

"Listen," he said, leaning closer, careful not to encroach too far. "There's something you might be able to help me with. I have reason to believe that Edwards has been doing something a little untoward. Shocking, I know, but it could be quite diverting if it proves true—and the person who uncovers such a thing would certainly be rewarded handsomely. You seem enterprising, and far too lively to be trapped in Fairmont House forever. If you hear anything . . . see anything . . . can I rely on you to pass it along?"

Emily was stuck on *rewarded handsomely*.

This could be the answer. She wouldn't need to lie low for weeks, hoping for another opportunity to steal something gaudy from the depths of a cupboard. Collecting secrets was far easier. There was no need to find somewhere in your room to stash the evidence. Captain Edwards was likely involved in some dull crime of a financial nature—some bending of the rules that wealthy people were so fond of—and she would be all too happy to cash in on his arrogant mistakes.

"Think about it," he said. Emily was pleased to discover that her face wasn't saying an enthusiastic yes on her behalf. "And don't tell the old man, whatever you decide. Stop back here again Saturday week, and we can continue this little chat. Have another drink. I'll count your fingers and thumbs to ensure you still have them all."

"I can manage counting to ten on my own," said Emily.

"Well, there you are," said the man, winking. "I knew I was looking at a woman of substance. Saturday, next week! Think about it."

"I will," said Emily.

He offered a hand to be shaken. "I'm Charles."

"Charles," said Emily, taking it briefly.

"And you are . . . ?"

"The governess."

Charles seemed to find this little act of resistance amusing.

"What sort of governess drinks in public houses and lets ugly, brazen strangers bend her ear?"

Emily drank the last of her second pint in one gulp, then set the glass back down and got to her feet.

"*This* sort."

She kept the note and the shillings clutched tightly in her hot fist all the way back to Fairmont House.

Chapter Eight

HELL HAD NOT YET BECOME A DESTINATION FOR ICE-SKATING and frost fairs, so Emily did not go looking for Captain Edwards herself.

She sought out Meera instead, thinking her the best intermediary for note-passing, already rehearsing the story she'd tell—that a nondescript messenger had given it to her on the road by the house, rather than a very describable man slipping it into her hand two drinks deep at the Rose and Crown.

She was on her way to the stairs, intending to go down to the housekeeper's office to see if she could find Meera there, when she instead saw what looked like a bundle of fabric crumpled at the bottom of the stairs. It took her another few seconds to realize what she was looking at.

"Grace?" she said, striding over to get a closer look. "What are you doing?"

For one horrible moment, she thought Grace was unconscious, or worse. Her limbs went cold with fear, her body reacting before her brain could; she knew it was Grace on the floor, but her mind saw Amy, fainted clean away on the path outside the house when she had come home from the Turners' to visit at Christmas, berries crushed bloodily into the stone, snow in her hair. Amy had looked just like this: too still, too small, hurting in a way Emily couldn't fix . . .

"Oh," said Grace, stirring. "Good afternoon, Amy. I was

just . . . I was on my way upstairs, but I needed to have a little rest. I shall be fine in a minute."

"Did you fall?" said Emily, catching her breath.

Grace looked as if she were in quite a lot of difficulty; she was half sitting, half lying against the bottom steps, her face flushed and damp.

"No," Grace said stubbornly. "I sat down! This is how I sit."

Emily thought again of Amy, insisting she was all right to go back to work—thinking she was doing an excellent job of hiding the fact that she was swaying on her feet, refusing Emily's arm when she offered it.

"Fine," Emily said. "I would also like to sit."

God save her from little martyrs who refused to be helped, but she could hardly trot away and leave her there. She might have been irritating, but she *was* only a child.

"You don't have to do that, really. I'll just . . ."

"I wouldn't have married Valancourt," Emily said after a few moments. "I think he's an idiot. And he lost all his money."

"Oh, but he's a hero in the end," Grace said, closing her eyes and smiling. "On second thought, I think he deserves another chance. Perhaps he'd be more discerning, the next time around."

"People do not change," said Emily. "If they do, they only get worse."

"I cannot believe that," said Grace. "Not least because, if that's the case, Aster will be a seasoned criminal by the time she turns one-and-twenty."

Emily snorted, and Grace's face lit up.

"She means well," she said, and then at the expression on Emily's face, rethought. "All right, not *well* exactly. I suppose I mean . . . she is good in ways that you do not see right away."

"She threatened to kill me the other day," said Emily.

Grace sighed, letting her head fall gently back against the step.

"Yes, she does tend to do that quite a lot." There was quiet as she pondered this. "Do you have any siblings?"

Emily wasn't going to tell her; she didn't owe Grace anything—explanations or intimacy or pieces of her heart—but it felt strange to deny Amy for any reason at all.

"I have a sister."

"Oh!" said Grace, looking pleased. "Then you *know*."

"For all *you* know, we might hate each other," said Emily.

"Do you?"

"No," Emily admitted. "No, I do not hate her at all."

Grace closed her eyes, and Emily realized that even having this conversation almost horizontally had stretched her a little too thin. There was a quiet creak on the upper landing, the sort of noise houses like this made all the time just because they could, but Emily glanced up anyway and found herself looking directly at Captain Edwards.

He was standing with one hand on the banister and one foot on the top step, as if he'd been arrested mid-movement. His brow was slightly furrowed, his lips pressed firmly together as he looked back at Emily, off guard and deep in thought. She had no idea how long he had been watching them like that, and expected that any moment he would come marching down the stairs to take charge of his daughter, ask after her health, and arrange to have her carried upstairs.

He did not move. His expression was the only thing that changed—a journey from puzzled focus to something much more neutral, a smoothing over of the lines that made his face irritatingly interesting.

"Miss Edwards?"

It was not Captain Edwards who had spoken; it was Joe, from the other direction. He sounded gruff as ever, but with an undercurrent of urgency. He had a crumpled list in his hand, as if he, too, might have been looking for Meera.

"Are you unwell?"

"I fell," said Grace, with a shrug. "Don't tell Father. He's . . . busy."

Joe was too preoccupied to notice that Captain Edwards was still standing just ten feet above them. Emily glanced back at him; his mouth was open as if he had been about to speak, but he closed it abruptly again. He seemed to have forgotten Emily entirely—he was watching Grace, his eyes tight as Joe went to help her up.

A second later, he had turned on his heel and vanished.

"Come on," said Joe. "Take my arm. Miss Laurence, get Meera."

"It's all right, Joe, really," said Grace, as he helped her to her feet. "There is no need for all this fuss. I felt light-headed. I suppose I didn't have enough at luncheon."

"Well, what did you do that for?" Joe said amiably, as they very slowly started to ascend the stairs. "It was plum cake. You *like* plum cake. What was wrong with my plum cake, eh?"

By the time Emily had found Meera, who was trying to fix one of the shutters in the parlor, she had almost forgotten about the note. After relaying Grace's small collapse, Emily pressed it into her hand as an afterthought. Meera tucked it away into her apron and then went to see about calling for the doctor.

Emily was familiar with the strange hush that fell over a house when a doctor came to call. It pulled to the surface a sickly anxiety that drowned out everything else and made her feel distracted and brittle. She was so desperate not to be there to see him come that she went down to the servants' dining room, found the discarded pack of playing cards that the others had probably been gambling merrily with the night before, and set up a game of patience.

She was somehow losing to herself when Meera discovered her.

"She'll be all right," Meera said, without prompting. Her apron was coming untied on one side, and she seemed to have a smear of preserves on her arm; she noticed both at once and tried to rectify them simultaneously. "She has just overdone it a little, and needs rest."

Emily nodded. "What did Captain Edwards say?"

"Say? I don't know," said Meera, as if this were a very odd question.

Emily supposed it was. She just couldn't get the picture of the captain standing silently at the top of the stairs out of her head. What sort of father wouldn't come rushing to his daughter's aid? Would sneak away rather than extend a hand, or a kind word? Even Emily's own father would have done better, although his only comfort would likely have been a ruffling of her hair and gruff advice to get straight back on her feet.

"Grace didn't want him to know," said Emily, and Meera sighed.

"I do not encourage the keeping of secrets in this house," she said.

It felt pointed enough that heat rose in Emily's cheeks, but Meera did not seem to be accusing her of anything. She sat down opposite Emily, taking the weight off her feet and letting out a long breath.

"Are you all right?"

"Me?" said Emily, blindsided.

"Are you settling in? Sleeping? Eating enough? Is there anything you miss from home, perhaps, that I could request from Joe?"

"Oh," said Emily. She had barely spared a thought for any of this; she was eating, she was sleeping, but whether it was *enough* had never been worth considering. "No. I mean . . . yes."

"Hmmm," said Meera, studying her. Emily thought of the barmaid's not particularly flattering description of the new governess at Fairmont House, and wondered if they all saw her that way: pale and ugly and strange, in dire need of feeding up. "Well, let me know if you need anything. And if . . . Well, I can fetch you something from the stillroom if you'd like something for the . . . the rash, on your hands."

Emily's hands curled protectively like startled hedgehogs. There was no rash, just the healing calluses from hard days of menial labor—but she was struck with suspicion that Meera had already guessed this, and was trying to be delicate about it.

It was ridiculous. Her hands were fine.

"I don't need anything," she said, and Meera looked at her far too closely before giving a little shrug and getting to her feet.

"In my experience, that is very rarely true," she said, "but each to their own, I suppose. Right, I ought to start the tea. I shouldn't think you'll be needed for lessons tomorrow morning, but Grace might wish for some company in the afternoon. Oh, and be careful if you show your face aboveground—Aster is in a bit of a difficult mood."

There was a letter addressed to *Miss Laurence* waiting in Emily's room when she finally ascended the stairs, keeping an eye out for Aster all the while, like a vole scanning for owls. As soon as she saw Amy's handwriting she snatched it up and took it to her bed, so that she could read it slowly from the comfort of her blankets.

Dear Emily,
You must think I am foolish indeed. You cannot fob me off by talking about your CURTAINS. Who cares about the fireplace, or the cornices! Who even taught you the word cornices!

What are the children really like? And the captain? The housekeeper was so kind when we corresponded—please do pass on my thanks to her for allowing this arrangement until I am feeling better. Incidentally—has there been any trouble on this front? I feel I agreed to this in such a malaise of fever that it all seemed like a play we were putting on. The reality is not particularly practical. Do they really not mind that you have never taken care of a child before? I will endeavor to get better faster, so that if complications do arise, they do not have time to come to a full simmer.

I know you think you are an acquired taste, and you do not like to stand still enough for anybody to be able to acquire you, but please remember to be a little sweeter than usual, if it doesn't turn your stomach.

Also, I don't know what you said to Mother before you left, but she keeps insisting I eat second helpings of everything practically at knifepoint, and creeping into the room and watching me when she thinks I'm asleep. It's very troubling.

I love you and I miss you. Thank you for doing this. Not just this.

Your affectionate (and bored) sister,
Amy

Chapter Nine

TWO WEEKS INTO EMILY'S LIFE AT FAIRMONT HOUSE, CAPTAIN Edwards decided to throw a dinner party.

This was clearly unusual behavior, because everybody was walking around looking as if they had never heard the phrase *dinner party* before in their lives. When Meera announced it at breakfast, Joe stood up, threw his napkin across the room, stood seething silently for a moment, and then sat down again.

"He's very pleased," Akia whispered to Emily. She seemed to be perfectly serious.

Emily had grown used to taking her meals with the servants. Sometimes Grace demanded her company for breakfast or luncheon in the schoolroom and Emily did stay, eating cake and drinking tea as Grace talked determinedly at her, but just as often Grace disappeared into Aster's room to eat—a place Emily would not have dared venture even with the king's militia covering her back—or went to eat with her father. Meera had suggested that Emily could eat in the schoolroom regardless of whether her charges were there or not, as the previous governesses had, but this just felt like additional fuss for no reason. She told Meera very firmly that she did not care, and nobody questioned it anymore when she appeared in the servants' dining room and took a seat at the very end of the table.

She had not been encouraging friendship from anybody at the house, but she discovered that some of its inhabitants didn't need encouragement. Apparently, her lack of propriety about eating arrangements had put them at ease enough that they thought she might be in the market for *friends*. They kept talking to her, trying to pull her into their little rituals and jokes, although they did not seem surprised when she stayed taciturn and distant. Meera chatted away about local people and places at a fast clip, interrupting herself constantly to explain who was related to whom, not that Emily was even attempting to catalog a single one of them; Akia kept telling her more and more ridiculous stories that could not *possibly* be true, not a bit put off by the fact that Emily never laughed; even Oliver offered her drinks and his pipe without a second thought, as if they were intimate enough friends to share spit.

She did speak to them—she could hardly get through the day without doing so—but she kept fraternizing to a minimum. It was probably the only way in which she was behaving like a real governess.

These people were too loyal to let slip any useful tidbit about Captain Edwards, and there was no real value in pretending to be far more agreeable than she actually was to get to know them, because now she had an escape route. If she could discover exactly what improper business Captain Edwards had tangled himself up in, and earn herself a quick payout that far exceeded a year's worth of wages at Fairmont House, she'd be away with the next post—long before they noticed that some of the captain's most hideous possessions had gone out walking.

The past week had not been fruitful—she'd barely seen the captain, not even when she tried repeating her nocturnal wanderings about the house when everybody else was preoccupied, keeping her hands to herself this time. She was not entirely sure how one went about obtaining secret information about somebody who seemed to be such a closed book. The only time they had been within breathing room of each other was at church, but they had traveled in separate carriages—Meera had been needed for some conversation about linens, so Emily had been relegated to the carriage with the servants—and sat in different pews, so the only view she had of him was his back. She had not been able to glean anything from the way he thumbed through his hymnal.

Aster, on the other hand, accidentally tore one of the pages halfway through the service, and Emily saw her slip it to Grace, who looked exceedingly guilty as she tucked it under a cushion.

"Joe," Meera was saying now, as they finished eating their breakfast, the upcoming dinner party still top billing. "If you can get me a list today, I'll speak to Mr. Khan personally and ensure we get the best of everything."

Oliver, who looked hungover, raised his head as if he were going to try to make a joke, then shook it and gave up.

"Did you have something you wished to say, Oliver?" said Meera primly.

"Mr. Khan," Oliver attempted valiantly. "You want to . . . touch mouths with him."

"That was disgusting, thank you, Oliver. Put sixpence in the jar just for nauseating me. All right, everybody, we have a lot of work to do! Amy . . . I hate to ask, but I'd be grateful for a little help once you have finished with your lessons for the day. We only have a few days to prepare, and it is impossible to get additional staff at such short notice. Nothing too onerous, I promise!"

Akia rolled her eyes, perhaps due to the fact that the more onerous tasks would probably be parceled out to her, but nobody complained. It seemed to be universally accepted that Meera was doing her absolute best. She would certainly not be shirking responsibilities or delegating everything to the rest of them; Emily was always discovering her doing jobs that were more suited to a maid of all work than a housekeeper. Just that morning, she had found Meera attempting to climb onto a dresser so that she could remove the world's smallest cobweb from the frame of a nautical painting; in Emily's opinion it had not been visible to the naked eye, and was certainly not worth risking your kneecaps for.

Emily had planned to set Grace up with some art materials and let her sketch all day again—drawing was one of a few helpful subjects that she had found easy to bluff, as it could be "taught" simply by telling Grace that a dog's nose had been drawn in the wrong place—but Grace, who was feeling much better, had torn her dress on the corner of a dresser and started musing about where fabric came from, anyway.

This was how Emily found herself explaining the concept and inner workings of textile mills. Grace, who had never imagined such things existed, was so curious that she insisted Emily gave her a full account, which Emily tried to do while pretending she had never set foot in such a place herself. It was hardly a sermon on the rules of etiquette, but Emily could not bring herself to care.

If things went her way, the Edwards sisters were not going to be her problem for much longer; and besides, it might do Grace some good to understand a little something of the real world. It was also pleasing, Emily had to admit, to feel like an expert on something other than the location of a dog's nose. She wasn't getting much of a chance to do that at Fairmont House.

Grace listened in rapt fascination the entire time, and then asked a long series of questions that included things like "What is a loom?" and "How exactly do *wages* work?"

Emily had no idea when she'd stopped finding these conversations so irritating. She supposed she had simply built up a
resistance to them. During her first week, Grace had seemed desperate to impress her, but since her fall on the stairs and Emily's
encounter with her there, she had relaxed somewhat. She spoke
to Emily as if they were old friends, was always genuinely pleased
to see her, and was often rather funny even if she did not mean to
be. There was something of Amy in her, too, that Emily was finding it increasingly difficult to ignore.

"You are in a good mood," Grace observed, when Emily had
run out of ways to explain mill equipment.

"No, I'm not," Emily said promptly. "Start drawing."

"I will draw, but I will not back down on the good mood,"
Grace said. "You *like* me! You like explaining *looms* to me!"

"Believe me, I derive no joy from realizing the depths of your
ignorance," said Emily, but Grace just laughed.

It was not a *good mood*. It was simply the ebbing of nerves
as she settled into the house, and the knowledge that she had
found a way out of it. If she was relieved that Grace had come
through her spell of illness relatively quickly and without seeming too worse for wear, it was only because anything else would
have complicated her life further.

Emily brought over a vase of flowers to be used as the subject
of a still life, and then sat enjoying the quiet as her charge bent
industriously over her etching. The flames were crackling gently
in the grate as Grace scratched softly away with her charcoal, all
sound in the room muffled by the thick rugs and the cheerful
tapestry on the wall. There was even a blanket draped over the
arm of Emily's chair that she could pull over herself if she was
feeling truly decadent.

It was such a luxury, just to sit near a fire in a well-appointed
room, warm enough and well-fed, that in her weakest moments
Emily could almost imagine herself accustomed to it—until she

thought of Amy at home, probably this minute a little hungry and a little cold, and felt disgusted with herself for entertaining the idea.

When lessons concluded for the day and Grace was sent off to prepare for dinner, Meera apologetically asked Emily to sit with Akia in the servants' dining room and polish silver. They carried boxes and boxes of it down and Akia started methodically taking it all out and making little symmetrical piles, humming softly as she did.

It would have been all too easy to slip something into her pocket when Akia turned away, but Emily was determined not to let her rashness get her into any more trouble—and besides, she could not tell the difference between a mediocre spoon and a spoon of merit.

"As you may have gathered, Mr. Khan the grocer is madly in love with Meera," Akia said to Emily, who hadn't asked. "He delivers her things *personally*. But she thinks herself far too sensible for love. I once told her a man had given me a flower, and she said, 'What for?' I told him that all he needs to do is explain to her that it makes *business sense* for them to get married, and she'll agree to terms and sign on the dotted line. He's too much of a romantic, though. He thinks he can woo her. She's unwooable."

"Mmmm," Emily said, as she polished a knife with climbing roses wrapped around the handle.

"Speaking of spectator sports, Mrs. Spencer is coming to the dinner party. Oliver and I have a bet running that pertains to her."

"Who's Mrs. Spencer?" said Emily, falling for the bait.

Akia looked slightly triumphant. "The future Mrs. Captain Edwards, by my wager. She's an heiress, and a widow. And Captain

Edwards is in need of an heiress. Apparently he and the late Mrs. Edwards married for love, but there is to be no more of that sort of nonsense under this roof."

Emily didn't scoff, but she wanted to. An enormous house, a governess, and four servants hardly seemed like dire financial straits.

"I mean it. This used to be a grand house. Fully staffed. The captain has sold half the furniture in the past few years. Sometimes I go to sit down, forgetting, and I just keep going until I hit the floor."

It wasn't as if Emily hadn't noticed the absence of furniture, but she was still curious.

"Why is he selling it?"

Akia put down the cutlery and slid a silver serving dish into polishing range.

"He had a moderate inheritance, but he really made something of himself in the navy. He wasn't supposed to come home so soon. Should have had a few more promotions under his belt before he ran aground."

"Then why would Mrs. Spencer marry him?" asked Emily.

Akia laughed. "Maybe she likes tall, broad, seaworn widowers. Or *papas*. Have you seen him without his shirt on?"

"No," said Emily, horrified by all of the above.

"Ah," said Akia, nodding sagely. "It will all make sense when you do."

Emily strongly doubted this, and was quite disturbed by the direction this conversation had taken. It had already been obvious that the servants of Fairmont House did not have as many boundaries as one might expect when it came to their relationship with their employer, but discussions of *shirtlessness* were beyond anything she could have imagined. She didn't want to think of Captain Edwards as a real person at all, and certainly not about what might be underneath his *shirt*.

"What happened?" Emily said, trying to move past this. "With the navy, I mean? Why did he come home early?"

"Maybe he realized that once you've seen one wave, you've seen them all," Akia said lightly, but Emily was not fooled: she knew more than she was letting on.

"It wasn't because of Grace's illness, then?"

Akia shrugged. "Perhaps. It's not really for me to say."

"He barely seems to notice that he *has* children," Emily said.

Akia stopped polishing and frowned at her. "I cannot agree with you there," she said. "There is nothing on this earth that Captain Edwards cares more about than those girls."

Emily thought of him hiding in the shadows of his own stairwell, fleeing the scene rather than comforting his younger daughter in her time of need, and then picked up another knife, secure and unshakable in the knowledge that no matter if Akia had been there longer, she was wrong and Emily was right.

Chapter Ten

᷒ᷗᷕᷜᷝ

ᴇᴍɪʟʏ ᴇɴᴅᴇᴅ ᴜᴘ ᴘᴀɪʀᴇᴅ ᴡɪᴛʜ ᴀᴋɪᴀ ᴀ ғᴇᴡ ᴛɪᴍᴇs ᴅᴜʀɪɴɢ the course of preparations for the dinner party. She learned that Akia's last position as a proper lady's maid had been somewhat of a living nightmare—screaming tantrums, hairbrushes thrown at her, a memorable occasion during which her mistress had locked her out of the house during a snowstorm—and that in comparison, the extra workload at Fairmont was no more than a mild irritation. From the sisterly way she spoke about the other maids in this previous house, Emily suspected that she had developed her habit of telling outrageous stories to keep up general morale.

Emily learned that Joe had been a ship's cook in the navy, and was used to the somewhat trying atmosphere in a galley, cooking for a hundred while all the knives in the room kept throwing themselves at you during dramatic swells. This mostly accounted for his odd demeanor.

"He doesn't know how to do his job without the threat of cannon fire," Akia said knowingly as they folded tablecloths, "so I think he sort of . . . creates the cannon fire, in his head."

Oliver had been dismissed by his previous master for some apparently minimal crime that Akia did not expand upon; that master had been a friend of the captain's, and apparently Captain Edwards had quietly taken him on afterward, despite the black mark of dismissal against him. This made no sense at all to Emily, who found Oliver far too loud and unreasonably enamored with horses, and could not see why anybody would go out of their way to hire him.

Meera was only a few years older than Captain Edwards, and had started at his father's house as a scullery maid when he was barely more than a child. That they had known each other for so long made sense of a few things—the fact that the captain had trusted Meera entirely with the hiring of a new governess, for one.

She learned all of this without having to ask. Akia was fond of speaking, but unlike Grace, she was a very accomplished story-teller. When she was funny, it was because she wanted to be, and as time went on Emily found herself holding back laughter on more than one occasion. She thought she was doing a relatively good job of staying detached and standoffish, rarely speaking un-less she was asked something directly, but she noticed that Akia had started darting glances at her when she told jokes, watching for Emily's reaction. She was starting to look far too pleased with herself; as if she had seen something on Emily's face that Emily had not been quick enough to hide.

The afternoon of the party, Emily walked into the kitchen and found that Oliver was "helping with the vegetables," which ap-parently entailed cutting the tops off and then throwing them at Akia, who was serenely weighing large quantities of fruit for the dessert.

"Meera told me you might need help," Emily said uncertainly, watching as the latest piece of carrot went sailing past Akia's head and landed somewhere near the fire.

"We're having an asparagus emergency," Oliver said, not look-ing particularly concerned. Emily glanced over at Joe, and saw that his neck was a furious, purplish red. "Do you happen to have any asparagus in your pockets?"

"No."

"Pity."

"Nothing ever weighs what I think it will weigh," said Akia, frowning. "But then I think maybe I am just a poor judge of weights. And heights. Oliver, how tall are you?"

"One and a quarter Graces," said Oliver. "Or seven cats."

"You see? I'd have said six cats."

Oliver shrugged, winding back his arm. "You do tend to underestimate me."

"Oliver," said Akia, "if you throw another piece of carrot at me, I will ram this pear so far down your throat you'll be pissing juice for a week."

"Jar," Oliver said, throwing another piece of carrot.

"Meera isn't here," said Akia, at the exact moment Meera came blustering into the room.

"Well, I did send a note, but I suppose they might not have seen it in time—oh, Amy, you look very nice today—so if it can't be asparagus, Joe, what should it be instead?"

"Asparagus," Joe said dangerously, not turning around.

"I cannot simply *magic* asparagus from thin air. I'm very sorry, I'm so sure I put it in the order. I can't believe I would have missed it."

Somebody knocked on the back door, and Akia went to answer it.

A handsome, middle-aged Indian man with a ready smile and a soft swell of a belly was standing there, looking hopeful, and in his hand was an entire basket of . . .

"Asparagus," Meera breathed. "Oh, *thank* you, Mr. Khan—you've saved the day, you have no idea!"

Mr. Khan seemed to have been angling for such a glowing reception, and grinned shyly from underneath his large, luxurious mustache as he handed over his wares.

"It was in the order, Miss Bhandari, but I'm afraid one of my boys missed it. It won't happen again, and I shall make it up to you. Perhaps I could call on you at some point this week, and I could bring you some—?"

"Oh, I'll be ever so busy this week," Meera said, putting the asparagus down next to Oliver and removing the knife from his hand so that he could not create any more tiny missiles.

Mr. Khan looked somewhat crestfallen. "Next week, then? Or perhaps I shall see you in the village?"

"Perhaps," said Meera. "Akia, there's a bit of carrot in your hair. When you are finished here, can you and Amy go and dress the girls?"

Mr. Khan gracefully accepted defeat, and Akia gave Emily a very knowing look as the door closed behind him.

When they went upstairs in search of said girls for dressing, Aster was nowhere to be found.

"She's probably taking a nap," Grace said, as Akia pinned her hair at the dressing table. "She doesn't like these things. Father doesn't let us join them for dinner—he just sort of presents us and then sends us away."

"Yes," said Akia. "I saw her earlier putting on her napping boots and a napping coat, and sneaking some food from the kitchen—in case she's hungry when she wakes up, I suppose."

"Sometimes it's best just to let her go," Grace said. "If I try to get her to stay, she just gets all . . . scratchy."

"Like a cat in a bag," said Emily.

"Yes! Exactly," said Grace. "Do they put cats in bags at mills?"

"What would be the practical application?" said Emily.

Grace thought for a moment. "To generate power," she said decisively. "Like a water mill."

"What have you two been talking about in those lessons of yours?" said Akia. "I don't recall there being a part about bagged cats in *The Mirror of Graces*."

"Have you been reading my etiquette books?" said Grace.

"Yes," said Akia. "They are . . . *very* funny."

Meera knocked on the door requesting help in the dining room, and Emily didn't get a chance to breathe again until the dinner party began. It was very obvious how understaffed Fairmont was when it came to entertaining fifteen people instead of three.

The dining room had been meticulously cleaned, the windows washed, the floors scrubbed, but now they had to lay the table, check for any water spots that needed last-minute polishing, arrange large sprays of yellow roses and purple asters from the garden into vases twice the size of Emily's head. Candles had to be lit, so many tall tapers that Akia nearly set her hair alight when she leaned over to get to the back of one of the elaborate candelabras.

It looked transformed when they had finished: so decadent it might have been a back room at Versailles. Meera did not have time to be pleased with herself, although she made sure to thank the rest of them before hurrying off to do whatever was next on her never-ending list of tasks.

Back downstairs, Meera, Akia, and Oliver prepared to serve the guests, while Emily was relegated to passing things to Joe in the kitchen, which was far more terrifying. She couldn't tell if she was doing a good or a bad job; Joe seemed generally furious at both himself and the world around him, and only communicated to her in single sentences, most of which were just the word "Spoon!" barked at her at high volume.

She didn't mind. It was like being back at the textile mill. She just kept her head down and waited for her next order. Let her body take over, while her mind blinked out. Hard, physical work like this made sense to her, even if it was in the service of something ridiculous.

When the time came, Emily came up to fetch Grace and present her to the guests in the drawing room. Aster had not been located, and Grace was clearly nervous about it; she kept fidgeting, pulling at her appallingly frilly sleeves, glancing around in the hope that her sister might be about to appear fully dressed and ready to be pleasant, which seemed to Emily about as likely as Joe embracing her and thanking her profusely for all her hard work.

She hadn't given a thought for her own appearance, except to wipe the spattered sauce from Joe's enthusiastic stirring from her cheek. When she beheld the guests, however, she suddenly felt as if she were wearing ... What was it Aster had said on that first day? Something about burlap sacks?

Her fingers itched with the desire to try to straighten her dress or fix her hair—but then she felt furious with herself for even considering such a thing. *She* was not the one who should be ashamed. If she looked a mess, it was simply because she had actually been *working*, something none of Captain Edwards's guests had likely done in their entire lives.

They didn't seem to care about her appearance, but that was probably because they didn't look at her at all. They cooed over Grace, who curtsied and said polite little things about their journeys and the weather, words more suited to somebody three times her age; they all laughed, obviously delighted. Emily mostly focused on the rug, which was a slightly faded scarlet color and probably Turkish, but when she did look up, her eyes landed on the person she assumed to be Augusta Spencer, who was sitting closest to the pianoforte. She was tall and full-bodied, with creamy skin and an impressive necklace of garnets that contrasted dramatically with her dark hair. She looked like a fresh cup of milk, or a silky, expensive horse.

Captain Edwards was sitting next to her, and he looked so striking in his Royal Navy uniform that Emily practically did a double take. His buttons were polished, the threads in the gold piping catching the light; the jacket made his shoulders look broader, too, although perhaps they had been this broad all along and Emily simply hadn't noticed. His hair had a slight wave to it, and the candlelight lent warmth and color to the parts that were still deep brown rather than silver. He wasn't looking at his daughter, or at Mrs. Spencer. He wasn't looking at anybody. He was holding himself very stiffly, as if he somehow found this extravagant dinner party he had demanded they throw to be rather stressful.

Poor thing. To have to cope with a *party*. To have to put on nice clothes, have six courses cooked for you, and be waited on hand and foot. The indignity of it all!

"And where is your elder daughter?" said one of the gentlemen, directing the question to the captain rather than to Emily.

Captain Edwards seemed to think Emily was exactly the right person to answer this, because he looked to her, eyebrows raised expectantly.

"She was tired," Emily said, "and sends her apologies."

This was good enough for the guests, but not for the captain, who was looking at Emily as if he knew very well that Aster would never send *apologies*, and that he considered her absence to be entirely Emily's fault.

This was unfair. She was a governess, not a sheepdog or a prison warden. She could hardly be blamed for not bringing Aster down to dinner when she had no idea if Aster still existed on this earthly plane.

"Do you happen to have a dog?" Grace was saying excitedly to one of the ladies. Her voice was leaning rather shrill and getting louder by the moment. It at least drew Captain Edwards's attention away from his disappointing governess. "I am ever so fond of dogs—I wish to have one of my own someday! I would like a brown one and I would call it Muffet, or Pudding, or Cyril . . . or if it was very large, I would call it Samson . . . and if it was very small, Blueberry . . . and if it was somewhere in the middle . . . well, I shall have to think!"

Captain Edwards winced, and Emily witnessed the exact moment that Grace looked to her father, probably hoping to see encouragement or endearment, and instead caught said wince like a slap. She was too young and too openhearted to hide the hurt on her face.

There was a pause, and then Captain Edwards cleared his throat.

"Miss Laurence," he said meaningfully to Emily. There was no mistaking what he wished her to do.

"Come along now, Grace," Emily said, going to her and putting a hand on her shoulder.

Grace was glancing about nervously like a stray dog about to be collared.

"Oh, I don't have to go yet, do I?" she said, shifting away from Emily's touch. "We were just getting to know one another! Father, might I stay a little longer?"

The adults laughed indulgently, and Captain Edwards grimaced.

"Listen to Miss Laurence, Grace."

"But it wasn't Miss Laurence who wanted me to go," Grace said insistently. "So if *you* do not mind—"

"Grace. Enough."

He didn't shout it, but it was stern enough that it was almost worse than a shout. Grace didn't resist this time when Emily gently guided her away, out of the drawing room and up the stairs.

"I won't go to bed," Grace said bitterly. "I mean it."

"Fine," said Emily. "What is it you wish to do instead?"

What Grace wished to do instead was to spy on the dinner party. It turned out that from the second floor above the entrance hall, they could see into half of the dining room on one side and half of the drawing room on the other, provided that they sat pressed up against the banisters like perverts outside a brothel, as Grace seemed determined to do.

"This is unseemly," Emily said, and Grace only laughed darkly like some creature of great evil, her forehead pressed so hard against the banister that it was likely to imprint the fretwork onto her skin. She seemed to have rallied from the disappointment at impressive speed.

"Interesting things happen so rarely around here," she said, sounding a bit squashed. "I want to see."

Emily sighed, but she sat down next to Grace and put her chin in her hands and found her eyes drifting to the drawing room just for something to do. It was preferable to being called back down to the kitchen to help with dessert. Meera, Akia, and Oliver kept passing through the entrance hall, back and forth with drinks and empty glasses, and then the entire party moved from the drawing room to the dining room and Emily watched Captain Edwards's stiff, uniformed shoulders as he shepherded his guests on. Just as he was about to step through the doorway, he looked sharply upward and caught Emily's eye.

She didn't know if she was supposed to be embarrassed to be discovered perched there, but it wasn't as if it had been *her* idea. He didn't look angry, exactly—more like he was slightly surprised to see them sitting there, side by side. Next to her, Grace fixed her posture: sat up straight, removed her head from the banisters. Captain Edwards's gaze dropped, and then he was gone.

When Akia passed underneath them on her way back from serving the soup, she also looked up, and smiled when she spotted them. Five minutes later she climbed up to deliver a large cushion to Grace and a large glass of wine to Emily.

"If anybody asks, you stole that yourself," she said sternly, already on her way back downstairs. "I'm not going down for crimes I didn't even get to enjoy."

Emily still didn't understand why Akia was being so kind when she had given her absolutely no encouragement, but she accepted the wine and sat sipping it as they listened to the sounds of a party under way, of clinking glasses and soft laughter and the fire crackling in the background.

It had a soporific effect. She didn't even realize that she had fallen asleep until she was being gently shaken awake by Grace, who was standing now, one end of the cushion in her hand and the other trailing on the floor.

"You drank all your wine and then you fell asleep," she said helpfully. "But I'm going to bed, and I thought you might not want to be discovered here . . . drooling."

Emily wiped her mouth, and her hand did indeed come away slightly wet.

"Good night!" said Grace, irritatingly perky.

It took Emily a little while to find the strength to stand. Her knees hurt. Her neck hurt. She felt very nine-and-twenty.

The party was still going in the drawing room, although from the stretches of quiet and the muted chatter it seemed that they had moved on to the sitting-and-smoking portion of the evening. Somebody was half-heartedly tapping away at the keys of the piano, but not attempting to strike up a real tune. Emily moved slowly away, hoping desperately that Captain Edwards had not crossed the hallway while she was sleeping and looked up again to see her fast asleep and salivating all over herself.

During her slow, creaking journey along the landing, she caught a glimpse of movement out of the window, and paused to investigate.

There were two people walking quickly across the lawn, with urgency that didn't match the attendance of a dinner party. At first they were nothing but shadowy blurs, but as they drew closer, the light from the house illuminated them and Emily realized who it was: Aster, wrapped in an enormous coat, and Oliver walking with her, positioned so that he could talk in her ear as they moved. It looked as if he was saying something very serious, from the expression on both of their faces. As they approached the house they moved out of sight; curious, Emily slipped quietly down the stairs and made her way toward the back entrance, careful not to be spotted by the inhabitants of the dining room.

When she reached them, they were standing together in a corner of the hallway, their heads very close together. *Too* close together. Oliver said something to Aster, and Aster muttered back in reply, their voices low and intimate. Oliver sighed, then put his hand on Aster's shoulder and gave her an affectionate squeeze before letting go.

When Aster turned around, Emily caught a quick glimpse of her face and saw that she looked almost on the verge of tears—but a glimpse was all she could risk, and she stepped quickly away, returning to her room with a dry mouth and a racing heart.

Chapter Eleven

"Aster," Emily said, knocking again. "I know you're in there. Open the door."

It was toward the end of the morning, and she had left Grace sketching a chair stacked with things she had gathered from around the room. When asked about the whereabouts of her sister, Grace had vaguely indicated that she was still sleeping—apparently this was quite a common occurrence, and likely the reason that Aster did not ever attend morning lessons. Of course, she didn't attend afternoon lessons, either, and her reasoning for that seemed to simply be that she'd rather not.

"*Aster*," Emily said again, knocking louder. For the love of God. She wouldn't have bothered at all, but for the simmering rage that had kept her awake, thinking of men who tried to touch things that didn't belong to them.

There had been a man at the mill. Older. Funny, friendly. *Fatherly.* He had sought her out straightaway. At first she thought he was simply looking out for her, but she realized later that he had sensed her vulnerability—the fact that she had never worked anywhere like this before, that her family had recently suffered a hardship—and had seen an opening. She had quickly grown wise to him—found ways to avoid him, to ensure there were always other people around. It had never been more than a hand lingering too long on her arm, or a wink, or a quiet word in her ear that could have been construed as friendliness.

There had been the time he'd cornered her in a back room,

but he'd barely taken a step toward her when they were interrupted. She felt as if she had escaped something by a hair's breadth, and shuddered whenever she slipped up and imagined what could have been.

Oliver wasn't some old, red-faced lech. He could only have been around Emily's age. But Aster was sixteen and angry, isolated— convinced she knew better than everybody around her. If Oliver *had* wanted to take advantage, he could not have picked a better target. There had been something very untoward about how close they had been the night before, thinking themselves safe from prying eyes.

"I'm coming in."

"Desist," Aster said croakily from inside the room. "And go away, while you're at it."

"I'm not visiting you because I am so desirous of your company," said Emily. "I'm coming in for one minute, and then you can sleep until Christmas for all I care."

Aster said something very rude, and Emily opened the door anyway.

"You cannot take a hint, can you," Aster said from halfway under the blankets. "How do you expect to teach anybody else when you have not even mastered the simple meaning of the word *no*."

"You didn't say *no*," said Emily. "You actually said *go away*, and the last time we spoke, *go and fuck yourself*."

"And yet here you remain," said Aster. "Unfucked."

Her room was a mess. She must have banned Akia and Meera from entering it altogether, for it to have fallen into such a bad state. There were mud tracks on the rug and piles of clothes on the chairs. She had somehow removed the glass of the ornate French mirror on the dresser, and probably done something dreadful with it. Piles of rags—Emily assumed they were rags, although some of them looked suspiciously expensive—were stiff with paint, and there were stacks of crumpled artworks on the windowsill.

"What were you doing with Oliver last night?"

Aster went very still, and then sat up, shedding pillows and blankets as she did.

"Have you been *spying* on me?"

"I have better things to do with my time—"

"Clearly."

"I didn't come here to be insulted. You have made it obvious that you provide delivery for that particular service. I came here to . . . Look, if something inappropriate is happening, you ought to . . . tell Meera about it. Or Akia. Your father. Anybody."

Aster somehow looked both derisive and incredulous. And sleepy. There was a lot happening on her face.

"Something *inappropriate*?"

"I know what I saw, Aster, and it did not look as if you were discussing the weather. I don't know what the two of you were doing out in the grounds, but—"

"You're right, you *don't* know. And you never will. I somehow doubt you have the imagination to even attempt a guess. It is absolutely none of your business, and I'd advise you to stay out of mine from now on."

Emily was so frustrated she could have shaken her. There was nothing in this for *her*. She didn't want any part of Aster's business!

"Fine," she said shortly. "But please recall that I warned you, when you realize how foolish you have been later on."

"Oh, *restrain* yourself. Oliver hasn't done anything wrong, you imbecile. And I am old enough to take care of myself. I need to go to luncheon—get out."

So irritated she could have spat fire, Emily got out.

This was the thanks she received for trying to do something good—for trying to help somebody who had been rude to her since the day she'd arrived! Insults hurled at her by a petulant adolescent who lived in a den of cushions like an animal. She wouldn't be making that mistake again.

She returned to an empty schoolroom, as Grace had also gone

for luncheon, and used the time to sort ruthlessly through the art supplies to give her hands something to do that wasn't wringing Aster's neck. All of the paintbrushes were very old, the bristles bent and pressed into odd shapes, as if somebody had bought them all new at the same time and never thought to replace them. The paints weren't in much better shape; they smelled musty and were crumbly to the touch, leaving little chalky stains on the desk and on Emily's fingers when she wasn't careful enough handling them.

A lot of things in the schoolroom seemed frozen in time, and it only took Emily half an hour of tidying to realize why: nothing had been bought new for the children in the four years since their mother had died. She was sure Meera would be horrified to learn this—that she would have sent away for new things at once if she'd known—but it must have just been one of those things that had been accidentally neglected as the house became more difficult to run. Mrs. Edwards had clearly been the one to make sure her daughters had new paintbrushes and books, and her husband had not stepped up to shoulder the responsibility in the past few years. He probably thought children entertained themselves with games of fetch or skeins of wool.

She'd make sure to tell Meera about the paint, to see if they could send for some more. Even if Aster certainly did not deserve it, it would do for Grace—and besides, it was what Amy would have done.

Actually, Amy would have traveled into the village and found out exactly where to procure new supplies, and likely blown all of her own wages on them, but Emily was not feeling quite *that* committed to her role.

That afternoon, Grace returned from luncheon looking cowed and listless.

"I was thinking Shakespeare," Emily said.

She had stacked up the volumes of collected works on the table; Grace picked one up from the top, glanced it over, and then put it back again.

"Very good," she said, sitting down. Emily waited for the rest, but apparently her sentence was finished.

"Which one?" said Emily. "You choose."

"Oh, I really don't mind. Whichever contains the least horrid father."

Ah. Emily wrinkled her nose, then sat down across the table.

"Potentially impossible. Shakespeare loved a horrid father. Although at least yours hasn't ordered your execution. Unless that's what happened at luncheon."

Grace blinked at her, and then sighed. "No. And . . . nothing really happened. I am the one being dreadful. Father isn't horrid. Please, forget I said anything."

"I see."

"I mean . . . I just thought . . . No, same as always, really."

"All right," Emily said slowly. She didn't know how to do this; providing comfort to children let down by their parents was not in her wheelhouse. She cringed away from the expectation internally, as if it were something cloying and sticky. The best she could offer was, "*Hamlet*? His father is vexing, but at least he's dead."

"*Hamlet* it is," said Grace.

The Edwards siblings seemed to be suffering from contrary afflictions: Grace too desperate to win her father's approval, and Aster attempting the exact opposite. The root of the problem was the same, but they were each giving their emotional responses their own personal flair.

Emily often found herself repeating, in her mind, that it was absolutely none of her business. She could not sell "father is emotionally distant with his children" to Charles when she next met him at the pub. It also seemed unlikely that noticing Aster sneaking around with Oliver would lead anywhere fruitful, but she knew she'd keep an eye on the valet from now on, just in case.

That night after dinner, when Akia offered her a drink—the implication being that she might actually stay seated with them long enough to drink it—she accepted.

Nobody made a fuss about it, to her great relief. They simply poured an extra glass of wine and passed it down the table.

"I simply do not think he's going to propose," Oliver said. "But I've been saying that all along."

"Oliver," Meera said reprovingly. "This is not a game for you to place bets on. This is Captain Edwards's private business."

"They went outside to 'look at the gardens' for a while after dinner," said Akia. "I thought he might do it then. But he just looked a bit . . . scared of her."

"When?" said Oliver.

"Hmmm?"

"When were they standing outside?"

Emily watched his expression carefully. He was aiming for neutrality and only missing by an inch or two.

"Oh, I don't know. Around eleven o'clock? I was going to bed. I'd be frightened of her, too . . . She puts me in mind of Salome, hungry for a head."

Joe looked up from his drink. "Salome didn't eat John the Baptist's head."

"She did in the version I tell."

"I just think, you know . . . piss or get off the pot," said Oliver. "I know, Meera. Sixpence. I'm running a little low on coins at the moment, as it is . . . I shall have to owe you."

"Captain Routley was there," said Akia. "I haven't seen him for a while."

Oliver patted down his pockets and then drew out a pipe. "Which one is Routley?"

"Short. Pretty. Mrs. Edwards used to say that he always looked like he was on the verge of crying."

"Oh *God*, yes. I can never tell if he looks twelve years old or fifty. Sort of like a baby in uniform, but also a bit like an elderly man in a dressing-up costume. Did we sense any discord there?"

"*Oliver*," said Meera.

"Don't you tire of saying my name like that, Meera?"

"I have a thousand *Oliver*s ready to go, and they will never be enough," said Meera. "Are you going to light that pipe or conduct an orchestra with it? Give it here."

"Why would there be discord?" said Emily.

As soon as she'd said it, she regretted it. She sounded far too eager for an answer. She was supposed to be keeping a low profile, not conducting an inquisition.

"That is *not* for us to say," said Meera, as Oliver relinquished his pipe so that Meera could light it and take a puff.

"Mostly because we don't know," said Akia. "But Captain Edwards does not seem particularly fond of the navy anymore. And who can blame him? If they really discharged him against his wishes, when he was doing so well—"

"He hasn't been discharged, he's still wearing the uniform," said Oliver. Emily tried not to stare; tried not to make it clear that she was trying to memorize every detail of this conversation in case she could barter it later. "Doesn't that mean he's still on duty?"

Joe grunted in assent. "You can't wear it furloughed, or dismissed. So he's neither."

"Well, there you go. Nobody would risk the embarrassment of wearing it if they'd been discharged. Or at least—Ben wouldn't."

"Jar," said Meera.

"For what crime, *jar*?"

"His name is Captain Edwards, Oliver. Not *Ben*."

"It's a swear jar! It's not a fucking *Ben* jar. Yes, fine, I see what I've done there, a schoolboy error . . . I owe you twice over, I suppose."

They sat in companionable silence until Joe cleared his throat.

"He'll propose," he said, surprising Emily. She wouldn't have thought Joe would have anything to say on the subject of his master's romantic affairs; half the time he didn't actually seem to be listening to them at all. Everybody else seemed to take this in their stride.

"Well, if he does, I shall be very pleased for him. And for *us*, if we are able to take on a full staff again." Meera sighed, somewhat wistfully. "We could have a groom again. A butler. A lady's maid for each lady."

"I'm not giving up the big room," Oliver said sternly. "I have arranged all of my belongings in piles that please me, and any sudden change will wreak havoc upon my nerves."

"You will do exactly as you are told," said Meera.

She turned to Emily, offering her Oliver's pipe. Emily declined.

"How have lessons been with the girls?"

"It's just been the one girl, mostly," said Emily. "And it has been . . . fine."

"Ah," said Meera sympathetically. "Yes, I didn't think you'd been seeing much of Aster. She can be—"

"A nightmare," said Oliver.

"Oliver!"

"I'm going to start an Oliver jar," said Oliver. "And *you* can owe *me* a thousand sixpences."

"She seems to be having a . . . difficult time," Emily said, which was so generous and diplomatic of her that she probably could have been tasked with negotiations with France. She watched Oliver's face as she said this. No hint of guilt or unease. But there was *something* there—as if he knew something the rest of them did not.

"She took it very hard when her mother passed on," said Akia. "Well . . . they all did, of course. But Aster has her own way of dealing with things."

"Mrs. Edwards never would have stood for it," said Meera. "It'll be four years next week. I miss that woman."

"Hear hear," said Joe, raising his glass.

The others mirrored him, and drank. Emily just watched them, her glass already empty.

It was hard to imagine the captain's late wife as a real person rather than a sad specter. For some reason she had at first imagined somebody prim and cold, as distant from the children as Captain Edwards was, a worthy mistress for a house like this— but now she knew that Mrs. Edwards was a keen gardener; a procurer of paints. That did not conjure up images of coolness and neglect. And besides, she could hardly imagine Meera toasting so sincerely to the memory of somebody so dreadful, even if she did have an overinflated sense of duty.

"Right," said Oliver, smacking his hand on the table. "I'm going to the pub. I'll shut up the house when I get back. Is anybody coming with me?"

"I will," said Akia. "If you swear to take up arms against the bigots, the starers, and the grabbers."

"You know I always do," said Oliver. "Joe?"

"One drink," said Joe. "No dancing on the tables. No arrests."

"Damn," said Oliver. "Then what's the point?"

Meera declined, her idea of fun being an empty to-do list and early to bed, and Emily made similar noises of refusal. She climbed the many stairs—so many stairs, *too* many stairs—and, once she was in the sanctuary of her room, fell quickly asleep.

Chapter Twelve

I⟳ FELT LIKE ONLY TEN MINUTES LATER THAT EMILY AWOKE to somebody shaking her arm urgently.

"Amy?" somebody was saying. "Amy, please wake up."

"What's wrong? Is she all right?" Emily said, addled by sleep, before she remembered that *she* was Amy.

Grace was looking down at her, tearful in the light of the single candle she was holding.

"No, she's not all right," she said, somewhat confusingly. "She's not in her bed. It must be two o'clock in the morning! Please, Amy, I don't know what to do."

"Aster isn't in her bed?" said Emily, catching up.

"Don't tell Father," said Grace urgently. "He'll be furious. I just need to find her, and then—"

"Are you sure she's not there?" Emily said, getting up. She pulled on her threadbare coat over her nightclothes and slipped clumsily into her shoes. "I'll look. She's probably in the house somewhere. Go back to bed, Grace. Now."

"I can't," said Grace, utterly miserable.

She followed Emily along the hallway and stood nervously outside the door as Emily went into Aster's room to check it thoroughly before she started dredging the house. It took a while to check under all the drifts and piles, but Aster was indeed missing from her bed.

There was no point waking Meera, or any of the others, if they had even made it back from the pub yet—Aster would probably be lurking somewhere in the depths of Fairmont, causing trouble on purpose.

As governess, Emily knew she might be considered *somewhat* responsible for her whereabouts, and wanted to put off conversations of that nature for as long as possible. She would simply search the house and gardens herself.

She went down to the ground floor and methodically walked from dining room to drawing room, parlor to hallway, checking everywhere—behind doors, curtains, furniture. In the dining room her candle illuminated a shadowy mass that looked so much like a person lurking in the dark, waiting for her, that her heart forgot to beat for a moment. When she drew closer, it became a coat that had been left unceremoniously tossed on a chair. This, surely, was a sign that Aster had been here; in the same way that bats left droppings and deer footprints, Aster left casual disregard for both people and property.

Eventually, Emily had to concede that Aster was not on the ground floor, unless she had become some sort of contortionist and crammed herself into a knee-high dresser or trunk. The longer this went on, the more likely it seemed that she would have to go and fetch Meera, and the thought filled her with rising dread that wasn't helped by how foreboding the house looked in the dark. Captain Edwards had seemed displeased enough that Aster had not attended the brief showing at the dinner party; how furious would he be if Emily had to break the news to him that he now had only half his children remaining?

Oliver might have been able to offer some insight into where Aster was, but Oliver was out—now that Emily thought of it, there was some chance that Aster might have gone to *meet* him.

She started searching faster.

Up on the first floor, she made it through the first two empty bedrooms without incident before she opened a door and realized she had accidentally walked into Captain Edwards's study—and even worse, that he was inside, sitting behind his desk.

"Miss . . . Laurence?" he said, seeming baffled by her presence. He had that undone look about him again, a middle-of-the-night haziness that made him look far less intimidating. He glanced down at what she was wearing—her coat hanging open, exposing the nightdress underneath—and then very quickly returned his gaze to her face with a slight twitch at the corner of his mouth.

Emily tucked her coat tighter around herself and grimaced.

"Sorry," she said, backing away. "I was just . . . I didn't realize this was—"

"Stop," said Captain Edwards, and Emily found herself obeying at once. "Explain."

"Aster is not in her bed."

Captain Edwards stared at her, the words hanging in the air between them, and then he exploded into action, shoving his chair roughly back and striding to the door.

"Where is Grace?"

"She's up by her room, but—"

"*Grace!*" Captain Edwards shouted.

He hadn't stopped moving; Emily followed him at a fast clip as he marched down the hallway and then took the stairs two at a time.

Grace looked exceptionally woebegone, her eyes enormous and glossy with tears.

"Where is she?" Captain Edwards said, apparently unmoved by his daughter's impression of a woodland creature.

"I don't know," Grace said in a very small voice. "I just checked her room and she wasn't—"

"Where," Captain Edwards said again, enunciating slowly, "is she?"

Grace bit her lip and seemed to be attempting a vow of silence, but it was broken after approximately three seconds under Captain Edwards's glare.

"I didn't think she'd actually do it! I told her the tide might come in, but she said . . ."

Apparently this was all the information he needed, because he immediately made for the stairs.

"Oh *no*," Grace said, watching him go with fresh tears on her cheeks. She turned to Emily, and her expression darkened into something akin to a cross kitten. "Why did you tell him? That was the one thing I asked of you!"

"The *one thing* . . . ?" Emily started, instantly vexed. "You knew more than you were letting on. You let me search the house when you knew exactly where she was!"

"But I *forbade* you from—"

"Damn it, Grace, if she's down by the water she could be in danger! You are being just as arrogant and selfish as your sister."

It was not what Amy would have said. It was not what anybody sensible would have said. Aster might not have cared to pass on the insults they had exchanged in the schoolroom, but Emily was running out of chances; Grace might go to her father and tell him exactly what Emily had shouted at her.

But Grace looked remorseful at once, and Emily's anger turned to sickly unease as she burst into fresh tears.

"I'm sorry," Grace sobbed, before rushing back into her bedroom and slamming the door.

At a loss for what else to do, Emily went downstairs, where she found Captain Edwards pulling on his coat.

"A lamp," he said to Emily, and after a moment's delay she realized that she was being given an order and went in search of one. Upon her return, she expected him to snatch it from her and make his way out into the night, but instead she found that the door was already open and he was striding across the lawn.

When she caught up with him, slightly breathless, he didn't even acknowledge her presence—which was particularly silly considering that very soon, the lamp in her hand became the only source of light in any direction.

They reached the cliffs and started rapidly descending a path that did not feel secure enough for Emily's liking. Captain Edwards had gone ahead, which did not make sense based on the logic of lamplight, but did mean that, when she stumbled on a loose rock and almost went crashing into him, he was able to brace against her and stop her from going over and rolling jauntily all the way down to the beach.

"Careful," he said, his voice clipped, as if she'd done it on purpose.

She only realized when she straightened up from being crumpled against him that he'd had to put a hand on her waist—her coat had fallen open again, and the thin, gauzy fabric of her nightgown was laughably insubstantial. She could feel the warmth of his fingers, which meant that *he* could feel the contours of her waist; it was a nightmare from which they both tried to recover quickly, springing apart so violently that Emily almost tripped again.

She judged it best not to speak, so the only sound as they made their way down to the beach and started walking along the stone-strewn sand was the soft roar of the sea and the crunching of their footsteps. There was a breeze nipping at her heels, the evening still warm but not *quite* balmy enough to be forgiving to somebody mostly clad in nightwear.

Emily had never been so close to the ocean, and was feeling somewhat overwhelmed by this assault on her senses and the knowledge that to her left was endless black water. When Captain Edwards stopped, she had to resist the urge to step in closer to him, so that he might shield her from the fine spray and the whipping wind.

"There," he said, nodding farther ahead toward the craggy face of the cliffs.

Emily didn't know what he was trying to show her, but she squinted into the dark to show willing. Nothing notable was forthcoming.

"There's a cave," he said, which added essential context.

"You think she's in a cave?" Emily said, as the lantern swayed in her hand with a subdued squeak.

Captain Edwards's expression was grim as they picked their way forward across sand that was boggy with salt water; it seemed that Grace's warning about high tides had been a portentous one, because the waves were sending it lapping right up to the entrance of the cave.

Inside was muffled and dank; there was rubbery seaweed underfoot, and the sounds of shuffling wings and a rhythmic dripping. The smell of salt and something unpleasant and rotten intensified the farther they delved. Emily was trying to pay heed to what she was stepping on, but even with the lamp it was somewhat impossible to understand what was going on under her feet.

"Take my arm," Captain Edwards said, sounding impatient.

"I'm fine," Emily snapped back, without thinking.

Captain Edwards did not reply, but she thought she saw him shaking his head out of the corner of her eye.

The cave went far deeper than Emily would have guessed, and around twenty yards in she realized that she could hear another sound: girlish laughter.

It was honestly quite haunting, echoing off the damp walls. She glanced over at Captain Edwards, but he looked both unsurprised and quietly furious.

The scene they discovered when they turned the corner looked a little like a Joseph Wright painting Emily had once seen reproduced, of people gathered around a scientific experiment by the light of a candle—except that in this case the experiment seemed to be drinking spirits, and the intrepid scientists were a group of girls around Aster's age, clearly hailing from the village. When they saw Emily and the captain come into view, they froze in startled silence.

"Aster," Captain Edwards said dangerously. "Get *up*."

At this, the girls scattered, getting to their feet with flushed cheeks and damp dresses and darting past Emily like mice fleeing a cat. Aster was the only one who did not stand; she was lounging against a jutting shelf of rock, wearing what looked like men's breeches and an untucked shirt.

She was obviously very drunk.

"Evening, Father," she said, her words slurred. She still had a bottle of spirits in her hand. Emily was quite impressed by her gumption; even she would have quavered under the thunderous expression on Captain Edwards's face. "Didn't expect to see you here . . . Do you come often? We must keep . . . missing each other."

"I will not speak to you like this," Captain Edwards said. "We are going home. Now."

"Fine," Aster said, sighing.

As she moved to get up, she lost her grip on the bottle, and after a short drop it smashed loudly against the rock by her foot. She frowned down at the pieces.

"Ah. Hmmm. That was . . . a different shape, just a moment ago."

When she tried to take a step forward, it became clear that she could not be responsible for her own feet. Captain Edwards went to her immediately, put an arm around her, and began the slow journey back out of the cave, Emily hurrying along beside them with the lamp lifted as high as possible until her arm felt as if it might fall off.

If she had thought the walk down to the cave felt neverending, the return journey explored new realms of torture.

Captain Edwards wasn't so much helping Aster along as he was holding her up, and it seemed that with every step they took, his silent fury intensified.

It didn't help that Aster kept talking.

"I have not done anything wrong," was her very strong opener. She started listing all the reasons why this was the case, frequently forgetting herself halfway through a sentence and skipping ahead to the next on her list, until she concluded with ". . . and besides, I have been under . . . under *considerable* strain at work."

"You do not have a job," said Emily.

Aster twisted around in her father's grip, almost earning herself a close encounter with the sand.

"Oh look, it's *Amy*! Well, perhaps I'll become a governess, seeing as they are letting just anybody do it these days."

She swung toward Emily for what was likely going to be an unfriendly pat on the shoulder, unbalanced, and did finally fall; Captain Edwards did not attempt to catch her. His hair was mussed and he had sand down the front of his shirt; he looked like a man who desperately wanted to swear, but was just about keeping himself in check.

"*Aster*—"

"If you are going to tell me to get up," Aster said loftily, "I cannot."

She closed her eyes, apparently quite content to stay on the beach until the tide bore her away.

Captain Edwards put his hands on his hips and stared down at his elder child. Emily expected him to start shouting in earnest, but he instead looked as if he were trying to solve a particularly depressing puzzle.

"I'll carry her," he said to Emily eventually, rolling up his sleeves. "Just . . . put the lamp down and help me get her up."

It was not quite that simple, but between them they did eventually manage to pull Aster to her feet. From there, Captain Edwards paused and took a thin breath in and out through his nose, as if he could not quite believe that his life had come to this. Then he lifted Aster up into his arms as if she were no more than a baby.

It could not have been easy. Aster was not small, so a considerable amount of muscle must have been required. Emily thought fleetingly of what Akia had said about the captain and shirtlessness, then banished the image immediately.

The journey up the crumbling path was complicated enough for Emily with her lantern; it must have been downright treacherous for Captain Edwards, with no hands at all available to break his fall. Emily stayed close, thinking that she would have to rush to his aid if he stumbled, or at least make a show of trying to catch Aster if he dropped her, but it only meant that she heard his breathing become ragged with labor, and the very soft curses he let slip under his breath as they approached the top.

"I would not have drowned," Aster said, once they were on flatter ground. Emily had thought her unconscious; she had not opened her eyes. "I would have been back before you knew it."

"No, Aster, you would not," the captain said, his voice strained. "I don't know what the hell you think you were doing—"

"Ah," said Aster. "Well. You . . . you keep your secrets, and I will keep mine."

Back at the house, it seemed that Grace had gone to fetch Meera; she and Joe were waiting in the entrance hall, Meera twisting her skirt into pulp and Joe so red he seemed to be glowing. Captain Edwards handed Aster over to them without a word. Emily noticed that despite his fury he did it with great care, cradling her head so that it did not droop, watching closely to ensure that Joe had his arms firmly around her before he finally let go.

"Everybody to bed," he said. Emily made to leave. "*Not* you."

Emily wasn't sure, for a moment, if it was her that he had been addressing, but this was cleared up when she caught his eye and saw that he was glaring directly at her. He strode away into the drawing room, and Emily followed, trying to keep her nerves in check. She would *not* let him see her apprehension. After all, unlike Aster, she genuinely *had* done nothing wrong.

His shirt was ruined, the sleeves rolled up to his elbows, and his chest was still heaving with effort. Emily could not quite bring herself to look at him; she focused determinedly at a spot on the wall behind his head instead.

"Miss Laurence," he said, "you were given charge of my children. That is your role here, is it not?"

"Yes," said Emily, when he seemed to expect an answer.

"Then do explain to me *why* we have just had to climb down into a *cave* to retrieve my elder daughter, in the middle of the night, drunk and in peril—"

"I certainly did not put her in a cave," said Emily. "I didn't even know there *was* a cave."

There was a dangerous silence.

"She is under *your* protection," said Captain Edwards. "Her well-being should be your most pressing concern, above all else. How could this have escaped your notice?"

"How could it have escaped yours?" Emily retorted, feeling hot and indignant and stupid. "You live here, just as I do. They are *your* children—not that you seem to want to know them at all. Aster has made it clear from the moment I arrived that she thinks me as low as vermin, not fit to set foot in this house. How could you expect me to know the warning signs that she is about to dash off to a cave when I have barely seen her at all?"

"Don't you *dare* speak to me that way about my children," Captain Edwards shouted, the anger that had been simmering finally coming to a head. He took a deep breath and then let it out slowly, scrubbing a hand across his face as he composed himself. "What do you mean, you have barely seen her? You have been teaching her, have you not?"

"No," said Emily, her voice still hard and brittle. "She refuses to be taught."

"A sixteen-year-old's refusal?" scoffed the captain. "Find a way. This cannot be allowed to continue—there will be no more disobedience, no more ruinous behavior. This is your one task, and if you are not able to complete it, you are of no use to me, to this house, or to my children."

"If it's so easy to overrule her refusal, why not do it yourself?" said Emily.

"Because that is why I *hired you*," said Captain Edwards. "Go to bed, Miss Laurence."

"But—"

"*Miss Laurence.*"

Akia was wrong. Emily didn't care how shapely his chest was under that shirt; it could not even go partway toward making up for being so wholly, incurably *vile*.

Chapter Thirteen

THE NEXT DAY WAS SATURDAY, AND EMILY WAS GRANTED THE afternoon off.

She intended to keep her appointment at the Rose and Crown.

She was glad to be out of the house, regardless of her destination. If she bumped into Aster, she would be forced to drag her kicking and screaming—or, more likely, limp and unimpressed and heckling Emily with cutting remarks—to lessons, and if she had the misfortune of crossing paths with Captain Edwards, he might treat her to another few verses of scolding about her inability to transform Aster into someone punctual and pleasant.

Meera had offered the gig, but the weather was fine, and Emily wanted to walk. There was only so much pent-up frustration that one could vent while pacing circles around the rooms of Fairmont House; a proper stomp along the coast was just what she needed to prevent her from skipping around sprinkling something flammable and then batting over a candle.

The *gall* of Captain Edwards, to blame *her* for Aster's exploits, when anybody could see that the girl was completely out of control! The *audacity* of placing all the responsibility on her shoulders, simply because he did not want to face up to the fact that he had produced such a monster! Every conversation she'd had with this man provided more proof that she should not feel an ounce of regret for selling him out to the highest—well, the *only*—bidder. If only he knew that he was digging his own grave every time he opened his mouth.

She was so caught up in elaborate violent fantasies that she had almost forgotten what she was looking for when she walked through the door of the pub, but the sound of the bell announcing her arrival brought her back to reality.

She found Charles in one of the strange dead ends on the other side of the bar. He was sitting at a tiny table that could barely fit two chairs around it, smoking his pipe; when he saw her, he removed it from his mouth and smiled as if he were genuinely pleased. He looked slightly out of place in this pub, halfway between a regular patron and a lost gentleman, his coat expensive but worn at the sleeves and lapels; perhaps he had fallen on hard times. Emily could certainly understand that.

"Governess," he said slowly. "I was almost starting to think I had dreamed you."

"Real, unfortunately," said Emily.

Charles laughed. "Not real enough to have a name."

"You may call me whatever you like," said Emily.

Charles lifted a finger to signal the barmaid, and a moment later there was a pint next to Emily's hand. "Then I shall call you *Miss Laurence.*"

Emily was momentarily taken aback before her faculties kicked in. Her last name was not so much a secret as to cause concern; he might have heard it from anybody who knew a member of staff at the house.

"As you wish," she said evenly.

"And I suppose you may continue to call me Charles."

"Is it not your name?"

"Oh, no, it is. Should I have come up with another? I quite like Charles."

"Charles is fine," said Emily, confused by the meandering route this conversation was taking when they had something serious to discuss. "Look—I have some information for you."

Charles took up his pipe to take another puff, and then watched her over the plume of smoke.

"Do go on."

"There was some sort of rift between Captain Edwards and the Royal Navy," Emily said, lowering her voice to a whisper. "A naval officer came to the house the other night for dinner, and the servants were discussing the possibility of . . . tension between them."

"Ah," said Charles. "Yes. Well. Therein lies the question."

"What question?"

"What *happened*," said Charles, "between Edwards and the navy?"

"Oh," said Emily, deflated. "So you knew already?"

"I did," Charles said, watching her thoughtfully. "But I am grateful to you nonetheless for telling me. It builds trust, you know? And how are we to go on without trust." He flashed Emily another leonine smile, as if she had truly impressed him. "Well. Have two sovereigns for your trouble, to start."

He slid the coins across the table toward her and Emily stared down at them. It was close to a month's wages, and he'd given it to her as if it was nothing.

"I have more," she said. "I mean . . . I wanted to see if this might be worth something, and I thought you might be able to help me."

She reached into her pocket and pulled out the baroque box, wrapped in a scrap of linen. Charles reached out in a leisurely fashion and flipped the fabric away from the top part of the box, then quickly replaced it.

"My my, you have been busy."

"Can you help? I thought it might need to be broken up. Gemstones sold separately."

"I can help," he said. "I have a man I can show it to, if it suits."

Emily nodded; he took the box and tucked it away into his jacket. "He will take a cut, but I'm afraid that's the price of business." He smiled again, leaning forward on the table, looking a little besotted. "Goodness—you certainly are my kind of girl."

Emily wasn't at all sure she wanted to be his kind of girl—or *anybody's* kind of girl—but she found herself smiling tentatively back. There was a strange rightness to the wrongness; a feeling that she fitted in better here, doing deals with a charming, dastardly stranger in a dark corner, than she ever could among the people of Fairmont House.

"Is your drink not to your liking?" said Charles, apparently feeling very laid-back about this clandestine meeting and the stolen goods in his pocket. "Or . . . something to eat, perhaps? The food is terrible, but if you take a great swig of your drink before you eat it, it becomes a sort of food-adjacent paste . . ."

"No," said Emily, taking a gulp of beer to show willing and then pushing it away. "Thank you. I should . . . I'll be getting back."

"Suit yourself," said Charles. "I will be away for a fortnight, on business. But the Saturday after my return, I hope to see you again. Perhaps you'll have something for me."

"I will," Emily said, feeling the weight of the coins in her palm and letting it fuel her determination to earn herself some more. It was all rather convenient, really—and the thought that she might soon be able to deal Captain Edwards some real damage was doing wonders for her mood.

When she got back to the house, she walked into the kitchen and discovered Oliver sitting there, smoking, the paper open in front of him. When he saw her, he sat up straighter and observed her progress across the room like a floppy-haired hawk as she went to retrieve the last of the pound cake.

"I heard there was a spot of trouble last night," he said.

"Mmm," Emily said noncommittally, mouth full of cake.

"Meera didn't say, but . . . was Aster . . . ?"

"Was Aster what?" Emily said, once she had swallowed. "What particular concern is it of yours?"

"Er . . . excuse me," said Oliver, affronted. "*Down*, girl. I'm asking a perfectly innocent question."

"Whatever you were doing sneaking back into the house the other night during dinner did not look particularly innocent." Emily watched his expression shift, his mouth go slack. "I *saw* you together, Oliver. I saw you put your hand on her."

"Whatever it is that you think you are accusing me of," Oliver said, "could not be further from the truth. I would *never*." His usual playfulness had vanished; he was now deathly serious, in a way that looked out of place on his face.

"I just want you to know that I'm keeping an eye on you," said Emily, delivering this parting blow as she left the room.

Oliver followed, speeding up until he was at her elbow.

"There is nothing to *keep an eye on*—and whatever it is you think you saw, let it go. Not for my sake, but for Aster's."

"Interesting that now you are so keen to protect her," said Emily. "The other night you seemed to be making her cry."

"Oh, for God's sake, Amy—how have I ended up a player in this drama of yours when I didn't even pay for admittance?"

They had reached the entrance hall now, but Oliver showed no signs of being shaken off. He was also now speaking at a volume closer to shouting.

"You are meddling in something you do not understand. Will you just *drop* it?"

"What is going on here?" said Captain Edwards. He had just stepped out of the drawing room, looking, as always, like the human embodiment of distant thunder.

"Ask him!" said Emily. "He's the one who's been—"

"*Amy*," Oliver said warningly.

Captain Edwards looked between them, unimpressed.

"Miss Laurence . . . please accompany me to my study."

Emily glowered openly at him, and he only raised an eyebrow back and gestured for her to lead the way.

It felt like a very long walk up the stairs and into the study. It wasn't as unnaturally neat and empty as some of the other rooms in the house; there were battered books on the shelves, a sextant and compass on the desk—as if it wasn't enough to just be *in* the Royal Navy, he had to accessorize nautically, too. On the wall was an enormous painting of a sunset over a mirror-calm ocean, a lone ship breaching the horizon. Emily sat down and waited for Captain Edwards to take his seat on the other side of the desk, but he stayed standing, searching for something in a stack of papers on a side table.

"You were arguing with Oliver," he said eventually.

"He was arguing with me, sir," said Emily, sounding petulant but beyond caring. "I saw him with Aster the other night. When you were . . . During your dinner party. They were outside together after dark, and Aster looked upset, and I thought that perhaps Oliver . . . I thought he might be . . . taking advantage."

Captain Edwards looked up at her, astonished. There was a fine scrape of stubble on his chin, mostly dark, but with a little gray around the edges; he was not taking care of himself in the ways that a gentleman should.

"Taking advantage?" he said. "Oliver?"

"You didn't see how they were together," said Emily, still breathing out pure exasperation. "And Aster is . . . I know what it's like, to feel angry and powerless and to rely on the kindness of a man who offers help, but if that man has ill intentions—"

"He doesn't," said Captain Edwards.

Emily was getting very tired of people acting as if she were making all of this up for fun and japes; she sat back hard in her chair and folded her arms.

"How on earth can you be so sure?"

"Because I know him. I have known him for a long time. That will have to be sufficient for you."

"I am not entirely sure that you understand the . . . the *dynamics* that could be at play here—"

"Right, of course," he said, his voice steely. "Because I . . . What was it you said before? I don't know my children at all?"

If he wanted her to squirm, she wasn't going to give him the satisfaction. She could stare just as well as he could, and so she did. He had brown eyes, nothing to write home about, ringed with the sort of naturally thick, dark lashes that only ever seemed to be gifted to men. The prolonged eye contact was starting to feel odd—Emily didn't spend a lot of time locking eyes with people, if she could help it. She was getting through it by pretending that his face was not really a face at all—perhaps just a statue or a portrait or an oddly shaped cloud—when his gaze dipped slightly, breaking the spell.

"Would you like a drink?"

Emily's staring renewed, for entirely different reasons. His voice had dropped out of its usual military register; it was softer, almost mellow.

"A drink?"

"Well, I'm going to have one," he said.

As she watched, he opened a drawer in the bottom of his desk and pulled out a bottle of whiskey. It was half-empty.

"Ah," he said, lifting it toward the light and tilting it, swirling the amber contents. "Hmmm. This was sealed."

"Aster," said Emily.

It wasn't a question, and Captain Edwards did not pass comment, although he did look a little more defeated.

He poured himself a generous measure, and then sat down, cradling his drink in his hand. Emily watched the slow, considered way he brought the glass to his lips and then savored the whiskey, letting out the tiniest exhalation when it hit his tongue.

"I cannot tell you all the reasons I trust Oliver," he said. "But I do. I trust him with Aster—with both of my children—and I know he would never let them come to any harm. And . . ." He broke off for a moment, considering. "I realize now that things with Aster have . . . progressed. I should not have been so quick to blame you, last night. I was upset."

It wasn't quite an apology, but it was *almost* one, even if he was talking as if every word pained him. Emily didn't know what to do with it.

"It seems that Grace is already very . . . fond of you," he said, watching her over the top of his glass, as if trying to figure out exactly how she could have tricked his daughter into feeling that way.

It was all suddenly too much. Emily didn't want Grace to be fond of her. She didn't want to care if Aster was intent on ruining her life, disappearing into caves and coming home drunk and barely conscious. It was none of her concern what Oliver got up to, and she certainly put no stock in what Captain Edwards thought of her. She didn't want him to be sorry. She didn't want him to look at her at all.

The entire point of being here had been to get in and out, making as little impression as possible—to be so invisible that she was beyond reproach or investigation. How could she ever manage that, if Grace started beaming every time she walked into a room, and Captain Edwards felt compelled to invite her into his study and offer *whiskey*, of all things?

She had thought herself so unremarkable that it would not be a problem, but these people insisted on wanting to know her, even as she resisted with every fiber of her being.

"Will that be all?" she said, knowing she was being impertinent, from the tilt of her chin to the fact that she wouldn't meet his eye.

"All?" he said, sounding momentarily as if he had lost command of the room. He recovered quickly. "Yes. That is all."

"Thank you," she said, getting up, still not looking at him. "Good afternoon, sir."

She left him sitting in his chair with his whiskey. On the way upstairs, she stole a gold and tortoiseshell snuffbox and a tiny carving of what looked like a saint from the back of a cabinet in the hallway, and didn't even stop to check if anybody was watching.

Chapter Fourteen

(O)LIVER WAS SULKING. FROM THE WAY EVERYBODY ELSE WAS reacting, it seemed that this was not an uncommon state of affairs, but Emily knew it to be aimed at her and therefore found it extra irritating.

He had ignored her all through dinner, but been unable to stop himself from cornering her in the hallway and asking, "What did he say?"

"He didn't say anything," Emily had replied, sick to the back teeth of all of them, and particularly hating the fact that he had placed himself between her and her exit. "And don't *crowd* me. Just for future reference, furtively demanding to know the details of conversations you weren't privy to does not make me any more convinced of your innocence."

Oliver had huffed away—huffed to church on Sunday, huffed past Emily anytime their paths crossed—and now at breakfast on Monday he was huffing still.

"Did you two kiss by accident?" Akia asked, pointing her fork at Emily and then at Oliver. Emily looked disgusted. Oliver did, too, which she was probably supposed to take as an insult. "No? All right. I'm just trying to work out what this strange tension is. Just regular, garden-variety hatred, then?"

"I don't hate her," said Oliver. "I'd have to think about her to hate her, and she's barely even a person to me."

"I kissed somebody by accident once," Akia said, ignoring him. "We were attempting to say good morning to each other in a corridor and both leaned in and somehow ended up in a mouth collision."

"Oliver," Meera said. "You are *two-and-thirty*. Please establish a firm grip on yourself or I will be forced to take you by the scruff myself."

After an intolerable breakfast came an intolerable lesson with Grace.

Aster was still not in attendance, now glaringly so; Emily had gone to knock for her and found that she was not in her room at all. Thinking of Captain Edwards watching her from the other side of his desk, she had actually gone in search of her mislaid pupil, and eventually determined that she was hiding in a locked storage room that usually housed linens.

Aster had pretended not to be there, which was ridiculous considering the fact that Emily could hear her breathing, but Emily had not recently come into possession of a battering ram, so she had admitted defeat for one more day.

Grace was still clearly smarting from their argument about Aster's escape, and had been in a skittish sort of mood ever since, skirting around Emily like a rabbit avoiding a trap. Emily had found it easiest to let Grace guide their lessons, so while she offered a few subjects when they started for the day, it was always Miss Edwards who chose their agenda. They were studying poetry that morning, but everything Grace selected was dire and gloomy, obsessed with death and meting out punishment.

"Grace," Emily said eventually, when she reached for a pen and Grace actually flinched. "Stop it."

"Stop what?"

"Stop acting as if I'm going to stab you with the sharp end of a paintbrush if you talk too loudly."

"I don't think you're going to stab me," Grace said. "I just don't want you to shout at me again."

"I didn't *shout* at you," Emily scoffed, but then she stopped to reflect. It might have been loud enough to qualify as shouting. "All right, I'm not going to shout at you . . . unless you truly deserve it. But what you did was very irritating. You should have told me that you suspected where Aster might be."

"But I—"

"Grace. You should have told me, and I was right to tell your father. Aster was in danger. He needed to know."

Grace chewed on her lip, and then nodded reluctantly.

"I just don't want him to . . . to only notice when we're doing something wrong."

"You are not being performance reviewed in your roles as his children," said Emily. "He is not going to dismiss you if you make a mistake."

"You don't know that," Grace said darkly.

Emily thought of what Akia had said, about Captain Edwards caring more for his children than anything else in the world. She had seen not a shred of proof that this was the case—and if she felt this way after just a fortnight at Fairmont, she could only imagine what sort of evidence Grace might have compiled to prove to herself that her father's love was conditional.

"I do know, actually," said Emily, even though she did not believe it. "Because he is your father, and he cares for you."

This was the sort of thing you said to children, regardless of the truth.

"I think he'd like me better if I was a horse," said Grace. Emily was caught so off guard that she snorted. Grace smiled tentatively back, but it soon slipped. "I know he loves me . . . I just wish he'd *talk* to me. When we sit down to eat he says exactly two things—'How are you, Grace?' and 'How are you, Aster?'—but I don't think he even listens to our replies, and then that's it for the next hour. Silence, unless I talk, and then usually only Aster replies. Mama *loved* to spend time with me. We used to go to the beach together, or plant flowers, or play with this doll's house up in the attic—sometimes we'd be up there for hours, hiding from everybody else, when Aster got older and started acting as if she was above playing. I'd almost rather Father *didn't* love me, but did enjoy my company."

This was too sad, even for Emily.

It was an awful thing for a child to be so astute; better to be foolish and happy than to *notice* things, and have your life made forever worse by that knowledge.

"No more of this. Buck up and stop being so maudlin. Weren't you going to paint my portrait?"

"All right," Grace said. "But you cannot glare at me the entire time in that odd way of yours. The portrait will turn out too Gothic, and I will have to burn it."

Emily finally caught a glimpse of Aster after luncheon. She was standing in the entrance hall, looking exhausted and sullen, having a conversation with Captain Edwards, who looked as stern as always but was at least talking softly. They had matching dark circles under their eyes; their shoulders sloped like puppets on threadbare strings. They seemed very alike, standing in profile, the captain looking down at Aster and Aster looking down at the floor.

Emily wondered if they had argued, or if the captain had found avoidance preferable; whatever had happened, they seemed to be over the worst of it now.

Grace came in wearing a blue silken bonnet and practically skipping, apparently in high spirits again, and Akia followed behind holding an armful of coats.

Emily hadn't meant to linger for so long. She was halfway to the kitchens when she heard somebody behind her, and turned to find that Captain Edwards had followed her.

Much like a dog chasing a pigeon, he did not seem to know what to do now that he had caught up.

He cleared his throat.

"I am taking the children out. To see . . . relatives. My cousin."

Emily nodded, and then waited, wondering if there was to be more. He really did look very tired.

"We will be gone all afternoon. So . . . your lessons will be postponed until the morrow."

"Well," said Emily. "All right."

"I can only apologize if this inconveniences you, Miss Laurence."

This was odd. What did he care of her inconvenience? They were his children, to do with what he wished. She could see no logical reason for him to follow her just for this awkward, stilted interlude. Perhaps he wanted some sort of gold medal for voluntarily spending more time with his own offspring, and was looking to her to bestow it.

"It is no inconvenience to me," Emily said. "I hope you . . . enjoy your time together."

"Yes," said Captain Edwards. "I think . . . Yes."

He hovered for a moment more, and then seemed to consider this strange interaction at an end, because he nodded to her and then turned and walked briskly away.

Emily waited until the bustle in the front hall had ceased and then went upstairs so that she could watch them from the first floor window. Aster climbed into the carriage first, as if eager to get this all over with, and then Grace took her father's arm so that she could be helped up, chattering melodically like a bird all the while. It was obvious how thrilled she was that her father had deigned to take them out, her delight written so plainly on her face that it was almost painful.

Captain Edwards was, as ever, harder to read, but when Emily caught a glimpse of his face he looked almost nervous, as if being trapped in a carriage with his children was tantamount to being interviewed for a job or undergoing a cross-examination in a court of law.

If Emily wasn't very much mistaken, he was *trying*.

Not that she cared. If they were going to be away all afternoon, the only thing she cared about was stealing something baked from the kitchen, taking a book down from the schoolroom shelves, and hiding with it in a corner where nobody could ask her to do a thing.

Unfortunately, Akia was in the schoolroom, tidying; Emily was obliged to hand over one of the raisin-studded biscuits she had pilfered and then make a vague effort to help.

Meera found them there twenty minutes later, while Akia was reading snatches from an etiquette book aloud to Emily and Emily was trying not to laugh.

"Shall we go down to the beach for an hour or so?" Meera said, surprising Emily, who had been expecting a rueful request for help in some other part of the house. "Captain Edwards will not mind, and we can catch up by the time they return. Joe won't come—he's busy doing something very violent to a rack of lamb. But I caught a glimpse of sun earlier, so we ought to throw ourselves at it while we can. And Amy hasn't properly seen the beach yet."

Emily thought this quite a tactful way to avoid discussing the time she *had* recently spent on the beach, seeking a drunk child in the company of a reticent man.

Meera packed a small picnic—mostly wine and fruit, with a few crumbly pieces of cake wrapped in paper—and they set off toward the cliffs. Oliver lagged behind them, hands in his pockets, looking artfully pale and hungover and noticeably avoiding Emily. It really was very sunny, although the wind kept chivvying clouds along and casting fast-moving shadows on the ground;

the tall grasses rippled back and forth as if pulled in warring currents, and it was all so bright and bracing that Emily felt a bit stunned, like a bat exposed to a lamp. They reached the chalky, sandy path that switchbacked its way dramatically down to sea level. Seeing it in daylight, Emily could hardly believe that she and Captain Edwards had made it down there without breaking their necks, let alone back up with Aster draped in her father's arms.

Emily had glimpsed the sea from atop the coastal path, and she had heard it rushing ominously nearby in the dark, but she had never stood and watched the waves rolling in, exhausting themselves against the shore and then gathering their strength to do it all over again. She found herself mesmerized by the rhythm of it, steady and inevitable, and only snapped out of it when Oliver said, "Oh dear, she's got the sea madness," in his nastiest little voice.

The sand was less mesmerizing. It was coarse, and rough, and somehow already in Emily's hair.

Meera laid out a blanket in the shade, and Akia immediately sat down on it and started eating grapes. Oliver took off his shoes and stockings and went to stand dramatically in the surf, squinting out to sea.

Emily went for a walk.

She was surprised how far the beach stretched ahead of her, endless curves and corners. There were some parts where rocks rose up out of the gray sand and partially blocked the way, but it turned out they weren't so hard to maneuver over, as long as they weren't all filled with water. In one such pool, she saw a crab the size of her fingernail making a dash for it as her shadow passed overhead. In another, she discovered a dead fish, its ribs protruding whitely from its rotting flesh. She passed the cave she had entered with Captain Edwards, as dark and ominous as ever, even in daylight.

Amy would have looked so right here, striding about, getting great lungfuls of sea air, letting the coast heal her from the inside out. She was the sort of person who delighted in ordinary things, finding a hundred different ways to brighten up her own day. Her first glimpse of the sea would have had her in quiet, smiling raptures for hours before she found the words to express to Emily just how wonderful it all was. Emily would have to try to describe the little scuttling crab to her; the way the sea stretched inexorably to a blurry horizon.

When she was far enough away from the others, she could get down to the real reason for her walk. The snuffbox and statuette she had swiped from the hall mantel were clutched tight in her pocket. She had wrapped them and hidden them in her trunk at first, as she had done with the hideous baroque contraption, but she had been overwhelmed by paranoia due to Oliver's pointed looks over the breakfast table and had ultimately decided to keep them on her person instead.

Thinking of the tide that had lapped threateningly at the entrance to the cave, she kept walking until she found a little stretch of beach that extended beyond the border of crushed shells, tangled seaweed, and miscellaneous debris that must have marked the waterline. She located a memorable jut of rock and reached down into the furry gray sand below it to scoop up a handful. It left a fist-sized hole, which stayed relatively structurally sound. She glanced around and then returned to her digging until she was satisfied that she had gone far enough. It was like grave burial mathematics, probably—if six feet was right for a person, then surely an entire foot for a couple of trinkets that were only a few inches across was, in actual fact, overkill.

Once she had laid her treasures inside and covered them up again, she dusted her hands mostly free of sand and made her way back toward the others, where she found them all lounging on the blanket.

"I don't understand how sea air could possibly be good for the lungs," Oliver was saying, as if he had read her mind. "It's just *wet*. Isn't wet *bad*? Nobody says you ought to go and sit in a damp, moldy cellar for your health, do they?"

"Mold is different," said Akia. "I think it sort of poisons you. Through the air."

"Delightful," said Meera. "Well, she won't come to the sea anyway. She doesn't like to travel. I think her last trip almost did her in." She noticed Emily approaching, and shuffled over to make room. "My aunt is unwell," she explained. "She was doing all right in India, but somebody convinced her that the doctors here were better. Now she's here with her daughter, it turns out they most certainly are *not*, and besides, the city air is no good for her. They cannot move away and have my cousin lose her position, so they are somewhat . . . stuck. I would hire her here, if we only had the budget for another maid."

"Oh," said Emily. "I'm sorry."

"No need to be sorry," Meera said cheerfully. "*You* didn't duff up her lungs. I'll send her what I can, and perhaps she can see about a short trip away from all the smoke. What do you think of our patch of sea, then?"

Emily had not quite grown used to Meera's habit of abruptly directing the conversation toward her.

"It's very . . . big."

"Goodness," said Oliver. "And this is the great mind teaching the next generation."

"Well, what do you want me to say, Oliver?" Emily snapped. "It encompasses an unknowable vastness? I wasn't aware I was supposed to be composing an additional verse for *The Rime of the Ancient Mariner*."

"God, please don't," said Akia. "I know that one. It's *so* long."

"I have had enough of this," said Meera. "Either shake hands and become friends, Oliver, or eat a grape and shut up."

"Oh, fine." Oliver sat up onto his knees and offered Emily a hand. "Look, I will agree to play nicely, but only if you admit that you jumped to vile conclusions about me for absolutely *no* discernible reason, and that you are very sorry for being such a toad."

"I will do no such thing," Emily said. She would never have admitted that Captain Edwards's surety that Oliver would never harm Aster had in fact swayed her opinion in his favor, but she supposed she could ease the disagreement in increments. "I *will* agree to be civil. I am sick of your pouting."

Akia laughed, and Meera elbowed her in the ribs to stop her.

"You really are the most cantankerous little weasel," said Oliver, but he grasped her hand anyway and shook it once, hard.

"Thank God," said Akia. "All right, who wants to play Stones?"

"I will," said Oliver.

"You cheat."

"How could I possibly cheat? It's not whist, Akia—it's throwing small stones at a bigger stone. A one-year-old could do it."

"You call dishonest points," said Akia. "You are overgenerous with yourself."

"As we should all be."

The game of Stones really was just throwing pebbles at a big stone, receiving a point for every time you hit the target, but it took up half an hour as they nibbled on fruit and cheese—and then Meera announced that their allotted slot for fun was over and it was time to return to the house to begin the evening's chores.

Without Grace to instruct, and with the schoolroom already tidy, Emily could have retired to her room to be alone. She could have gone wandering by herself, making the best of the fine weather. Instead, she found herself drifting into the kitchen, ostensibly looking for something to eat, and then wandering through to the tiny housekeeper's office, where she found Meera now elbow-deep in lists.

"Do you need something, Amy? Just give me a moment, I am holding ten numbers in my head and if I let one drop, it will start somewhat of a cascade."

Emily did not need anything, and was suddenly embarrassed to have come here, interrupting the real work Meera was doing. Meera finished writing something with a flourish and then put down her pen.

"I am all yours."

"Oh, I wasn't . . . I just thought I would check if you . . . needed me for anything."

Meera gave her a slightly puzzled smile. "Not at all. It is *very* kind of you to offer, though."

Emily had not felt kind. She had simply felt bored. If Meera misconstrued her actions as kindness, that was her problem.

"I know you have been working hard with Grace, Amy, and that you would do the same with Aster if only she were within arm's reach. Please, your time is your own."

"It isn't real hard work," Emily said, before she could stop herself. "I mean . . . not like the kind of work *you* do."

"Whatever makes you say that? I believe instructing young ladies is one of the most important things you can do. You might not get a chronic back problem out of it, but I am sure it puts strain on other things."

"Do you have a chronic back problem?"

"Oh, yes," said Meera. "But all the best people do." She was studying Emily's face very closely; whatever had pulled Emily like a magnet to seek company had vanished, and she suddenly felt as if she had awoken from a spell that had led her into the lion's den. "You know, we have never employed a governess before who was willing to get her hands dirty. I had never imagined such a person existed, but . . . here you are."

"Yes," said Emily, trying to keep the disquiet out of her voice. "Sorry. I'll just be going."

"Do not *apologize*," said Meera, shuffling her papers into a neat pile. "You are unique, Miss Laurence, and we are grateful to have you."

Emily let out a disbelieving little huff. "I am not entirely sure that Captain Edwards feels the same way."

Meera tilted her head to one side and considered her again. "I don't think that's true."

"Have I lasted longer than the last governess, yet?"

"Well," said Meera slowly. "The *previous* governess did not believe that Grace was truly ill. She thought that it was a sort of laziness of character, and that she could fix her with endless *walking*, especially when she was feeling under the weather. Grace was too determined to cure herself to tell anybody what was happening. She collapsed in the garden and was in bed for a month. I have never seen Captain Edwards so angry."

"Oh," said Emily. "I didn't know."

"I know *you* will not do anything so foolish. I mean it, Amy. We are *all* so pleased that you are here."

Emily wasn't sure if she said anything in reply, or if it just came out as garbled nonsense. She exited as if pursued by a constable, and only felt able to breathe again once she was up in her room, sitting on her bed, where she should have gone in the first place.

When her heart had ceased hammering, she sat down to write to Amy, placing the two gold sovereigns next to her on the desk, where they gleamed ostentatiously in the light.

Dear Amy,

Nobody minds that I am here in your place, and you should not be worrying yourself about it; they are too kind for their own good and would probably be grateful for me even if I were teaching the children how to smash windows and set things alight like tiny Luddites (actually, not a bad idea—we need more baby revolutionaries in the world).

I have barely seen the captain, so please insert here whichever mental picture of him you prefer; an elderly sea dog, a young whippersnapper dashing about on boats. Whatever pleases you will suit.

Re my being an acquired taste—nobody here is sampling me, thank you very much, so my taste is neither here nor there.

Do you remember when you fell in that puddle outside Jimson's and the water went so far up under your dress you said it had entered via the exit and you were no longer thirsty, and I laughed so hard I almost made a show of myself?

The sea is a bit like that puddle, so no need to worry that you're missing anything. Everything smells sort of fishy, and the air is so salty that I might as well be brushing my hair with a comb of fish ribs.

I am sure you are feeling better and sprightly, but in case you do need to call for the doctor so you can flirt with him and tell him off for being so damnably expensive, I have enclosed some money. Do not run off and spend it all at once on peppermints or give it to a charity that makes little peg legs for three-legged dogs.

All my love, really and truly, because nobody else deserves it,

Emily

Chapter Fifteen

ASTER APPEARED IN THE SCHOOLROOM THE NEXT DAY.
She didn't say anything, and Emily didn't expect her to; the
fact that she had actually come to lessons without Emily having
to go and hunt her down seemed monumental enough. Captain
Edwards must have said something to her—encouragement or
threats—although it felt more likely that he had employed the
stick rather than the carrot. Whatever the reason, Aster sat down
next to Grace at the table and immediately slumped forward,
resting her head on her arms and watching Emily out of the corner of her eye.

Attendance did not extend to participation, then.

Emily had been skimming a book on Tudor history before
bed, which meant that she was just about equipped to get Grace
talking about belligerent kings and their wars. All Grace wanted
to talk about was Henry VIII's wives, with the kind of alarming
fascination for violent detail that often presented in children.

"I would think," Grace said enthusiastically, "that if you were
a man's second wife called Anne or *third* wife called Catherine,
you might start to wonder."

Aster snorted. "If you agreed to be a man's third wife at all,
you have only yourself to blame."

"Unfortunately," Emily said, trying to encourage this neutral
participation without scaring Aster off, "the fact of these women's
positions—"

"Oh, please, do impart some knowledge about *women's*

positions," said Aster. "You are so learned, I can hardly restrain myself from applause."

Ah, well. So much for that, then.

It was much of the same until luncheon; afterward, when they both returned, Emily did not bother to try to engage Aster at all. She simply fetched the sketching things and dumped them on the table.

Aster looked suspicious, as if Emily must have some hidden agenda for allowing her to make art rather than discuss gouty kings. Anything that got Aster to stop talking was its own reward.

It worked. Grace chattered away as she drew, telling Emily about the relatives they had gone to visit and how wonderful their elderly Skye terrier was, and Aster picked up her graphite and started making decisive, bold lines on the page. She seemed to be drawing entirely from memory, or perhaps her imagination.

Emily tried not to pay too much attention in case Aster caught her looking and mistook it for interest, but something darkly beautiful was blossoming from under that pencil, and it was the sort of thing you wanted to bear witness to, even if the artist *was* profoundly annoying.

From some angles it looked like a house, from others a ship. When Aster ran out of graphite, Emily placed another within her reach as if by accident, and Aster picked it up without pause and kept drawing.

"Oh, Aster," Grace said, when she came to look over her sister's shoulder. "That is terrifying. I love it."

"Thanks," Aster said gruffly, going a bit red. "Leave off, you'll smudge it."

When Grace did sit back down, she fell heavily into her seat, landing slightly off-kilter.

"Grace?" Emily said sharply.

"I'm all right!" Grace said cheerfully, adjusting herself. "I suppose I still haven't mastered the art of sitting, but I have high hopes that I'll get there before I come out into society. People will look at me and say—there goes Miss Edwards the younger, master of sitting, sitter extraordinaire. People will come from all around to marvel at my seat."

Now that Emily was looking at her, Grace had the tightly drawn together edges of a person who was only *attempting* to appear well. She was doing such a strange impression of vigor and good health that the whole thing became uncanny: smile too big, expression too rigid. Hands white at the knuckles where she was pretending to hold casually on to the edge of the table.

Aster was looking, too.

"We're done for today," Aster said abruptly. "Come on."

She stood up and held a hand out for Grace; Grace didn't move.

"I haven't finished my work of art," she said. "It's the latest in my dog series. I am going through somewhat of a canine period."

"Later," said Aster. "Come on, Gracie. Read some of that horrid poetry you like to me while I nap."

It was obvious that Grace had not been fooled by any of this, but she got up anyway and allowed herself to be accompanied from the room, Aster gently contorting herself so that she could prop her sister up like a scaffold.

Perhaps Emily should have followed to ensure that Grace made it safely into bed, but there was not a doubt in her mind that Aster would take care of her. She knew exactly how that felt—could have told Aster so, let her know that this was something they shared, if Aster weren't so doggedly committed to being such an interminable arse.

She found herself in the kitchen, and when Joe saw her with her hands and head clearly empty, he gave her a very large turnip as if he were handing over a baton.

"Peel and cut," he said. "Thin. Even."

"I am . . . busy."

"No you aren't. Where are the girls?"

Emily wrinkled her brow. "Resting."

"Thin and even," he said again, as if that settled matters.

It was absolutely not Emily's job to cut turnips into any sort of shape and thickness, but he did have that knife, so she sat down and did it anyway. Joe didn't try to talk to her further; he just went back to his own station to continue with whatever dark magic produced the delicious dinners they ate every evening. When Emily had finished her turnip, quite proud of her work, she showed it to Joe. He nodded once, then handed her an entire basket of turnips.

Emily rather thought that such excellent turnip-cutting should have warranted reward rather than punishment, but she supposed she had proved herself too talented in the arena of vegetable dissection to be allowed to walk free without repeating the trick.

"She's a good girl," Joe said ten minutes later, apropos of absolutely nothing.

"Who?" said Emily.

"Grace," said Joe. "Aster's not the kind of good most people see, but she deserves a fair shot anyway."

"Right," said Emily. "Yes. Of course."

Joe turned around to look at her, his ruddy face concertinaed into a frown that seemed to involve every single one of his facial muscles.

"You just be careful not to break their hearts," said Joe.

Emily let out an odd bark of laughter. "Me? Why on earth would—?"

"Be careful," Joe said slowly, and then he turned and went back to his cooking.

It was so unnerving that Emily was still feeling out of sorts when she finished the last of the turnips, and slipped from the kitchen before Joe could hand her a cauliflower and tell her to start pruning.

That evening, after a late dinner and a good while spent sitting around nursing their drinks, Emily offered to deal with the fires. There were three lit on the ground floor alone—a monstrous extravagance of fuel for August, even if the weather was unseasonably dire. Meera gave her a startled, unconvinced look before agreeing, and then made sure she knew exactly how to do it without filling the room with smoke or coating the carpet in ashes.

It was irritating, repetitive work, but it meant that Emily had an excuse to enter every room under the cover of darkness without witnesses, and that made it worth every second. The hour was already very late, but she did not hurry.

Captain Edwards's study was her real target, but she didn't rush there first. Instead, she made sure that she had completed every room in proper order so as to be convincing if questioned. When she did eventually reach the study, she closed the door behind her and felt a little thrill course through her as she turned to face his inner sanctum. The room was truly empty, the house silent; she had made sure of that this time, so as not to risk another run-in with the captain, hiding in the corner with a book like a dull and cantankerous ghoul. There was always the chance that he might spring out of bed and come rushing downstairs to attend to some business, but she thought it unlikely enough that she only kept an ear out for urgent creaking in the corridor.

She did at least start by attending to the fire, leaving the job half-done, so that if she were discovered she could claim to have been momentarily distracted from the legitimate work that had brought her here in the first place.

The captain had obviously tidied up before leaving, and it

made Emily's job easier; there was no need to rifle through endless piles of paper, only to open each drawer and decipher from context clues which carefully regimented section she had discovered. There was a drawer for papers relating to the house, one that seemed to be entirely filled with invitations to social occasions, some of which didn't even have the seal broken. Emily's heart sped up when she came across what appeared to be official correspondence from the Royal Navy. She picked up the pile and carefully spread it out across the desk, so that she could inspect each in turn and then put them back where she had found them. Captain Edwards seemed the sort to know exactly where he'd put his letters, and in what order. He also probably cataloged his stockings and his stocks, and, when struck down with a cold, allowed himself exactly three sneezes per fit. Any more would be indulgent and perverse.

From what Emily could see, these letters contained nothing of interest. Most of them just seemed to be conveying orders, using military terms she didn't understand. Two of them were about past promotions, and were written in such stilted and formal language that Emily was surprised they were trying to express good news rather than instructions for replacing a pipe valve.

She carefully stacked the letters and replaced them, and then tried to open the bottom drawer in the desk, only to find that it had been locked. A *lock* suggested that there might be something within worth having.

Emily gave it a good rattle, hoping it might be old enough that it gave in and admitted her without the formality of a key, but had no such luck. The keyhole was tiny—a silly size, really—and searching for a key that would have been more suited to a doll's house was not likely to be fruitful.

She tried anyway, sweeping her hands over the desk, going to the narrow table by the wall and inspecting the base of the globe, the space behind the books of nautical maps: all empty.

Her hand went to her hair, and she felt about for a pin. One of the tricks she'd picked up at the mill, from a boy of about ten, was that some locks could be persuaded to open with the application of anything that vaguely resembled a key.

Even her narrow pin was too cumbersome to open this lock.

It was frustrating, but still . . . she had a lead. It seemed extremely likely that Captain Edwards was storing his most sensitive papers in that drawer, and if she could get her hands on even a single incriminating letter or document, it would change everything. Charles had given her two gold sovereigns just for proving herself trustworthy—she couldn't imagine how much he might hand over if she came into possession of something real.

She still had no earthly idea what Captain Edwards could have done that would be so damning, because she couldn't imagine him doing much of interest at all. Perhaps it was one of those crimes that one heard about without ever really understanding what it was—something to do with taxes, or a particularly dull flavor of embezzlement.

The matter of the key would have to wait for another day. Emily dealt with the fire and was halfway to the next room when she heard something fall heavily to the floor in the ground floor hallway below.

She froze, listening, wondering if she had accidentally discovered an intruder, or if Oliver had sneaked out to the pub and come back too soused to remember that he was an employee of this house, rather than its master.

When somebody spoke it was not Oliver.

"Shit."

It was instead, unmistakably, Captain Edwards.

Emily thought she might have misheard him, but then he said it again: the long, drawn-out, half-whispered "shiiit" of somebody who had recently made an error in judgment.

She crept to the top of the stairs and then abruptly stopped attempting to be discreet when she saw the state he was in.

He was crouching down, attempting to right the candelabra he had knocked to the floor, but seemed to be having some trouble remembering where his own fingers were and what he was supposed to be doing with them. He gave up the candelabra as a bad lot and sat fully down on the floor, with a heavy, childlike ungainliness that was so out of character Emily laughed.

It was a quiet, slightly unkind laugh. By all rights, he shouldn't have heard it. He was clearly very drunk. But he had also presumably been drilled in the Royal Navy to be alert to potential threats, and apparently this meant he had a very good ear for muffled laughter.

"Oliver?" he said, squinting up at her.

This, Emily found deeply offensive.

"No," she said reluctantly. "It's . . . Miss Laurence, sir."

"Ah," he said. "Of course it is."

"Should I . . . go and fetch Oliver?" Emily asked, hopeful that this suggestion might bring a swift end to this encounter.

"No, no, don't bother Oliver, I am perfectly . . ." Captain Edwards trailed off. What he *was perfectly* was in evidence. Perfectly, entirely drunk. The Platonic ideal of three sheets to the wind. Perfectly incapable of standing up.

Emily did not want to help Captain Edwards. She didn't want to talk to him, or even to be within a twenty-foot range of him. She did, however, wish to stay employed long enough to earn good money from his downfall, and this was what she kept her mind firmly fixed on as she descended the stairs and went to offer him a hand.

"Oh," he said affably. "No, I couldn't possibly . . ."

"It's just a hand, sir," said Emily.

"It's *your* hand," said Captain Edwards.

The best that could be said of this statement was that it was accurate. Emily was starting to get rather annoyed.

"Well, if it is somehow repulsive to you, I will retract the offer and leave you here to—"

Captain Edwards took her hand. He wasn't wearing a glove. Emily wasn't wearing a glove. After her insistence that it was *just a hand*, and that grasping it did not require extensive deliberation, the feeling of his fingers on hers was far more complex than she had anticipated.

It was the *way* he did it. It wasn't brusque and practical, as he usually was. He was being . . . gentler than he had any right to be. Careful, as if she should be handled delicately. It was the way someone might take your hand before they leaned over to press a kiss to the fine skin over your knuckles, or before they ducked their head and led you out onto the dance floor.

It was horribly intimate, and Emily wanted to shake him off at once. Instead, she dug her heels in and helped pull him to a stand, trying not to notice the way he rested his weight on her for a second before he stepped away and released her, and very much noticing it anyway.

"Thank you," he said, his voice low and confidential despite the fact that there was nobody around to bear witness to any of this.

"You're bleeding," said Emily.

He held his other hand up in front of his face and frowned at it. His knuckles were bruised, the skin split in a way that Emily recognized as a sure sign that they had recently connected with somebody's face.

"It's nothing," said Captain Edwards. "Only that . . . some people are determined to fill their leisure time passing judgment upon others . . . absolutely incapable of extending the humanity they cling to as an inalienable right to . . . to *anybody* who is not their perfect mirror. It is all so very dull, and sometimes to break up the monotony you just . . ." He trailed off, still looking at his hand.

"I see," said Emily, not really seeing at all. "If you come into the kitchen, I think Meera keeps things there for when Joe slices off prime cuts of his fingers."

"Ha," said Captain Edwards. "Yes. All right."

He followed her as meekly as a lamb, and when they reached the empty kitchen, he pulled up a chair and collapsed into it gratefully, as if he would have returned to the floor if they had arrived at their destination but a moment later. The surfaces had all been diligently scrubbed, the dinner things cleaned and put away. Emily lit a candle, wondering why her hands were slightly jittery. In the light, she could see that his face was bruised around the eye socket, a mottled red that would likely mature to a rich, moody purple.

She rummaged until she found the bandages as yet unbloodied by Joe, and then handed them awkwardly to Captain Edwards. He looked down at them as if gathering the strength to act, and then started winding them around his hand. He kept losing the tension, so that they sagged, then having to start over again. Eventually Emily rolled her eyes and sat down next to him, pulling his hand toward her in as businesslike a fashion as she could manage.

"You don't seem very happy here," he said to Emily, as she frowned over her work.

"I don't see what that has to do with anything," she replied without thinking. She reached the end of her winding and tied a knot so tight that Captain Edwards winced. "Sorry."

"Monstrous as I am, of course, in the tradition of men at the helms of . . . of large boats and slightly smaller houses . . . I do not wish for you to suffer under my roof."

Emily gave him a doubtful, unimpressed sort of look. There seemed little chance he'd remember the details of this conversation in the morning.

"Well, it's suffer under your roof or suffer elsewhere. Sorry if I ruin the view."

"No, that is . . . not what I meant." Captain Edwards was looking at her very directly from under a wayward lock of hair, one of the ones not yet streaked with silver, and she kept having to look away. "Did you have trouble at your last house?"

"Trouble?" Emily said, confused by the turn this conversation had taken. "No, I don't . . . Why would you think that?"

"The other day when we were talking . . . some might say arguing, although I certainly wouldn't be one of them . . . you mentioned men with ill intentions, and I wasn't sure . . ."

"Oh," said Emily, trying to remember exactly what she had said, feeling irritated with herself that she had brought it up at all. "No. I mean, it wasn't at my last house."

Captain Edwards nodded seriously. "I suppose there's no way to say that would not be tolerated here without it sounding . . . well . . . But I have said it anyway."

Emily continued to be baffled. "You have."

"But you are resolved not to be happy here, anyway, so it is of no consequence."

Emily looked sharply up at him and saw that he seemed to be joking.

"You are happy, obviously. Happy people often find themselves coming home with split knuckles," she said, feeling brazen. "Unable to pick themselves up from the hallway floor. The calling card of a person at peace and content, the Tuesday evening drinking binge."

For a second, Emily thought she had miscalculated, but then Captain Edwards laughed quietly. It transformed his whole face: his eyes crinkled, the furrows at his brow smoothed. He looked younger. Alive. There was something about that laugh that tugged at Emily's stomach, a sort of horrified pleasure that she had been the one to cause it.

Or maybe she was just hungry. That was probably it.

"You are very impertinent," Captain Edwards said, as if it was a neutral trait.

Emily shrugged, then remembered herself and picked up the scissors so that she could cut the end of the bandage and free him from her grip. She had to lean in close to do it, so that she didn't accidentally slip and cut him, and for reasons unbeknownst to her, she found that he had leaned in a fraction closer to her, too.

"I admire impertinence," he said thoughtfully. "You wear it well. I almost believe you'd stab me with those, if I truly deserved it."

She didn't look up at him. That felt far too intimate and dangerous. She simply focused all her effort on the slide and cut of the scissors, to distract from the fact that she was so close she could actually smell him—sea salt and wet grass and sweet whiskey—and that his breath was ruffling the loose strands of her hair.

He must have been very drunk to have forgotten himself like this and leaned in so very close. Or perhaps his head simply felt too heavy, his neck too weary to hold it up properly anymore, like a baby's.

"There," said Emily, abruptly sitting back and dropping the scissors onto the table. "I've finished."

"Mmm," said Captain Edwards thoughtfully. He leaned back in the chair and pushed his hair out of his eyes, blinking hard as if trying to sober himself up. "Yes. You have. And *I* have embarrassed myself terribly, haven't I."

"I wouldn't know," said Emily. "I wasn't there."

"No, not out there," said Captain Edwards dismissively. "Here."

"Here?" said Emily.

"Yes." There was no premeditation behind his words; nothing about them was practiced, or intentional. He genuinely seemed to be speaking almost as soon as a thought occurred to him, which was why Emily was so stunned by what he said next. "I think it must have been the way I was looking at you."

Emily knocked the scissors from the table as she stood, and was gone almost before they hit the floor.

Chapter Sixteen

N OBODY CARED TO LOOK AT EMILY, AND SHE LIKED IT THAT way. Or at least—she thought she did. She had always been sure of it before.

There had been a few people who had caught her notice when she and Amy were no more than giggling children, but the realities of life had soon put a damper on any *romantic* leanings she might have had, and things were neater that way. Simpler.

Her body was not intended for indulgences like pleasure; it was a machine she had put to work, and it carried all the evidence of that work with it as she grew older. She had a scar on her wrist from the knife of an overenthusiastic young piecer at the mill, calluses on her fingers, ropy muscles in her arms from hard use that were so unlike the soft, supple arms of a *lady*. She hadn't been ornamental since childhood, and the idea that anybody could enjoy *looking* at her now was completely absurd.

Captain Edwards must have been even more drunk than she had fathomed. And . . . perhaps a little lonely. Maybe he had made such advances to every woman in his employ at some point. No matter what he said about *respect*, you never could tell what a man might decide to do with an idle mind and too much power at his disposal.

She woke up the next morning to the instant realization that it would have been the *perfect* opportunity to probe about his problems with the Royal Navy, to see if a well-timed question might bring it all tumbling out of him. She was kicking herself for getting so caught up in the strangeness of the situation that she had not seized the chance; she could not afford to be so foolish, with so much at stake. She would not make that mistake again.

"Could you take this to Meera?" Oliver said when he passed Emily in the hall, after she had exhausted herself with two hours of Edward VI with the girls and then sent them off to eat luncheon. He was holding a crate of something that looked rather heavy.

"You take it to Meera," Emily said primly.

"Oh, it's like that, is it? All right, roll up your sleeves, let's have this out like gentlemen."

"Gentlemen do not brawl in the corridor," said Emily.

Oliver smirked. "Tell that to Ben. Have you seen the black eye on him? He wouldn't say how he procured it, but I'm sure he was fighting for someone's honor. Deeply, *genuinely* impressive. Sort of looks like a ferret, but just on the one side."

"Charming."

"Hideous, actually. Go on, do me a favor, take the crate—think of how you can lord it over me at a later date. You'll love that."

Emily rolled her eyes, but she received the crate anyway and then staggered through the kitchen and into the servants' dining room with it, so she could place it on the table.

"What's that?" Meera said, coming from her office to investigate.

"I have not the faintest idea," said Emily.

Meera fetched something to help lever it open; inside, they found lots of enormous paintbrushes, of the type that you might use to paint rooms or furniture.

"Oh," said Meera, puzzled. "Hmmm. I am not entirely sure—oh, *no*." She clapped a hand to her face, looking thunderstruck. "This is not what I ordered. I am sure of it! I have a receipt somewhere—let me . . ." She left the room, and reappeared scanning some paper in her hand. She looked crestfallen. "No, this is right—*I* was wrong. I must not have been paying attention."

"What were you trying to order?" Emily said, picking up one of the paintbrushes and looking it over.

"Paintbrushes," said Meera. "But . . . small ones. For art. The girls. Captain Edwards said that Grace had been dropping hints. You should have told me how dire things were, Amy! I know we are not exactly sitting atop mountains of gold, but we can stretch to a few art supplies."

Emily had meant to tell her. She had just had other things on her mind. Like theft, and espionage.

"Except now I have spent the money on something entirely wrong," Meera said. "A silly mistake, really. I should have been more careful. Leave those there, and I will tell Oliver to see about sending them back . . . Oh, drat."

There was a knock at the back door, and Meera went to see about it; she was still staring at the receipt in her hand, as if it might be about to turn into the correct order, when she walked into the kitchen. Emily saw what was about to happen, but it was too late to stop her. Joe was turning around, holding an enormous pot of stock, and when they collided, it spilled spectacularly all down Meera's apron, drenching her through to her stockings and leaving a large, meaty puddle on the floor.

"You all right?" Joe said, hefting the pot so he could put it down.

"No, I'm fine—it's not that hot," Meera said, her voice pitched very high.

Whoever was at the back door gave up knocking and nudged it open. Emily saw Mr. Khan standing there, a box of something in his hands, looking as nervous and hopeful as the last time he'd come to visit. It was like watching a puppy line up voluntarily to be kicked.

"Miss Bhandari . . ." he said, and then, "*Oh*, my goodness."

"Just give me a moment, Mr. Khan," Meera said.

She attempted to take a step toward her office, but didn't account for the stock underfoot; she fell spectacularly, skidding as she tried to keep her balance and then pitching headlong toward the stone floor.

Mr. Khan dropped the box and caught her.

It was probably one of the finest moments of his life, and could have been very romantic, if Meera had not immediately burst into tears.

"Oh," he said, looking very panicked. "Miss . . . Miss Bhandari, I am so sorry, I just—"

"Not your fault," said Joe. "Inevitable. The nose has hit the grindstone. Meera, here." He passed her a handful of clean rags, and Meera pulled away from Mr. Khan and sat down in the nearest chair, mopping at herself ineffectually. "I'll have Akia fetch some dry clothes."

He left to find her—although Emily suspected that he was also leaving so that he would not have to bear witness to any more weeping—and Mr. Khan sat down next to Meera, looking deeply concerned.

"I apologize, Mr. Khan, this is not at all becoming . . ." Meera said through her tears. "If you will just give me a moment, I will regain control of myself."

"Not at all! You are always working too hard, Miss Bhandari—an affliction I suffer from myself. I can never judge when I have gone too far, because the more I work, the better business becomes—but we are only human, after all."

Emily decided that the best possible course of action was to make some tea. She busied herself with the hot water and the collection of crockery, trying not to listen to Meera and Mr. Khan speaking to each other quietly behind her. After a minute or so, Meera's hiccuping sobs subsided. She even laughed wetly at something the grocer was saying.

Fine work, Mr. Khan, Emily thought, as she set the tea to steep.

"Oh, Meera, what have you done to yourself?" Akia said, when she came in holding a fresh set of clothes, Joe behind her. "Ah. Well. I see Mr. Khan has been doing a very good job of looking after you. Look, Amy has been unfathomably pleasant and made you some tea—you drink that and I will arrange a bath, all right?"

Mr. Khan went a little red.

"Akia," Meera said, noticing. "Please. We have company."

"Oh, sorry. Mr. Khan, please rest assured that Meera has never taken a bath in her life, she finds the whole thing vulgar and beneath her—"

"*Akia,*" Meera said, but she did not seem truly vexed. She was smiling, in fact, as she wiped the tears from her cheeks. "Oh, dear. This day."

She was sipping her cup of tea when Captain Edwards entered, wearing the sort of scruffy, worn-out clothes that had caused Emily to mistake him for a groom on her very first day. He stopped short when he saw the scene in front of him: Meera red-eyed and stocked, Mr. Khan's chair so close, Joe mopping at the floor.

"Hmmm," he said. "I . . . Never mind."

"Did you need something?" said Meera.

"I . . . Is there something amiss?"

"No. I mean, yes. I am afraid I ordered the wrong paint-brushes," said Meera. She was attempting to put on a brave face, but a little wobble had returned to her voice.

Captain Edwards's brow furrowed. His black eye really was quite spectacular: a half-moon from cheekbone to eyebrow, in pretty shades of bloodied lavender and gorse yellow. He exchanged a glance with Joe, who only gave him a very small shrug.

"Meera," he said gently. "They are only paintbrushes."

Meera smiled in a watery sort of way. "*Did* you need something?"

"I just wanted somebody to . . . I was in the garden, but I . . ."

"Amy," Meera said, looking at her imploringly, "if you would . . . ?"

So much for staying as far away from the captain as possible; Emily could hardly refuse to help him, and so she simply nodded, and if Captain Edwards stood awkwardly for a second in the doorway before nodding, too, she could only hope that nobody else in the room noticed.

They walked silently out into the back garden, Captain Edwards keeping such an exaggerated distance that Emily felt a bit like a pariah. They came to a stop by the first flower bed, in which an enormous peach-colored rose seemed to be trying to eat itself.

"You know it wasn't just about the paintbrushes," Emily said.

Captain Edwards nodded seriously, keeping his eyes on the flowers.

"This is foolish, really," he said suddenly. "Usually I talk things through with Meera, because she has a way of . . ." He waved his hand slightly.

"Untangling?" said Emily.

"Yes. Yes, exactly," said Captain Edwards. "I wanted to do something with the garden. Not to get rid of what's here," he added quickly, "but to . . . cut back the overgrowth. Remove only what cannot be salvaged. Give the rest some space to grow. We can only do a little this year before the cold sets in, but we could plan for the future. Miranda would have . . . Well, the garden was her domain, really. But it might be time to assume the mantle."

He said all of this tentatively, as if Emily might be about to scoff at him and tell him that this was a ridiculous endeavor.

"I think that sounds . . . good," she said instead, very carefully.

"Yes?" he said, looking at her properly.

"Yes."

He let out a long breath. "Fine. Good. All right."

They walked down the garden slowly, Captain Edwards intermittently pointing out the places where the plants would have to be removed completely, suggesting what he might put there instead. That the plentiful asters were to remain seemed to go without saying. He did not really need Emily's input—she knew less about gardening than she did the rules of etiquette—but it seemed enough just that she was listening.

"Joe does a little out here when he can," he said, when they were walking back up the other side. "But he hardly has the time, and I would never ask him to do more. He planted zinnias on the end here, but they won't be back . . . These, though, the black-eyed Susans . . ."

He winced very slightly with his unblemished eye and his bruised one, clearly regretting his choice of words.

"It is hardly noticeable," Emily lied.

"Unless you look," said Captain Edwards.

"Oliver said you were fighting for somebody's honor."

The captain grimaced.

"No? So it was just recreational boxing, was it?"

"Somebody said something . . . unkind."

"About who?"

"Oliver, actually."

"So you were fighting for *Oliver's* honor," Emily said, more pleased than she should have been.

"Not quite how I would put it," said Captain Edwards.

"What were they saying about Oliver?"

"Nothing worth repeating," said the captain. "People often do seem very *concerned* with each other's private lives in a way that . . . Well, I have never understood it."

Emily shrugged. "Nor have I. It is not my business what anybody else does, in the same way that it is not *their* business what

I might do. I cannot abide gossip. There are far more pressing things to be concerned about."

Captain Edwards studied her closely before he replied—so closely that Emily began to feel a little alarmed.

"Yes. Well . . . indeed." He hesitated. "Last night . . . I am not sure that I . . . that I behaved particularly—"

"Please," said Emily. "Don't mention it." She was very happy to put everything that had happened in the dark of the kitchen behind her. "You were saying something about . . . zinnias?"

"Yes," said Captain Edwards, visibly relieved. "I thought we might try them again, when the frost thaws . . ."

It wasn't so bad, just listening to him talk about flowers. Around half an hour had passed when he realized that she should have been back in the schoolroom, and he sent her off with profuse apologies, much more at ease than he had been when they had started out into the garden.

Emily discovered that it was not such a nightmare having Aster in the schoolroom, as long as she was almost entirely left to her own devices. There was still the occasional remark—a jab at Emily's dress, something cutting about her expertise in whatever they were reading that day—but if Aster had pencil or paintbrush in her hand, she was too distracted to give her all to the job of pestering Emily.

A week passed like this without incident. Emily strode about the schoolroom all day, and then sat awash in the familiar chatter around the dining table at night. Sometimes she smoked Oliver's pipe, when it was passed to her. Other times she had a few too many glasses of wine and laughed openly at Akia's stories, or volunteered some part of her day up to Meera without much digging.

She had no more news for Charles at the Rose and Crown,

and it nagged at the back of her mind—but she did have wages tucked under the mattress in her room, salve for her hands that had simply appeared one day on her bedside table, and two expensive trinkets buried on the beach for when the time came.

Seven days after Aster returned to the schoolroom, she left a painting on the table instead of squirreling it away in her room as she usually did. She had titled it *Death of the Governess*, and probably thought it very threatening. It depicted someone who looked suspiciously like Emily in the process of violently drowning.

It was really rather good. Emily propped it up on her bedroom mantel, so that she could look at it every morning and remember how important it was that she survived.

Chapter Seventeen

IN THE FIRST WEEK OF SEPTEMBER, A SHIP SCRAPED THE coast. It was so close to the house that Emily could stand at the window on the top floor landing and see the dark spikes of the bobbing masts, far too close.

"It'll hit the rocks," Meera said grimly, standing behind her with her arms crossed. "Mark my words. They've miscalculated. There's no getting out of this cove once you come in, not in a vessel that size. That's a Royal Navy frigate."

Mere moments later, Oliver came rushing up the stairs two at a time to tell them that Captain Edwards had called all of the household downstairs.

"You look very sweaty, Oliver," said Emily.

Oliver narrowed his eyes at her, but did not rise to it.

"I had to sprint to catch a messenger for the captain. He says the ship is going to wreck, and we'll need all hands down on the beach."

"Our beach?" said Meera. "He thinks it'll come in here?"

"He's dragging the rowing boat down there right now," said Oliver. "So either he just fancied going for a jaunt in a storm, or he's planning to row out there himself and start fishing unfortunates out of the water."

"Damn," said Meera.

"Jar," said Oliver.

"How can you think of the jar at a time like this?"

"My sentiments daily, Meera."

Emily was instructed to stay behind and mind the girls, which meant telling Grace to come away from the window and sit down four times, until she gave up entirely and went to stand at Grace's shoulder. They watched as Joe and Oliver carried a second rowing boat excruciatingly slowly toward the cliffs, buffeted by sharp gusts of unpredictable wind. It looked as if it was threatening to rain, which was exactly the sort of complication you didn't need on the cusp of a shipwreck; it was only two o'clock, but looking at the dim sky, it almost seemed as if the sun had already set.

A little while later, a cart pulled up with another boat on the back, coming to an abrupt stop and almost throwing its occupants out onto the grass. Several men piled out and started shouting at one another, until they had negotiated who would be carrying the boat and who would be shouldering ropes instead.

Meera rushed out to meet them, and the men stood speaking urgently as she pointed toward the cliffs. They set off quickly in the right direction, looking like a little regiment of ants, determined and full of purpose. Meera followed them. Akia came out, too, laden with blankets and baskets, and went after them at speed.

Once she had disappeared, Emily was left with the feeling that they were going to somewhat miss out on the action up here, while everybody else was off playing the hero.

Aster had apparently decided the same thing—a moment later, she went striding out across the lawn, wearing a hat and one of her father's old coats.

"Ah," said Emily.

The day's lesson had somewhat broken down as they watched the ship draw nearer, and she had presumed Aster to be watching from another window.

"We might as well go, then," said Grace cheerfully. "You can hardly keep an eye on both of us if one of us is liable to get lost at sea."

"I will go and fetch her back," said Emily, "and you will stay here."

"You cannot leave me in the house alone," said Grace. "What if there are . . . brigands?"

"In the schoolroom?"

"Breaking down the back door," said Grace, grinning. "Impersonating Joe by grunting so I let them in. Taking me hostage for a vast ransom."

"Oh, *fine*," said Emily. "But you must wear at least two coats. Are you sure you're feeling—?"

"If you finish that sentence I will scream," Grace said serenely.

She seemed to lose some of that serenity as they walked toward the beach, heads bowed against the wind, needle-thin rain now stinging their cheeks and turning them a mottled pink.

"We can go back," Emily said. "Or . . . I could carry you?"

"I don't need to be carried," said Grace, blinking rain out of her lashes. "And I sincerely doubt your ability to do so. But if you could just . . . give me your arm."

It was probably very stupid to have agreed to take her, but the idea of the beach swarming with people had set quiet alarm bells ringing in the back of Emily's mind. The likelihood that they'd come across her little stash of buried goods was not high, but she would feel better seeing with her own eyes that nobody was straying too close to the rock, and that wind or tide had not betrayed her and uncovered her secret.

By the time they reached the shore, the shipwreck was in full swing.

It was actually very horrible. Emily was surprised by the enormity of it all: seeing something as vast and sturdy as a ship come up against the elements and lose violently; the shouts of terror from those in the water; the stony, strained determination on the faces of those bundling into the tiny rowing boats, bullishly intent on hope. Everybody was soaked through and grim, their clothes plastered to their bodies, the urgency palpable as they crossed to and fro. The storm clouds that were pressing down on them would have seemed apt if this were a painting, but in reality they just made everything seem all the more dire and hopeless.

Others must have come from the village or the nearby cottages with their boats, because there were at least ten or fifteen now. Emily could see some of them in the distance, closer to the wreck. The ship itself had come up so high on the rocks that the keel was fully out of the water, the whole thing listing to starboard as the hull threatened to break in half completely with a deep, yawning groan.

There were men still on it, clinging desperately to what they could, holding out hope for a boat. There were men who had already let go and were trying to swim away from the rocks, reaching desperately toward the shore. There were also men who did not seem to be moving, beyond the sway of the waves; Emily tried not to look too closely at them, turning back to the beach instead.

She watched hopelessly as a group of boys no older than Grace and Aster dragged their boat into the surf and then jumped in, two of them picking up the oars and immediately beginning to row out, not a flicker of hesitation on their faces.

"Where's Aster?" Emily asked Meera, when she found her in the fray.

Some very wet people were shivering in the sand, blankets draped over their shoulders, and Meera and Akia were handing out little parcels of bread and cheese.

"Eat it," Meera said to the nearest man, who was whey-faced and shaking. "For the shock." She turned to Emily, saw Grace at her side, and sighed. "Aster? I had no idea she was here. Grace, come here and help me, would you?"

She sat Grace down in the shelter of an overhanging rock and set her to organizing the food as Emily marched off across the beach, searching every face for a sign of Aster. It would have been a lot easier if every single one of these men and boys hadn't been wearing old, dull-colored coats and almost identical hats. As far as she could see, nobody was straying near her particular rock; now that she was here among the chaos, she felt silly for even thinking it. These people were far too busy with matters of life and death to notice if a few stolen goods popped up out of the sand.

When she finally did discover the elder Edwards sibling, it was too late: Aster caught her eye and then looked determinedly away again as the rowing boat she was sitting in with two strange men set out into the cresting waves.

"Thrice fucked and goddamn it," Emily gritted out, grateful that Meera was nowhere nearby to demand a shilling or three. She didn't realize until she felt the water splashing halfway up her skirts that she had been walking toward the boat, as if she stood a chance of grabbing it and dragging it back. Now she was damp *and* cold *and* liable to be shouted at again for letting one of her charges drift out to sea like a discarded ale bottle.

One of the boats making its way back to shore seemed to be overloaded. It was borne aloft by a particularly violent wave, and as it came crashing down the other side, somebody fell out of it. One moment they were clinging to the edge of the boat, the next they were overboard; Emily couldn't tell if they had gone silently or if the wind had swallowed their shout.

She turned around, looking for somebody to tell, but there was nobody close enough in any condition to help. By the time she turned back, she saw that a man in the boat had stood up and leaped into the unforgiving water.

Emily watched the gray, choppy surf, waiting for them to resurface; in the distance, lightning forked across the sky, eliciting shouts of dismay from those on the beach behind her. She couldn't remember where the two men had gone in, so she scanned the waves, until they blurred into a maelstrom of panic and spray and dark water.

It took so long that she had almost lost hope when she saw them break the surface, one after the other in quick succession, struggling to keep their heads above the water, and then grapple jerkily toward the shore. She only realized it was Captain Edwards she was looking at, towing the half-drowned man behind him, when he was close enough to shout for aid.

When they were able to stand, Captain Edwards got to his feet and then pulled the smaller man bodily from the water and walked toward Emily, seemingly powered by sheer force of will.

"*You!*" he shouted to her, forgetting either her name or perhaps that he had ever encountered her before at all. "We need help!"

Already wet, Emily met them knee-deep in the water and lent her shoulder for the waterlogged stranger to lean on. Propped up between the two of them, he made it up onto the shore. Captain Edwards eased him down onto the beach and turned him over onto his side just in time as he vomited feebly onto the sand.

The captain was drenched through, seawater still dripping from his chin and the dark, clinging whorls of his hair. He had removed everything but shirt and breeches and must have been freezing, but he didn't even seem to have noticed.

"Get him warm!" he shouted to Emily, over the sound of the ship in the distance beginning to break in half with a great, reverberating creak.

"Aster is out there," Emily said. "I saw her leaving. I . . . She's in one of the boats."

She watched him process this as just one more piece of urgent information among a whole flotilla.

"Get him warm," he said again, and then he was off to meet another boat, to help those inside to shore before climbing into it himself to relieve the man who had been rowing, and cast off back into hell again.

Emily delivered blankets to the vomiting man, and Akia came with food. Soon Emily found herself part of the rescue machine, slotting into place, moving automatically until her mind narrowed to a single purpose and her hands were numb with cold. She met the boats; she brought those who could walk to the relative shelter up the beach and blanketed them and fed them. Then it was back down into the sea to retrieve more sailors, who looked so glad to be on dry land that she wondered if they'd ever make it out on another sea voyage again.

One man, with wide eyes and a salt-and-pepper beard, would not stop clinging to her, even when Meera tried to prise his hands from her arm; it seemed as if he was worried that he might be swept away again without Emily there to anchor him.

Another seemed in surprisingly good spirits, telling jokes and talking in her ear with chattering teeth as they went.

"I have . . . n-never been fished out of the sea by a lady before," he said. "Are you p-perhaps a m-mermaid?"

"I am not a mermaid," Emily said firmly.

"But you have such l-lovely yellow hair."

"You should perhaps save your energy for getting warm, sir, rather than for flirting."

"I'd rather die flirting," he said, trying to wink. It sent him into spasms of shivers, which finally quieted him down.

Down in the surf, two of the rescuers—burly men from the village who had lost their hats—pulled the first body from the water. They wrapped him in a blanket and carried him down the beach, away from the survivors. The second came out just a few moments later.

Nobody felt much like joking after that.

"Joe is going back up to the house to fetch more supplies," Meera said, when Emily delivered a cabin boy to her, who looked barely twelve. "Go with him. And take this boy with you, will you?"

"Take them all," said Captain Edwards. He had come to fetch a blanket, although by the careful way he was carrying it, it didn't seem to be for him. "Take them all up to the house, if they can walk, and put them in every room with a fire going. Then light the rest. I'll send Aster when I've pulled her out of that boat."

Meera looked on the verge of questioning this, but it was only a brief ripple of uncertainty, and then it was gone.

"Up to the house," she said. "All right. Grace, you go with Amy and Joe. Stick to them like glue, all right?"

"They aren't brigands," Grace said. She was comparatively warm and dry, but was still starting to shiver under her many coats. "They're just sailors."

"Exactly," said Meera. "Like glue, all right?"

Chapter Eighteen

Emily wasn't sure how exactly they made it up the cliffs and to the house. She was primarily concerned with keeping Grace moving, although she had to stop a few times to encourage some poor trembling sailor who looked ready to give up and die where he fell.

The chaos didn't stop when she made it across the threshold.

She deposited Grace in the kitchen with Joe, who had immediately set about warming vast pans of broth, and then walked through each room, stoking the fires and pulling the curtains shut to try to preserve as much warmth as possible. Men huddled in sodden little piles around the hearths, leaving sand and puddles of seawater all over absolutely everything. They at least had the good sense not to sit on the furniture.

When they were all settled and there was nothing more Emily could practically do, she returned to Joe and Grace and found herself on another production line. She was so exhausted that she just accepted whatever she was given without comment, did as she was told, chopped vegetables, and portioned up soup, then helped Akia carry it upstairs to the men, who grabbed on as if they were still drowning and this soup was to be their savior.

Ten minutes after she had returned downstairs to the kitchen, Emily looked up from her work to discover that Captain Edwards was standing next to her. He had changed his clothes and was chopping carrots with mechanical precision, hair still wet, exhaustion that rivaled her own only showing around his eyes.

He was standing so close to her that his arm brushed hers whenever he reached for a new carrot. She hadn't even noticed.

"Joe wants them thinner than that," she said. "Quicker to cook."

Captain Edwards glanced up at her, his expression unreadable. When he spoke, his voice was monotonous and hoarse.

"Are you giving me orders in my own kitchen?"

"It's *Joe's* kitchen," said Emily. "Still not thin enough. Look at mine if you want to see how to do it."

Emily wasn't sure if Captain Edwards knocked her arm by accident, or if he had just intentionally given her a gentle nudge of reproach before he resumed chopping. She darted a look at him and found him looking as inscrutable as ever; he was at least cutting the carrots correctly this time.

They worked together side by side like that for at least an hour, and developed a rhythm that stopped them from bumping into each other; Captain Edwards noticed every time Emily ran out of vegetables to chop, and rolled some more toward her. It was almost companionable, if Emily put aside the fact that every time their arms brushed now she felt a strange, shivery jolt run up her from wrist to elbow.

She remembered him drunk at this same table, leaning toward her, soft and unguarded. It had been hard to reconcile that man with the one she had dealt with in the past, but today it made sense to her that he might reside somewhere in the middle.

"Is Aster all right?" Emily said suddenly, pausing with her knife hovering in the air.

"I had to drag her out of the water by the scruff of her neck, so she is not best pleased with me, but . . . yes. Otherwise, she is all right."

They didn't speak again except to deal with vegetable practicalities, but Emily was very aware of him the entire time; when he moved away to do something across the kitchen she felt his absence, and when he returned it was as if everything had been put in its correct place. She volunteered to transport soup once it was ready, and each time she returned from going upstairs, she saw Captain Edwards glance up at her before he returned to his work.

It was on Emily's fourth trip upstairs to deliver soup that Meera looked from Emily to Akia and then ordered them both to sit down and eat a bowl themselves.

There were sailors talking in clusters in the halls, sitting on the stairs, leaving damp spots on the walls if they could find a place to lean; some of them were quiet and subdued, others clearly furious, looking for somebody to blame for what had happened. There was actually a brief scuffle by the stairs, which was broken up immediately when every officer in the vicinity went rushing to quell it.

The smell of damp clothes and hair, seaweed, and the general fug of sailors was thick in the air. Those standing closest to the fires were steaming gently, which certainly did not help matters, although they looked as if they were being imbued with a second lease of life as they warmed their hands by the flames.

Emily wondered where they had put the injured. The dead. Were they still on that beach? Had they been painstakingly carried up the hill and laid out somewhere—in the garden, perhaps, among Mrs. Edwards's asters and roses? Now that the men were drying off a little, it was harder for some of them to hide the fact that they were crying.

Emily considered going upstairs to her room for a moment of quiet, but the number of wet bodies she'd have to push past to get there, followed by the insurmountable challenge of stairs when she was this tired, was too much. She sat down in the drawing room instead, choosing the quietest possible corner, and Akia sat down next to her.

"I have forgotten how to use a spoon," she said thinly.

"No you haven't," said Emily—but then, just in case, "It goes in your mouth. And the soup goes in the spoon."

"And *then* where does the soup go?" Akia said, but she was too tired to joke in earnest. She took a few mouthfuls and then set down her spoon and closed her eyes. "There's a man dying in the other drawing room."

Emily put her spoon down, too, and watched the exhausted sailors talk among themselves. They weren't trying to be quiet, even for her and Akia's sake. She could hear the two nearest locked in a fierce debate about how likely it was that they would still get paid their prize money. It seemed inappropriate in the extreme, but then, Emily supposed that this was how it all worked—still a job, even when your particularly bad day at sea was a literal wreck. You could not feed your family on platitudes and good wishes and watery soup.

Captain Edwards came up to join them, a bowl of soup in his own hand that he never touched. He used it more like a prop—an excuse to look down, to pick up the spoon, to never quite let it reach his mouth while he avoided eye contact with these officers whom Emily presumed must be his distant comrades. He was so-ciable, talking to almost everybody, without really saying much at all. He simply exchanged a few words and then let people talk *at* him while he did his very successful soup-miming routine.

She heard a few people remark on his black eye, expressing their concern, and each time he shrugged it off without bothering to ex-plain that he had not injured himself during the day's events, but rather during a drunken altercation, most likely in a public house.

Emily supposed she could not blame him for keeping them in the dark.

As Captain Edwards walked over to the fireplace, shifting his bowl so that he could shake another hand, a man sitting by the leg of the sofa turned to his companion and nodded his head in the captain's direction.

"That's Edwards," he said, his voice a quiet rasp. "The one I was telling you about."

Emily's ears pricked up. She set down her spoon and glanced at Akia to see if she was listening, but found she was half-asleep over her bowl.

"He's the one who—?"

"Shh," said the first man. "It's only guesses and rumors."

"You wouldn't think so, to look at him. Especially not after today."

"No," said the first man. "Those are the worst kind."

They were openly staring at him, and Emily saw the moment he noticed from over by the hearth. His head barely turned, but he put his shoulders back and stood a little stiffer, guard firmly up.

When Emily got up to resume her duties, she accidentally kicked the man by the sofa in the leg, and ignored the sound of his muffled oaths as she swept from the room.

Chapter Nineteen

"THERE'S ONE IN THE STABLES," OLIVER SAID TO MEERA, HIS voice high and agitated. "There's one in the *parlor*, sitting at the table and asking for tea."

"One of them asked if we could bring the gig around for him so that he could go to the pub," Emily added. "He would have walked, he said, but he thinks that his leg might be broken."

"You see?" said Oliver. "They're all horrible. They all treat me like they have a corner table at Brooks's and I'm their personal waiter. This is ridiculous. Either they go or I do."

"It's been one night," Meera said, sounding more tired with every syllable. Emily hadn't seen her sit down since the ship had hit those rocks, and very much doubted that she had been able to get any sleep. "They'll be gone by tomorrow."

"Not soon enough," said Oliver. "Here. Have a sixpence."

He handed one to Meera, who just looked at it, confused. "Why?"

"Because they can all go and *fuck* themselves," Oliver said, enunciating every word. "I'm off to see to the horses, and if you happen to find a man dead in there once I've finished, I'll thank you to just kick some hay over him and leave him for me to deal with at a later date."

"What will you do with the body?" said Joe.

"We're not running that low on supplies," said Meera. "No dead officers in the stew. I have to draw a line somewhere."

"A bold ruling," said Akia, "but a fair and just one."

The crew of HMS *Unicorn*—a name that had caused Oliver to choke on his own soup, and keep choking as a strapping officer with very large arms patted him forcefully on the back—had bedded down as best they could in the ground floor rooms overnight, and it had thrown the entire house into acute disarray. Captain Edwards had slept in Grace's room with both of his children, not due to lack of beds but as a precaution against around a hundred strange men in the house, and Meera had insisted that Akia and Emily share a room for the same reason.

"You can sleep closest to the door," Akia had said as she tied her headscarf, "so that when they come to ravish and kill us, you can be my human buffer while I climb out of the window."

Emily didn't really believe that anybody was going to burst through the door in the night, but she hadn't slept well regardless. The only reason she had been able to drift off at all had been that the sound of Akia's gentle breathing in the dark beside her had reminded her so much of Amy. She had awoken far too early and thought herself at home for a moment, before she opened her eyes and remembered.

It seemed that none of their guests had slept either. The house was a wreck of its own this morning, with sailors wandering aimlessly through the halls. Absolutely everything was *gritty*, and reeked of the sea and wet boots and various bodily odors.

"I hope they never leave," Grace said, as they sat in the schoolroom. The door was firmly closed, but it didn't matter; at least ten men were smoking at the front of the house at all times, blazing their way through all of the captain's rarely touched tobacco, so Grace always had people to spy on. "It's so exciting! Perhaps one of them will glance up and see me sitting at the window, and the light will catch me just right, and he will decide to marry me."

"Ugh," said Aster. "That's vile, Grace."

Aster had been in an unspecified amount of trouble for rushing away into the sea when she should have been carefully tucked up inside the house, but it seemed that Captain Edwards had been too busy to deal out punishment; he had also not yet reprimanded Emily for losing track of her in the first place, and she was starting to think that it might actually never come. Perhaps he had finally realized what everybody else in the house was already well apprised of—that no force on earth could keep Aster anywhere she did not want to be for very long.

"If any of them make the vaguest of advances in your direction," Emily said, "they'll be killed three times over by the time they reach you."

"Three?" said Aster, absentmindedly flicking a scrap of paper in Emily's direction.

"Your father, Joe, Akia. Oh, and Meera, too, if she wasn't buried under her task list."

"Five, then," said Aster. "I'm faster than Father. But there won't be any man left to re-murder when I'm through."

"I am fourteen years old," said Grace. "I am almost a woman, and I cannot put off thoughts of marriage for too much longer."

"Yes you can," said Aster and Emily, at the exact same time and with identical tones of finality.

Aster glanced sideways at her, looking mildly disgusted; Emily just blinked calmly back at her until she rolled her eyes and looked away.

"Just because I am sometimes ill," Grace said, going pink, "doesn't mean I am not a real person, or that I cannot have any romantic feelings, or—"

"No," said Aster. "It's not that. Sorry, Gracie. And I mean . . . of course you can do all those things. Just not yet. You're still a baby."

"You are only two years my senior, and nobody thinks you're a baby!" said Grace indignantly.

"Yes," said Aster. "But that's just because I'm horrible."

She flashed her sister a grin, and Emily tried not to smile to herself as she reached for a book.

There was something horrifyingly endearing about how determined Aster was to tell all the world that she was terrible, now that Emily had seen enough of her softer side to know that this was not entirely true. Terrible people did not dote on their sisters, try to keep them safe from harm, jump into boats, and head out into the volatile ocean to try to save the lives of men they had never met.

"Come on," said Emily. "No more talk of marriage, lest I vomit. Let's read some poetry."

She did not add that the poetry was just as likely to induce her to lose her breakfast.

They made their way line by line through a really rather horrible poem by Nash Nicholson; by the end of it Aster was asleep by the fire, and Grace seemed to have given up on romance completely.

"Akia is going to come and eat luncheon with you," Emily said on her way out of the door. "Do *not* leave this room."

From her chair by the fire, Aster gave a sleepy mock salute without opening her eyes.

Now that the sailors were not reeling from their brush with death, their behavior was deteriorating. Emily felt all eyes on her as she walked down the stairs; every single one of the men in the entrance hall looked up as she descended and then tracked her progress across the hallway, like bedraggled beagles eyeing a fox. Their conversations quieted, as if they needed all of their concentration to engage in uncomfortable staring, and only started up again once she had left the room.

She told herself that they were not talking about her, but very distinctly heard the word *governess* tossed about, before an outbreak of unkind laughter.

Just yesterday she had been working herself to the bone for their survival; today, she wished to toss them all back in the sea and wave merrily to them as they sank to the murky bottom.

In the kitchen, Joe handed Emily two bowls of dubious stew.

"One's for the boss," he said.

"Right," said Emily. "And where is . . . the boss?"

"He's in his study," said Akia. "Hiding."

Emily took the bowls up the stairs, her head held high and her elbows out so that she could jab them into the sides of any of the men who got in her way. They seemed to get the idea after their comrades suffered the first few bruising knocks to the ribs; she left them swearing quietly in her wake, and the rest of the men parted to let her through, taking the opportunity to ogle at her at close quarters.

Once she reached Captain Edwards's study, she realized she had no hands to knock, and tried instead to announce her arrival. There was no answer—but then, a crowd of sailors was standing in the entrance hall having a raucous conversation. She tried again, giving the door a shove with one of her much-abused elbows, and thought she heard a voice raised inside. Deciding it must have been an invitation to enter, she shoved open the door.

She realized her mistake very abruptly when she found herself face-to-face with Captain Edwards, who was standing beside his desk in dire need of a shirt.

"Oh," Emily said. "God."

The captain's shoulders really were very broad, even without the help of his uniform, and he was lightly muscled in a way that somehow looked accidental, as if he hadn't done it on purpose and was probably quite embarrassed to find himself looking this way. There was a scar on his inner bicep, a silvery-white curve of puckered flesh, like somebody had taken a slice out of him with a wickedly sharp blade.

Akia had been right about the shirtlessness. It changed things. Emily's gaze was somewhat stuck on the dusting of dark hair that trailed from pectorals to navel when Captain Edwards cleared his throat and turned away.

"Miss Laurence," he said. "If you could . . . just give me a moment, I . . ."

"Sorry," said Emily. "I was . . . Joe told me to . . . and I thought you had . . . shirt."

Captain Edwards did not respond. Emily turned away as he reached for the shirt that was sitting folded on his desk, and then waited in excruciating silence, the stew bowls hot in her hands.

"Some of the high-ranking officers asked if they could make use of my dressing room," he said.

Emily was momentarily confused, before she realized this explained his use of his study as a place to rid himself of clothes.

"Is that for me?"

She turned, and found him now wearing all appropriate garments, reaching out a hand toward her. She stared at said hand for at least two full seconds before realizing that he was gesturing for the bowl.

"Yes," she said, putting it down on the desk rather than handing it to him. "I'll just . . . I'll leave you to . . ."

She was backing away from him as if he were a slow tiger when he inclined his head toward the chair by the desk.

"Stay," he said. "Eat."

It wasn't really a request, but he said it gently enough that it didn't sound fully like a command, either. Emily supposed he was just too tired to put the required force into it, his resources depleted just like the rest of them. He had barely stopped moving during the rescue efforts, bodily carrying the people who could not stand, and he had been up late ensuring that everybody had a place to sleep. Emily had seen him delivering a newspaper to someone she presumed to be the *Unicorn*'s captain on her way to bed.

She pulled up the chair and sat down. He sat, too. There was another hideous silence. Emily didn't even want to put spoon to bowl, in case she made a loud sound and their predicament worsened. She waited until he started to eat, and then realized that her pronounced hesitation probably made it look as if she'd poisoned the food.

It was all very irritating. She shouldn't care—*didn't* care—if they had nothing to say to each other. Why would they?

"It's good," he lied. It wasn't *bad* stew, but it was mostly made of scraps at this point, stretched thin enough to feed an entire ship's crew with Mr. Khan's extra emergency deliveries that morning. They had probably cleared out months' worth of supplies from the larder. Captain Edwards didn't seem to mind. "Joe is either going to resign or burn the house down when they all finally leave."

"Why not both?" said Emily.

"Well . . ." said Captain Edwards. "Indeed."

They ate some more stew, Emily working up the required courage to probe. In her experience, fatigue loosened people's tongues. It did not feel quite right to exploit this moment of weakness—but then again, there was no point quibbling over the ethics of your *methods* when trying to conduct espionage for profit.

"Is it strange for you to have a house full of sailors?"

Captain Edwards didn't flinch. "No. After so much time spent at sea, why would it be?"

"Some of them don't seem particularly friendly," she said carefully. "I didn't eavesdrop on purpose, but I heard them being a little . . . unkind."

"Ah," said Captain Edwards. "Well . . . sailors. Things work quite differently aboard ships, even in the Royal Navy."

"But they were saying—"

"You worked hard yesterday," he said, cutting her off. "You seem particularly adept at looking after people. Not just children."

The idea that Emily was good at looking after children at all was absurd, but she let it slide, because she could hardly protest that she was not at all qualified for the job he was paying her to do. That she had tricked him into believing her to be kind and competent frankly lowered him in her estimations.

"I'm used to it," she said anyway. He looked up at her, a question in the lift of his eyebrows, and Emily shrugged. "My sister. She's . . . been unwell."

Captain Edwards nodded. "Is she expected to recover?"

This was so blunt and painful that Emily was left reeling. What a question to ask of a practical stranger over watery stew! How little tact did this man have, that he thought it an appropriate thing to say to her, when she herself didn't dare think about the answer in case it tempted fate? She hadn't even meant to tell him about Amy in the first place.

"I'd rather not discuss it," she said, and he nodded again.

They stewed.

"My wife was terrible at being unwell," he said after a few more mouthfuls. "In complete denial. Couldn't get out of bed, but was convinced we were still going ahead with a ball the next weekend, and that she'd be there. I suppose . . . in retrospect, perhaps it wasn't denial. Something more like . . . hope."

"And you didn't have any?" asked Emily.

Captain Edwards's mouth tightened. "No, I suppose I didn't. I am pragmatic. To a fault, she always said. I knew the odds. I had never supposed myself a likely beneficiary for a miracle."

"But Grace beat those odds," said Emily.

"Yes," said Captain Edwards. "A miracle after all."

They ate for a while longer, Emily looking out of the window at the scudding clouds. The storm had cleared, but the air still felt brisk and unsettled.

Captain Edwards put his spoon down so abruptly that Emily's gaze snapped back to him.

"Listen, Miss Laurence, I am aware that my children are sometimes . . . difficult—"

"Difficult," Emily repeated, bristling slightly at the word. She had been described that way since childhood, and had found it meant that she refused to bow and scrape, or to be agreeable to those who didn't deserve it. *Difficult* had been hurt, and wasn't stupid enough to let it happen again. *Difficult* had teeth, and knew how to use them. No matter that she would have used that exact word and *many* more to describe Aster quite recently; now she knew better, and the captain should, too. "They have been through more than any child should at that age. And . . . and Aster has probably tried to be something of a parent to Grace, in their mother's absence." Emily knew all too well how *that* went.

"Grace *has* a parent," said Captain Edwards. He seemed very taken aback by the turn this conversation had taken.

"Perhaps what you are willing to give is not enough."

Captain Edwards pushed away his bowl.

"I'm not entirely sure what you mean by that, Miss Laurence."

"I mean that a sibling who is also struggling and a . . . a household full of *paid staff* cannot substitute for a parent who smiles when their children enter a room."

"Now *that's* enough," Captain Edwards said sharply. "You don't know what you're talking about. You have been here a little over a month. I am here every day."

"You *are* here every day," said Emily. "*Right* here. In your study. Hiding from them."

"I do not hide. I have been trying, I have been—"

"It is not *enough*. Grace is desperate for you to be her friend, Aster is trying to set fire to her life because she's so unhappy, and you refuse to . . ."

Captain Edwards shifted, head up and shoulders back, and suddenly looked every inch a man of the Royal Navy.

"Miss Laurence, I don't recall inviting you to pass comment on my relationship with my children."

"No, but you did invite me into this house, to sit with Grace every day and see firsthand exactly how desperately she needs you. Aster, too, in her own way. They've already lost their mother, for God's sake. Don't you think you ought to take a stab at being their father?"

"Stop this," said Captain Edwards, his voice hard and his eyes blazing. "Just . . . *stop*."

Sometimes, when Emily was behaving badly, she imagined recounting the story to Amy exactly as it happened. Amy, being Amy, would never be able to hide her disappointment if Emily had badly misstepped, or her righteous indignation on behalf of her sister if Emily was, in fact, in the right. Often she knew that if she ever *did* tell Amy what she had said or done, she'd have to twist or omit some details to get her on side.

For example: speaking up on behalf of Captain Edwards's slightly neglected children? Amy-approved.

Shouting at a still-grieving man that he was a poor excuse for a father? Probably not.

Captain Edwards's hands were fists on the table. His eyes were still fixed on Emily. She expected him to be furious at her—to finally dismiss her on the spot—but instead he closed his eyes and let all the air leave him at once. He passed a hand over his brow and through his hair, and then leaned his elbow on the desk, his hand supporting his chin as he surveyed her. Emily couldn't imagine how she'd ever thought his eyes were boring. Yes, they were only brown, but there was so much contained within them. Right now they were intent, *searching*; he used them to such effect that she felt as if she had been pinned to her seat. She had never felt so thoroughly caught off guard by the way somebody *looked* at her before.

"Miranda was always the one who dealt with the children," he said heavily. "She was willful, and she was brilliant, and she had always wanted to be a mother. She knew how to love . . . openly, unashamedly. She was always the one who had . . . feelings."

"You have feelings," said Emily. It came out a lot more accusatory than she had intended.

Captain Edwards looked at her so oddly then that she didn't know what to make of it. It was almost as if he were too tired for artifice or ceremony. If his face was usually shuttered, right now it was wide open.

She didn't want him to be *open*. She hadn't even asked to be let in.

"I had never planned to do this without her," he said quietly. "I don't know how to navigate it. Everything . . . makes sense at sea. There's an order to life. Even when things go astray, I know what I'm doing—what's expected of me. Here . . . I am adrift."

Emily forgave him the sea metaphors. He looked so pained all of a sudden that she didn't think she should count them against him.

"Why don't you go back to your ship, then?"

"Ah," said Captain Edwards. "That's . . . difficult."

"Why?"

"Because part of me wishes to be there. But it's not necessarily a place where I will be welcomed with open arms."

"And that's because . . . ? Look, I heard what they were saying about you," Emily said, dangling the bait.

"A fair and objective judgment, I am sure," Captain Edwards said, closing off slightly, his voice clipped once again. "The truth is relatively simple. My primary crime was that I . . . interpreted an order as I saw fit. Disobeying a direct order is a case for the court martial, and a sentence of death is not unheard of, but in this case things were . . . murky. I did not wish to send my officers to a certain death on an already sinking ship, and so I held them back and engaged from afar."

This did not seem all that horrifying to Emily, although admittedly, she had never set foot on a ship, and was not up-to-date on the quirks of maritime law. Captain Edwards sighed thinly.

"The secondary crime, for which nobody has the slightest bit of proof, is that they think I engaged in a brief liaison with a fellow officer, around six months ago. He was one of the men I refused to send forth to die, you see, which . . . complicated matters."

Emily froze.

She had expected some dull misdemeanor like *disobeying orders*, because she had by now ruled out a financial crime due to Fairmont's evident lack of funds; she had never begun to imagine that it might be so personal in nature.

"And . . . did you? Have a . . . a liaison with him?"

"Yes," said Captain Edwards, watching her very carefully. "As it happens, I did. I would not have sent him to die regardless, but it did make the entire thing seem quite urgent. Incidentally, the sentence *is* death for engaging in such activities, but the commodore would not believe it of me and chose not to act based on rumor and gossip."

This was it. This was the information Emily had been looking for—the secret she could probably exchange for an entire bag of gold sovereigns. There had been no need to go looking for a key, or to snoop through the captain's private correspondence for clues. He had simply told her, without suspicion or duress. She could go from this room and pack her bag, march straight into the pub on Saturday afternoon to meet Charles, and then be back at home with Amy on Sunday.

The problem was that Emily really had been expecting some bland crime—some breaking of the rules of the Royal Navy that would be scandalous in certain circles, but barely interesting enough for her to follow the basic premise, like this issue with orders interpreted as he saw fit. It would have been terribly easy to give something like that over to Charles to do whatever he wished with it, without feeling even a modicum of guilt. What were the lives of rich fraudsters to her? Why should he not be punished for having everything and deciding to bend the rules anyway?

This was nothing of the sort. It was not even a crime, really, in Emily's eyes. She truly had never cared to pass judgment on anybody for the private desires of their hearts—it was, frankly, none of her business—and she could not do so now. Besides, even though she had long ago shut up that part of her heart, on the rare occasion that she *had* noticed somebody standing at the loom on the other side of the mill with their sleeves rolled up to their elbows, or passing her in the street in town with an air of confidence about them, their *gender* had seemed entirely irrelevant.

Captain Edwards was guilty of many things—being too rich, too careless, and too oblivious to the broken hearts of his own children—and *those* things he should have been ashamed of. Emily certainly would have been embarrassed, had it been her. But this? A fleeting romance with a fellow officer? In the grand scheme of things, it felt of very little consequence.

The captain certainly did not seem to think it shameful—but he had picked up his spoon again and returned to his stew, and Emily wondered if he were perhaps using it as an excuse to hide his face while he waited for her to speak.

"What was his name?"

Captain Edwards didn't look up, but he did relax minutely.

"Wakefield."

"And you called him by his last name?" said Emily. "Romantic."

Captain Edwards laughed quietly, and Emily's chest lightened.

"So . . . did they send you home?" she said.

"Yes . . . well . . . It was suggested that I should take a few months at home and remarry as a matter of urgency. I didn't mind as much as I ought to have. I suppose my disillusionment with the Royal Navy began the moment I set foot on deck for the first time. And . . . it was marginally better than being summarily executed."

"So, are you going to?"

"To what?"

"To remarry."

Captain Edwards lifted his shoulder very slightly, in the merest suggestion of a shrug, as if it was none of his business what happened to him next.

"I expect so."

"And then will you return to your ship?"

Captain Edwards rubbed the stubble at his jaw thoughtfully with his free hand.

"That remains to be seen."

"And this . . . this fellow officer . . . ?"

She had to wait for him to finish his mouthful before he spoke.

"Yes. We parted ways. I suppose I should count myself lucky that it would be possible for me to find happiness in the confines of marriage again. He is . . . not so fortunate."

Emily grimaced. "Will *he* marry?"

"He already has. He is not in the . . . financial position to weather being cast out of polite society. Even if they cannot find cause to execute us, they can certainly find other ways to do lasting damage." He straightened up in his seat, putting back his shoulders and schooling his expression. "I find the fuss ridiculous, but I am in favor of keeping my head and my house, especially after everything the children have been through."

Downstairs, there was a burst of raucous laughter, a sudden reminder that the house was full of the Royal Navy's finest. Or . . . probably *not* their finest, as they'd managed to ram their ship into a large, stationary rock. Emily was finished with her stew. Captain Edwards did not seem to be making any more headway with his. Emily was about to take his bowl and excuse herself, but curiosity won out.

"Why are you telling me all of this?" she said.

She had thought him a relatively intelligent man, but here he was, handing her everything she needed to destroy him.

Captain Edwards smiled at her. It was a small smile, sad and rusty from lack of practice. Like his laughter, it rendered him utterly transformed. Human. Handsome.

"Because you asked," he said. "And . . . because I haven't shared a meal with somebody like this for a very long time."

Chapter Twenty

Emily's beliefs and values were very important to her. There were things she clung to: that the French revolutionaries had the right idea about what to do with wealthy people, even if they had gone somewhat off the rails after the initial idea; that the impoverished and working class of England were treated abominably, and that all should strive toward more equal distribution of wealth so that the rich didn't sup on strawberries while the poor choked on coal fumes; that her sister's well-being was of greater importance than the life of anybody else in this country, due to the fact that she was goodness personified and had been dealt a monstrously unfair hand.

She did *not* have a particular code of conduct when it came to her own personal dealings with other people. She did not care if everyone thought her spiky, unpleasant, and rude. She did not harbor any aspiration to be *beloved*. In pursuit of her own ends, she was dogged and single-minded, hardly noticing if she stepped on a few feet along the way.

She knew all of these things about herself and had made peace with them a long time ago.

Her certainty about her own character meant that she very rarely experienced any kind of moral conundrum; the qualities of being both headstrong and never in *any* situation with the aim of making friends did not give rise to the need for much umming and ahhing about the path ahead.

Now, however, as Emily lay in bed—alone, now that the sail-

ors were departing, and Akia had returned to her own room—
she realized that she was stuck.

In the grand scheme of things, telling Charles about Captain
Edwards's admission would not tip the scales of the world in
any direction. He was still relatively wealthy. If his commanding
officers had already given him the benefit of the doubt, and he
did in fact remarry quickly, she was sure he would survive, even
if his good name did not. Grace and Aster could weather the indignity of being reduced to living with only *one* drawing room.

What Emily *did* take issue with was the fact that, in ratting him
out, she would be taking the side of the worst of the Royal Navy—
unfortunate in the extreme—and those who filled their days with
moralizing and hand-wringing about who people ought to *love,*
something so embarrassing and petty that Emily wanted no part in
it. His comrade, Wakefield, might also be at risk of greater harm than
Captain Edwards; she was not entirely sure what would become of
him, but she could not pretend that he would escape unscathed.

It would be worth anything to help Amy. That she was sure of.
But if she ever told Amy exactly what she had done to secure doctor's visits for a year, she knew with utmost certainty that Amy
would never speak to her again.

Amy cared very much whose toes she stepped on. She was the
sort to keep her eyes on the ground, just in case.

This, Emily was sure, was why she was finding the idea of
going to the Rose and Crown again so difficult. It had nothing to
do with the memory of Captain Edwards sitting across from her,
smiling in a way that made her feel . . . warm. Happy. Hopeful.

That was all, quite frankly, disgusting.

"Did I ever tell you about the time I accidentally bought a horse
instead of pork chops?" Akia said conversationally, as she pulled
back the curtains in the schoolroom to give the windows a quick

lick with a cloth. Through the glass, Emily could see some of the last of the shipwrecked sailors departing by wagon.

"No," said Emily, putting away books. "Probably best if you—"

"The horse was alive," said Akia. "But very old. I did think it was expensive for chops, though."

"At what point did you realize your mistake?"

"Before we put it in the marinade," said Akia. "No, I'm joking. I worked it out at the market, when I was expecting to be handed a parcel of chops and they gave me a halter with a horse attached to it instead."

Emily laughed. "Does anything normal ever happen to you?"

"Sadly, yes," said Akia. "*Too* much normality. I could do with more horse-chops days."

Grace came into the room and threw herself down into an armchair; it was so unlike her that both Emily and Akia stared at her, waiting to discover what had caused such dramatics.

"I am in love," she said.

"Not this again," said Emily.

"Again?" said Akia. "Good Lord. Have you been breaking hearts?"

"No," said Grace. "Simply having mine broken."

Emily sighed. "Grace, the sailors are mostly twice your age, and the ones who aren't probably haven't discovered what a girl *is* yet."

"Officer Calthorpe would never dare be so old," said Grace insistently. "And I am *sure* he knows what a girl is."

"You didn't talk to him, did you?" Emily said quickly.

It was just the sort of thing Grace might do: launch herself at an officer and ask him if he had a dog and if he'd like to marry her, not realizing how disastrous the consequences might be.

"No," said Grace. "But I opened my window and listened to him talking to his friend. He said that Father is very handsome, and wondered if he did not get lonely in this house—which is silly, of course, because if Father wanted company he could come to me and Aster, and you two, and Oliver, Meera—"

"Yes, yes," Emily said. "Remind me to explain the use of *et cetera* today."

"Do you not think that the house developed a certain . . . miasma," Akia said to Grace, "while they were here? Are you not looking forward to air less foul?"

"Maybe," Grace said diplomatically. "But I will miss their ridiculous arguments, and the way they liked to shove each other, and all of the excellent swearing."

Aster, it seemed, had also fallen in love, but in a very different way. She came storming in and sat down in the other armchair, cross-armed and frowny.

"I wish to be a sailor," she announced. "I think my true calling is the sea."

"Aster," said Emily. "You just saw how dangerous it can be at sea. Did you really look upon that shipwreck and think, 'Oh, how splendid, I must get myself aboard one of those at once'?"

"Yes, actually," said Aster, scuffing the rug with her shoe. "Don't be a bore, Amy. Let's have something maritime today."

"*The Rime of the Ancient Mariner* it is," said Emily.

"Christ," said Akia. "And that is very much my cue to leave."

Putting the house back together took days, and Emily was pulled in to help without anybody questioning if it was right for her to do so; they had long moved past such things, and Emily slightly missed the days when Meera would hesitate before asking her to muck in with some menial task.

She was helping Akia in the drawing room over luncheon when Meera burst into the room with such violence that Akia dropped her cloth.

"I need to borrow one of you," she said, with the wide eyes

and ragged breathing of somebody on the verge of a domestic-chores-related breakdown. "Now."

"And *I* have to finish scrubbing the Royal Navy from the rooms," Akia said, with an apologetic shrug. "They're filthy. Unless we've decided we don't care about rooms anymore. I wouldn't mind, but they are quite a key component of the house."

"No, no, you carry on . . . Amy? The captain did say you might be best suited."

"Well, I'm expecting the children." Emily was quite looking forward to an afternoon of doing next to nothing while Grace read her book and Aster painted abstract depictions of Emily's own death, and was wary of being dragged into real work.

"Can they get by on their own for a few hours?"

"I suppose so."

"Excellent! Wonderful! Can you meet Captain Edwards downstairs? He's bringing the gig out himself."

"Oh," said Emily. "Why? Where are we . . . Why can't you go? Or Oliver?"

"Oliver is at the horse doctor, I have to stay here to accept deliveries, and Joe is up to his eyes in soufflés and apparently must stand and watch them the entire time they cook or the world will end. And besides, Captain Edwards needs a woman."

"I'll say," Akia muttered.

"*Akia—*"

"Is Oliver at the horse doctor because they couldn't find a muzzle big enough to fit him at the regular doctor?"

"He is at the horse doctor with a horse," said Meera. "As you well know."

"It seems more likely to me that he refused to be examined by a physician without his head stuck in a big bag of food to distract him," said Akia. "But if you say so."

"Amy," Meera said imploringly. "Downstairs."

"Fine," said Emily. "I'll fetch my cloak."

She had not imagined that she would be forced into close proximity with Captain Edwards so soon after their revelatory conversation about his misdemeanors in the Royal Navy, and even though she knew he would be waiting for her, it was still somewhat disconcerting to walk out of the door and find him standing there, offering a hand to help her climb up into the small carriage.

He didn't say good afternoon, so Emily didn't say good afternoon, and it led to an interesting silence as he urged the horse on—a silence that did not seem to be affecting him at all. They had been traveling for at least five minutes when he finally spoke.

"I feel the urgency of this afternoon's expedition has been overstated."

Emily thought of Meera's wild-eyed panic.

"Oh?"

"Grace has been requesting a new dress for some time," he said, sounding as if this concept was entirely foreign to him, "and as I am planning to host some people at the house soon, I thought it best to appease her. Apparently this requires the . . . acquisition of fabric."

"Yes," said Emily. "They do tend to be made of fabric."

Captain Edwards glanced sharply at her. He seemed to be trying to ascertain whether she was making fun of him—which she was, a little. An urgent trip to buy fabric for a dress was not what she had expected based on Meera's failing death grip on her own sanity—but then, Meera was a perfectionist to a fault, and was likely kicking herself for not having predicted through sorcery that Grace would soon require a new dress for a party.

"When we arrive, if you could perhaps cease making me an object of mockery for a few moments, I would appreciate your help selecting something appropriate."

"What about Aster?" asked Emily, thinking of the jealous little spats she'd had with Amy when they were children over things exactly like this. "Does she want a new dress? It only seems fair."

"Hmmm," said Captain Edwards. "No. I rather think not."

"All right. Well, what did Grace ask for?" said Emily, trying to picture any of the dresses Grace had worn. They all blurred into a big cloud of pastel silk.

"I intended it to be . . . a surprise." This, too, sounded strange coming out of his mouth. He did not seem like somebody who had ever intentionally engineered a surprise that hadn't ended in a hundred dead and a ship at the bottom of the ocean.

"Well, it certainly will be that," said Emily.

She was exactly the wrong person to bring on an expedition to the haberdashery. She had once cared very much for dresses, but had quickly abandoned her interest when it became clear that new ones were not to be on the horizon, and had decided to look down on the whole thing as silliness and frippery.

"The mockery, Miss Laurence. Just a little less of it, if you please."

She was hardly mocking him at all, but she shut her mouth and they traveled the rest of the way in peaceful quiet. She ducked her head slightly when they eventually passed the Rose and Crown, as if Captain Edwards might know just from seeing the two of them together that she had been up to no good there, and only straightened up when they were pulling into the village proper.

It was rather busy for a Friday morning of no consequence; Emily spotted a handful of sailors standing by the door to the inn, and wondered if this was one of the places the shipwrecked men had scattered to.

Captain Edwards noticed, too. He pulled the horse to a stop as far away from the inn as possible and helped Emily out of the carriage with perfect cordiality. Then he walked with purpose toward Bimpton's, which had such a silly name that Emily had to restrain herself from laughing when she saw it painstakingly painted on the sign.

Inside, there were a few women perusing the ribbons; they

looked up at Captain Edwards and immediately set to whispering to one another, darting glances and small smiles at him as they did.

He looked rather as if he was dying inside, and immediately walked up to the velvet and stared very hard at it.

"It's September," said Emily, when she caught up with him.

"Yes?" said Captain Edwards.

"You usually do not wear a velvet dress in September unless you wish to suffocate luxuriously."

"Oh," said Captain Edwards, sounding a little flustered. "Right. Fine. What do you wear in September?"

"I'm sure there's somebody who works here who can help us," Emily said, peering into a back room through the half-open door. "I can ring the bell—"

"No." Captain Edwards had stopped her from ringing said bell by gently touching her arm, and when he realized what he'd done he frowned down at his own fingers and immediately released her. "No. You can help me."

"All right," said Emily, leading him toward the many varieties of cotton and muslin. "But I am far from an expert, so it is very much your funeral."

"If only it were," muttered Captain Edwards. "Nobody would take issue with velvet."

Emily bit back a laugh and then gestured to the rolls of cloth. "Here."

"What do you mean, *here*," he said tersely. "This is . . . twenty types of fabric. I need it narrowed down a little beyond *here*."

"Well, she likes pink and blue," said Emily. "So perhaps start there."

"I think I might be color-blind," said Captain Edwards.

He sounded so genuinely miserable that Emily rolled her eyes and started making some choices for him; he relaxed somewhat, and stood silently at her shoulder while she deliberated.

She had been so glad, as a child, that more color seemed to be coming into fashion; she remembered coveting gowns of rosy peach and Pomona green before she learned that the whims of fashion were now very much out of her family's reach. Now she briefly fingered a pale gold satin before landing on something soft and lustrous and blue.

"This?" Captain Edwards said.

He tentatively reached for the fabric as well, and for a second they were both holding it, their hands almost brushing.

"Maybe," said Emily.

"What do *you* like?"

"I don't know," Emily said, immediately removing her hand and taking a step back. She hadn't thought about what she *liked* in years—just what she needed, or, more accurately, what *Amy* needed.

"Well, if you were picking out a dress," Captain Edwards said impatiently, "would this be the one?"

"I just told you, I don't know!" Emily said, too loudly and too curtly. Captain Edwards blinked at her, and she lowered her voice. Behind her, she heard a little noise of exclamation from one of the ribbon ladies. "You must understand very little about the lives of working people, Captain Edwards, if you think we are constantly in need of the latest woven silks and painted satin."

"Of course," Captain Edwards said, sounding as if he regretted the day he had learned to talk. "Then I think . . . this will do. Are we supposed to procure . . . ribbon? Grace usually seems to have two or five about her person."

"Yes," said Emily.

She could see the shop assistant approaching, gazing hungrily at Captain Edwards, although whether this was due to his looks or the likelihood that he was about to spend a lot of money, she could not tell and, at this moment, did not care.

"I think this lady will help you. Excuse me."

Out in the square, she could breathe a little easier. She watched two little blond girls walking together hand in hand, wearing matching dresses, the fabric plain but the love in the stitching evident even from afar. Somebody had carefully curled their hair and tied it with ribbons.

She didn't begrudge them, but she did feel a dull, creeping ache in her chest. From behind, the girls could have been her and Amy.

Had she ever felt cherished? Beautiful? She couldn't remember. She had felt useful, instead, which had taken the place of everything else.

The ringing of the shop bell brought her back to reality, and she looked up to find that Captain Edwards was standing there, holding a large box, looking slightly dazed.

"If she had at least pulled a knife on me," he said, "I could have been robbed without the loss of my dignity."

"You should have worn a worse coat," said Emily. "Although I imagine everybody knows you on sight, anyway."

"I shouldn't think so," said Captain Edwards. "I rarely come to the village."

"Trust me," Emily said. "They know."

Back in the gig, Captain Edwards seemed to recover some of his composure. He certainly relaxed once they reached the edge of the village, with nothing but rolling coast ahead of them until Fairmont.

"Why did you not just send someone for the fabric another time?" Emily said, watching gulls wheel overhead, buffeted by the wind.

He considered for a while before he answered. "I wanted her to know that I picked it out myself."

He hadn't *actually* picked it out himself, but she supposed that he had done the next best thing, and that it was probably the thought that counted. Better that he come home bearing a box full of something lovely he'd been directed toward, than that he came home with mountains of lime-green taffeta he'd grabbed out of panic.

It was also obvious *why* he wanted Grace to know he had picked it out himself, and after all the shouting she'd done at him about his lack of connection with his children, Emily felt a strange stab of pride. She couldn't tell whether it was her own pride for standing up to him, or—heaven forbid—if she actually felt a little proud of *him* for listening.

Not that Grace's affection should or could be bought—but Emily already knew she'd be thrilled that he had tried. And it wasn't much. But it was a start.

"Go on, say it," he said dryly. "I didn't really pick it out myself. It doesn't count."

"I think it counts," said Emily.

When he smiled tentatively at her, the ache in her chest returned so suddenly that she bit down on the inside of her cheek rather than smile back.

It was surprisingly easy to talk to him all the way home.

Chapter Twenty-one

IN THE KITCHEN OVER BREAKFAST THE NEXT MORNING, AKIA had to nudge Emily from her thoughts with the poke of a spoon.

"Amy? Are you listening? I said your name three times."

"What?"

"I said there's going to be a *ball*. As if we haven't got enough to do, cleaning sand out of every crevice of this house."

"Not just of the house," Oliver said darkly.

"Please do not discuss your crevices at the breakfast table," said Meera.

"At least they let us join in for the last few dances," said Akia.

"Well. *They* don't. The captain does. Everybody else looks horrified every time."

"I seem to recall that last time, you almost danced away with a proposal of marriage from a very handsome gentleman who would not stop talking about pineapples," said Oliver. "He didn't look *horrified*."

Akia looked a little coy. "*That* is my private business."

"*Aha*," said Oliver. "So you *have* seen him again."

"I could not possibly comment," said Akia, but she was smiling into her tea. "All I will say on the matter is that I cannot be wooed with just one or two pineapples."

"I can," said Oliver. "Next time, send him my way."

"Amy," said Meera. "I know it's your day off, but when you're back this evening . . . I'm sorry to ask, but they really did get sand and seawater all over everything."

Emily almost wanted to tell her that she would stay and help all day, just to remove the option of the Rose and Crown from her mind altogether, but she could not. She was exceedingly anxious about her meeting with Charles; she had still not been able to decide what she should and should not say, and could not imagine that the decision would become easier in the moment, knowing that he might have enough money in his pocket to change her and Amy's lives.

She went to her bedroom and readied herself, pulling on the cloak that was too warm for September but too new to replace, fixing the pins in her disappointing hair and then pulling them out again.

On her way back downstairs, she heard an odd, muffled gasp coming from Aster's bedroom. Reluctant to interfere where she knew she wasn't wanted, she hovered, thinking that if there was nothing more, she could carry on her way and pretend she hadn't heard anything at all.

Instead, she heard the sound of something hitting the floor, and Aster's extensive swearing in response.

She would just go in to make sure Aster wasn't doing anything unforgivably stupid, be condescended to or shouted at (or both) for a minute or so, and then she would leave.

"Good God," Emily said, when she had opened the door. "Aster, put those down at *once*."

Aster lowered the sewing scissors a fraction, but in every meaningful way, it was already too late.

She had taken them to her hair and cut off an enormous chunk of it, leaving her with a stubby crop by her temple and a foot and a half of it on the floor beneath her stool.

"I did it," she said, sounding both horrified and in awe of herself.

As Emily watched, tears escaped from under her lashes and slid down her cheeks. She lifted the scissors again, and Emily took a step forward with her hand raised, as if Aster were brandishing a gun.

"Aster! If you stop now you might be able to hide it."

"I don't want to hide it," said Aster.

She cut again, and more long brown hair fluttered to the floor. This seemed to inspire her, and she started hacking indiscriminately, not seeming to mind what length she lost and what she left behind.

There was nothing Emily could do but watch.

Some of the urgency seemed to leave Aster, and she turned to look in the mirror that she had propped up on the dressing table behind her. Her face was an odd war of emotions: she looked defiant and terrified, amazed and utterly spooked.

"Oh," she said. "It looks . . . It's not quite what I . . ."

To Emily's horror, Aster started crying properly, her shoulders shaking as she looked down at the scissors and then back up at her reflection.

"What did you . . . *want* it to look like?" said Emily.

Aster put down the scissors, dropped her head into her hands, and didn't answer.

Emily approached very carefully. She had no idea what to do with Aster in this sort of mood. She had no idea Aster was *capable* of such a mood.

"Go away," Aster said, when Emily was at her shoulder, which was more familiar territory.

"Give me the scissors and I'll try to fix it," Emily said. "You look ridiculous."

Aster squinted up at her, red-eyed and waterlogged, and then wordlessly handed her the scissors.

"I wanted it . . . short," she said. "But not too short. Like Father's."

"Not too short," Emily repeated incredulously. "Just like a *man's* hair."

"Yes," Aster said, catching Emily's eye in the mirror. "Exactly like a man's hair."

Emily sighed, and picked up one of the badly shorn locks.

"Fine. But you are not to complain. I am not an expert."

"In this or anything else," said Aster, with enough of her usual fire that Emily didn't feel too guilty about roughly shoving her head into place so that she could start cutting.

She had cut her own hair before, and Amy's, but this was different. It felt like there was a lot riding on it. She didn't know *what* exactly, but she knew that it was important. Aster closed her eyes and stayed absolutely, rigidly still the entire time she was cutting, and when Emily rapped her on the shoulder to indicate that she was finished, she stayed as she was, as if she were too frightened to look.

When she finally did, it was like watching a fire catch when you were freezing, or the very first peek of a blazing dawn. Aster lit up entirely. She reached up to touch her hair and then stayed like that, running her fingers through it, marveling at how quickly she ran out of length.

Emily wasn't sure how even it was, but Aster *did* look more like her father than ever, so she supposed that was something.

"You are a terrible hairdresser," said Aster.

Emily rolled her eyes and let the scissors drop onto the dressing table, making to leave.

Aster stopped her with a hand on her wrist.

"But . . . thank you."

Emily gritted her teeth and didn't yank herself away. She just nodded.

"I'm sure some people will still think you look . . . beautiful," she offered.

Aster shook her head, turning back to look at herself in the mirror again.

"Well. Dashing, at least."

That seemed more like it. Aster almost *grinned*. She was still holding on to Emily's wrist, as if it were a lifeline.

"I need to go and talk to Father," she said, perfectly balanced between nerves and steel. "Will you . . . ? Can you come with me?"

Emily's stomach lurched uncomfortably. Aster's grip on her arm suddenly felt too much.

"I don't know," she said. "I have to go to . . . I'm expected somewhere. It's my day off."

Aster let go of her. Her face shuttered. Her shoulders bunched.

"Fine," she said. "That's fine. You can go."

"Aster."

"Just go, please. I don't . . . I don't actually recall *inviting* you into my room."

It was half-hearted, but Emily didn't bother arguing. She left, and went downstairs to the back entrance, feeling sick with indecision.

She wasn't going to go. Or . . . perhaps she would, but she wouldn't give everything away. No. This was foolish. She wouldn't go at all.

But what did Captain Edwards owe her, really? A few weeks at Fairmont House and it was as if she was forgetting why she was here . . . who she *was*. Nobody else would make that mistake, and she would do well to remember that.

She arrived at the pub at a little after two o'clock, and found Charles exactly where she'd left him after their last meeting. She could almost have believed that he'd never left the place; that he was tied to it like a ghost with a narrow haunting jurisdiction.

"Good afternoon, Emily," he said. "You've got a bit of hair stuck to your chin. Not yours, I'd wager, unless you are growing a beard."

Emily removed the hair and sat down.

It took her approximately three seconds to realize that he had called her *Emily*, and it hit her like a blow; her face flushed hot, her mind was wiped shockingly blank, her limbs were momentarily unavailable.

Charles's face was almost entirely neutral, but she could see how pleased he was with himself by the glint in his eye and the way his finger was tapping against the table in anticipation.

Emily could not begin to fathom how he had found out her true name, and her mind raced ahead to what *else* he might know—where her family lived, her late father's name, *Amy's* name—as he watched her very carefully.

"Good afternoon," she said eventually.

If Charles was disappointed that she had not risen to the bait, he worked hard not to let it show.

"There is no need to look quite so startled," he said, his voice dropping into a register that was low and friendly. "Your secret's safe with me."

Emily nodded, trying to relax her shoulders, but something had shifted: he had thought to investigate her background, to seek more about her when she only had his first name and the fact that he seemed overly fond of this pub. He had somehow found out what nobody at Fairmont had, and it was the sort of information that had the potential to be incendiary.

Charles looked at her expectantly.

"Usually," he said, "it is you who insist that we get down to business at once. If you have mellowed, I am very happy for you, but it just so happens I am in somewhat of a rush today. Do you have something for me, or are you just here for the pleasure of my company? Here, I'll get you a drink."

He called for the barmaid in that way of his—a flick of his fingers—but today Emily did not find it at all charming; it was imperious, in a way that grated on her nerves. A tankard appeared, but Emily did not touch it. He seemed to be enjoying himself. Emily decidedly was not.

"Go on, then," he prompted.

"There was a shipwreck," Emily said. "HMS *Unicorn*. The sailors ended up staying at the house."

"Ah," said Charles. "I heard about that, but I wasn't entirely sure where they'd ended up. I don't suppose the captain was very happy about that."

"He invited them," said Emily.

"Well, he loves to make his life harder," said Charles. "Heard something interesting during their stay, did you?"

He might have just been fishing, but perhaps he could see it on Emily's face—everything she had that she wasn't telling him. It all felt so complicated now. Gone was her certainty—her purpose. When she had first buried those things at the beach she had thought to fetch them before she met him again, but in all the mess of the captain and Aster, she had forgotten.

"Did you sell the box?" she asked, stalling for time. "The one I gave you. The parts."

"Not yet," said Charles. "But I have an interested buyer I intend to meet with soon. I'm sure I'll have something for you next time, but in return . . . I really think you might have something for me."

"You still have it?" Emily said. "I would have thought—"

"Look," said Charles, his smooth demeanor faltering. "Do you have anything for me or not?"

"You were supposed to sell the parts," Emily said bullishly.

"I am not a *fence*," Charles snapped back. "I am doing you a favor. I asked you to retrieve information for me, you made it clear that you were *more* than willing, and now you are sitting there looking ten shades of suspicious and offering me nothing."

Emily continued to offer him nothing.

She could not believe that she had ever taken any kind of pleasure in this man's company. Before, she had seen it as a partnership of sorts—had felt that she and Charles were cut from the same cloth. Now she realized that he saw her as nothing more than a tool, something blunt to use to get at what he wanted.

Could she really lay bare all of Captain Edwards's most closely guarded secrets to be used by this man in any way he saw fit?

"Well," he said, drumming his fingers on the table and then leaning back in his seat. "As it so happens, I caught up with an old navy friend of my own last week. He told me *exactly* what he thinks went on. By the looks of you, I think you might know, too, Emily—there is no point playing coy, or nursing your offended sensibilities. Now that we are on the same page, all we need is a little proof."

Proof.

There might be none at all. Or there might be a stack of personal correspondence in that drawer of Captain Edwards's—she'd know exactly what to look for, now. *Wakefield.*

"To what end?" said Emily, trying to keep her voice calm and even. "Do you wish to see him hanged? Or do you plan to blackmail him?"

"That is none of your concern, really," said Charles breezily. "You know the man, now. You know the house. Do you think you can bring me proof or not?"

She probably could—but in that moment, she knew with certainty that she would not.

"Look," said Charles. "I am still very willing to help you, Emily. But I cannot do it for no return. And now that we know each other better, I'm sure there are things about *you* that you would prefer kept quiet."

Emily straightened up a little in her seat. It was not quite a threat, but the intent was there—the promise of something more, if she did not behave. He did *not* know her well, but he certainly knew something that nobody else did: that she was a liar, and a thief.

"He must have a study, some place where he writes his letters—why don't you start there?"

Emily could have laughed aloud. She had been granted a reprieve, for now, simply because he did not believe her intelligent enough to know what she was looking for. A *study*. How clever! It never could have occurred to her—a *study*. After all his flattery, Charles thought her no more than a desperate fool, incapable of connecting the boldest of dots.

She supposed she *had* been a desperate fool, just not in precisely the ways he imagined. She had backed herself into this corner. If Amy could have seen her now, she would have been rightly horrified; one day she would have to tell her sister what she had done here, and the thought of it flooded her with shame.

All she could do now was try to buy herself a little time.

It took every ounce of her willpower to nod, seriously, as if the suggestion of a study was actually a very useful one.

"All right," she said. "A study. I'll look."

"There's a good girl," said Charles. "I'll see about selling that box of yours—and I'll meet you here in a fortnight."

He got to his feet and gave her a quick pat on the shoulder.

Emily thought, with burning passion, about breaking every one of his fingers.

He smiled at her on his way out, and winked.

"I think this is all going to work out *marvelously*."

Chapter Twenty-two

THE HOUSE FELT STRANGELY QUIET WHEN EMILY RETURNED. As soon as she crossed the threshold, her thoughts flew to Aster.

She half ran up the stairs, ignoring Akia's questioning look from down the hallway, where she was exiting a room with an armful of bed linen, and only stopped when she saw that the door to Captain Edwards's study was slightly ajar.

She couldn't hear anything coming from inside. When she moved closer, the room shifted into view.

Aster was there, standing by the desk. Captain Edwards was there, too, his coat on the floor, as if it had fallen from the back of his chair.

They were embracing, Aster's head buried in her father's shoulder. It looked as if they had possibly been that way for quite some time. Neither of them looked up, and Emily stepped quickly away, trying to quiet her labored breathing.

A little way down the corridor, she found Grace sitting on the floor, cross-legged. It was not at *all* ladylike. For once, she looked something close to her age.

"What are you doing down there?" Emily asked her quietly.

Grace looked up and shrugged, her face softly puzzled.

"Apparently I have a brother," she said.

"A brother?" said Emily.

"Aster," Grace clarified.

Aster.

Emily thought of Aster's face in the mirror, freed from all that hair. Aster in the boat among all those men and boys, shoulders raised and chin lifted, draped in Captain Edwards's coat. It fitted at once, in a way the coat hadn't yet. Aster. Aster, Grace's brother. Aster, Captain Edwards's son.

Back at the mill, Emily had worked alongside Alexander, a quick wit with a knack for untangling the looms. Occasionally they had exchanged friendly words—and then one day, Alexander had vanished. She had been Alexandra when she returned six months later, her grown-out hair tucked under a bonnet just like Emily's, her pay cut in half. She and Emily had picked up exactly where they had left off, working side by side on the factory floor.

It had been jarring for a moment. Unexpected. But unexpected did not mean wrong, and it was easy to adapt. Just like a great many things, it was none of her business.

Emily sat down next to Grace on the floor and rested her head against the wall.

Everybody in this house seemed absolutely determined to surprise her.

"And how do you feel about that?"

"I'm not sure," said Grace. "Who's he going to marry? And, actually, does that mean . . . is he really going to be a sailor?"

Emily laughed, more out of shock than anything.

"I wouldn't worry about any of that, Grace."

"All right," said Grace. "Goodness. A brother. A brother for Grace. I think I like it."

"Come on," said Emily. "Let's go to the schoolroom, shall we? And then Aster can join us when he's ready."

"If you think he's coming to lessons today when he has a most excellent excuse to abstain," Grace said, as Emily helped her to her feet, "then you are the world's greatest optimist, and likely deserve a medal."

Everybody knew by dinnertime.

Emily was a little on edge, waiting to see if there might be odd looks or off-color remarks once they'd started drinking their wine, but she had underestimated these people; once Meera had broached the subject, there was nothing but gentle good cheer.

"Can't say I understand it," said Joe, "but if Aster's happy . . ."

"Do you know how hard it has been to say *nothing*?" Oliver said. "To give *nothing* away? I am the world's worst secret-keeper, but he kept stealing my damned clothes, so of course when I asked him about it he just *told* me everything, and I had to walk around feeling like my head was going to explode—"

"Aster told *you*?" said Meera. "But why?"

"Well, you know," said Oliver. "Not quite birds of a feather, but . . . birds who drink from the same fountain, you know?"

Emily did not, in fact, know—but this gave her plenty of reason to suspect.

"Poor boy," said Akia. "With only you to confide in. Did you give him one of your famous speeches about confidence that always make me long for death by the end?"

"No," said Oliver. "Well . . . sort of. Not one big speech. A few little speechettes, along the way."

Emily put down her wineglass.

"Hold on. That night when I saw you two together, after the dinner party—"

"And you accused me of being a vile scoundrel? Oh, yes, that was very delightful of you. He kept trying to run away, but not getting very far. I've had to fetch him back three bloody times."

They all laughed at his outrage, and Akia patted him on the

knee. It was a sign of the spirit of the evening that Meera didn't even make him put a sixpence in the jar.

"You did well, Oliver," she said. "Thank you."

"Hear hear," said Joe, with a little tilt of his glass.

"I suppose he won't come to the ball next week," said Meera, going from laughter to logistics in an instant. "I shall have to ask."

"Is it optional?" said Emily.

"Not for *you*," said Akia. "I am going to do your hair."

Emily started protesting, but there was a loud and immediate consensus that she *had* to attend the ball. She was a little taken aback by their insistence. Nobody but Amy had ever been so enthusiastic about an evening spent in her company.

"Fine, fine," said Emily. "But I shall complain the whole time."

"No you won't," said Meera. "You'll sulk and stew on it inside your head, and be almost civil on the rare occasions you speak, as always."

Emily felt slightly startled. She didn't like being nailed down like this—or the idea that Meera had noticed how often there was a storm brewing below Emily's surface, only kept from breaking over everybody else's heads because she mostly turned it inward and let lightning strike where nobody else could see.

"But I don't have anything to wear," Emily said, and Meera smiled.

"I'll see what I can do."

What she could do, apparently, was let slip to the children that Emily didn't have a smart enough dress for a ball, because apparently it reached Grace, who told Aster. When Emily got to the schoolroom the next day after church, thinking of doing some reading, she had barely sat down before Aster strode in with an enormous armful of fabric and dumped it unceremoniously onto the desk in front of her.

"Here," he said. "Go wild."

"What is this?" said Emily, urgently moving an inkwell away from an eruption of crushed pink satin.

"All the formal dresses I have never worn," said Aster. "Take your pick. I wouldn't recommend the green—you'd look quite dead in it."

"Aster," Emily said, her instinct to immediately refuse. "I can't—"

"Yes you can," said Aster.

He was wearing clothes that clearly hadn't yet been tailored for him—soft brown breeches, a crisp shirt, a creamy gold and carmine-red waistcoat unfastened and hanging loose—but he looked more comfortable in his own skin than Emily had ever seen before. There was still a wariness to him—a sense that any moment he might throw up his guard or duck for cover—but it didn't seem to be weighing so heavily now. He was certainly being marginally more pleasant.

"Look . . ." he began. "I know I've been a prick, and I still think *you're* a bit of a prick, and I'm not . . . *good* at talking about things. But I suppose I am sorry. And grateful. For the haircut."

"For the haircut," Emily said. "Right. It looks . . . good, by the way."

"It looks fine," said Aster. "Don't get carried away, you're not that skilled a barber. Anyway . . . truce?"

He held out a hand to shake, looking solemn, and Emily took it and gave it a single solid pump, trying not to look amused by the entire endeavor. It was clear that Aster was trying to do things *properly*.

"Anyway," said Aster. "Have a look. See which you'd like."

"Just tell me which you like the least and I'll have that one."

"Ugh," said Aster. "No thank you. I'm not helping you choose which dress to seduce my *father* in."

"To *seduce* your . . . ?"

Emily had to get a handle on her horrified spluttering as

Grace entered; her face lit up in a way that made Emily afraid for her life.

"Are we *trying on dresses*?" she half shrieked. Emily winced. "Can I help choose?"

"Yes," said Emily, distracted. "Aster, about what you just said, I really think—"

"Revolting," said Aster. "Transparent. Goodbye."

"What's revolting and transparent?" Grace said, as Aster exited the room looking dreadfully smug.

"This dress," said Emily, plucking at something puce and unappealing. "Look, will you just choose one for me?"

Grace pressed a hand to her chest and looked at Emily with enormous, reverent eyes.

"It would be my *greatest* honor."

Grace chose a dress in palest periwinkle blue, with gathered sleeves and a spiderweb-thin covering of organza at the bodice. There were tiny flowers stitched along the neckline and at the waist, but otherwise it was mercifully simple. Emily didn't even bother looking at herself in the mirror; she just weathered Grace's gasps and applause and then immediately went to take it off again.

"It matches your eyes," Grace said, which Emily found mildly hilarious; her eyes were the dullest possible blue, bleached of all vibrancy. The ocular equivalent of an overcast day. No dress could possibly hope to change that.

The ball was to be in a week's time, and in the meantime the house became almost uninhabitable. It seemed that Meera was taking it as a personal challenge to see how far she could stretch the budget—and her colleagues—to pull off something quite spectacular. She kept asking Emily to do strange things at irregular intervals: one day it was running out to the garden to cut some of the late-blooming roses and great handfuls of asters so that she could experiment with floral arrangements; the next it was measuring the tablecloths to see just how far they could be stretched.

"She asked me to stand at one end of the ballroom next to a candelabra and pretend I was having a private conversation with someone," Akia said, when their paths crossed in the hall after the tablecloths incident. "And then I had to move away inch by inch, so that she could work out exactly how far you had to go before you were in shadow. Apparently clandestine shadows are *key* to throwing a good ball."

It seemed that Captain Edwards had also been busy, although Emily doubted that Meera had managed to get him measuring tablecloths or standing next to candelabras. She came across him completely by accident a few days before the ball, when she had been sent into the strawberry drawing room in search of a particular vase that Meera wanted for her flowers. He was hiding in that same corner again, reading.

"Oh," she said. "I was just . . . Meera sent me for something."

"No, carry on," he said.

She went to the windowsill and located the vase in question. It reminded her too strongly of the night he'd caught her stealing; she could only hope that it did not jog his memory, too, and prompt a conversation with Meera about the box that had never quite made it to her.

"Everybody seems very busy," he remarked, now only pretending to read.

"Yes," said Emily. "As you may recall, you announced a ball."

"I did," Captain Edwards said gravely.

"And yet it is not you who is being sent to find vases, or trim the tassels on the drawing room curtains."

"Trim the . . . ?" He glanced up from his book, horrified for a moment, before he realized that Emily was joking and his face softened. "Yes. You're right. I have not been of much use. I have . . . also been busy."

"Doing what?" said Emily.

"Talking to my children," the captain said, with such a nervous twist to his expression that Emily laughed.

"Oh, the horror," she said. "I hope you will recover in time for your dance."

"It has not actually been . . . quite as difficult as I had anticipated," he said. "They are very funny. They take after their mother in that regard."

"I could have told you they were funny a month ago," said Emily.

"Yes. Well. The next time we quarrel about my failings, you may strike this one off the list of complaints."

"That will barely make a dent in the list."

Captain Edwards raised an eyebrow. "Really? Fascinating."

Emily did not really know what to do with this, or with the odd little jump of her stomach when he looked at her like that.

"I'll just . . ." She gestured toward the door. Captain Edwards nodded, but he did not seem quite done with her yet.

"You haven't been avoiding me?" he said, phrasing it somewhere halfway between a statement and a question. He seemed to be compensating for how vulnerable it was by trying to make it sound like an order.

"No," said Emily firmly. "If only I had the *time* to avoid you. When my days clear up a little, I'll see if I can schedule it in."

He smiled at her—a true smile, relieved and open and warm—and Emily allowed herself to wonder if that moment in the kitchen when he had been injured, their conversations in his study and the garden, his arm bumping hers as they prepared endless soup, had actually . . . *meant* something. Not the casual drunk advances of a lonely man, or an ordinary rapport between master and governess, but something fragile and important that she had not fully grasped, busy as she had been trying to ruin his life.

But the thought was only fleeting, and then it was gone.

Chapter Twenty-three

EMILY REALLY DID CONSIDER FEIGNING ILLNESS WHEN THE evening of the ball finally came. She would have been content to slink off to her room and enjoy an evening of peace and quiet while the others made merry, but none of the servants would hear of it.

"What do you usually do with your hair?"

Akia had cornered Emily and somehow herded her up into her bedroom. She had been gently forced down onto the footstool in front of the mirror, and not allowed to get back up again.

Emily's hair had a loose, uneven natural curl, and she usually pinned it up in the simplest bun possible, not bothering to try to shape it into something more extravagant.

Apparently, this would not do.

"You will embarrass yourself, and embarrass me by association," Akia said. "Also, you will look like one of those sad dogs with the long floppy ears."

"Oh, thanks ever so much," said Emily.

She allowed herself to be yanked this way and that until Akia had installed meticulous rows of curling papers.

"Do not fuss with those," Akia said happily. "Or I'm afraid I shall have to kill you. The last person who ruined my curling papers after I had put them in was dead the very next day."

Emily stared at her in the mirror.

"*Dead?*"

"Well, it was unrelated. She was very old. Trouble with her heart. But still . . . consider it a warning."

"I will not touch the curling papers on pain of death," Emily
said.

Being forced to sit and look at her reflection for so long was its
own sort of torture. Akia insisted that she had good bone struc-
ture, whatever that meant, and that her eyes were very arresting.
Emily could not see it. She thought the barmaid back at the Rose
and Crown had the true measure of her: scrawny, odd-looking.
Big lampy eyes.

There were still things to be done, and Emily had to do them
all with her hair pinned up on top of her head like a balding lion.
Mr. Khan arrived while Emily was standing just outside the back
door, taking a few moments to herself to breathe, which meant
she had a front row seat as he asked Meera if she was excited for
the ball, if she had planned what she would wear, and then ex-
pressed his belief that she looked beautiful regardless.

He had chosen the worst possible timing. All Meera said in
response to *this* was, "I thought we had ordered forty oranges?
You've given us thirty-eight."

Emily's conversation with Charles, and the revelation that he
knew her real name, had left her feeling nervous and jumpy. Oliver tapped her on the shoulder to get her attention while she was
haphazardly arranging flowers into vases and she almost cut *his*
stem off.

"Christ," he said, backing away with his hands up. "You almost sliced me a new arsehole. Does the army know about you?"

If Charles had indeed sold the box, at least his only physical evidence of her crimes was gone—but it also meant that Emily was
now a true thief, with no way for her to undo what she had done.
Every time she thought of it, some urgent ball-related task would
come up and she would get dragged back into bustle and activity,
with absolutely no time to think on it until the fleeting moments
between laying her head on the pillow and falling asleep.

"Careful," Aster said in the hall, a few hours before the guests were due to arrive. "If you insist on looking like you're having *that* much fun, everybody will want a turn."

Emily's face remained stony. Everybody seemed to think they had the right to *comment* on her now, and she was finding it highly vexing.

"And where will *you* be tonight?"

Aster grinned. "Struck down with a large helping of Generic Malady," he said, pressing the back of his hand to his forehead in mock-distress. "A plague of Hairlessness. A terrible case of the Trousers."

"So your plan is to hide?"

"That's right," said Aster. "Hide. Eat some of Joe's cake. Entertain myself by imagining all the ways in which you are inevitably embarrassing yourself. Have fun—don't do anything I wouldn't do."

"There's nothing you wouldn't do," said Emily.

"So true, you lucky thing," said Aster. "Your hair is ridiculous, by the way."

The papers had done their job, and Emily now had a full head of curls so enthusiastic that they kept bouncing merrily in the periphery of her vision. She did *not* feel ready for a ball. She felt like a poodle with a nervous condition.

As the guests began to fill the ground floor and Emily made her escape, Akia managed to snare her again and come at her with a comb, attacking on all fronts until her hair had been tamed and she looked less like she was about to win the consolation prize in a dog show.

"There you go!" Akia was wearing a sunshine-gold dress that looked beautiful against her skin, and had a matching floral pin tucked into her own braided hair. "Lovely."

Emily snorted. She had *never* been lovely, and it was unlikely that she was about to start now.

"Yes, I know, you're not lovely; you're the *toughest* governess in town," said Akia, laughing openly at her. "But right now you have a pretty dress to wear and a genius has fixed your hair, so why don't you imagine you're somebody pleasant and lower yourself to having fun, just for one night?"

Emily's answering nod was not particularly convincing. It was probably the tensed jaw and the gritted teeth that did it.

"Well, close enough," said Akia. "Come on. Let's finish up in the kitchen and then go to a *ball*."

Meera had worked a miracle.

The ballroom had been utterly transformed. Emily had helped, of course, but she had been stretched too thin to step back and appreciate the full effect, and the last time she'd seen it there had still been ladders and crates of decorative miscellany cluttering the place.

Now it looked enormous, the furniture gone, arrangements of creamy roses and bright forget-me-nots scattered across every available surface. There were crowds of candles on the mantel, and freestanding candelabras arranged strategically to create little pockets of gold light and Meera's carefully arranged shadowy, clandestine corners. A table groaning with Joe's finest refreshments had been placed along the west wall, and there was a string trio playing something lively near the hearth.

The guests were in high spirits, laughing and dancing and flitting from group to group. The amount of extravagance in the room—encircling necks and wrists, lining men's coats, from fine brocade shoes and expensive lace trimmings—was staggering, and it turned Emily's stomach. A man in an excessive jacket stood piling his plate high with food—food enough to last him an hour, as if he was trying to ensure that there was nothing left for the rest of the guests. A woman wearing an elaborate floral hat, with a bodice so high and narrow that it was practically no more than a ribbon, dropped a glass on the floor and laughed when it shattered, walking away as if it had nothing to do with her at all.

Emily's first task of the night was to shepherd Grace in so that she might curtsy and smile and impress all who looked upon her. It was hoped that letting her attend for five or ten minutes might sate her appetite for party-going, and that she would then retire in peace to bed.

Emily harbored strong doubts. They knew not what they were about to unleash.

Grace looked very sweet in her party dress, and she did curtsy and exchange pleasantries with some of Captain Edwards's friends, although admittedly there were rather too many questions about their canine companions. The captain himself was busy across the room; Grace used this as an excuse to stay for much longer than she had been instructed, but eventually Emily managed to pull her away. Ensuring that she actually got into her bed was impossible; Emily left her, instead, with strict instructions to only stay up for another few hours, and impressed on her that *if* she did sneak down to catch another glimpse of the guests, it was of the utmost imperative that she did not get caught.

Emily went to check her ridiculous hair, then sat in her room listening to the sound of music and hubbub below with as much apprehension as if it were screaming and cannon fire. When Akia finally came to fetch her so that they could attend for the last few dances, she accepted her fate with a grim face and a stout heart.

"You do know that nobody is going to perform surgery on you," Akia said in her ear, her voice light and full of laughter.

Emily just swallowed, and braced herself for something potentially far worse.

Without Grace, she had nobody to hide behind; she was no longer just the governess, but a *woman* attending a ball.

It was dreadful. If it weren't for Akia by her side, she would have sprinted for the exit.

Only now, standing next to one of the candelabras that Meera had so meticulously measured, did it occur to Emily to wonder *why* Captain Edwards would choose to throw a ball when his finances could barely stretch to cover such a thing.

And then Mrs. Augusta Spencer glided across the room, beautiful enough to draw all eyes and a little sigh of longing from a rather drunk man standing near Emily's elbow—and it all made sense.

This ball was for *her*. Perhaps, Emily thought, with a sickening little cramp in her chest, he would propose to her tonight. Emily felt as if she ought to have been forewarned, somehow, but there was no reason he should have told her. She was not entitled to the private machinations of his heart.

She was his employee. Staff. Any hints of candor or affection in her direction had been solely due to the fact that he'd needed somebody to talk to, and she'd sometimes happened to be nearby. If Oliver had been the one to tie up his hand or bring him soup, she was sure the captain would have unburdened himself in his valet's direction instead, and *Oliver* would not have presumed Captain Edwards to feel anything approaching romantic in his direction.

Although . . . Oliver *was* at this very moment ensconced in one of the dark corners with a young blond man who kept laughing quietly at his jokes, and he had the sort of nervous, electrified gaze that indicated there might indeed be romance on the cards that evening—so what did Emily know?

"I need a drink," she said to Akia. "Can we . . . ?"

"Here," said a stranger in an apron, offering her a tray.

"Er . . . thank you," said Emily, taking a glass and handing one to Akia, too, before the maid moved on. "Who on earth is that?"

"*What?* That's Sarah. She works here," Akia said, looking horror-struck. "Please tell me you recognize *Sarah*."

Emily gaped after her for a moment before her mouth snapped shut.

"You're making fun of me," she said.

"I am," said Akia. "It's just so *easy*. Sarah works for Mrs. Spencer—Meera called in some extra help so we could join in for these dances. You didn't think these people were going to serve *themselves*, did you?"

Emily felt that old, hot hatred boiling up inside her again, watching them waste food and spill drinks and act as if the serving staff didn't exist. She had somehow let herself forget—lulled by the comforts of the house, the informality, mollified by the fact that Captain Edwards was not actually as rich as she had imagined him to be. Now, as she watched an elderly woman positively dripping with diamonds frown at Meera from across the room, she wanted to take all their decadence and haughtiness and frippery and crush it beneath her heel.

"Oh dear," Akia said. "You have a murderous look about you. Farewell."

She crossed the room to talk to Meera, leaving Emily standing on the edge of the revelry, feeling spiky and foolish and *wrong*.

It didn't matter how nice a dress Grace had chosen for her, or how carefully Akia had arranged her hair—she didn't belong here. She didn't *want* to belong here. She probably looked ridiculous in this outfit, which was worth more than she had ever earned in her life; the other guests were likely sniggering at her from behind their fans, enjoying the spectacle of the plain governess playing at somebody worth dancing with.

Enough of this. She wouldn't give them the chance. She had no idea what she had been thinking, agreeing to come to a *ball* in the first place.

Emily swiped a second glass of wine and stalked from the room, barely stopping to apologize when her elbow knocked a gentleman entering from the hall. She kept going until she reached the stairs. The first drink vanished far too quickly; she left the empty glass balanced on the banister, knowing she'd probably be the one who had to deal with it later.

Five steps and two more gulps of wine later, she heard some-one call her name.

Emily turned, trying to push down all that wrath and outrage until she was a slate wiped clean.

It didn't really matter that Captain Edwards's face changed when he saw her—that his eyes widened, and his mouth dropped open maybe a quarter or a third of an inch. It didn't matter that his eyes swept down her body and back up again, from her ridic-ulous dress to her silly hair, and then came to land on her face with an expression that looked almost like quiet wonder.

It didn't matter because she was marching upstairs to change back into her own clothes and be where she belonged. Deluding herself that it meant anything that he might like her *dress*, or be somewhat impressed by what Akia had managed to do with her hair, was folly.

"Miss Laurence," he said again. He had to clear his throat be-fore doing it. "Meera was asking after you in the ballroom."

"Are you a messenger now?" Emily said, apparently throwing caution not just to the wind but off the edge of the cliffs.

Captain Edwards barely seemed to register the slight. He had the same half-dazed look that Emily had once seen on Amy, when a large bucket had fallen from a shelf and knocked her hard on the temple. He wasn't wearing his uniform tonight, but he was wearing an unfussy blue-black jacket fitted perfectly to the lines of his shoulders, which was almost as bad.

"More like a gooseherd," he said benignly. And then, far less benignly, "Or a lion tamer."

"I am not a goose." Emily knocked back the wine and walked reluctantly back down the stairs.

"Jury's out on the lion, though," Captain Edwards said in a low, resonant voice as she passed him.

It made her feel oddly hot and shivery all over. She was keenly aware of him at her back as she reentered the drawing room, and felt the loss when he peeled away to talk to somebody else.

By the time she reached Meera and Akia, Emily could feel that her face was flushed without having to touch it. Meera looked from the glass in her hand to her pink cheeks and made a jovial attempt at disapproval.

"Three sheets to the wind, is it? Or have we lost count of sheets."

"This is only my second drink," Emily said defensively.

"Of the past two minutes," said Akia.

"What was it that you wanted?" Emily said. "Captain Edwards said you needed me."

"Oh, I don't need you," Meera said, smiling wickedly. "I just saw you leaving, and after all our hard work, I couldn't stand for *that*. Come on, they're starting another dance."

She all but *shoved* Emily into the line, and Emily didn't have time to protest that she didn't really know *how* to dance, which was only number three on her list of reasons why this was her worst nightmare come to life.

Luckily for Emily, the dance was not complicated. Luckily for Meera, she'd had the presence of mind to push Akia into the fray, too, so that Emily was not on her own, and was therefore slightly less inclined to murder the housekeeper later. She was certain she made a few very obvious missteps, but everybody else was too soused to notice; she ended up being swung around on the arms of two different gentlemen, one young and giddy and the other older and very, very drunk.

The younger, giddier one, who was likely five years Emily's junior, had the audacity to ask her for another dance after the first had finished. Emily stared at him, convinced he must be joking, and only believed this wasn't some elaborate trick when the music started again and he reached for her hand. *He* was not a good dancer, but that only helped to soothe Emily's nerves; she wouldn't have admitted it with a bayonet to her throat, but there was something freeing about dancing like this, blending into the row of ladies on either side of her, as if she, too, had not a care in the world.

It was probably just the wine.

Her high spirits abated when she saw who had joined the end of the line. Captain Edwards was dancing with Mrs. Augusta Spencer.

They looked . . . *perfect* together. Mrs. Spencer's elegance and poise were the ideal match for Captain Edwards's solemnity and stature, and Emily could see some of the guests watching, muttering among themselves and smiling, enjoying the spectacle of an exciting union about to come to fruition.

Emily tried not to look at them. She tried not to notice when Mrs. Spencer smiled at Captain Edwards, and Captain Edwards smiled back.

She went to get some more wine between dances, and had only taken one sip when Meera removed it from her hand and gave it to Akia, who drank it down in one.

"Excuse me," Emily said. "That was very rude."

"Letting you drink unabated in polite company feels rather like handing a torch to a child and sending them off into a hay barn," said Meera. "You set plenty of fires without needing libations, Amy."

Amy. Emily was suddenly on the verge of telling her the truth, for no reason she could fathom.

"Meera . . ." Emily started, but both Meera and Akia had seen something over her shoulder and immediately buried their faces in drinks and pivoted away as Emily turned to see what the matter was.

"Miss Laurence." There was that errant thrill of pleasure again, finger-walking up the length of her spine. Captain Edwards's color was up from the dancing. Perhaps he had also been drinking. "Would you . . . ?"

It took Emily such a long time to grasp his meaning that she would not have been surprised if he had given up and walked away. Once she did, however, the part of her that always longed to *push* at him won out again.

"Would I . . . ?" she said, daring him to actually say it. "I'm afraid I don't understand."

Captain Edwards narrowed his eyes, but there was no real anger in his expression.

"Miss Laurence, would you care to dance?"

Chapter Twenty-four

"To dance?" Emily said, disbelievingly. "Here? In front of all of your . . . society friends?"

"I traditionally dance with the staff," he said. "Well—the *female* staff," he amended. "Not that I haven't tried asking Joe."

"Far be it from me to keep you from tradition," said Emily, but it had lessened her anticipation somewhat to realize that he had not, in fact, singled her out. This was all just part of the show: the kind and benevolent master of the house deigning to entertain the little people, for one night of the year. She hadn't made any sort of move closer to him, or to the dance floor, and when Captain Edwards held his hand out to her she almost didn't take it.

"Please," he said.

That one word, spoken quietly enough that it was for Emily alone, broke her resolve. She took his hand and glanced back over at Meera and Akia, both of whom were watching with their heads together, definitely discussing her in muttered tones.

It was easy to roll her eyes and feign amused reluctance until they actually reached the floor, but the melody the musicians were starting to play was slow, and the steps were unfamiliar, and Emily was suddenly foundering.

"I . . . can't dance," she said, stepping in closer to Captain Edwards to make sure he heard and understood her. "I mean it. I don't know the steps. You're going to lose an ankle."

He looked at her seriously, ignoring the fact that others around them had begun to move. He didn't look like Grace and

Aster's father tonight. He looked like . . . a man at a ball. A bright-eyed, mussed-haired *suitor*.

"I can get by with just the one."

When they joined the dance, Emily's panic was coming to a head. He didn't *understand*. When would she have ever learned how to dance like this? She missed the first steps, her gaze stuck on the lady next to her as she attempted to copy her; after her second blunder, she was tempted to turn around and walk right back out of the ballroom, feeling frustration rising in her throat.

But then Captain Edwards found her hand again and tugged it just a little, so that Emily was forced to take a step closer; she looked up and caught his eye, and found that if she kept watching him, it wasn't so difficult to work out where to put her feet.

His hands guided her at her wrist and waist, pulling her in and then pushing her away in time to the swell of the music, and whenever she found herself unmoored it wasn't long before he was holding her again, keeping time for them both.

It was only halfway through that Emily realized none of the other partners were dancing like that; they would meet in a per-functory sort of way, a quick grasp of hands before parting, only the boldest among them daring to linger with fingers trailing along wrists or the seams of bodices.

Even the boldest weren't touching each other as much as Captain Edwards was touching *her*.

The realization sparked unfamiliar, prickling heat wherever he placed his hands, no matter how chaste his touch was, and Emily was so overcome that it took all her willpower and concentration to keep dancing rather than come to an abrupt standstill. Even through sleeve or dress or glove, it felt as if his fingers were pressing into bare, unclothed skin.

It was almost too much—the sweeping violin, and the wine hot in her chest, and Captain Edwards watching her so carefully as he led her—and then suddenly it *was* too much. She became aware of herself within the room again: aware that people were gawping at her, eager to see who Captain Edwards was dancing so closely with. The dance hadn't finished when Emily stepped away, pushing back her hair and smoothing her dress in an attempt to put right everything that had been disarranged. She sensed a few sidelong glances, a few mutters of surprise, but she left them all behind as she finally escaped.

She was out of the front door and halfway down the drive when she came to a stop, the air chilling the skin of her arms not encased in ridiculous borrowed gloves, her breathing harsh and loud in the near-windless night.

That had been stupid. And *unfair*. How dare Captain Edwards dance with her like that—so intimately, so attentively, as if it really *mattered* to him—in front of absolutely everybody, probably imagining that he was doing her some sort of favor? The shame welled up in her and spilled, flooding her with icy regret.

Somebody was calling her name from the house.

No. Not *her* name. Amy's name.

Captain Edwards was standing in the doorway, haloed all over by warm light. She started walking away again, with no destination in mind.

"Amy," he said again. "Please."

Emily was shaking her head. Both at the *Amy* and at the *please*. She hadn't run out here because she'd wanted to be chased and caught; if that had been the point, she'd have gone slowly, and not ruined both her shoes and her hair in the process.

The captain caught up with her where the drive became the road, and Emily suddenly felt so foolish she didn't want him to look at her.

"I didn't want to dance," she said, crossing her arms as if she might be able to keep all her feelings safely in her chest that way.

"I'm sorry."

"I told you I can't dance, and you wouldn't listen to me—did it even occur to you that you might be embarrassing me? And . . . and I have no desire to be trotted out as a *charity* case, evidence of your goodwill, that you'll deign to take the hand of a lowly governess one night of the year. Did you clean off your glove afterward, where nobody could see? Will you laugh about it with your real guests?"

"Of course not," Captain Edwards said, his voice as tight as a plucked bowstring. "Amy—"

"No," Emily said. "Do *not* call me that."

She wasn't looking at his face, but she saw his body half flinch away from her. Good. Fine.

"Again, I offer my sincere apologies." He was using his captain's voice—his man-of-the-house voice. "I can assure you that I had no desire to upset or embarrass you. I have apologized twice over—I don't know what more you want from me."

"I want to know *why*," Emily said. She hated that it came out with so much feeling. "Why did you dance with me like *that*?"

Captain Edwards took a slow, careful step closer to her.

"I danced with you because I wanted to dance with you." He still sounded stiff and formal, but Emily could hear something else in there, too—an undercurrent of true emotion. "I overstepped. It was inappropriate in the extreme, and if I made you feel . . . if I gave you the impression that I . . . I have apologized, Miss Laurence. The mistake will never be repeated."

"You think that just because you are the head of this household," Emily said, running too hot to slow down, "you can do whatever you want, without consequence. I might be an employee, *Captain*, but I am still a person—not a prop, not a gimmick—and I am still a *woman*, even if my reputation can take a little harder wear than the Mrs. Spencers of the world."

"Believe me," Captain Edwards said roughly. "I do not need reminding that you are a woman."

This hung strangely in the air between them, and Emily was

surprised to find that in an instant, her anger was transformed into something else entirely.

It made absolutely no sense that standing here, shouting at him, genuinely incensed by his behavior, she also wanted to press her hands to those broad shoulders—to make a mess of his collar, to force him to stop playing at captain and just be a man at a ball again. His face was slightly flushed from dancing, one hand raised, as if he were thinking of reaching for her but choosing restraint.

When she finally did touch him, hands splayed flat across his collarbones in a strange, dazed wonder at her own daring, all his restraint seemed to leave him in a rush; his body bent toward her at once, as if he had been waiting at the very edge of his nerve for permission, and then his hand was at her waist again like it had been on the dance floor, fisting in all that silky blue so that he could pull her closer. His other hand slid to cup the back of her neck and she felt his fingers there, sure and careful, as he kissed her.

Emily *really* hadn't been sure that he wanted her. He had said and done enough to make her wonder, but she had no idea whether it was all just a bit of fun for him, a minor flirtation to ease the passing of the days that could never really turn into action.

He certainly wanted her now. He was kissing her without hesitation or reserve, long-simmering heat in the drag of his lips and the curl of his fingers, which were now sliding into her hair, and there was nothing measured or controlled about the way he gathered her to him so that their bodies were pressed flush together without an inch of space between them.

Emily let herself feel it—feel both wanted and heady with want, feel the hard lines of his body as he drew her close—until his hand slipped from her hair and he pulled back just for a moment, allowing her brain to sputter back to life with great, heavy reluctance.

"Wait," Captain Edwards said, as if he had read and understood the change in her expression immediately. "Don't—"

"This is a mistake," Emily said.

Captain Edwards's grip on her waist tightened, as if he could keep her there, and Emily's eyes half shut as she took a moment to gather herself. His fingers were *very* distracting.

"I need to . . . I have to go."

Captain Edwards released her, but he didn't move away.

"I will escort you back to the ballroom," he said, his voice tight. "But later, Miss Laurence, when the guests have departed—"

"That's *enough*."

Emily didn't want to hear what he was going to say next. That she should come to his room, perhaps? Or maybe that was too risky— too likely to be spotted by some other member of staff or, God forbid, one of the children. The garden, then. The stables. Some place he could kiss her, and touch her, and know that he could get away with it. Somewhere he could hide her, so that he could return her to her proper place once he was finished with her, leaving everybody else none the wiser.

He didn't really think she was *beautiful*. He just thought she was useful, in this particular regard.

The world made sense again.

"Miss Laurence, please. I need to—"

"Miss Laurence?" said an unfamiliar voice.

Emily had been so caught up in both her desire and her anger in rapid succession that she hadn't noticed a messenger riding up the road to meet them; if the expression on Captain Edwards's face was anything to go by, he hadn't either. They both stared at the young man, and he looked slightly panicked.

"Er," he said haltingly. "I have a . . . a letter? An urgent note, for a Miss Emily Laurence. I thought I heard him say that was . . . you."

"Yes," Emily said quickly. "I am. I mean . . . it is. I'm Emily Laurence."

He leaned down to hand her the note, and Emily's heart jolted uncomfortably in her chest when she recognized her mother's very unfortunate handwriting.

Forgetting Captain Edwards was there at all, she broke the seal and read as quickly as she could manage, navigating her mother's spilled ink and irritating tangents. When she deciphered the letter's meaning, her fingers went so shockingly numb that she almost dropped it.

Amy had taken a turn. She was much worse. Emily was called home, *just in case.*

She thought she was going to be sick, but instead, she opened her mouth and swore so violently that the messenger immediately turned his horse and scarpered.

Captain Edwards was watching her. He did not seem particularly taken aback by her language. Not that she would have cared if he was; nothing here mattered at all, suddenly. Her heart was at home, bedridden with fever, and every second she spent here was time wasted.

"Miss Laurence?" Captain Edwards said.

"My sister," Emily managed. "Amy is unwell, I must . . . I need to go."

"Amy," he said slowly.

Emily realized her mistake. It was of no consequence.

She was already gone.

Chapter Twenty-five

Meera wouldn't let Emily leave without pressing a month's wages into her hand, and Joe wouldn't let her go without an enormous basket of food. Captain Edwards seemed to be hiding from her. Oliver insisted that she'd be a damned fool if she walked to the pub in the dark to catch the early morning post, and had her wait for an excruciating half an hour while he set up the gig, and then insisted on driving.

"I can drive myself and have somebody bring this back to the house when I'm gone," she said, as he hauled her trunk up and then offered her an arm. "You don't have to do this."

"No, I don't," he mused. "But I'd probably look like an unfeeling bastard if I didn't, wouldn't I? Come on, the horse is getting cold."

He was quite a terrifying driver, but there was nobody for miles around for him to crash into, so Emily held on to her limbs and her luggage and found herself barely able to register the cliffs, or the bumps in the road, or the view of the sunrise just peeking above the horizon in the distance.

As they approached the pub, Emily looked at Oliver properly for the first time since they'd left and noticed a very distinctive bruise on his neck, as if somebody had forgotten how to kiss and had taken a bite out of him instead. She thought of the blond he'd been flirting with in the corner, and wondered if the exact size and shape of Oliver's injury would match up to the man's dental records.

"Oliver," she said, too tired to consider her words properly, "did that man bite you?"

"Hmmm?" said Oliver, trying to glance down at his own neck and obviously failing. "Ah. Yes. Not hard enough, frankly."

"Oh," said Emily. "That's . . . nice."

"I should hope not," said Oliver. "Christ, look at your face. You must feel like you've accidentally wandered into hell."

"Does Captain Edwards know?"

"*Ben?* Ha! Yes—Ben knows. We have been in each other's confidences about such things for a long time. It was the reason he took me on, when I was cast unceremoniously out of my previous house for kissing the butler. His nurse when he was a boy was of that persuasion, too, you know. Lives with a lifelong *friend*. Carries the wrong sort of umbrella."

The sunrise was putting on its very best show, and Emily was too distracted to see it at all, except in the way it made Oliver the color of ripe peaches and bitten grapes.

"I really am sorry I accused you of . . . being inappropriate. With Aster."

Oliver let out a long sigh, actually bothering to glance over to the left and right as they reached a crossroads.

"No, no, I think you were right. I mean, you were *wrong*—I was simply trying to make sure he had somebody to talk to, and to stop him from making an enormous mess of his life before he'd even had the chance to be himself properly—but if *I'd* seen anybody else sneaking about in the dead of night with one of those children, I'd have garroted him myself. They're lucky to have you."

Emily did not want to hear this. It occurred to her, in a sudden rush of jumbled feeling, that it might be for the best if she never returned to Fairmont House. She would not have to worry then about what to say to Charles, the next time they met; she would not have to untangle the mess of Captain Edwards and how she felt about him; she would not have to explain why she had been calling herself *Amy*, now that her story was beginning to fall apart. She would have to find another job—perhaps even go back to the dreaded mill—but that had always been inevitable. It would be somewhat of a relief to leave all her lies behind her, and better for everyone at Fairmont, too. The next governess would not be so stupid as to accept the friendship of a dastardly stranger in a pub. The next governess would never set foot in a pub at all.

Emily bit down on the meat of her mouth and pushed away the thought of Aster handing her the scissors; Grace's face brightening every time her governess walked into the room. They would be fine. They already *had* a family. Emily was going home to hers.

Logistics took over once she reached the Rose and Crown, and she had no idea if she wished Oliver farewell or said anything to him at all before she was bundling herself into a carriage that, to her great relief, only had a single elderly man inside. He nodded at her and then closed his eyes to go to sleep, leaving Emily to sit and look out of the window as her mind spiraled.

If the doctor hadn't been called, she would have to do that first, perhaps go straight to his house, as it was only slightly out of her way—but if he *had* already been summoned then she was wasting precious minutes with this detour, and she would feel every one of them as she rushed home, trying to make up for lost time. She would have to use all of her Fairmont wages to pay him. Amy still might have the two sovereigns from Charles that she'd sent home—she had probably refused to spend them on the things she so sorely needed—but then, if there was nothing left, what about a funeral? She would not let Amy go without, but they could hardly wait for Emily to find some other place of employment for long enough to pay for it, which meant they would likely have to take some sort of loan, and then—

She cut herself off, feeling violently guilty for even thinking of a *funeral*.

She supposed somebody had to. Her mother would be next to useless. With Amy gone, it would almost be as if Emily had no family left at all.

She had always mocked her mother's superstitions, but she knocked her knuckles twice against the wooden doorframe of the carriage to try to undo her thoughts of grave plots and flowers.

Unfortunately, her mind could not be tricked into perfect blankness, and in trying to distract herself, her thoughts kept straying back to the captain. As they rushed alongside fields and lanes and Emily watched the flashing white tails of rabbits, flocks of crows wheeling, smoke rising from the stacks of distant farmhouses and villages, she wondered what he might be doing back at Fairmont House. Hiding in his study? Breakfasting with the children?

She could not delude herself into imagining that he was thinking of her. More likely, he was writing to arrange a next meeting with Mrs. Spencer. *She* made sense at Fairmont. They would marry, and with the Royal Navy appeased, the captain would return to his ship. Everybody would be exactly where they ought, as if Emily's trip to the coast had never really happened.

She thought of Amy, pictured her standing on the beach—a place she had never been, and now might not get the chance to visit—and then settled right back into spiraling again for the length of the journey home.

In the end, Emily went straight to the house.

It looked even smaller now than it had before. There was damage to the brickwork up near the roof, overgrown ivy trying to force its way through one of the upstairs windows; when Emily went to open the door, it stuck in the frame, and she had to give it a hard shove to gain entrance.

Inside it was clean. The stone floor had been swept; the rug with the little burn marks where sparks had escaped from the hearth looked freshly beaten. There was even a cup with a bouquet of wild flowers on the table.

The possible meanings of this turned Emily's insides to melting ice; had somebody brought flowers to express their sympathy? Had her mother cleaned, knowing they might soon have visitors?

Emily's movements were suddenly erratic and fumbling as she put down her trunk and stumbled toward the stairs, taking them two at a time and almost slipping when she reached the top.

The door to the bedroom she shared with Amy was closed.

When she opened it, she found her mother sitting beside the bed, in the chair Amy often read in.

She was holding Amy's hand.

"*Amy*," Emily choked out, going to her at once. "I'm home."

She wasn't unconscious, as Emily had feared, but she did have a high, clammy fever and a sickly green tinge to her skin that made Emily want to wrap her up in blankets and run away with her, as if they could outpace whatever was coming for her. She had grown thinner, too, her hands like little claws, all pale skin and jutting bone.

"Em," Amy said weakly, as their mother got up and shuffled from the room with a pat to Emily's shoulder that she barely noticed. "You didn't need to come, you fool."

"Oh, shut up," Emily said. "I was sick and tired of the coast, anyway. Always too cold, even in the height of summer. The people were dull and the house was ugly and I missed your face. Look, I have an entire basket of rich people's food here—take your pick. I'd try the chicken—I think they fatten them on plum cake and cream."

Amy smiled thinly, and let Emily prattle on as she unpacked the food and presented it, her descriptions of its origin getting more ridiculous each time.

"What are they like?" Amy said hoarsely. "Were the children good? Was Captain Edwards reasonable?"

"Ah," said Emily, with a brief and uncomfortable memory of the captain's hand tightening in her hair. "Yes . . . sort of. They would have *loved* you. Me, they tolerated. Now, let me tell you about this pie . . ."

Amy could not eat the pie. She could not do much of anything. Even lying there listening to Emily seemed to take something from her that she could not afford to give, so Emily soon lapsed into silence and sat vigil instead.

When Amy fell asleep, Emily slipped from the room and met her mother downstairs, cutting a meager pile of vegetables by the fire.

"Amy told me the doctor has been here," she said, not sitting down. "What did he say?"

Her mother sighed. "More of the usual. She needs rest, she needs good food . . . She needs some miracle medicine that only he can provide, but it will cost us the earth and we cannot have it until next week."

Emily did not ask what they were going to do. She did not collapse into her mother's arms, weeping. She would have to figure this out herself. She would need to—

"You could at least pretend to be glad to see me," said her mother.

Emily blinked at her. "I . . . am."

"Mmm," said her mother. "She has not been alone while you have been gone, Emily. I have been here."

It was on the tip of Emily's tongue to say that it was almost the same thing, but she stopped herself. That was not fair.

If the Edwards family had shown her anything these past months, it was that everybody wore their grief differently: Grace, inclined to love even harder; Aster, feeling angry and alone; the captain, retreating into himself, not able to reach out for his own family, who would understand the most.

Emily had always been the sort to leap into action—to see what could be done, to make plans and try to think ten steps ahead.

But that was *Emily's* way, not her mother's. And while Emily would never be able to completely forgive her for her lack of effort, she could at least understand that mourning her father had been something entirely different for her mother, who had lost a husband. She was mourning still, in a way that Emily was not.

If forgiveness was out of reach, she could at least extend a little grace.

"Thank you," Emily said quietly.

Her mother nodded, short and sharp, and then went back to her vegetables.

Emily did not sleep. She sat in the chair, watching Amy breathing, and did sums in her head. They could summon the doctor again a handful more times, but it would do no good if he had nothing useful to say. They could put their hopes into whatever this *medicine* was that he was selling, but it would likely use up every last bit of her wages. The two sovereigns she had sent home had already been spent. They at least had good food from Fairmont to sustain them for a few days; if only Amy was able to sit up and eat it.

In the morning, not long after the muted peach of sunrise, there was a firm rap at the front door. Emily's mother answered it, and a minute later a man in a very nice coat with a polished leather bag knocked on the half-open bedroom door and waited to be admitted.

"Miss Laurence?" he said. "And Miss Laurence. I suppose I can assume that the one abed is the one in need of assistance."

"Who . . . are you?" Emily said, confused.

"Dr. Abingley," said the man, putting down his bag and opening it with a snap. "Your mother mentioned that you have already seen a local doctor, but I wonder if you might be in need of a second opinion."

"Yes," said Amy. Emily hadn't realized she was awake. Her face was flushed and her voice was thin, but at least she was talking. "Dr. . . . Johnson. He said there was nothing to be done but rest, but then . . . we did lack the means to pay him to say much more."

"All right," said Dr. Abingley, ignoring this obvious indication that they certainly had no more money to pay *him* than they did Dr. Johnson. "Let's have a look at you, then. Miss Laurence, you are very welcome to stay and chaperone, but if you could move aside . . ."

Emily watched, stilling the questions on her tongue, as he subjected Amy to a gentle, thorough examination, and then quizzed her for upward of half an hour about the nature of her illness. She had never known a doctor so willing to stay put for so long, without glancing pointedly at his pocket watch or implying that more funds would need to be forthcoming if he were to stay any longer.

"Right," Dr. Abingley said, once he had finished. "I can give you something for the fever and inflammation, and that should calm things down. You'll need to take medicine daily, and a change in diet is in order. Miss Laurence, I will speak with you downstairs in a moment."

"Am I dying?" Amy said, with a sort of calm, measured interest that made Emily's heart hurt.

"No," said Dr. Abingley. "I don't expect so, unless you plan on colliding with a carriage or leaning too far out of your window after I'm gone. There are a few things I want to discuss with some colleagues of mine, to get their recommendations. I will return in a few days with my findings, and to see how you are getting on. How does that sound?"

Amy blinked at him, and then closed her eyes. "That sounds just fine."

Emily walked from the room and burst into tears in the darkness of the corridor, pressing the back of her hand to her mouth to try to stifle her sobs. She could still hear Dr. Abingley talking to Amy in that brusque, reassuring voice. She could have listened to it forever.

She went downstairs and took a drink to compose herself, and then wiped her face and stood up straight and listened attentively when Dr. Abingley came down to give her instructions, nodding and agreeing as if she had the means to produce endless fresh vegetables and good-quality meat for Amy to eat.

Mrs. Laurence sat in the corner, listening, and after he had departed, she looked at Emily with a frown.

"Where did he come from, then?"

"I . . . don't know," said Emily.

"And how on earth are we to pay him?"

"He didn't seem to want paying," said Emily.

The days continued in a strange fug, during which Emily was practically glued to the chair at Amy's bedside. She helped her to drink, and to take her medicine. She helped their mother clean her as best she could with a damp cloth, ignoring Amy's weak complaints. She spent what felt like months, or years, watching for the rise and fall of Amy's chest and being grateful every time it came, and only slept when her mother relieved her.

"Stop watching me, you crackpot," Amy murmured a few days later, as day slipped into evening outside the window. "I cannot sleep if I'm worried you'll be looming over me the entire time."

"Come over here and fight me, then," Emily said.

"I will in a moment," said Amy. "Just gathering my strength, and then you're in a world of trouble."

Emily smiled, and they lapsed into silence until Amy's eye cracked open.

"Who sent the doctor?" she said.

The answer, which had been slowly dawning on Emily for the past few days, was almost unbearable.

"Captain Edwards."

"Captain *Edwards*?" said Amy, her other eye flying open as this caught her interest. "Goodness. Did you ask him to—?"

"No," Emily said emphatically. "God, no. But his daughter is unwell, and she has a doctor, so I suppose the captain thought . . ."

"Oh, Emily," Amy said. "What have you done?"

Emily bristled. "What do you mean, *what have I done*?"

"You are practically *blushing*, which I have never seen you do before," said Amy. "Have you also succumbed to fever, or have you . . . ? You didn't . . . ?"

"Nothing happened." Emily had apparently become a worse liar during her time away, because Amy snorted. "All right. We . . . There was a . . . a *moment*. The night before I left. But it didn't mean anything. He's just some rich toff who thinks he can have anything he wants, and . . . and I am certainly not stupid enough to risk anything by believing that he really *likes* me."

"Oh," said Amy. "Is he horrid, then?"

"Yes," said Emily. "Well . . . no, actually. I'm not sure. He has certainly never been the least bit forceful with me, if that's what you mean. But . . . if he were truly a good man, he wouldn't have kissed me."

"He *kissed* you?" Amy said.

She was looking so animated now that Emily was worried she might burn through all her energy in one fell swoop.

"Calm down—it meant absolutely nothing," Emily said. "Just a wealthy man's whim. I suppose he would have kissed anybody."

Amy did not seem willing to believe this.

"Or perhaps he likes you," she said. "Perhaps he has fallen madly in love with you, despite your differences in station, and wishes to whisk you off to the altar and bring you back as the lady of Fairmont House, to—"

"Amy," Emily said sharply. "Stop it. I mean it."

Her sister did not know the whole truth of the matter: her lies, her meetings with Charles, the fact that she had been at Fairmont under Amy's own name. If she knew the extent of it all, she would not think it so romantic. She would understand exactly why Captain Edwards could never really love her, had he also known the truth.

She *would* tell Amy. Just not at a time when the shock was likely to spike her fever.

"Oh, fine," Amy grumbled. "But you are being a terrible bore. What would be so strange about him liking you? *I* like you, and I have wonderful taste."

"You are a saint," said Emily. "And probably some sort of earthbound angel, or something equally distasteful."

"Oh, you stop," said Amy. "I hate it when you talk like this."

"I am telling the truth."

"Emily," Amy said, sitting up on her elbows. "I'm *not* anything even close to an angel. I have plenty of terrible thoughts. I am selfish, sometimes. You make me less of a person when you do this. You act as if I am perfect, and put me on a pedestal, and use me to flagellate yourself—if *I* am good, then you must be bad. But I don't want to be any of that to you. I certainly do not want to be an ideal you use to martyr yourself. I just want to be your sister."

"You *are* my sister," said Emily. "Look, lie back down, that doctor said you needed rest—"

"You are," Amy barreled on, "quite frequently a bit of an arse, but you are not *bad*, no matter how much you insist so, and you deserve to have good things. No, don't look at me like that, I mean it. You have always done everything for me and nothing for yourself, and I am sick to death of it. It's starting to reflect very poorly on me, you know."

Emily looked at her fondly, despite this ridiculous tirade.

"Don't say 'sick to death,' you idiot. You're tempting fate."

"Well, all I'm saying is, perhaps he likes you! And there's no use me warning you to be careful, because you are always far *too* careful. I'm surprised you let him close enough to kiss you without maiming him."

"Who says I didn't maim him," Emily said. "Lie *down*."

"Agree with me that you deserve a little joy in your life first," Amy said. "Or I will get up and start dancing a jig until you do."

"No you won't," Emily said warningly, but Amy raised her eyebrows in overt threat and Emily sighed. "I deserve a little joy in my life," she said tonelessly.

"That was dreadful," said Amy, with a long sigh. "Next time, try to believe it, just a little."

"Fine," Emily lied.

She pulled a blanket over her legs and leaned back into her chair as Amy closed her eyes and almost instantly fell asleep.

Chapter Twenty-six

THE DOCTOR DID INDEED RETURN LATER IN THE WEEK TO check on Amy. The Laurence household also received a delivery of food: baskets of plump fruit and vegetables; a freshly killed goose; bouquets of fragrant herbs and a pot of golden honey tied neatly in linen ribbon.

This was about the point at which Emily went from a daze of sheer relief to extremely, potently furious, in almost an instant.

"What's the problem?" Amy sat at the kitchen table surrounded by an exhaustive array of groceries. Emily had helped her there, not sure at all that she should be out of bed. "You look all . . . chompy."

"The problem," Emily said, picking up a very shiny apple and then putting it back down again, "is that we don't need *charity*."

"Oh, Emily," said Amy. "Why not let him be kind, if he wants to? I like charity. I'm going to eat all this delicious charity, and grow big and strong enough to put you in a headlock when you get like this."

It wasn't that Emily didn't want Amy to have everything she needed—of *course* she did—but the idea of Captain Edwards and Meera conspiring to send this food to her, taking care to order all the things that the doctor had recommended, made her feel squirmy and ashamed and profoundly irritated.

She thought of the expression on his face when she'd named her sister, his realization that she'd been operating under a false name. Had he not realized the implications of this? Had he decided to willfully ignore them? Why was he insisting on this extravagant show of wealth in her direction, if he knew her to be some sort of fraud?

Amy *was* looking better, though. There was some more natural color in her cheeks, and she could hold a conversation without exhausting herself, and even read short passages of her favorite books. Emily felt quite able to leave her and go out for some air; to walk down to the market on Saturday to look for a few small delicacies that might cheer Amy up, and experience the horror of being known when Thomas from the fruit and vegetable stall and Mary at the pie stand insisted on saying good day to her and asking how she had been.

She even walked past the mill. It was odd that it felt so familiar and yet, at the same time, very far away; just one wall between her and the work that had bent her back day after day for years. She would likely be back there in a matter of weeks, groveling for her old position, assuring the foreman that she was back for the long run.

She could not pretend that she did not dread it, but *this* was real life. Not whatever had happened at Fairmont House.

Meera had written. Emily had not opened the letter. She would need to respond at some point, to make it clear that she had vacated her position—but every time she thought of doing it, she put it off for just a little while longer.

It would feel like severing something, and she was not quite ready to cut that line for good.

They ate the last of the goose on Saturday night, and their mother stewed the apples for after. As they sat by the fire before bed, Emily watched Amy curled up in her chair, reading a book under an enormous blanket, and felt so overwhelmed by how much she loved her that she almost couldn't stand it.

Emily knew it was almost time to face the practicalities of what needed to be done next: finding a job, sorting out a budget.

Making the money in her drawer last for as long as physically possible, and arranging a means to replenish it.

She dressed herself one cool Tuesday morning, ate a thick crust of bread and the last of the slightly brown apples, and opened the front door to find—

"*Oliver?*"

"Oh," said Oliver. "Yes . . . good. I wasn't sure if this was—but it is."

Just two weeks away from Fairmont House had made it all feel like somewhat of a dream; she didn't know what to make of the valet standing on her front doorstep, impeccably turned out, peering past her into her house with an expression of barely suppressed shock on his face.

She stepped out and firmly closed the door.

"What is it?"

"Ah . . ." he said, seeming to remember that he wasn't just here to snoop. "You're needed."

"I . . . I'm not coming back, Oliver. I was planning to hand in my notice."

"Were you? You could have told Meera sooner, you wretch. Anyway . . . you're being brought back in for one last job—Grace is missing."

Grace? *Missing?*

Emily could not make sense of this. *Aster* missing made perfect sense, but Grace would never be so irresponsible as to wander off alone.

This thought led to a spike of panic, because it was true—she *wouldn't* wander off alone. Which meant that something truly terrible might have befallen her.

"Why do you need me?" Emily said, as if she hadn't already made her mind up to go.

"Captain's orders," said Oliver. "Come on. Throw some things in a trunk—we might need you to stay for a few days."

Emily went to tell her sister. Amy understood at once and bid her to go with haste.

"And you will be all right?" Emily said, reluctant to let go of her hand.

"I know you are not particularly impressed by our mother," said Amy, "but she is perfectly capable of feeding me. And besides, you are *not* to use me as an excuse to loiter here when I really am feeling much better. *Go.*"

Emily left all the money she had on the dresser by the bed and then went to join Oliver in the gig.

"How long has she been missing?" Emily asked, over the racket of speeding horses.

"She hasn't been seen since yesterday afternoon," said Oliver. "We've been searching the grounds, but Ben thought you might have better luck, as the two of you have been thick as thieves lately."

Emily somewhat doubted this. She did not know the house and grounds any better than the rest of them, and while she and Grace had become relatively close in the time Emily had been at Fairmont House, Grace loved *all* the staff just as much, if not more.

"How is your sister?" Oliver said.

It sounded odd, coming from him. Too kind and earnest. It felt wrong that he even knew she *had* a sister. Emily wondered what else he might know by now, if the captain had shared what he'd learned about her just before she had fled back home.

"She will be all right." For some reason, saying it to him made it feel more true. "At the house, are they . . . ? Is Captain Edwards engaged?"

Oliver looked at her sideways, faint amusement playing about his mouth.

"Not yet," he said, which sort of answered her question, and sort of told her nothing at all.

He told her, instead, about the moment they'd realized Grace was gone, and all the places they had already checked. When she was caught up, they lapsed into silence. To Emily's surprise, it felt comforting to sit with him. Companionable.

When had *Oliver* become her *companion*?

Emily hadn't expected to be making this journey again, and it felt strange, as if she was stealing a glimpse of something she no longer had the right to. When they reached the familiar land around Fairmont, she almost didn't want to look at it, didn't want to acknowledge that she really had returned. She wanted it to feel natural when she slipped away again in a day or two, leaving no mark, and letting the house leave no mark on her.

When they entered, Meera met them, her usually neat hair in disarray and her mind clearly just as scattered.

"Oh! Amy, you're here!"

If Emily was still Amy to Meera, Captain Edwards must not have told anybody about her lies. Good. That was one less complication.

"If you just . . ." Meera's voice trailed off. "Sorry, the constable is here and I'm just bringing him some tea."

Emily couldn't help it; she flinched at the news that a man of the law was sitting in the drawing room, just a few feet away. It only occurred to her now that this all could have been a trap— Captain Edwards's way of luring her back here to be arrested, if Charles had become frustrated by her lack of attendance at the Rose and Crown this past week and decided to reveal her as a thief. Perhaps the captain *had* thought it of note that she had been using a false name, and was dragging her back here to face the consequences.

She took a step backward, feeling cornered, but then Aster

came rushing down the stairs two at a time, ran over to Emily, and actually gave her a brief, tight *hug*.

"You're back," he said. "Good. Where do you think she is?"

"Ah," Emily said, still reeling from the hug, watching as Meera bore the tea tray away into the drawing room for the constable. "I don't know."

"Oh," said Aster, deflating. "I thought for certain she might have said something to you. There's nowhere she likes to go to be alone? No secret hiding place?"

"She would have told *you*, if there were," said Emily. "Not me."

"I wouldn't be so sure." His lip was bleeding slightly, as if he'd been worrying at it with his teeth. "She keeps some things secret, even from me. She doesn't want to bother me. All right, Oliver— let's go back down to the beach and keep walking."

"She can't have made it very far," said Emily, thinking of that long stretch of coast—but Aster's face twisted into a pained grimace, and Emily realized that he wasn't entirely sure that they weren't looking for a *body*.

That threw everything into sharp relief, and Emily went hurriedly upstairs to put her trunk down in her old room. She stood in the hall, trying desperately to recall the conversations she'd had with Grace, even the most banal and mundane. There had been something about her mother, she thought—afternoons playing on the beach? But Aster and Oliver already had that covered.

It was useless to search the rooms of the house again, but she did. She paid special attention to the sort of nooks that might fit a Grace-sized person, even if they could not hold an adult: cupboards, sills, even the trunk in Meera's office, as if Meera would not have noticed Grace folding herself in. It was all for naught.

In the garden she met Joe, who was heading to the back road through the gate. There was a scattering of trees out there, but they were easy enough to search and had obviously been gone over before. Grace was not sitting on a branch like a pigeon. She was not curled in the hollow of a trunk like a woodland creature.

"Captain's in the village," Joe said grimly. "Mustering people to start walking the fields between, in case she tried to get there for some reason."

"Why would she go to the village?" said Emily, as they turned back toward the house, defeat in the sag of their shoulders.

"Don't know," said Joe. "Perhaps she was going after some-one."

His look at her was a little too pointed.

"Oh, don't. Do you know what's so . . . so hideous, so *vexing* about all this?" Emily said, as Joe held open the gate for her. "We probably would have *found* her already if she'd just been allowed to get a bloody dog."

"Hmmph," said Joe, which was his way of agreeing whole-heartedly.

Back at the house, Emily ascended the stairs to the servants' quarters at the top of the house. She would have felt bad about intruding into their rooms, but the doors had been left open, cupboards already thrown wide. There was no Grace to be found in any of them.

She was almost at the stairs, thinking that she would try to find Meera and ask what she should do next, when she happened to glance up at the battered wooden ladder resting lopsidedly against the wall at the end of the hall. If dragged upright, it would have led right up into the rafters themselves, a place Emily had never found cause to go.

Hadn't Grace once said something to her about the attic?

On instinct, Emily righted the ladder, grasped the rungs, and began to climb.

What she found was really no more than a crawl space, not big enough for an adult to stand upright and with only as much light as managed to creep in from below. There was a lantern, but it had burned out, and over by an assortment of crates and boxes, Emily found Grace curled up on what seemed to be a pile of dresses.

"Grace?" Emily said, her voice rising urgently.

She fell to her knees and forced herself to slow down and take stock: yes, Grace was breathing. No, she did not appear outwardly hurt.

"Grace," Emily said again, giving her a gentle shake. "Wake up."

"Oh," Grace said, rousing slowly and then squinting up at her dustily. "*Oh!* Amy!"

She threw herself at Emily, so that Emily had to catch her; they sat like that for a long minute, Grace apparently unwilling to let her go.

"What the hell are you doing up here?" said Emily, once Grace had finally relinquished her iron grip. "Everybody's looking for you. They sent for the constable!"

"Oh no," Grace said, her face crumpling. "I really didn't mean . . . I just wanted to come up here for a while to be alone, with Mama's things, and then I fell asleep after all that crying . . . but I must have done something wrong with the ladder, because it wasn't where I had left it, so I couldn't climb down. I did try calling for Meera and the others this morning, but I don't think they heard me."

"We'd better go and tell them you haven't drowned," Emily said. "Do you think you can make it down?"

"I want to stay a little longer," Grace said, going from sleepy to pouty in an instant.

"Oh, for God's sake," said Emily, her patience wearing thin. "What on earth for? I came all the way here to get you—I'm not leaving you up here covered in dust in an attic, and if I tell your father where you are, I'm sure he'll come and drag you down himself."

"Stop being horrid," Grace said. "It's not *you*."

"It most certainly *is* me," said Emily. "Look, I'm not going to be your governess anymore, Grace—"

"You're not?" said Grace, with a little intake of breath that half broke Emily's heart.

"No. I'm sorry. But it means I can finally speak plainly. I am rash and impatient, and I have a very short temper that you'd do best not to incur. Let's *go*."

To her surprise, Grace started laughing.

"What?"

"It's funny to me," Grace said breathlessly, "that you think you were *ever* not telling me things plainly. Or that you thought you hid your . . . your short *temper*. You are so silly."

"No, I'm not," Emily said.

She did *feel* somewhat silly, though, and confused—if Grace had seen her for what she was all along, why had she been so willing to love her?

"You are, I'm afraid," said Grace. All of a sudden, her laughter dissolved into tears; Emily was left with emotional whiplash, wondering how she had missed the signs. "Oh, goodness. I don't want you to leave. I don't want to go back downstairs. I don't want Father to marry Mrs. Spencer—I'm sure she's agreeable enough, but she has barely spoken a word to me. It would be like having a stranger in the house. She came to visit the other day, and then I overheard Akia talking to Meera about it. About how she is going to be my new *mother*."

Mrs. Spencer. Emily tried not to care, but she felt a stab of something in her chest that snagged and twisted. She was being foolish. What did it matter to her who the captain married, anyway? It was certainly never going to be her, and Mrs. Spencer was as good as anyone.

"You'll be fine. I was a stranger in the house. You liked me, even though you could apparently tell that I was dreadful from the off."

"Dreadful? No, you were never dreadful," said Grace. "Irascible, perhaps. Curmudgeonly. Cantankerous."

"This is not an exercise in vocabulary," grumbled Emily.

"Well," Grace said with a wet laugh, "*you'd* hardly recognize it, even if it were. You didn't teach us anything from the lesson books!"

"You don't need teaching," said Emily. "Well . . . not *vocabulary*, anyway. But clearly you have a lot to learn about common sense."

"I will come down when I'm ready," Grace said, a little sniffily, before leaning into misery again. "Amy, I am tired of everything being so hard. I miss Mama. And . . . I do not want to be ill. I do not want illness to be the first and last thing everybody sees when they look at me. I do not want to have *limits*, when I am only fourteen! I should be running about like a spring lamb. I should be . . . I don't know. What if *I* want to sneak down to the caves to meet girls from the village and drink spirits? How will I do that, if there's a chance I won't make it up the hill again?"

"Has Aster been doing that again?" Emily asked, briefly amused despite herself.

Grace sighed, and nodded.

"Well, I have no doubt that he'll volunteer to carry you, if you really do want to spend your evenings on a cold beach running your reputation into the ground. Your father, however, would *not* be amused."

"Amy—"

"Emily," said Emily, more gently than she thought herself

capable of being. "My name is Emily. My younger sister is called Amy. She's the one who was supposed to be your governess, and she would have done an absolutely marvelous job of it. She wouldn't have had screaming matches with Aster, or allowed swearing in the schoolroom. *She* would have done vocabulary exercises. But she's . . . she's been unwell, too, for quite a long time, so she couldn't make it. I came in her place. But Amy is *wonderful*, Grace, and being ill . . . It is usually the last thing you notice about her. Everybody loves her. She is kind, intelligent, wickedly funny . . . She never turns away a person in need . . . She *adores* children, which I have never understood and never will. Do not look at me like that, Grace—of course I like *you*, but you are barely a child anymore, you talk like you're fifty years old. I'd trust you to run the country. Anyway . . . I won't pretend to understand how you're feeling, but please just know that I do not think of you as *Grace, who is ill*, and neither does anybody else in this house. I think of you as . . . Grace, who is always open to making a new friend, who is quick-witted and an enormous pain in the neck, with an alarming passion for the frivolities of fashion and a wicked side she pretends does not exist. And . . . yes, besides those things, you are also ill."

"Emily?" Grace said slowly. "Your name is Emily?"

"Yes," said Emily, feeling her shoulders lighten. "It is."

"Was everything else you've said to me true?" said Grace, very seriously.

She was searching Emily's eyes, intent, leaving Emily no room to escape.

"Yes," she said. "Well . . . if you ever found me amenable or pleasant, that was me doing my best impression of my sister. And . . . I am not really a governess. I worked in a mill before I came here. But otherwise . . . I imagine so, yes."

"All right," said Grace, taking a deep breath and wiping her face delicately with her fingers.

There was a long pause before she spoke, and Emily could almost see the wheels turning in her mind. She was struck by the thought that she very desperately wanted Grace to know all this, and love her anyway.

"Emily," Grace said again. "I believe you. Despite what you might think, you *have* been a good governess, you know. The best I've ever had. And . . . and I think I'd like to go downstairs."

Chapter Twenty-seven

"BUT I DON'T UNDERSTAND." MEERA WAS STANDING BY THE fire, arms crossed, her face a kindly puzzle, but a puzzle nonetheless. "You are not who I was corresponding with?"

"No," said Emily.

She was sitting at the kitchen table with an untouched cup of tea in front of her, the household staff gathered around, staring at her as if she were on trial. Joe, at least, wasn't staring. He *was* chopping things aggressively, though, with the unspoken implication that after the radishes, she might be next.

"And your name is *Emily*?" said Akia.

"Yes," said Emily. "My sister is Amy. She's been unwell. She's the . . . She should have been here. Not me."

"Right," said Meera. "Well. I suppose—"

"Er . . . Excuse me," said Oliver. "No. We're not just going to let this go! She's been lying this entire time, and she accused *me* of being untrustworthy, and I refuse to walk away from this room without so much as a gentle bust-up."

"If you didn't want me back," said Emily, "you didn't have to come and fetch me."

Meera shook her head. "Not everything has to come to fisticuffs and dramatics, Oliver."

"I should have tipped you out of the carriage when we were going over the cliffs—"

"Perhaps you should have."

"Enough!" Meera exclaimed. "None of this is for us to decide.

Amy . . . Emily . . . *Miss Laurence*. Captain Edwards has finished speaking to Grace, and would like to see you in his study."

Emily sighed. She would rather they *had* just punched her or hurled her from the carriage. Anything was better than being forced to *talk* about it.

"That's right," said Akia, with a wink. "Belligerent sighing ought to get him on side. You are the very picture of penitence."

Emily wanted to direct quite a rude gesture at her, but Akia *had* been the one to make her the tea, and seemed to be taking the fact that Emily had lied about who she was very much in her stride.

"It is no different to me if your name begins with A or E," she'd said, when Grace had been returned to her proper place and Akia had shepherded Emily down to the kitchen to wait. "Did you accidentally take my scarf with you when you ran away, though? My neck's been cold."

Emily sort of wished Akia could have accompanied her now to the captain's study. The walk upstairs had never felt so long. She waited an age before knocking, and then immediately heard him say "Come in" from the other side of the door, as if he'd been aware of her standing there, just a few inches away from reentering his life.

He was dressed properly, formally—Emily hated that she was unable to rid the image of him looking quite the opposite from her mind, although at least it only flashed briefly before her eyes before she firmly pushed it away—but he looked hollowed out and weary. He must have been up all night looking for Grace. She wondered if he had shouted at her, or if he'd taken her into his arms and listened to her. Once, she would have assumed the former. Now she wasn't so sure.

"Take a seat," he said.

Emily did, but only because she had been planning on doing so anyway. He wasn't the only one who was tired.

"I didn't ask for your charity," she said, before he had a chance to speak again.

He paused, his brow furrowing, as if he had no earthly idea what she was talking about.

"Ah," he said eventually. "Well—"

"I know people like you think you can just throw money at things and the problems will go away, but that's not quite how it works. It might seem somewhat . . . *poetic* or heroic to you to try to save the day, but I can assure you that there is absolutely nothing romantic about any of this. And besides, I can look after my own sister."

"When did we commence arguing?" Captain Edwards said. "I must have missed the starting gun."

"I'm not stupid," Emily said, sitting up as straight as she could manage in this ridiculous soft chair. "You sent the doctor because of some . . . weight on your conscience, some passing guilt you felt after what happened at the ball, but there is no need. I am not so easy to hurt, sir. I can hand in my notice right now. We can part ways, and you can feel safe in the knowledge that I will never think of you again."

Captain Edwards let out a long breath, and for a second Emily thought he was going to bristle and snarl and join her at her level, which was hovering somewhere between rightfully angry and irrationally irate.

He did not.

"That is the last thing I want," he said. "And the last thing I intended. I sent the doctor in case he would be of any use. I did not mean it as an insult to you, or a comment on your ability to care for your sister. I know you are perfectly capable, Miss Laurence. And as for the ball—"

"Let's not talk about it," Emily said, her voice a little strangled.

"All right," Captain Edwards said slowly. "Then what *would* you like to discuss?"

"Me? I thought . . . Did you not summon me here to dismiss me?"

"Dismiss you?" said Captain Edwards. "How can I? You have just said that you wish to quit."

"But . . . you know I lied," Emily countered, all too aware that she was arguing against her own interests but unable to stop.

"Yes. Grace has just made clear some of the finer points."

"So you *know* I am not the governess you and Meera hired, and that I lied about my name, and came here under false pretenses."

"Yes," he said, infuriatingly calm. "I do. I know that you came here because your sister could not, to fill a post that desperately needed filling. I know that you have been taking care of the children, in your own way. They adore you—"

"They don't know any better."

"You and I both know *that's* not true," he said, with the hint of a laugh. "They are terribly discerning when it comes to governesses in particular. Aster, in fact, warned me before your arrival that if you were found wanting, he would set fire to your bed and give you a splendid Viking send-off. I believe he offered to play the horn."

"He probably thought you weren't listening."

"I was listening," said Captain Edwards. "I haven't always known . . . I *don't* always know how they would like me to respond. But I am trying. I have been trying."

"Fine," said Emily, unsure how they'd been blown so thoroughly off course. "All right. So we can consider this business . . . concluded."

"Actually," said Captain Edwards, "I wanted to ask if you'd reconsider."

"Reconsider what?"

"Staying."

"Don't be ridiculous," said Emily.

It had made so much sense to leave—why was he making this so *difficult*? They had kissed, she had rightfully departed, approximately half of her secrets had been laid bare, and now he wanted to rehash it all? Start again? If he knew how thoroughly Emily had almost betrayed him, he wouldn't be looking at her like that, stern and steady with a touch of fondness showing in the corners of his eyes and mouth. She could tell him now—tell him the entire truth of her meetings with Charles and the things she had buried down at the beach—and hope he at least gave her a head start when he called for the constable to turn around and come right back.

Even with such a surprising capacity for forgiveness, he would need to draw the line somewhere, and Emily would only half hate him for it.

"Emily," he said, and hearing him say her true name was wonderful and excruciating. "You kissed me."

Emily burned with shame. Because it was true—she *had* been the one to kiss him. He had asked her to dance, he had been the one on the verge of proposing something far more indecent, but she could not pretend that he had made advances on her out of nowhere and that she had rejected him out of hand, even if that did make more sense to her than what had really happened. She had touched him first. She had lifted her head so that he could meet her.

"I told you I didn't want to talk about that."

"Then don't talk."

The atmosphere had been slipping sideways, but suddenly it fell off a cliff into dangerous waters. His gaze was burning into her from the other side of the desk. He was watching her intently, waiting for her to react. To make a move.

To kiss him, Emily thought, and then she let out a breath of a laugh. She was angry again. Good. She could use that.

"What . . . ? Are you asking me to do it again? Now? Here? I know I am too old to be courted, Captain Edwards, but that does not mean I am happy to throw everything away so that I might entertain you while you wait to marry."

"That's not—"

"Or do you wish to marry *me*? To take your governess to wife because for some ungodly reason you like it when we scrap? To throw away *your* reputation, when I know it is in such desperate need of shoring up?"

He stared at her. "Would that be so absurd?"

"*Yes*," Emily said, feeling winded. "It is absurd. Captain—"

"My name is Ben," he said, each word carefully enunciated. Why was he so insistent on all this unendurable eye contact?

"I am not going to call you *Ben!*" Emily shouted. "And we both know I am never going to be your *wife*, so let's end this now and be done with it."

"Emily—"

"*Captain Edwards.*" She said it with finality, and he made a small frustrated noise and then relented, leaning back in his chair and observing her with open incredulity.

Of course he would think he was offering her something wonderful: a dalliance with him; empty promises of matrimony. Emily just wasn't foolish enough to believe it would ever end well for somebody like her. Even if Captain Edwards did prove to be the ridiculous sort of romantic who'd try to do right by her—next to impossible—Charles from the Rose and Crown could put a stop to any happiness as soon as it dared to bloom.

"It seems," he said, "that I have once again misconstrued the situation. I will let it rest. But I will not rescind my invitation for you to stay. Grace and Aster would like to continue their education with you."

"What education?" Emily said derisively.

"Grace has never been allowed to spend so long reading the books she is truly interested in," Captain Edwards said, his voice like cut glass now. "And Aster has been enjoying spending time focused on his painting. I have high hopes that he might benefit from the proximity to you and Grace and absorb some knowledge accidentally."

"If he learns anything from me," said Emily, "it certainly will be an accident."

"Stop trying to talk everybody in this house out of wanting you," Captain Edwards said sharply. "Will you stay or not?"

He'd be married sooner rather than later, Emily thought suddenly. He was clearly desperate for companionship, and now that she had rebuffed his farce of an offer, he'd marry Augusta Spencer and the children would have somebody mother-shaped again and wouldn't need her. It might only take a month—two, at most.

Another two months' wages was hard to refuse. Amy was doing better, but there was no saying whether it would last, or how long it would be before she could work again. Charles might know her real name, but now so did everybody in Fairmont—perhaps with less ammunition to use against her, and with no more information forthcoming from her, he would divert his energy elsewhere. Perhaps he thought her a fool, incapable of following basic directions to a desk drawer, and no longer a worthy partner in crime. Perhaps he had given up on the whole endeavor entirely. Once Mrs. Spencer was the new Mrs. Edwards, she could cut herself free from this place without anybody coming to drag her back again.

"I will stay a little while longer," said Emily, and Captain Edwards nodded. He seemed reluctant to speak again, as if by opening his mouth he might scare her away. Presumably, she was dismissed.

She got up immediately and went from the room, hearing what sounded like an abrupt, exasperated sigh as she closed the door behind her.

Chapter Twenty-eight

"Oh, look," said Oliver, when Emily returned to the kitchen. "It's Emily the liar! Have a drink."

It was barely evening, certainly not the end of the working day, but Meera didn't seem to mind. She was, in fact, also holding a glass of wine.

"Are you double-dismissed?" Oliver said cheerfully, handing Emily a drink while she stood frozen by the table, feeling wrong-footed and confused. "I . . . I was never dismissed," she said haltingly. "I left of my own accord."

"That's the spirit," said Oliver. "Now, I know you're a sensitive soul, open and loving and prone to hysterics, but do try to keep a stiff upper lip—we have something for you."

"Something for me?" said Emily, wary.

"Oh, it's not much. Oliver, you shouldn't have said anything," said Meera crossly. "We just thought . . . Oliver told us what you said, about leaving, and we thought you might be going tomorrow, so we pulled together some . . . for you and your sister, you know, because she hasn't been well . . . It's not much, but—"

"For God's sake, Meera," said Akia. "You're downplaying it so much she's going to expect a turd in a basket. It's just some food and things."

Meera put down her drink and went to fetch it.

It was *not* just some food and things. It was an enormous basket overflowing with supplies.

"I told Captain Edwards I didn't want any—"

"Ben isn't getting the credit for this," Oliver said scornfully. "*We* did this. Don't pull that face at me, Meera—I am *not* going to do a good deed and not be lauded for it. I am only *in* it for the lauding."

Emily reached for the basket, running her hand over the things inside. Her fingers landed on some handmade mittens, and she thought of Amy's cold, narrow fingers by the fire in winter, the way that she could never quite get them warm, as if her blood had better places to be.

She burst into tears.

It was the most mortifying thing that had ever happened to her, and she immediately tried to get up and leave, but Meera came to envelop her in a hug and she found herself trapped there, sobbing a wet patch onto the housekeeper's shoulder.

"There, there," Meera said, rubbing her back, "it's all right. Nobody's looking."

"I'm looking," said Oliver. "Jesus Christ, I was joking about the hysterics, Emily."

"Shut up, Oliver," Akia said pleasantly. "Have another drink."

Emily wished they wouldn't insist on being so kind to her—even Oliver, in his own way, although it might have looked like pure belligerence to anybody else. It was unbearable. She wasn't crying just because of Captain Edwards, or the gift basket, or even the niggling worry of Charles at the Rose and Crown—it was the *too-much-ness* of it all: the unendurable weight of everything, the thought of Amy exclaiming in delight over those mittens and wearing them until they wore out, if they were all very lucky, and the knowledge that even if life was hard and devastating and unfair, Emily would have to get back up and endure it anyway. She had never *stopped* enduring it; her worry about the Laurence family's survival was a constant background hum that plagued her days and her nights equally, and she was so very tired of it all.

"Let's have another drink," said Meera, and Emily found herself released from the housekeeper's iron grip and free to run for the door.

She sat down in a chair instead, and wiped her eyes on her sleeve. At Meera's prompting, she downed her first glass of wine in one gulp, and almost managed to smile when Akia refilled it.

"I gave a man a fake name once," Akia said, with a wistful smile.

"Oh, here we go," said Oliver.

"Fine, then, I shan't tell it."

"No," said Emily, desperate for some levity. "Please do."

"It was at my last house, and there was a gentleman who was the son of some wealthy old merchant who often used to visit . . . He hated socializing and would hide during the dinner parties until his father came to drag him out. I would often spot him curled up behind a curtain or sitting behind a side table and leave him a drink. One night he heard me placing a glass on the other side of the curtain and he asked me to stay and talk, so I did, and then it became a habit of ours, conversing through the fabric whenever I could find the time . . . We became rather good friends. I thought he might end our acquaintance if I told him who I truly was, so I told him I was called Lady Hestia for some reason, and he said his name was Bill. Of course, it turned out that he knew who I was all along, because the week I handed in my notice he stopped me in the hallway and gave me a letter addressed to Lady Hestia, and said he would miss our little chats, and that I had given him the courage to try life on the other side of the curtain. I do wonder how he is, sometimes. I still call him Bill in my head, although I always knew his name was actually Theophilus Elderspot."

"But . . . that wasn't funny at all," Emily said, her throat feeling dangerously tight again.

"No," said Meera. "That was actually very lovely."

"There is no need to seem so surprised," said Akia. "*I* am very lovely."

"This is why you should almost *always* lie," said Oliver. "If it's not funny, at least it's interesting. Except when you do it, obviously, Emily."

This exchange had given Emily enough time to drink another half a glass of wine and compose herself.

"I didn't mean to put you in a difficult position," she said, mostly to Meera. "By lying, I mean."

"What was the captain's verdict?" said Meera.

"He wants me to stay," said Emily.

"What's yours?" Joe said from behind her.

Emily had forgotten he was in the room, and did her best impression of a cat startled by a cucumber.

"Um . . ." she said, when her heart had ceased racing. "Staying. For now."

Joe nodded. "That's decided, then. Two chickens tonight, Meera."

"Two chickens," Meera repeated, patting Emily on the hand and giving her an encouraging smile.

Chapter Twenty-nine

"MRS. SPENCER SPEAKS FRENCH," GRACE SAID, AS SHE SAT sandwiched between Aster and Emily, all three of them painting. Well . . . the children were painting. Emily was occasionally letting her brush wander across the page by accident, and had produced something that looked like the visual representation of a headache. "And Spanish. She told me so."

"Delightful," said Aster, head down over an arresting painting that was vaguely nautical. "She can condescend to us in three languages, then."

"Aster, I have made up my mind to be very grown-up about this," Grace said reprovingly. "I would appreciate it if you did the same."

"*Oui, madame*," said Aster. "You're missing out the most important detail, though."

"What's that?"

"She has a dog."

"She has a *what*?" Grace shrieked, almost upsetting her water glass. "What sort of dog is it? How tall? What color? Is it a puppy? How many legs?"

"Just the one," said Aster. "A miracle and a tragedy."

"Don't be such a broken brick, Aster! Did you see the dog? Was it here?"

"When would I have seen the dog?" Aster said, the tip of his tongue sticking out as he spread dark paint with a flourish. "I don't exist, remember?"

Grace had explained to Emily in a rush before Aster arrived in the schoolroom that news of Aster's gentlemanhood had not yet been broken to Mrs. Spencer, or to anybody outside Fairmont House, and that they intended it to stay that way for the time being. Emily wondered if Mrs. Spencer was the type to reject a proposal because of such news. Captain Edwards certainly did not seem the sort to feel embarrassed or ashamed of it.

"She's coming again tomorrow," Grace said. "I do *so* hope she brings it! Perhaps I could ask Father to write to her and request that the dog comes? Expressly invite it?"

"You do that," said Aster. "Emily, does this look like a seagull or a cloud? No, wait, don't tell me—I actually think it's better this way."

It looked like half a spider.

Emily put down her paintbrush and cleared her throat.

"Mrs. Spencer is coming tomorrow?"

"Yes," said Grace. "And I think *this time* he really will ask her to marry him."

"Father invited her and a few other dullards for dinner," said Aster. "Why such interest, Emily? Do you plan to arm wrestle her for Father's love? Between you and me, I think you'd win. He likes you."

"Aster," Emily said sharply.

"Are you really in love with Father?" Grace said, abandoning her own painting, which had been a rather upsetting portrait of Emily.

"No," Emily said firmly. "And Aster should stop joking about it, because it's completely inappropriate and deeply unfunny."

"It's medium funny," said Aster. "More so when you go all red and start spluttering denials."

"I would root for you in the arm wrestling," Grace said thoughtfully. "Although . . . I could do it in better conscience if you had a dog."

"Forget the dog," said Aster. "It's a fortune Father needs."

"Don't say such dreadful things, Aster! I'm sure he wants to fall in love. Emily, if you *do* wrestle—"

"There will be no wrestling of any kind," said Emily. "And we should stop speculating about your father's private business. Finish your paintings."

"Mine feels passé to me now," Grace sighed. "Shall we practice our French?"

"Go on, then," said Aster.

"*Où est votre chien?*" said Grace, her accent perfect. "*Quel est le nom de votre chien? Puis-je s'il vous plaît caresser votre chien?*"*

"*Où sont les autres pattes de votre chien?*"† said Aster.

"Aster," said Grace. "I *said* don't be *une brique*."‡

Emily was distracted all day; so distracted, in fact, that when her lessons were finished and she was making her way downstairs to the kitchen, she almost bumped into Captain Edwards in the entrance hall. Every time she thought of him, she was catapulted back into his study and thoroughly tormented by the memory of their last encounter—his poorly judged flirting, her rather effective shouting—so the idea of having to make polite small talk was about as appealing to her as the garlic paste Oliver had been hand-feeding to the sickly horse in the stable.

Emily managed to stop before he noticed her, but had to stay completely still to avoid detection, which meant she was watching from the stairs like an alarmed gargoyle as he crossed to the mirror to stare dispassionately at his reflection.

He looked as good as he always did, dressed for formality, but

---

* "Where's your dog? What is your dog's name? Can I please pet your dog?"
† "Where are your dog's other paws?"
‡ A brick.

apparently he seemed to find something wanting; he pushed a lock of mostly gray hair away from his face and straightened his collar, then sighed quietly.

His demeanor was more fitting for somebody about to go into battle or do Oliver's horse paste duties than a man on the verge of proposing. Emily lingered for longer than she should have, captivated by the sight of him without his armor on, wondering if he was giving himself some sort of motivational speech in his head as his eyes searched his own face and his brow furrowed.

If there *had* been a speech, apparently it had worked. He put his shoulders back, returned his expression to careful neutrality, and then went on his way.

Emily stopped to look at her own reflection in the mirror on her way past, but quickly thought better of it when she saw the state of her hair, and hurried off to the kitchen to help Meera with preparations for dinner.

Later that evening, when the guests had arrived, Emily ushered Grace down to be presented in the drawing room. They left Aster happily ensconced in his room with his painting and some pilfered ginger ale, tunelessly humming something that Emily highly suspected was a very bawdy drinking song.

Emily hadn't bothered asking Grace not to bring up the dog, as it seemed very important to her, but she did feel a twinge of regret when they entered the drawing room and Grace navigated a small clutch of men in their most expensive autumn suits and made a beeline for Mrs. Augusta Spencer as if they had debts to settle.

Mrs. Spencer, to her credit, took it in her stride. She was wearing a shade of puce that would have made Emily look like a corpse, but she somehow looked well in it.

"Good evening, Mrs. Spencer," Grace said, with a perfect curtsy. "I hope you are well. And I hope that your dog is well."

"My . . . dog is very well," said Mrs. Spencer, with a slightly confused smile.

"We can continue to converse in French, if you wish," Grace said, so seriously that the two men standing with Captain Edwards laughed.

"*Français, ma chérie?*"

"*Oui*," said Grace. "*J'adore les chiens.*"*

"Your accent is wonderful. Your governess has taught you well."

"Oh, no, Emily doesn't teach me French," Grace said, laughing as if Mrs. Spencer would be in on the joke.

"What does she teach you, then?" said Mrs. Spencer, smiling at Emily, who almost wished for another shipwreck to save her from this conversation urgently.

"Arguing, mostly," said Grace. "And a bit of thinking. The other day she told me you can open almost any locked door with the right size of hairpin."

"I think Mrs. Spencer has heard enough, Grace," Emily said, over the sound of more gentlemanly guffaws.

She dared glance at Captain Edwards and saw that he was affecting disapproval but had covered his mouth with a gloved hand, as if he might actually be smiling a little behind it.

"I haven't asked her how many legs her dog has yet," Grace said, in an attempt at a whisper that carried magnificently.

Emily finally managed to usher her from the drawing room and back up to the schoolroom, where Grace sat by the fire and read an apparently very amusing French book, and tried very falteringly to translate the jokes to Emily until it was time to go to bed.

Emily felt too antsy to go to bed herself, even though Meera had assured her that they could go without her help for one small

---

* "I love dogs."

dinner party. Instead, she wandered through the kitchen and immediately got into Joe's way, which hastened her out of the door and into the grounds.

It was still light outside, the sky a milky sort of lavender, as Emily walked a loop of the house. She should have felt somewhat settled, now that she had a plan in place to stay at Fairmont a while longer and then slip out once she was no longer needed, but she had been feeling unaccountably *fidgety* and agitated since her conversation with Captain Edwards. Going home to her family had felt like the end of something; returning was like opening the door again, when she had intended to keep it firmly shut. The problem was that she had glimpsed something through that door, and now it was impossible to pretend she hadn't.

It was sort of like when she had seen the captain without his shirt, except that this glimpsing was metaphorical, and the captain sans shirt had been *very* real . . .

"Good evening," said a woman's voice.

Emily jumped, and then internally chastised herself. She had let her guard down so thoroughly since arriving at Fairmont House that there could have been an entire regiment of officers standing on the back steps waiting to arrest her and she wouldn't have noticed.

It wasn't an entire regiment of officers, though. It was Mrs. Augusta Spencer. She had a shawl draped over her shoulders, and she was smoking a pipe.

"Terrible habit, I know," she said, wrinkling her beautiful nose. "Not at all proper, but it does calm my nerves. Do you want . . . ?"

She seemed to be offering Emily the pipe. Emily was almost too shocked to say no, but when she eventually managed to shake her head, Mrs. Spencer just shrugged genially.

"You're the governess, aren't you?"

"Miss Laurence," said Emily.

"Ah," said Mrs. Spencer. "I remember."

She took a deep drag on her pipe, and then expelled a large cloud of smoke like a silk-clad chimney.

"What are the children really like?" she asked. "Don't coddle me—I'd love to know."

"They're . . . good," said Emily. "Well, Aster can be pigheaded and Grace sometimes veers toward the ridiculous, but if you don't mind that, they are perfectly pleasant."

"Not a coddler, then," said Mrs. Spencer, amused. "Does that mean you're the nasty sort? My governesses were always one of the two."

"If those are the only options, then . . . probably," said Emily, and she sounded so glum that Mrs. Spencer laughed.

"I was testing you. I know you aren't nasty, and now I know you're humble to boot. Captain Edwards says he cannot imagine the house without you." She was looking out over the grounds in the failing light, with a smile that seemed to be fading just as rapidly. "I suppose it would have been all right here. Ah, well."

Emily did not attempt to parse her meaning; she was still reeling from the thought that Captain Edwards had been *discussing* her with this woman.

"Do you plan to stay on, for the long haul?"

"Oh, no," said Emily. "Only to see Captain Edwards married. I suppose that works out well—you can vet the next governess yourself."

She laughed. It sounded like wind chimes.

"Why on earth would I do that?"

"I thought you were . . . engaged to be married," Emily said, stumbling over her words slightly. "Or that you intended to be so, soon."

"Ah . . . no," said Mrs. Spencer. "Not at all, actually. I cannot even remember whose idea it was in the first place, because neither of us have ever been particularly keen. Still, we did insist on being sensible and *talking* about it. We entertained the idea for a while, but we have decided against it." She sighed. "I'm afraid I tend to prefer horrible men."

Emily blinked, taken aback by this sudden turn.

"And you don't think he's . . . horrible enough?"

"Good heavens, no. Not an ounce."

"Oh," said Emily. "I see."

"Well, you *do* see, don't you? The people who work in houses like this always do. My lady's maid would tell you that I'm difficult, spoiled . . . set in my ways. She could have told me it was never going to work out. It's been six years since my husband died, and while I didn't enjoy burying him, I am adjusting rather well to the rest." Mrs. Spencer put down her pipe and sighed, stretching her arms indulgently. It made her look like a very attractive cat. "What about you? What would *you* say about the master of the house?"

"Nothing," said Emily.

"Well, very good, then. He's lucky to have you. He talks a lot about what a boon you've been for the children—I know he will find it very difficult to lose you. I suppose . . . I suppose eventually he'll find somebody strong and spirited to marry. That's what he needs—a bit of fire, a bit of cheering up. I've never seen somebody so terribly, obviously *sad*."

When she got to her feet, the movement was so graceful she seemed to be flowing, like water. Emily found herself quite captivated.

"Good evening, Miss Laurence. Be careful if you're going to stay out here—there's a very hungry-looking woodlouse on the rail just by your left elbow."

Emily sat down on the steps Mrs. Spencer had vacated, and although she remained unmolested by the woodlouse, she felt just as shaken and out of sorts as if she had been.

Chapter Thirty

Aster was still awake when Emily went to check on the children, a habit she had picked up since *both* of them had gone missing from their beds on separate occasions.

"He isn't engaged, is he," Aster said conversationally, when Emily opened his door a crack to find him sitting by the fire still dressed, scratching out a letter with very haphazard handwriting.

"No," said Emily, without thinking. "Well . . . I shouldn't think so."

"I knew it," Aster said, with distracted triumph. "Damn. This ink is too . . . inky."

"Aster," Emily said. "When you were . . . Before, when you were saying . . . with the arm wrestling. You were . . . jesting, weren't you?"

"I didn't actually think you were going to arm wrestle her, if that's what you're asking," said Aster. "But no, I was perfectly serious about the rest."

"What rest?" said Emily, with great trepidation.

"Oh, that you are secretly madly in love with Father, and that he obviously feels the same about you, and the two of you are enacting some sort of dramatic Shakespearean play where you are kept apart by class and station and other reasons that are sort of silly, in the end."

"Differences in class and station are not . . . *silly*," Emily said faintly. "This country is obsessed with them."

"Oh, well, yes, but it is also obsessed with manners, and teaching ladies nothing and gentlemen the worst parts of everything, and ensuring that everybody is in the *proper* clothes, and designating anything even the slightest bit different as *evil*. You cannot let what people *think* dictate how you live your life—nobody would ever do anything interesting. And when it comes to love . . . you know. The heart wants what it wants. And the heart is also terminally stupid. A dangerous combination."

"You're wrong," Emily said. "About all of it. There's no Shakespeare, there's no . . . *love*."

"That's just what the character in the play would say right about now," said Aster. "Although I imagine it'd be much less pithy. They do tend to drone on. Close the door on your way out, will you? I need to finish writing this letter soon or I will be in terrible trouble."

"Trouble with whom?"

Aster smiled a horrible, leonine grin. "One of my *many* admirers."

"Ugh," said Emily, which was irritating, because it was just what Aster *wanted* her to say.

Once out in the hallway, she leaned against the wall and closed her eyes, listening to the sound of people saying their goodbyes down by the front door. She heard Mrs. Spencer's lilting, velvety voice above the hubbub, saying that the captain *must* thank the cook for her. She could only imagine how red in the face Joe would get if Captain Edwards did march down to the kitchens to convey her effusive thanks. She wondered how the captain was feeling; relieved, perhaps, as he said farewell to his guests? Would he go to his study, loosen his stock, and pour himself a drink? She thought of how he had looked before the party, tired and strained and completely without pretense, and felt a strange sort of protectiveness in his direction, which was ridiculous. He did not need protecting, and *Emily* was not qualified to be his knight in secondhand armor even if he did.

Aster had got it all wrong. She was not in *love* with Captain Edwards, and the idea that he might feel anything beyond vaguely attracted to her as a person-shaped diversion was fanciful at best. Emotions had been running too high in this house, and things had become muddled.

Besides, wanting to kiss somebody was not the same as being in love with them. Even if you wanted to kiss them very, very badly . . . and worse still, wanted to ask them what was wrong, and actually cared about the answer. She could go to him now, in his study; knock on the door and feel sure that he would grant her entrance, even if it was technically very untoward; sit down in the chair opposite him, ask for a drink of her own; and then perhaps pick a small fight with him to get things going . . .

"Are you napping?" said Akia. Emily jumped a little, opening her eyes to find that Akia was offering her a letter. "I thought only large animals were able to sleep standing up. Horses. Elephants."

"Birds," said Emily, taking the letter.

"Don't be a fool, Emily, elephants aren't birds," said Akia, looking pleased with herself. "I think they might actually be very large, hairless cats. That just came for you."

The letter was not written in any hand Emily recognized; she thanked Akia absentmindedly and opened it as she walked, unfolding it as she entered her bedroom.

Miss Emily Laurence,

I cannot help but notice that you failed to make our last appointment. It is my fault for not making myself clear: the consequences should you fail to attend again will be far more severe. I still have something of yours—or, not of yours—in my possession.

It is in both of our best interests for us to continue our friendship.

I will see you on Saturday. Don't forget. I certainly will not.

Please send my regards to your sister.

Emily had not even closed the door. She did so as if in a trance, and then sat down heavily on the end of her bed.

She had completely misconstrued the situation, and her position in it. She had thought that Charles might write her off completely and move on to some more fruitful endeavor with a better chance of return; that he might have sold the box she had given him, and therefore had nothing left to hold over her.

She had underestimated his doggedness, and perhaps too the strength of his vendetta against the captain. He was not going to let this go. She was not free after all. Perhaps she never could be.

The letter crumpled in her fist as she tried to remember to breathe. She usually kept such a tight grip on herself that it was deeply alarming to find her thoughts spiraling out of control. Why had she ever thought herself clever enough to get away with any of this? What rank foolishness had led her here? She had always been able to find answers and solutions, and had thought that it proved that she was *sturdy* and *capable* in ways her father never had been, but now it was becoming startlingly clear to her that she had only ever been an idiot, mere moments from disaster.

Amy. She had done it for *Amy*. But that felt foolish now, too: the plan of a child, to snatch and grab and run, rather than to be sensible and keep her head as her sister would have done.

She was being blackmailed by a known blackmailer. She wanted to kick herself almost as much as she wanted to kick him.

She scanned the letter again. The part about the box was clear enough. If she did not go to him with the evidence he had demanded to damn Captain Edwards, he would reveal her to be a thief. After how kind Meera and the others had been to her, the thought tore through her like the slip of a knife. They might have been lenient at Fairmont, but breaking the trust of everybody within and stealing something of immense value was not a small transgression that could be easily ignored. And if Charles told the captain how readily she had agreed to uncover and profit from his secrets . . .

It was more than enough reason for them to want to package her up in light restraints, deliver her personally to the constable, and then wash their hands of her completely.

Without Emily, Amy and her mother would be in real danger, neither of them able to find the sort of work Emily could. There would be no more doctors, no more good food—no more food at all.

That could not be allowed to happen.

Emily packed quietly. It wasn't hard; she hadn't been back long enough to truly spread herself out across the room and claim it as hers again. She felt a little sick every time she looked at the hamper of goods that she had placed on the dresser, ready to be sent home. She would deliver it herself now, along with the news that they should urgently look for other lodgings, lest someone come looking for her. She was not going to underestimate Charles ever again.

It would not be so bad to leave their house. There were other mills where Emily could find work; places where she could start again. Perhaps they could even move closer to the sea, and Amy could finally stand in the surf and breathe in the spray herself. This was what Emily focused on as she folded her things with shaking hands, and then closed the trunk and tucked it behind the door.

Just before dawn would be best. She could be up and out before the others awoke, and by the time she had walked to the village it would not be long until the regular post came to take her away. They would assume her still abed. She might be well on her way by the time Akia knocked on her door to inquire if she'd be bothering to do her job that day.

It was unpleasant to imagine anything further, so she didn't.

She tried to harden her heart against Fairmont and the people inside it, the way it had been so easy to do when she first arrived—

the way she had been doing her entire life—but this time it didn't work. The comforting numbness would not come. As she lay in her bed, far too worked up to sleep, she was plagued by the stirrings of a dangerous thought. When she let it break free, it threatened to engulf her.

Why shouldn't she have something for herself, just this once, before everything came tumbling down?

It didn't matter if she wasn't destined to be some swooning heroine in a play, the way Aster had described it; if nobody would ever cast her as the recipient of true, passionate love. That had never been her fate anyway.

She almost didn't realize where her feet were taking her until she found herself outside the captain's study. When she knocked, there was no answer. When she pushed the door open, she found the room dark, the fire burned down to chalky embers.

He wasn't lingering in either of the drawing rooms. He wasn't anywhere to be found on the ground floor as a whole. With a sense of purpose that made no earthly sense, Emily walked the second floor corridor until she came to a stop by a door she had never approached before.

The captain was still dressed when he answered it, which was a small mercy.

"What is it?" he said. "Aster? Grace?"

"No," said Emily. "I just . . . wanted to talk to you."

To his credit, he acted as if she had approached him politely in his study at two o'clock in the afternoon, not appeared outside his bedroom door past midnight with a look in her eye like a fox bedeviling a rabbit. When she stepped past him into the room, he looked mildly suspicious, as if this might all be part of some elaborate prank—but when she came to a stop in the middle of the room with her arms folded, he let go of the door and walked warily toward her.

His room was rather plain. Emily wondered if it had been a

guest room at one point, because there were hardly any flourishes at all. The bed seemed good quality, the curtains thick and dark, but there was not much to recommend it otherwise. The wallpaper looked deep, turbulent blue in the low light, and Emily found herself looking at it rather than at the captain while she tried to gather her faculties to speak.

"You and Mrs. Spencer should be engaged," she said.

He actually *rolled his eyes* at her like a petulant child and went to sit down at his dressing table, as if she weren't there at all.

"Should we indeed?" he said. "Well, I am terribly sorry to disappoint you."

"I only meant to stay until you were married," Emily plowed on, "but now that there are no plans for a wedding, I cannot just wait around until you manage to find another heiress who suits your purpose."

"Fine," said Captain Edwards.

"As long as you understand—"

"Miss Laurence," Captain Edwards said, turning to look at her from his chair. "I most certainly do *not* understand, and likely never will. You seem determined to run from my house, even when you have so recently agreed to stay, and I will not ask you to extend your suffering if it is still so disagreeable to you. If you wish to go, then *go*. I have made my own wishes perfectly clear."

It was her cue to leave. She didn't.

"Your wish for me to stay?"

"Yes."

"For the children?"

"Yes."

"And . . . for your own . . . entertainment."

Captain Edwards stood up. "For God's sake, Emily."

Emily. There was still something so weighty about hearing him say her real name; it sank into her chest and lit her on fire. It made her want to fight him harder.

"You were all too happy to speak plainly about this before—"

"I told you I would let it lie," Captain Edwards said, his voice rising. "I said I had misunderstood, I apologized, and I don't understand why you insist on bringing this up again unless it is to humiliate me."

"To humiliate *you*?"

"I made it perfectly clear that I loved you, and you made it equally clear that my feelings were not returned!"

This was delivered with such force that, for a moment, Emily was trying to work out exactly how she had been insulted. When she realized what he had actually said, she gaped openly at him, incensed.

"You most certainly did *not*," she exclaimed, when she was able. "At which point did you think you were telling me you loved me? Was it when you were trying to *seduce* me in your study? Was it when you were making preposterous noises about *marriage*, a promise you could never hope to keep?"

"Yes," Captain Edwards said forcefully. "When I asked you to dance, and I asked you to stay, and when I wanted to kiss you, I was telling you and *telling* you. And . . . if you had let me, I would have told you that the idea of the two of us, betrothed, does not seem preposterous to me at all."

Emily felt a little sick. "Well, it *is* preposterous. You need . . . You need *funds*. Someone of status. I cannot give you anything at all."

"If you don't want me, Emily, then why are you still standing here at all?"

She did want him. Obviously. But she had told him too many lies for there to ever be anything real between them. It was impossible, and the impossibility of it was breaking her heart.

She had never before been sorry for anything she'd done to help her family, to help Amy—but standing there, she wished she could turn back the clock and refuse Charles's offer; that she could put that hideous baroque box back on the shelf where it belonged. Captain Edwards was trying to give her something she thought she had never wanted for herself. Now that it was within reach, she knew the truth—that she had told herself she needed nothing, again and again, so that it didn't hurt when her hands remained empty.

"You know me to be a liar," she said, trying to keep her voice steady. "You know I came into this house under a false name, under false pretenses—and you think you *love* me?"

"What I *know* is that you are prickly, stubborn—funny when you want to be, and cutting when you don't. I know that you care very deeply for people, and I know that you want to kill me for saying so. I know that this house felt empty without you while you were gone. Are you trying to tell me that all of that is a lie?"

"No," said Emily, shaking her head. "But you don't understand. There are things that I have done that you would not so easily forgive—"

"I think you would say anything to try to dissuade me. That perhaps you find it almost . . . repulsive that I am *not* to be dissuaded."

"Yes," Emily said. "Yes, I do, because it is foolish of you to think that you know me or could *love* me after a few months of my acquaintance, and doubly foolish for you to think you know the depths of my sins. I could have killed a man!"

Captain Edwards laughed, a little huff of disbelief, and it broke the escalating tension somewhat. "*Have* you killed a man?"

"No!"

He stepped toward her. "Do you want to tell me what it is you've done that you think is so unforgivable?"

She did. She wanted to tell him, so that it could be done with and he could go ahead and start hating her, but she was feeling weak and tired and at war with herself with no idea what each side was actually fighting for.

". . . No."

"Then let me ask you, now that you know exactly how I feel with no room for misunderstandings—what do you want, Emily?"

She did not know herself, or have a hope of putting anything she was feeling into words—so she kissed him. Again.

She was not unaware of the fact that it was a very bad idea, or that it was becoming somewhat of a pattern, but it was hard to think too much about the morality of it all when he immediately pulled her into his chest and held her there, as if he'd simply wanted to embrace her as much as he'd wanted to kiss her. It was too sweet, too kind—and Emily didn't feel worthy of either of those things.

She kissed him hard, and pressed herself closer, and felt his breath catch in his chest as her hands found their way up into his hair. She found that she liked knowing that she could do this to him—that she could bite down gently on his lip and feel him shudder in response, and that when she pulled away, his eyes flew open so that he could look at her, fierce and molten.

"What are you doing?" he said, the words coming out in a gruff half whisper.

"What I want," said Emily.

She walked him backward to the edge of his bed, and marveled at how willingly he went, how easy it was to move this man so much taller and broader than her; he was watching her carefully as he sat down, following her lead, and yet he sounded so surprised when she sank down onto his lap that she could have laughed.

She *did* laugh. It sounded breathless and wild, and nothing like her.

"Emily—"

"Captain."

"For the love of God, call me Ben."

"All right," Emily said. "*Ben.*"

The sound of his name on her lips seemed to have the same effect she'd experienced when he called her *Emily*, because he let slip a groan that made her feel reckless and stupid. Or—even *more* reckless and stupid, because nothing she was doing made sense. What could possibly be compelling her to put a hand to his jaw and tilt it up toward her so that she could kiss him, soft and slow, until he grew impatient, just like she hoped he would, and surged up to meet her properly? Why was she easing the jacket from his shoulders, and then unbuttoning his waistcoat, so that she could run her hands over his thin shirt and better feel the rapid rise and fall of his chest?

Captain Edwards—*Ben*—pulled back only so that he could kiss her lightly on the jaw, and then her neck, and she found herself tilting her head back and leaning into his hands, which were holding her fast by the waist.

"Emily," he murmured, "you're—"

"Don't," Emily said. "No words."

"But I—"

"I can't marry you," she said, in a breathy rush.

He stilled and moved to look up at her, his hair mussed, his eyes intent on hers; it was agony.

"Then you should probably remove yourself from my lap."

He didn't let go of her waist, and she didn't get up; they just looked at each other, at an impasse, neither willing to move an inch, until Emily shifted against him almost by accident and he responded with another low, involuntary noise that made her want to *eat* him.

His hand dropped to her thigh, and for a moment it was all she could feel—his palm on her skin, caught maddeningly between desperation and restraint.

It was baffling. It was intoxicating.

"Do you really want me to leave?" she said.

She knew his *body's* answer, if not his mind's; he was leaning toward her even as he ordered her away, as if the message hadn't managed to reach his limbs yet.

"Obviously not," said Captain Edwards, very strained. "But I am not a . . . a thoughtless cad of twenty, who would shame you for the sake of my own lack of . . . of *decency*, and self-control."

"Not even if I asked you to?" said Emily, letting her hand fall to *his* thigh, ostensibly to steady herself, and enjoying the way his eyes closed for a moment as he gathered himself.

"Not even if you *begged* me to."

Emily sincerely doubted that this was the case. In fact, based on the look on his face, she rather thought he was trying to goad her into doing a little unseemly begging.

He would be left disappointed. She was not the begging type.

"You are absurd," she said instead. "You should take what you want, when it's so freely offered."

"Now you really are insulting me," Captain Edwards snapped back, "if you think me capable of being so cruel."

The mood had shifted into familiar, aggravating territory, and Emily really did make to get up. She was stopped by the captain's hands, which tightened on her waist so that he could hold her in place and kiss her again, fierce and fleeting, before he let her go.

"Not even if I begged, was it not?" Emily said, raising her eyebrows at him as he stared up at her from the bed, everything about him in utter disarray.

"You are incorrigible."

Emily neatened her dress and combed her hair back with her fingers, trying to at least *look* nonchalant and in control, even if she wasn't either. She did not want to leave the room, because then it would all be over. None of this could exist in the real world, or at any respectable hour of the day; it was a strange, fleeting moment, and it was already gone. It felt so obvious, she was amazed he hadn't realized that she had been trying to say goodbye.

"I just . . . I don't think it needs to be such a moral *quandary*. It could have been very simple."

Captain Edwards shook his head, looking grave. Emily wanted to pull his shirt completely off and draw him down into the bedclothes. She wanted to shout at him until he saw sense. She wanted to run.

"Whatever it was to *you*," he said, "it could never have been simple for me."

Chapter Thirty-one

Emily left fairmont the moment the sky lightened from deep black to a touch of navy. She did not hesitate or look back. There was no point, now she knew for certain that she would never be returning. It would just be rubbing salt into the wound, and her visit to the captain's room had been more than enough of that.

It was very hard to walk with her trunk *and* the basket of goods Meera and the others had provided, but like many things Emily had faced in her life, it was still a whisker short of impossible, and that whisker made all the difference. She simply had to take rests every now and then, to put her things down and shake out her arms and try not to get frustrated about the fact that she was getting in her own way.

When the village finally came into view she was hot with effort, and although she was certainly not *crying*, the wind had made her eyes smart and water so much that she looked as if she had been.

"Christ," said the innkeeper at the Rose and Crown, when she met him outside, rolling a barrel in through a side door. "Are you after doing something dramatic?"

"No," said Emily. "Just catching the post."

"So . . . you aren't running from an overenthusiastic paramour, or fleeing the scene of a crime, or . . . or escaping from a haunted manor, with ghosts and that?"

Yes, thought Emily. *All three, actually*.

"Just the post," she said out loud.

"Ah well," said the innkeeper. "You're early. You can wait inside, if you like. There's tea."

Emily dragged her things inside, more excited at the prospect of a chair to sit in than any sort of tea that the Rose and Crown might provide. She chose a table in the corner, collapsed brokenly into the chair, and was just trying to do something about her windblown hair and wet cheeks when she realized that somebody was watching her from across the room.

When she looked up to meet their gaze, her stomach plummeted directly through the dirty flagstones and landed somewhere in the vicinity of the ocean floor.

Charles was sitting with a newspaper in one hand and a cup of tea in the other, his face lit by the harsh light of a candle stub.

She sat frozen, too appalled to make her face pretend otherwise, as he slowly put down his cup and approached her table.

"Miss Laurence," he said, sitting down in the chair next to her.

Emily did not respond. She barely breathed. She was as still as she would have been if confronted by some sort of predator in the wild, who would eat her hands if she made the slightest wrong move.

"You are early," Charles said quietly. "Although . . . by the look of your luggage, you weren't planning on making our appointment at all. How very hurtful."

Emily's mouth came unstuck. "Why are you *here*?"

Charles looked slightly bemused. "I do not live nearby, Emily. I lodge here before our meetings. You can see why I find it so dreadfully rude when you do not attend, when I have gone to the trouble of commuting. I am not a great sleeper, so I often come down early for breakfast . . . and how fortuitous that I do, and that our paths have crossed."

"I do not have anything for you," Emily said in a rush, to avoid drawing this torturous conversation out for any longer than necessary. "There was nothing to find. I looked, but . . . I cannot help you. I have left the captain's employ. I can be of no further use."

"Hmmm," said Charles, frowning. He seemed irritated that she had not played along with his false niceties and asked him if he was enjoying his tea or the weather. "I hardly think that's true. You simply need to dig a little deeper to get to the truth." He ran a hand across his mouth, considering her at his leisure. "Do they even know you've left? This time of the morning, it rather looks as if you're . . . sneaking out. Turn around and walk back to Fairmont, Miss Laurence, and do as I have asked, and all will be well."

"I cannot," said Emily, because it was true.

"Cannot or will not? Your cowardice, which is more than evident, is not enough to excuse you, I'm afraid."

"It is not *cowardice*—"

Charles abruptly misplaced his temper. "You are attempting to sneak out of the house like a fleeing rat *and* renege on your agreement with me. You are a coward, Miss Laurence, and a shirker, and although you clearly have no regard for your responsibilities to others, perhaps you will understand if I speak plainly: *you owe me.*"

Despite all her attempts at restraint, Emily's temper vanished into the same abyss as Charles's had.

"I am *not* a coward, or a— I am not *any* of those things. You might have poked around in my life to retrieve a few facts meant to bully me into obedience, but you have made it very clear that you know absolutely *nothing* about me."

Charles clenched his fists, tensing until his entire being looked red and taut, and then slapped his palms against the table so loudly that Emily flinched.

"Let us go and speak to the constable," he said, trying to regain some of that earlier joviality. "And get all of this straightened out."

"How will *you* explain yourself?" Emily countered, not able to hide the shake in her voice. "If you tell everybody I have been stealing—how did *you* come to be in possession of the stolen goods? Why have we been meeting here, if you are not involved in something untoward? I'm sure there are plenty of witnesses who would attest to that fact."

"I don't think that's a risk you can afford to take, Miss Laurence," said Charles. "But by all means, continue digging your grave. The quality of prisons in the county is really rather troubling—you can give me a firsthand account when you get out. *If* you get out. I'm afraid they tend to forget who they've got in there, after the first few months. I only fear for the toll it would take on your sister's health, should you—"

"Do not talk about my sister," Emily said, the words coming out of her knife sharp.

"You were disappointingly easy to look up," said Charles, seeming to enjoy the fact that Emily was emanating waves of pure hatred at him from across the table. "A *mill* worker from an unremarkable town with a dead, unscrupulous father and an ailing sister. No wonder you started grabbing for everything that wasn't tied down when you came to a house like Fairmont. It must have been like another world."

Emily stood abruptly. Over by the bar, the innkeeper was watching them. "That's *enough*. Stop, or I'll—"

"You'll . . . what?" Charles leaned in horribly close. Emily felt disarmed, suddenly, and dizzy—she had promised herself that she would never be back in this position, at the mercy of some *man* who wanted to use her for his own ends, and yet somehow she had ended up right back here, powerless and cornered. She did not think that he would put his hands on her—but there were plentiful ways he could hurt her without needing to lift a finger. "You will do nothing, as you well know. I may not be a gentleman, but I have some standing—you have nothing. You are a poor, plain girl, good for nothing but what you can beg or steal. Run, if you wish, like the little rat you are—I won't stop you. But I will catch up with you, Emily. *Everything* will catch up with you in the end."

"You disgust me," Emily spat, her breath coming in great, shuddering gasps as she grabbed her trunk, dragging it with both hands toward the door.

"I really don't care," said Charles, with a nasty sneer of a smile. "I am going to finish my cup of tea, Miss Laurence, and read my paper, and then I am going to Fairmont House. I would advise you to return at once, and to take up your position again before anybody knows about this little error in judgment. If I arrive and you are *not* there, well . . . Captain Edwards and I will have *much* to discuss."

Emily succeeded in heaving the door open one-handed and fled into the dawn light, the one tear she had allowed to fall quickly drying on her cheek.

Emily had managed to cover the entrance hall with mud again. She had dropped her trunk multiple times on the journey, and the act of dragging it across the threshold had left brownish-gray muck smeared all over the tiles.

Beneath her feet, Meera and the others would already be working, urging the house into motion. She wondered if Meera would tut when she came upstairs and saw what Emily had done, or if her mind would be so preoccupied by what was to come next that she would barely notice the mess Emily had made.

She had been foolhardy. She had been reckless. She had made many unforgivable mistakes, some of which would surely be beyond redemption.

She had never been, and would never be, a coward.

Meera was in her office.

"I need to speak to Captain Edwards," Emily said, knowing how strange and stilted she sounded. "Could you please ask him to come down?"

"Ask him to—are you well, Emily?" Meera said, putting down the papers she was holding. She needed another candle in here; she was being far too hard on her eyes.

"I just need to speak to him," said Emily. "Meera. Please."

"All right," Meera said seriously. She got up with a little sound of protest, as if her knees hurt, and on her way out she put a reassuring hand on Emily's shoulder for a second before she was gone.

With a pang of sadness so overwhelming it almost winded her, Emily remembered that she had left the basket of gifts that the staff had so painstakingly put together under the table at the Rose and Crown.

She avoided the kitchen—she could hear Akia chatting happily to Joe inside, and could not face either of them at the moment—and went to sit in the empty servants' dining room, her despair overwhelming.

When Meera finally returned, she looked puzzled.

"Captain Edwards has come down, Emily, but—there's a man here to see you. He said it's urgent."

"He looks like a mean pirate," said Akia, coming in behind her. "And I mean that in a bad way *and* a good way."

"Why is your trunk in the hall?" said Meera.

Emily still could have run. It was not too late, and it was, after all, what a real thief would have done. She had come here to scam these people, and although she had done a very poor job of it, sprinting for the door while they all shouted after her would have been a fitting end.

"I'm sorry," she said instead. Meera and Akia both made noises of consternation as she got up and walked past them, ready to meet her doom.

Oliver was standing in the entrance hall when she reached it. Captain Edwards was not. When she looked to Oliver questioningly, he nodded out of the open front door, looking puzzled, but had the uncharacteristic good sense to stay quiet.

Charles was there in the driveway, dismounting from his horse, just as he'd promised—and Captain Edwards was there to receive him.

"Ah," said Charles, jovial in the way that only a true bastard could be under the circumstances, "there she is. Miss Laurence, good morning."

"Do not speak to her," Captain Edwards said. Emily was surprised by the contempt in his tone.

"But she's exactly who I have come to speak with," said Charles, his smile only faltering a little. "Miss Laurence, as I was just trying to explain to the good captain, I was simply here to call upon—"

"Mr. Pine, I have made it perfectly clear that you are not welcome in my house, on my grounds, or anywhere in my vicinity. I will not allow you to bother my children's governess."

Emily's mind stalled. Captain Edwards had spoken to Charles? Had banished him from the *house*? She suddenly recalled the note that he had given to her, all those weeks ago, addressed to Captain Edwards—foolish as it was, she'd not considered since what might have been inside.

"Your *governess* and I are in fact acquainted, Captain," said Charles. Emily noticed that he seemed somewhat cowed in Captain Edwards's presence, in a way he had never been with her. "You cannot begrudge her a private conversation with a friend, can you?"

"A friend?" Captain Edwards said, uncertainty creeping into his tone.

"No," Emily said, unable to bear this a moment longer. "We are not friends."

"Miss Laurence?" Charles said. Emily wished she could have enjoyed seeing him falter, genuinely wrong-footed by the turn things were taking, but she was too busy ruining her own life to do so.

"He has come here to blackmail me," Emily said, addressing Captain Edwards, who was watching her with acute focus.

"To blackmail you," Captain Edwards repeated slowly.

"Yes. I wanted to talk to you first, I came here to tell you . . . but that doesn't matter now." She turned to Charles. "Charles. Mr.—Mr. Pine. If you could just give us a moment to speak privately."

"Oh, I don't think that'll be necessary," said Charles. He seemed to believe that he was taking charge again. "I am more than happy to relay our agreement to the captain; I can ensure that no details are left out."

Captain Edwards looked lost. "What . . . *agreement* could possibly exist between you?"

"I can explain," Emily said, knowing she sounded panicked— but Captain Edwards shook his head.

"This man is a villain and a reprobate. He was dismissed from the Royal Navy when I reported his appalling conduct—abject cruelty, inflicting suffering on others for his own amusement. He has been attempting to extort money from me for months, threatening to reveal information about my personal life and my dealings in the navy, and requesting that I buy his silence. While I am very interested in the prospect of never having to hear him speak again, I was *not* interested in purchasing what he was selling. I have never believed him truly in possession of any information at all." Emily's heart was racing. If he knew Charles Pine to be a villain, he was only about to receive the disappointment of a lifetime when he realized that Emily was one, too. "If he is *blackmailing* you, Miss Laurence, then I feel certain that he is the only one at fault here."

Emily took a deep breath, but before she could speak, Charles cut in.

"The game is up, I'm afraid, Miss Laurence." He turned to the captain. "The truth is that Emily here came to me almost the moment she started in your employ, Captain, looking for somebody to sell your secrets to. I was only too happy to oblige."

"That's not how it happened," Emily said desperately. "I was . . . I was only looking to—"

"We have been meeting in the Rose and Crown every fortnight to discuss your exploits, your transgressions, your private life," Charles said. "You can ask around, if you'd like. There are plenty of *witnesses* who would attest to that fact. Emily here was just about to rummage around in your correspondence and bring me some proof."

Captain Edwards's face didn't fall, but it looked as if the last of his hope had drained away, leaving him devoid of any feeling at all.

"Miss Laurence," he said stiffly. "Is this true?"

"I have been meeting him," Emily said, bitter with hatred for both herself and Charles goddamned Pine. "I did . . . I did make an . . . agreement with him. But I haven't told him anything of substance, I swear. I met him before I got to know you, and I thought you would be somebody else entirely, and then by the time I *did* know you it was far too late. It was . . . I needed money, and I . . . I did it for Amy."

Shock passed over his face like a wave, and then was gone. He turned to Charles.

"Get off my land, Mr. Pine, and away from my house, and my family, and my staff, or I will call for the constable."

"Oh, *please* do call for the constable," Charles said, staying where he was. "Then we can discuss the crimes your homely governess hasn't shared with you. There is no civilizing gutter scum, Captain, and the sooner you realize that—"

Captain Edwards stepped neatly forward and punched him in the face. Emily had just been considering doing the same thing, and was so surprised to see the captain's fist connect instead that for a moment she almost believed she had done it herself.

Charles staggered backward toward his horse, hands groping for nothing, blood pouring from his nose in a steady stream.

"I thought I had made myself clear," the captain said, his words like thunder. "Remove yourself from my land or I will be obliged to remove you myself."

"She's a liar and a thief," Charles said, spluttering scarlet through his fingers, "and she's made a fool of you, *Captain*. If you have any sense, you'll see to it that she's hanged."

Captain Edwards and Emily both moved toward him, but he was already scrambling inelegantly onto his horse. Emily stood with balled fists and a heart full of venom and watched as Charles rode away, putting off the moment she had to look at Captain Edwards again.

When she did, he was staring right at her, his jaw set and his eyes tight. He might have looked almost neutral to somebody who didn't know him.

All the venom in Emily's heart drained away.

"Come with me," she said quickly, before he could speak.

All things considered, it was a miracle that he followed her.

Chapter Thirty-two

Emily didn't dare look back at him as she made her way to the cliffs and down the sandy, hazardous steps. Even when she reached the lopsided rock that marked the spot, she kept her eyes fixed firmly on the ground.

She dug in the sand until her fingers hit something cold and solid, and then she hauled up the statuette and the snuffbox and presented them to Captain Edwards, who was standing watching her with his face blank and his hands behind his back as if he was on duty.

"I stole these," she said, the breeze whipping her hair into her mouth so that she had to drag it out again, tasting salt and something bitter. "And that box of your wife's, the . . . the baroque one you saw me with that first week. I asked him to sell it for me, and I had planned to do the same with these, before . . . I didn't think you'd miss them, and . . . honestly, you *didn't* miss them, you *wouldn't* . . . but . . . that's why he called me a thief. Because I was one. I am one."

Captain Edwards sighed, squinting out at the sea as if it was doing something terribly interesting, and then he sat down heavily in the sand next to where Emily was crouching. She sat, too, and they both watched the waves come in as she waited for him to speak.

"It is not the stolen things I mind," he said eventually. "Because you're right. I didn't miss them. I suppose we could have sold them ourselves, but in the grand scheme of things . . . they hardly matter. No, it's . . . hmmm. I suppose . . . I suppose it's the fact that I trusted you completely."

He didn't even sound angry, which was so gut-wrenchingly awful that Emily wanted to shout at him, to throw insults until he raised his voice and fought with her, just as she deserved.

"I swear to you on everything I hold dear—which is really just my sister, so I suppose I swear on her—that I did not speak a word to him of anything you told me in confidence. I stole three things from you, and I tried to take things that mattered more, but all I ever told him was that you were at odds with the navy, which he already knew. As soon as I realized what he actually wanted, it was over. I lied about who I was when I arrived here, but you know the extent of that already. And . . . and I couldn't agree to marry you, if you ever really intended such a thing, because you didn't know the whole truth. Now you do. That is everything."

Captain Edwards didn't say anything, and Emily wavered.

"Well . . . not *everything*. I suppose there is also the fact that I think I might possibly love you, in my own way—but I'm not entirely sure how you're supposed to tell. I have never been that sort of person. I am at *least* eighty percent dreadful, which you have seen for yourself—and I think perhaps I was just not meant for things like . . . *kissing* and flowers and . . . and the holding of hands. Not that it matters now, of course."

She tried to give him his cold, wet things, but he didn't even look down, so she awkwardly deposited them next to him and stood up, shedding sand as she did.

She suddenly didn't want to hear his verdict, or to look at him at all—she wanted to put an end to this, to write it off as an ugly misadventure that she had escaped from by the skin of her teeth, a cautionary tale about the dangers of crossing the line and daring to believe there might be something better out there for someone like her.

He didn't come after her as she walked away up the beach. She thought of him sitting in the sand with the proof of her deception beside him, and felt so unbearably sad that she sped up, half running back to the house, as if she could outpace that mental picture and put everything behind her.

At Fairmont, she found all of the staff in the entrance hall, deep in conversation. They looked up expectantly when she entered, and she noticed that Aster was standing on the stairs, frowning down at her and looking much older than he actually was, a miniature master of the house.

"Are you all right?" Meera said, reaching for Emily's arm so that she could rub it fortifyingly. "We heard there was some sort of—"

"We heard that a man came looking for you and then the captain turned his face inside out," Akia said, not quite managing to hide the fact that she found this thrilling. "On your behalf."

"No," said Emily. "No, that isn't quite—"

"I wish I could have hit him," Oliver said gloomily. "I've been feeling punchy for absolutely ages, it would have been very nourishing for my soul. Do you think he'll be back?"

"I need to borrow the gig," Emily blurted out. "I need to go to the village. Now."

"Now?" said Meera. "Emily, do you not think you should—?"

"Now," Emily said, turning to Oliver. "Please."

"Well . . . Christ. I suppose proximity to you increases the likelihood that I might get into a little fisticuffs today, so I will do it," he said magnanimously. "Just give me a moment to put on new stockings. These ones don't match."

He went to do so, and Akia tilted her head and looked at Emily far too discerningly.

"You know," she said quietly, "there's a lot of capacity for forgiveness in this house. Too much, perhaps. I once set fire to the curtains in the drawing room, and probably should have been dismissed at once."

"*That* was not your fault," said Meera. "How were you to know that Oliver had soaked them in alcohol? In fact, *Oliver* should have been dismissed for drinking spirits in the window alcove."

Akia shrugged. "You see? This is exactly the sort of thing I'm talking about. And, look—nothing is on *fire*, Emily."

This was not quite true, although the fire was of a decidedly metaphorical nature.

Emily almost reached for her trunk, but then she thought of how much they would all exclaim and throw more questions at her if they knew she was really leaving for good this time, and could not quite bear it. They could send on her things, if they wished. They were hardly worth taking, anyway.

Aster came sauntering down the stairs toward her, hands in his pockets as if he were feeling rather casual—but he betrayed himself with the hawklike intensity on his face.

"You'll be back?" he said to her in an undertone, as if he already knew the answer.

"I don't know," Emily said quietly in reply.

"Well," said Aster, "the best of luck to you, then. Terrible governess—slightly better friend."

He gripped Emily's elbow briefly and then let it go.

"I don't think these stockings match either," said Oliver, appearing once more, looking exactly the same as he had done previously, "but I suppose it will be hard to tell, when they are covered in the viscera of your enemies."

Emily didn't laugh. She just nodded, and walked out and around to the stables with her heart in her mouth and her hands unable to keep still. She was so eager to get away before the captain returned that it felt almost as if *he* were her enemy—as if her life depended on outpacing him, on preventing any further punishment via the look of disappointment on his face. It was worse than if he *had* called for the constable to come and clap her in irons.

She wasn't running away this time. Not really. There was a difference between fleeing for the exit and knowing when the time had come to politely excuse yourself from somebody's life and shut the door behind you.

Grace came rushing around the corner as she was climbing into the gig.

"You aren't leaving? Aster said . . . I thought I wouldn't catch you, and . . ."

Emily stepped back onto the ground and allowed Grace to cannon into her, a tiny missile comprised of hair and ribbon and lace. When Grace threw her arms around Emily's waist, Emily pulled her close and allowed herself a brief, bright moment of fierce, uncomplicated love.

"You were my favorite," Grace said into her shoulder.

Emily looked up past her at the sky and blinked, very hard, to keep her tears at bay.

She cleared her throat.

"I would say 'be good,'" she said, "but you hardly need to be told. So perhaps be a little bad, all right? Just for me."

When Grace finally let go and stepped away, Emily climbed up into the gig next to Oliver and tried not to look back.

She failed.

As they reached the end of the drive, she twisted in her seat and watched Grace waving her off with all her might. She kept waving until they crested the hill and Fairmont slipped out of sight.

Chapter Thirty-three

(O)LIVER WAS APPARENTLY ATTEMPTING TO CHEER HER UP.

He would not stop talking to her about the fights he'd been in; there had not been many of them, and he had rarely prevailed, but from the way he told the stories, he had clearly cast himself as some sort of avenging knight, taking up arms over any and all perceived slights. Most of these battles had taken place at the Rose and Crown, and were fought over spilled drinks or ill-advised comments, and in all of them Oliver seemed to be the one at fault in the first instance.

"And then I said to him," he was saying now, as they ascended the last small hillock before they began their true approach to the village, "that I had never even *met* his sister, but that if I ever did, I would be certain to tell her that she was just as handsome as her brother, although hopefully in possession of better hair and a more reasonable temper—"

"Oliver," Emily said, "would you mind if we were just . . . quiet?"

Oliver considered this.

"Yes, actually, I would. So anyway, he hit me with a *lit candle*, of all things, and the wax was warm so it just bent in half, and I am always unable to stop myself from hysterical laughter once it has begun . . ."

Emily tried to block him out with sheer force of will, and focus on the sound of the horse snorting amiably and the wheels trundling beneath her. She didn't want to think about everything she was leaving behind. She was going home to Amy. That had always been the only thing that truly mattered.

"Oh, hang on," Oliver said suddenly, pulling the horse to a stop. "The dramatics continue. What is going *on* with you today? You are absolutely exuding spectacle—I almost feel I should take notes."

Emily had no idea what he was talking about until she swiveled around in her seat and saw what he had seen: Captain Edwards, on horseback, galloping toward them at full speed, with his head down and his horse's mane whipping dramatically in the wind.

Before, she had not been able to look at him. Now, she could not look away.

When he reached them, he pulled up so suddenly that the horse reared, and Oliver gave a bark of disbelieving laughter.

"What is it now?" he called to Captain Edwards. "Brigands at the house? Another mysterious visitor? Has Emily received a letter informing her that she's inherited half the county?"

"Do shut up, Oliver," Captain Edwards said, his breathing ragged as he dismounted.

"I would offer to give you some privacy," Oliver said to Emily, "but I don't want to, so I shan't."

Emily climbed down from the gig so that she could at least put ten feet between them, and Captain Edwards strode to meet her.

"You have not received a letter informing you that you have inherited half the county," he said, still very out of breath. "I thought I should make that clear first, in case—"

"Yes," said Emily. "I know."

Now that he was standing in front of her again, her desire to run had evaporated like mist on a hot day. Of course she didn't want to leave him; she just didn't want to stay long enough to be sent away.

"Well," said Captain Edwards. "I thought about what you said. About Charles. And . . . I believe you."

"You didn't have to think for very long," said Emily.

"No," he said. "I didn't."

A weight lifted so suddenly from Emily's shoulders that she felt loose and buoyant. It felt almost like absolution.

"Good," she said, nodding mechanically. "That's good. To know."

"I have already told *you* everything—almost everything," he said, the words coming out in a rush, as if he were worried he might not have the chance to say them all, "but there is one thing—I am leaving. *We* are leaving. I don't want to cling to the house until it is taken from me by force. I am finished with the navy. I was never particularly fond of polite society. Aster needs somewhere he can have a fresh start. I'm not sure where we'll go, but . . . we *will* go."

"Oh," said Emily, unsure why he was telling her this but not wishing to seem rude. "Well, that sounds . . . pleasant."

Captain Edwards was looking at her as if she had just told him to go fuck himself, which she was relatively certain she had not.

"Emily," he said. "I am asking you to come with us."

"That is . . . kind of you," Emily said. "But I do not think I can remain your governess, after all of this. It would be rather uncomfortable for everybody involved."

"Not as a governess," Captain Edwards said slowly. He looked very serious, as if he were explaining to somebody on a sinking ship how to loosen a life raft. "As my wife."

Apparently they were not far enough away from Oliver to make this conversation truly private, because he let out a choked-off sound that Emily heard quite clearly before she opened her mouth and laughed.

It was an odd, breathless laugh, the sort she had not been capable of before Fairmont House, with more than a hint of hysteria in it.

"You cannot be serious," she said. "You *cannot* be serious! You have just discovered that I *stole* from you, that I was meeting with somebody who was trying to *blackmail* you, and you ask me to be your *wife*?"

"I told you I had thought about this—"

"For how long? Ten minutes?"

She heard Oliver snort out another laugh behind her, and resolved to ignore him.

"Fifteen, or perhaps twenty," Captain Edwards said defensively, "but I know my own mind and am strong in my convictions, and I have already asked you *twice* even if you refused to hear it. Will you stop being so stubborn and actually *consider* it, before you try to run away again? Because I do not believe you are half as terrible as you think you are, and I am willing to take a chance on whatever it is you feel that *might* be something like love, and . . . and I *do* want to give you flowers and hold your damned hand, even if the idea is somewhat repugnant to you. Although obviously . . . I would prefer if it were . . . not."

Emily was ready to shout at him, but this knocked the wind from her sails. She took a breath, and closed her mouth so that she could think.

"Amy will always be my first priority," she said. "And . . . my mother, I suppose. Wherever we went, we would have to take that into consideration."

"Yes," said Captain Edwards. "Done."

"And I could never be a *lady*, no matter where we go. I refuse to take on airs and graces, or pretend to be somebody I am not, for the sake of you or anybody else."

Captain Edwards nodded. "I told you I am done with society, and I mean it. Besides, we could never afford another ball, even if we wanted one."

"And . . . the other staff," said Emily, lowering her voice so that Oliver could not overhear her. "You cannot abandon them on a whim because you wish to leave the house."

"I would never," said Captain Edwards.

Emily had run out of considerations, but for one.

"You cannot really wish to marry me, Ben," she said, sounding as tired as she felt. "We would only argue all the time. We cannot even get through a proposal without arguing."

Captain Edwards's face broke into one of his rare and utterly devastating smiles, and Emily tried to keep her head about it.

"I rather enjoy arguing with you," he said, with a small shrug. "It rarely feels like true conflict. More like . . . friendly sparring, even if you do occasionally draw blood."

"Is that really what you want in a wife? Regular risk of minor injury?"

"Emily, what I want in a wife is somebody who treats me as an equal, because we *are* equals. I like that you do not trifle with small talk and niceties, or care about appearing polite, because you are fiercely loyal to those you *do* care for, and that is worth far more to me than an even temperament or good social graces. I cannot blame you for something you didn't actually do, and I cannot find it in me to be angry about a few ill-judged meetings with Mr. Pine and a handful of trinkets you stole without anybody noticing. I only wish you knew that I would have given you anything you wanted, if you had only asked."

"I do not want charity," Emily said automatically. It came out a little husky, because her throat was feeling strangely tight.

"It is not *charity*, Emily. People do not pity you. We all know you are more than capable of providing for yourself, for your sister. Has it never occurred to you that people might wish to help you out of friendship? Out of *love*?"

"You cannot understand how it feels," Emily said sharply.

"No," said Captain Edwards. "I know. But . . . I know how I feel about *you*."

Emily sort of wished that her heart could have swelled at these words, and that she could have simply swooned a little and kissed him and felt so swept up in the moment that she could return his declarations of love, but it was truly impossible for her to be anybody but herself, so instead she did what came naturally: she felt a sharp thrill of joy, a healthy helping of discomfort as her body tried to cringe away from his words, and then she stepped forward so that he might kiss her.

It was much easier than talking, and it might have conveyed some of what she felt: that she, despite her horror that he loved her, loved him, too, in her own, far less simple way, and had run out of angles to try to argue him out of it. She hoped he got the gist.

He certainly seemed to. He did not kiss her like he was saying goodbye. He was smiling into it, kissing her with a slow, leisurely happiness that made Emily flush bright red, one of his hands in her hair and the other at her back, holding her steady.

"Shall I punch *him*?" Oliver called from the carriage. "He is impugning your honor a bit, Emily, in front of God and the seagulls and anybody who passes. Just say the word. I'm not afraid to be dismissed—I'm too valuable an asset."

Captain Edwards only removed his hand from Emily's back so that he could level a very rude gesture at Oliver. Emily laughed abruptly, and then stopped laughing even more abruptly when the captain's hands slid to her waist so that he could pull her closer, Oliver be damned.

Chapter Thirty-four

IT WAS JOE WHO THOUGHT OF A FREE HOSPITAL, AND MRS. Augusta Spencer, of all people, who said she'd put up the funding. Apparently she'd been looking for a charitable endeavor, and this one was as good as any. She was to buy the house and immediately donate it. Emily was glad of the increased opportunities to stare at her when she visited to discuss finances.

The house would be stripped of the last of its furniture and trinkets, everything that wasn't nailed down and a few things that were. Once it had all been sold, the Edwards family would vacate the premises and allow it to be converted to its new use.

There were a few conditions involved; negotiations that took place between Captain Edwards and the local board of governors and Mrs. Spencer herself, who only deigned to visit to discuss the plans when she had been assured that there would be bottles of wine opened to lubricate proceedings.

Negotiations also had to take place between the captain and Emily.

He was the one who suggested that, if she felt well enough, Amy might like employment at the hospital. They could make her position part of the deal: Amy could set her own hours, and take time to rest when required. Emily's mother would be there to keep an eye on her, but Emily was trying to stop hovering so much over her sister, or as Amy put it, "Stop appointing yourself the king of all my business, including when and how often I go to the toilet."

Captain Edwards had been talking about traveling the continent. It was the sort of thing Emily had heard people discuss wistfully in the past—seeing the ruins of Rome, the sparkling Aegean Sea—but it had never been stated so matter-of-factly as Captain Edwards did, with the means and the knowledge to actually do such a thing. As soon as he had suggested it, Emily had felt a restless longing spring up inside her, a desire to go at *once*.

She was starting to imagine what she might *like* to do, rather than what she *had* to do. It was difficult to unlearn; she was plagued by a nagging feeling that she had forgotten something, and that everything was all going to come tumbling down if she did not urgently recall it.

Traveling, however, felt like a very good place to start.

She would have liked to imagine Amy at her side as their ship pulled into some far-flung, mysterious port, but she wasn't entirely sure it would be to her sister's liking. She would come if Emily begged her to, but Emily had no desire to drag her around the world under duress. Amy working at the hospital, though, Emily could imagine. In fact, she could picture the expression that would blaze across Amy's face the instant she was asked.

Sea air and lodgings and a job doing something she loved, with time to rest when she needed it.

Emily wanted to kiss Captain Edwards for thinking of it, so she did.

A wedding was a uniquely strange thing to be facing when you had never considered having one before. It was like suddenly being told that you were to head up an expedition to the Arctic, or that your expertise was needed in an operating theater when you had not a jot of medical knowledge. Suddenly Emily was a *bride*, without having done any of the prerequisite dreaming about it, and it was coming as quite a shock.

As soon as she'd heard, Meera had developed a slightly manic glint in her eye and started talking very quickly while rapidly writing down notes. Emily had backed away from her, and from the idea of the wedding and the breakfast and all the other little details that needed organizing. She had been mostly hiding since.

Tomorrow, hiding would become impractical, as she would be due at the business end of a church, and she was finding it difficult to sleep.

She had been moved into an extravagant guest bedroom, just for one night. All the bedrooms had been turned over and refreshed, the cushions beaten, the windows left open to expel some of the dust—Amy and their mother would be arriving in the morning, as would a handful of Captain Edwards's cousins. Emily had found it more than a little ridiculous when Meera insisted that she should sleep in one of the beds she had just helped Akia make.

"You shouldn't be making beds at all," Meera said ruefully, and Emily had almost hit her with a pillow.

"I am becoming somebody's wife," she had said grimly, "not an incompetent ninny incapable of stripping a bed."

Now, after hours of twisting said bedsheets into knots, Emily gave up on sleep entirely and pulled on her shawl so that she could pad barefoot down the hall and make her predicament somebody else's problem.

When Captain Edwards opened the door, he had clearly already been asleep.

"Emily," he said, everything about him soft and unfocused. He was only wearing a nightshirt, which skimmed his knees. "What is it?"

"I don't know if anybody has told you, but we're getting married tomorrow," Emily said, walking past him into his bedroom, despite the fact that she had very much not been invited in.

"Yes," he said, rubbing his eyes as he let the door close. "I plan to be there. Awake. Well rested. Please vacate my bed."

"No," Emily said.

She did not feel quite as nonchalant about sitting on his un-made bedsheets as she was trying to make out; they were warm, and they smelled of him, and she knew she wasn't supposed to be lying down on them the night before they were to be married. The lying-down-on-bedsheets part traditionally happened after-ward, as far as she knew.

"Emily—"

"Ben."

He narrowed his eyes at her but then came to sit down next to her on the bed.

"You've been married before," she said, enjoying looking at him in profile and the fact that she was allowed to stare at him like this. His hair was sticking up slightly on one side as if he'd been sleeping on it, and she found it excruciatingly endearing. "I haven't. I have no idea what to expect."

"It's mostly just arguing over what to have for dinner." He was still trying to seem irritated but was failing completely. "You'll be fine. *We* will be fine."

"Easy for you to say," said Emily, crossing her arms over her chest and radiating petulance in his direction. "*You* know what you're getting yourself into."

Captain Edwards sighed, and then to Emily's surprise, he lay down next to her and felt across the bedclothes until he found her hand and squeezed it.

"What is it that you are so particularly concerned about?"

There was quite a lot, but there was one thing in particular at the forefront of her mind right now.

No matter what he said to her—how kind his words were, how much he insisted on trying to tell her that she was *handsome* or *beautiful*, words that made her wince—it was still impossible for her to truly believe that he saw her that way. What if they married, and on their wedding night he realized that she wasn't soft and delicate at all; that she was the sort of person who belonged hard at work with her hands, not *reclining* in a man's bed for the purposes of pleasure?

She would have preferred to be shot in both kneecaps rather than speak any of this out loud, and so she did the thing that she so often did when words failed her, and kissed him. She had to turn over onto her side and lean over him to do it. He returned the kiss very briefly before pushing her away, leaving her looking down at him with her cheeks flushed and her brows furrowed.

"You did not answer my question."

"I did," Emily said. "Sort of."

Captain Edwards frowned up at her, and then his eyebrows jolted fractionally upward as he seemed to catch her meaning.

"Oh," he said, reaching up to touch his fingers to her chin. "Well."

Emily didn't want him to keep looking at her like that, so careful and *kind*, so she just kissed him again, and when he didn't push her away she screwed her courage to the sticking place and actually moved on top of him. He froze at once, and she pulled away, feeling slightly wronged.

"What?" she said, as matter-of-factly as if they were arguing over tea in the drawing room.

"Emily," he said, low and strained, "we are to be married *to-morrow*. Would it not be wiser to—"

"Damn being wise," Emily said, noticing a slight lift of his chin when she swore. "Show me. That time I was here before, when we . . . Show me the rest."

She expected him to say no—to push her away again and perhaps walk her back to her room, firmly closing the door with her on the other side of it—but instead he eased himself up the bed and sat back against the pillows, leaving her stranded, kneeling over nothing, feeling like a fool.

"Come here," he said, and she didn't have it in her to say

something cutting in reply, not least because she was worried it would bring him back to his senses.

He reached for her when she was most of the way there and pulled her properly into his lap. There was only his nightshirt and Emily's shift between them, and she suddenly became acutely aware that they were naked but for two thin layers of soft cotton; he exhaled sharply at the exact moment she felt her limbs flush with something hot and heady.

She leaned down to kiss him, hungrily and with purpose, but he was faster; he swept the hair away from the side of her neck and then his mouth was on her, kissing roughly down the line of her throat.

Emily couldn't help it. She gasped.

It was so mortifying that she actually considered getting up and leaving, but he only laughed quietly—even the feeling of that was incredible, sending little shocks of pleasure skittering across her skin—and redoubled his efforts, his hands sliding down her back to her waist.

"This is just . . . more kissing," she said, trying to sound disapproving, which was undercut somewhat by the fact that she was arching her neck to ensure that he could continue. "That's not what—"

Captain Edwards's hand suddenly dipped from the curve of her waist to the flat plane of her hip; his thumb found her hip bone and he *pressed*, which very effectively cut her off mid-sentence.

"Is this more what you meant?" he said, his voice low and edged with amusement.

Emily had had quite enough of making him *laugh*. She pulled back so that she could look him directly in the eye—he looked a little sleepy still, and far too pleased with himself—and then she acted on instinct and rolled her hips very slightly.

"*Christ*, Emily," he said brokenly; apparently it felt just as good to him as it did to her, because his eyes half closed for a moment, and when they opened again there was nothing sleepy about them.

She did it again.

This time, it punched a noise out of him, and it sounded so rich and rasping and *good* that Emily suddenly understood exactly what it was that she wanted. She wanted to make him lose himself so completely to the feeling of her that he forgot everything else; to be the one taking the lead, making *him* gasp, unguarded and helpless.

Without allowing herself time to change her mind, she reached down and pulled her shift off over her head, not paying any heed to where it landed.

"*Fuck.*"

She could tell that it had slipped out of him completely without forethought, and she had to work very hard not to break into a genuine smile.

She didn't know if she was truly beautiful. She didn't know if she'd ever be able to look at herself that way—to catch a glimpse of herself in the mirror and not immediately want to look away, seeing only the scuffs and scars that life had inflicted on her.

But Ben wasn't looking at her like that at all. He was looking at her with bewildered, open wonder, his eyes traveling reverently down her body until he seemed to remember himself and return to her face.

"What the hell are you doing?" He sounded so pained that Emily did smile.

"You tell me," Emily said. "You're the one who's done this before."

"You are quite genuinely terrifying," said Captain Edwards.

"Good," said Emily.

His nightshirt was already rucked up a little, and she took the edge of it carefully between her fingers and gave it a slight tug. It was a question: Captain Edwards just watched her, apparently unable to say anything, but his head jerked slightly in assent, and she pulled it up as far as his chest before he removed her hands and did it himself. She kissed him to ease the strangeness of it, and he sank back against the pillows and ran his hands through her hair, one after the other.

It occurred to Emily that he probably thought it the only safe place to *put* his hands, but without their nightclothes everything was just hot skin against hot skin now, and she thought she might go mad if he didn't touch her properly.

"This is good," she said quietly into the inch of space between their mouths, "and tomorrow we'll be married, so just . . . pretend we already are. Yes?"

Captain Edwards just said her name, but it was much less of an admonishment and more of a dazed exhalation.

"Ben," she said quietly; he shuddered minutely beneath her. "Please."

"God help me," he said, sounding completely wrecked, but apparently God wasn't listening; he took her by the waist and gently turned her onto her side, so that they were face-to-face, pulling the blanket up over them both in an attempt at some decency.

"Tell me," he said seriously, "if you change your mind, if you want to stop, and we can simply go to sleep like sensible people. Don't look at me like that, Emily, I mean it."

"Look at you like what?" Emily said, wondering what her face was doing—she certainly had no idea.

"Like this is an argument you're determined to win. If it's too much—"

"I'll tell you," she conceded.

It wasn't too much when he ran his hand, very slowly, down from shoulder to ribs and to her hip again; it was *almost* too much, but exquisitely so, when he made gentle circles across her skin with his thumb and fingertips, each time dipping lower until her breath caught and she had to press her forehead into his shoulder to try to gather herself.

It was an impossible task, because then he was kissing across her collarbone and down her chest, his hands in constant motion until she was so overwhelmed she couldn't do anything except breathe shallowly into the crook of his neck, her hand digging tightly into his broad back and his name caught between her teeth.

"Show me how to touch you," she said.

He didn't try to fight her at all, this time—he just took her hand and did as she'd asked, and she experienced that fierce rush of heat and pride again as he closed his eyes, overcome, and choked out her name.

In the end, it wasn't anywhere near as strange as Emily had thought it might be, especially after they had been unclothed and entangled for so long; it was just even more of a good thing, so good that the sound of her name on his lips became almost unintelligible, and her teeth left a neat row of indents in the soft skin of his shoulder.

Afterward, she lay ensconced in his arms, both of them tired and slow and stupid, and Emily turned to look at his face—cheeks flushed, hair a mess, eyes heavy-lidded and looking back at her with an easy happiness—and smiled.

"You really do like me," she said, not able to keep the bewilderment out of her voice, and he laughed.

"I do."

She screwed up her face. "And you think I'm . . . *beautiful*."

"And all the rest."

He was mostly wrong, of course—but startlingly, she believed him.

"Well . . . I was right to come here. I think I feel ready to get married now."

"Good for you," said Captain Edwards. "I don't. It's about three o'clock in the morning, and they'll come to dress us at eight."

"I should probably go back to my own bed," Emily said, not moving.

"Yes," said Captain Edwards, burying his face in her hair and tightening his arms around her, so that she couldn't leave even if she wanted to. "All things considered, you probably should."

Chapter Thirty-five

"Do pirates need pelisses?" Grace said, picking up an expensive-looking blush-pink coat and looking at it dubiously. "I thought they usually wore big leathery-looking things. And nine guns. And black boots."

"For the last time, Grace, we are not going to be pirates," said Emily.

She had been cajoled into packing duty and had gone unwillingly to meet her fate, which was apparently to be shown every single item Grace owned and asked if it befitted a life on the high seas.

"We are getting a ship, though, so I ought to adopt the customs."

"We are not *getting* a ship—ships are very expensive. We are simply going to be . . . guests on a ship, for a while."

"That's what they call hostages," said Aster, from over on the sofa, where he was reading one of his father's books about rigging. "*Guests.* Are we to be held hostage? I suppose we might be able to negotiate. Give them Grace, so we can keep me."

"If you give me to a pirate I will be *so* vexed, Aster," Grace said crossly. "I will never forgive you."

"I'll live," said Aster.

They were not conducting themselves as if they were leaving that afternoon, and yet they very much were: it was giving Emily a headache.

Meera had offered to oversee the last of the packing, but the housekeeper was very busy with her own situation, namely the fact that Mr. Khan had finally tentatively proposed—with a sort of business presentation, Oliver had told her, a rundown of all the ways in which he might add value to her life—and they were to be married within the fortnight. For somebody who had been so impervious, she seemed delighted. She had also happily taken charge of converting Fairmont House to its new, far more useful purpose, and was expecting her aunt and cousin to arrive any day in advance of her nuptials, with an invitation to stay for as long as they wanted—perhaps even forever. Joe had also decided to stay, which had led to floods of tears from Grace and a few quiet ones from the cook himself, but Emily could not think of anything he would find more satisfying than trying to heal hundreds of people with the power of his broth. Oliver and Akia would be accompanying them on their voyage.

"I bet they don't have swearing jars on ships," Oliver had said dreamily. "In fact, I bet they *give* you sixpence if you say something really inventive. I will have to start working on my obscenities."

Amy was still wobbly, still too thin and quick to tire, but she was so excited about the prospect of a hospital that Emily had been slightly afraid of her. Their mother, too, had taken to the idea with far more enthusiasm than Emily would ever have expected. Meera had embraced them both like old friends at the wedding, and on their return to the house they had sat in the kitchen, making their way through an enormous sticky ginger cake and endless cups of tea while they plotted. Emily had decided it was best to leave them to it. More frightening than this union had been the moment Grace met Amy; they were both immediately so in love with each other that Emily felt rather as if she were intruding on something by standing in the vicinity.

The thought of leaving Amy again still hurt urgently whenever she considered the reality of it, but it was easier knowing she would be here, with people Emily trusted, doing something she loved and probably not even sparing Emily a thought. They would write. And Emily would be back. She just didn't know when.

They were to travel with the ship to Spain, because Grace had always wished to see it, and then perhaps Italy, because Aster had heard that Lord Byron might be there doing various horrible things that might be amusing to catch a glimpse of, and then after Italy they might make a plan to return to England, if it suited them, or to travel onward, if it did not.

The world, which had felt so small to Emily for so long, was suddenly wide open. She didn't know what to do with it all, but she supposed she would figure it out as she went.

There was a swift knock on the door.

"For the benefit of everybody in the schoolroom," Ben said from the other side of it, "we are departing in an hour, and anything that is left behind will be donated to the patients of the hospital with no hope of return."

"I'm donating Grace," called Aster.

Grace threw a hat at him. "I cannot be donated; I am one of a kind!"

"Well, just as long as you've decided within the hour," said Ben.

Emily didn't have to see him to know that he was smiling; just the slightest quirk of the corner of his mouth, as if he was trying to repress his amusement. He had been smiling like that a lot lately. Often he didn't bother repressing anything at all.

When the time came for goodbyes, Emily insisted on behaving as if they were simply going into the village for the day and would be back in time for supper. She allowed a handshake from Joe, a crushing hug from Meera, and a gentle one from her mother, and when she reached Amy, she found herself crying.

"You are such an embarrassment," said Amy, more than a little tearful herself. "All these people are going to think you've gone soft. Do you not have a reputation to uphold? You will be back so soon I won't really have time to miss you."

"I'll miss you," Emily said into her shoulder. "I always miss you."

"You will be in Rome looking at all the statues of nude men," Amy said, taking her by the shoulders and giving her a small shake, followed by another brief hug. "You won't think of me at all, except, I hope, to sketch them for me and post your drawings home."

They had hired an enormous carriage to take them all—the six of them and their many bags and trunks—and even with all that extra room they had to cram inside to fit, Emily practically sitting in Ben's lap while Aster made gagging noises and pretended to hang himself every time there was a bump in the road and Emily had to cling to her husband for stability.

When they reached the docks, the air outside smelled like a thousand different things, only half of them unpleasant. The ships were so enormous and grand as they waited to set sail that Emily found herself frozen in place, watching them bob gently in the harbor swell, unable to believe that she was about to set foot on one and suddenly very unsure about the physics of the whole thing.

Ben came to stand next to her, and slid his hand into hers. He didn't look nervous about the physics. He was smiling like he had just seen a very old, dear friend.

"What if it sinks?" said Emily.

"Unlikely," said Ben. "But you are traveling with the Royal Navy's finest turncoat, and I will see us all safely to shore."

"What if we get halfway around the Bay of Biscay and decide we hate each other?"

"I thought we were already in agreement that we hate each other," Ben said affably. "Was that not part of our wedding vows? I did ask him to put it in."

"Ben—"

"Emily."

"I have never traveled more than three hours from home before," she said, wincing as she offered up this total, vulnerable scrap of honesty. It was something she was trying to do more often, and it still stung every time. "I am a little . . ."

"Grace will take care of you," said Ben. "Aster, too, in his own way, although I suppose he does favor the tough love. I wouldn't rely on Oliver or Akia—I heard them discussing sailors' drinking games before we left, and they were rather upset when I told them I had not learned any during my time at sea."

"Is that true?" asked Emily, leaning into him so that he might put his arm around her and hold her close. He obliged.

"No," Ben said, with a sigh. "But I was not ready to explain to either of them that the game *I* played most often in my youth involved gambling for the removal of clothing, and I don't think I ever will be."

Emily laughed, and Ben pressed a kiss to her temple and then released her so that they could approach their ship, the *Porpoise*. Ben had tried to tell her many things about it when he had booked their passage, heavily discounted due to old favors owed, and she had pretended to listen and come away knowing absolutely nothing.

The gray, grizzled captain was waiting for them on board; Ben strode onto the gangplank and then realized that Emily was not behind him.

He turned to look at her, silhouetted against the bright autumn sun and billowing sails, and held out his hand.

Emily rolled her eyes, smiling despite herself, and took it.

Acknowledgments

THIS BOOK IS QUITE PREOCCUPIED WITH CHRONIC ILLNESS because I have been quite preoccupied with chronic illness these past few years, although I'm lucky enough to be in a period of better health at the time of writing. I just wanted to take a moment to say that living with a long-term illness or chronic pain is a big bitch, and I send love and good days to all those reading this who know what I'm talking about.

This is my fourth novel published in two years (this doesn't sound right, but it is! I checked!). That means I've written four sets of acknowledgments since 2021, and I'm running out of fresh new faces to thank. Please indulge me while I tip my hat to the series regulars.

A million big sexy thank-yous to my agent, Chloe Seager, and the rest of the team at Madeleine Milburn. Thank you to my wonderful editors, Sarah Bauer and Katie Lumsden, Eleanor Stammeijer, Abigail Walton, Casey Davoren, and the rest of the team at Bonnier. Thank you to Steve, a perpetual lifesaver!

I'm lucky enough to have an incredible team at SMPG over in the U.S., who works ridiculously hard even though I'm all the way over here in England and they could TOTALLY get away with a little slacking. Thank you to the brilliant Sarah Cantin, Drue VanDuker, Meghan Harrington, Rivka Holler, and Anne Marie Tallberg.

Thank you to my early readers, Maggie, Georgina, Parrish, Mireille, and Photine, for wading through this book when it was still lumpy and misshapen and providing invaluable feedback. Thank you to Louisa Cannell for the amazing cover illustration, and may I just say re: the captain . . . hubba hubba, etc.

I've needed a big human scaffold of emotional support during the past two years of this career, and holding me up at the top of the "I can't do this anymore, why did I ever think I could be a writer?" pyramid: my sister, Hannah, and my partner, Nick. Thank you for roast dinners and film nights and takeaways and picnics and lasagnas. Apparently we do most of our bonding over food. Huge thanks also to my parents, Rosianna, Sanne, Kez, and all of the talented fellow authors who've let me vent in your DMs.

Lastly, thank you to my beautiful old cat, Felicity "Fliss" Croucher (who is vomiting as I write this, but has hopefully stopped vomiting by the time you're reading it), *Breverton's Nautical Curiosities*, *The Sound of Music*, the band MUNA, Classic FM, *Our Flag Means Death*, and Coke Zero Cherry.

About the Author

Hannah Croucher

Lex Croucher is the author of *Reputation, Infamous,* and the YA novel *Gwen & Art Are Not in Love.* Lex grew up in Surrey reading a lot of books and making friends with strangers on the internet, and now lives in London.